COLD ENOUGH TO FREEZE COWS

Also by Lorraine Jenkin

CHOCOLATE MOUSSE AND TWO SPOONS

EATING BLACKBIRDS

COLD ENOUGH TO FREEZE COWS

by
Lorraine Jenkin

HONNO MODERN FICTION

First published by Honno in 2010
'Ailsa Craig', Heol y Cawl, Dinas Powys,
South Glamorgan, Wales, CF64 4AH.
1 2 3 4 5 6 7 8 9 10

A catalogue record for this book is available from
the British Library.

Published with the financial support of the
Welsh Books Council.

ISBN 978-1-906784-17-1

Cover illustration © Louise Gardiner
Cover design: Graham Preston
Text design: Jenks Design
Printed in Great Britain by Gomer Press

For Huw, for Charlotte, for Maude…
and now for baby Billi, too.

With many thanks to all those that helped with the making of
Cold Enough to Freeze Cows

CHAPTER 1

Fel bol buwch ddu – like a black cow's belly

Iestyn Bevan got up from the table and walked towards the back door. He pulled on the jumper and overshirt that were one inside the other on the hook, and ground his feet into the enormous wellies that stood in a puddle of water on the tiles.

He didn't want to go back out into the weather. His bones had been getting warm, finally, and the aching was subsiding. However, he knew by now that it was like needing the toilet in the night: no matter how much you didn't want to get up and go, you were far better to just get on with it. The need was never going to go away and ignoring it just prolonged the agony.

"Out to check the barn, boy?" asked his dad from his usual spot in the chair by the Rayburn.

"Yeah," grunted Iestyn, "just a last look round." Somehow his dad's unbelievably flexible neck permitted his eyes to follow Iestyn across the kitchen as he fetched his beanie hat, which sat in a puddle on the work surface.

"Check that old girl in the pen, eh, Iest? She wasn't looking too good earlier." Iestyn's father, Tomos, had a knack of allowing his body to sit perfectly still in the chair with just his head moving, revolving from side to side.

"Yep, no probs." He would have checked her anyway, having spotted earlier that she was looking none too bright.

1

"Good boy," said Tomos and his head returned to look at the small television perched on top of the dresser, once more meeting up with the alignment of his exhausted body and allowing every osteopath in the land to breathe a sigh of relief. Iestyn knew what it was like: when you spent your whole day slogging in the cold, after you'd finally sat down you moved as little of your body as possible.

Iestyn's mother, Isla, smiled at him and got to her feet, "I'll have a brew ready for when you get back." Iestyn smiled in return as she filled the kettle that had nearly steamed away all its contents and returned it to the hotplate of the Rayburn.

Isla sat back down and picked up her knitting. Her chair faced away from the television, so instead of watching it she assumed her usual concentrated frown as she listened to what was happening, knitting for her niece's children, for Iestyn, for her husband, Tomos, and finally for herself.

Iestyn reached for his coat on the peg in the porch and slung it, still wet, onto his back. The cold damp collar and cuffs touched his skin and he shuddered. Cursing for the thousandth time that no one had replaced that outdoor light, he grabbed the torch from the shelf and followed its feeble beam into the night.

He slopped along the path round the side of the house, the rain driving down his neck. He instinctively knew where the gutters were spilling out, but the duck shit he skidded on was unexpected. He cursed as he grabbed for a handhold and scraped his knuckles on the rusty corrugated iron cladding that protected the farmhouse from the worst of the easterly weather.

He trudged up the steps, knowing exactly where to step, which treads were loose, which were uneven and which were missing and had been for the last few years.

At the top of the slope, Iestyn wrenched open the barn door and felt for the lights. The sweet smell of the hay and the warmth from the sheep soothed him. He hung his wet coat on a nail and threw the torch down into a pile of old feed sacks.

As he moved amongst the pens, he looked over the sheep which were divided into groups or singles by hurdles and other more makeshift barriers. Some jumped to their feet as he approached, darting to the back of their pens, others eyed him warily, but stayed crouched in the warm hay. His father had been moaning about the severity of the winter and had predicted that because the weather had been so bad, the lambs would be born with stunted legs as their mothers had spent so much time crouched low to the ground. However, Iestyn knew that his father predicted such a thing most winters, so he felt a little more optimistic.

Iestyn made his way over to the ewe that Tomos had mentioned. Although to the layman most of the sheep looked the same, Iestyn knew exactly which one his father had meant when he had mentioned the "scraggy old" ewe. She tried to stand up as he approached and then hobbled off to the corner of the pen. He grabbed the rickety hurdle and stepped over it, his six-foot-two frame clearing the top rail easily.

He darted at the sheep and caught her. Her eyes were a little dull and her hooves were a bit smelly but she seemed OK. Certainly not worth doing anything about it anyway – father would rather eat her than get the vet out. Despite the Ministry and its paperwork, plenty of hobbling, crouching, or infertile sheep ended up lying with a handful of herbs shoved up their arse on the Bevans' table of a Sunday.

Kneeling down with the sheep, Iestyn felt the breeze racing under the wall of the barn. His grandfather had patched an old door opening with a tin sheet as a temporary measure about twenty-five years ago and it still rattled under the slightest breeze. He shivered: he'd been soaked through three times already and by the evening he'd been struggling to get warm. He pulled the collar of his shirt up and shuddered as that was wet too, a puddle of rainwater trickling down his neck.

He checked his watch – he'd been in here for forty minutes: that tea would be stewed to buggery by now. He made his way back to the door and shrugged his coat back on. He flicked the light switch off and the place plunged back into pitch darkness, not a streetlight for three miles. Iestyn cursed that he had not picked up his torch first as he fumbled round amongst the feed sacks and flicked away a mouse as it ran over his hand.

He slipped and slid down the path back to the house, no longer trying to avoid the puddles or the mud, vowing as he did every night to put a bulb in that bloody porch light first thing in the morning…

His mother and father were in exactly the same position as they had been when he left them earlier, his mother just being another couple of inches further on in her knitting. She looked up and his father craned his neck around and peeped over the chair.

"All right, love?"

"All right, boy?"

"Yeah."

"How was that ewe?"

"Oh, she'll be OK, bit ropey, but all right I think. I've stuck some more straw in her pen, cosy her up a bit."

Iestyn shook off his wellies and padded across the tiles, his long cream socks flopping out in front of him. He eased himself into his chair and accepted the cup of stewed tea from his mother with a smile. She waited beside him as he drained it and it was refilled without a comment. A thickly buttered scone was put beside his refilled cup.

"Thanks," he muttered, and picked up his scone. "Blimey, Mam, I think I've stopped growing now, you know!"

She smiled back. It was their little joke. Scones had filled him, his father and his brother, Joe, for as long as he could remember and there were always piles of them for when they had come in from outside. The scones had grown larger and larger as the years had gone by and Iestyn and Joe had grown into two large men. But this one was possibly the biggest ever.

"Well," laughed his mum, "I suppose I wasn't concentrating."

"Watching bloody *Pobl y Cwm*," quipped a voice from behind the chair wings, "that's why my sandwich didn't have any butter in and the chickens didn't get fed and..." Tomos peered around and winked at Iestyn and Isla laughed.

"Well, maybe one day he'll learn how to make his own sandwiches?"

"Hey, now, let's not get silly," said Tomos, "no need to go that far. Oh, and Iestyn, Joe phoned. He and Sima are coming down Christmas Eve – having Christmas day here and then heading off skiing for New Year. Off for a winter break, flying out with some old friends from Cardiff and then they'll call back through again on their way back to London."

"Another winter break? That bloke has so many winter breaks I'm surprised that he has time for a normal week to actually do any work!"

"He's had another bonus," said Isla proudly, "so he's going to treat Sima."

Joe was the son that was always boasted about in the local shop, the one who topped the Christmas card news and the one whose homecoming was more of an occasion. He would always turn up in a new car, usually one that was so low slung that it could be heard scraping its way up the mile-long track. He would nearly always have a gorgeous woman in the passenger seat and often a different one to the time before – although in fairness, the beautiful Sima would be on her third visit now. Iestyn remembered the first time that the tall, willowy Sima came to the farm. Her exotic looks had taken his father by surprise and Iestyn had chuckled at his slow deliberate English and then shrivelled with embarrassment as she replied, "Is-it-because-you-are-first-language-Welsh-that-you-talk-so-slowly?" in a broad Cockney accent. She'd winked at Iestyn as he giggled, then she'd laughed and patted Tomos on the arm, "I'm only joking," she laughed. "I know that sometimes people are not quite sure what to do with me! Let's start again: Sima Arshad born in England to Pakistani parents, I'm very pleased to meet you!"

"Tomos!" Isla had clucked, "Silly arse! Sima, love, pleased to meet you *wherever* you're from! Take no notice of Tomos, he's never been further than Cardiff in his life..." Joe had laughed again when he got a nudge from his mother, "Joe, m'n, you could have *told* us..."

Iestyn loved Joe. He was good fun and always full of tales of a life that was very different to Iestyn's. He told stories about the City, the bars, his fifth floor flat – sorry, luxury condominium – the clubs and the women. Iestyn had never sought to follow Joe; he'd always wanted to work on the farm, and that is what he had done, but he sometimes envied Joe his escapades and opportunities. He loved Pencwmhir, but wouldn't it be nice to sit on a balcony overlooking the Thames with a glass of champagne and someone as beautiful as Sima at his side just occasionally?

Instead, he supped his *paned* with his mother and father, chatting as they always did about the farm, the animals, any work that had to be done and the latest gossip from the local village, Bwlch y Garreg. Occasionally he would nudge the dog, snoring at his feet, with his toe.

Although he presumed that even Sima would fart and twitch in her sleep now and then, lying beside her would surely be a far more pleasant experience than having that Jack Russell snoozing beside his chair.

"That bloody dog," said Tomos, frowning. "Has he been eating chicken shit again?"

Louisa Harrison settled at her desk and switched on her lamp. She pressed the button on her computer and felt the usual surge of expectation as it whirred into being. As it sorted itself out, she busied herself in her bedroom, shutting her curtains against the foul December weather and removing her work clothes in favour of her pyjamas and dressing gown. As she sorted her outfit into those things that were destined for the wash basket and those that would be acceptable for another day, the door tapped and her mum's grey bob peeped round.

"Brought your tea up, love."

"Thanks, Mum," said Louisa without really looking at her, and she went back to wriggling the mouse in the attempt to get her system to boot up quicker. Her mother put the cup onto the mouse mat and Louisa frowned and picked it up and put it very deliberately onto the coaster.

"Sorry, love," dithered her mum, "I didn't realise it was your computer mat."

"Mouse mat," stated Louisa, as she stared at her screen.

"Sorry, *mouse* mat," said her mother and without thinking took a damp cloth from a loop on the back of her jeans and deftly wiped the surface of the desk, whipping round the keyboard and collecting the three specks of dust that had dared to gather there since she'd dusted earlier.

"Mum! For goodness sake!" snapped Louisa. "Can't it wait until tomorrow?"

"Yes, yes, of course it can. Sorry, love, wasn't thinking."

Louisa nodded and carried on staring at the screen. She hated waiting for so long. She could feel her mother standing behind her looking over her shoulder. Eventually she had to turn and look at her and raise her eyebrows and at last her mother took the hint. Wiping the shelf as she went, Esther walked slowly from the room and left her daughter in peace.

Louisa shook her head and returned to the screen and sighed. *Right. Let's get down to it.* There was another knock at the door.

"Sorry, love, I forgot to ask about your sandwiches for tomorrow."

Louisa rolled her eyes and groaned. "Oh, anything. Whatever."

"Cheese and tomato?"

"No, um, tuna, mayo and spring onion will be fine. Bit less pepper this time though, please."

"OK, love." And Esther clicked the door shut once more.

Louisa was feeling quite excited. As part of the Advanced Computer Studies course she was taking through her workplace personal advancement programme, the tutor, Herbie, had set the class the task of writing a blog for their Christmas homework.

"I want you to not just *use* the computer. I want you to *get involved* with it. *Interact* with it, yeah?"

Herbie got on her nerves. He was a bit of a hippy turned techno-head and it was as if the two didn't sit well together. Occasionally he would flick the flimsy ponytail that had managed to grow out the back of his neck and say, "Yeah?" as if that might mean that he wasn't betraying his roots. However, despite this, she was enjoying the course and had received positive feedback about her assignments.

To Louisa's annoyance, however, her mother had recently started attending a Computers For Beginners evening class, so that they could "help each other". Louisa knew that she would now no doubt spend much of her free time messing about with paper-jams, showing Esther how to save files, delete files, click on a mouse etcetera, etcetera, etcetera...

At last the Internet was up and ready to go. Louisa typed in the URL of her own blog, which she had set up in class, and then sat back as it flicked to the screen. *Bingo! It had worked!* The pastel shades made her nod – yes, they looked good. All she now needed to do was write something.

"It doesn't have to be much, and it doesn't have to be a literary masterpiece," Herbie had said. "Just a diary about your day, or something like that. I want to feel like I am getting to *know* you:

getting to know what makes you tick, yeah? I want you to use the tag lines, use the titles – you know the score? Let's get to it!"

Louisa had sat in the chair in the side of the class and wracked her brains as to how she could draw him in (yeah?). By the time she was ready to start typing, Herbie had checked the clock and seeing that they could legitimately "rap", as he called it, he leapt away to mingle with Rachel and Rosie, the two young women who sat next to each other at the front of the class and giggled together as if they were still at school. Louisa had spotted Herbie trying to arrange himself so that he could take quick glimpses down Rosie's top as he helped her with one of her many technical problems. Pretty pathetic really – shame that he didn't involve the rest of the class in his "rap" – everyone else had to chat amongst themselves.

"I'm going to write about what I am reading," said Moira, the woman who had sat next to Louisa.

Louisa had nodded, bored. Why had she ended up sat next to Moira? Rachel and Rosie were now laughing with Tom, the funny guy sat on the row behind them. How come she, Louisa, had Moira, with Barry and Robin behind her? They never really did any more than smile at her. It wasn't fair really; she'd have a lot more interesting things to say to Tom than Rachel or Rosie would – and she didn't have such an obvious fake tan. From where she had sat, she could see a tide-line behind Rosie's ear.

As she sat in her bedroom contemplating her text, Louisa shuffled the items on her desk. Her pen caddy, a photo of dear old Tibby in a frame, a clean pad of paper and a calculator. What on earth was there to write about?

She was twenty-six and worked in the bank in the neighbouring town of Tan-y-Bryn. She had worked there since leaving school and had been promoted twice and was now Chief Cashier with one girl beneath her. She lived at home with her parents in the Welsh hamlet of Anweledig and had been saving for her own house since she'd started her job. The plan had been that she would probably be buying it with a husband and therefore she hadn't actually started looking for something to spend her deposit on yet. She played badminton (very occasionally) on a Tuesday night, had her computer class on the

Thursday and usually accompanied her parents to the golf club on Saturday night for a meal, after her dad had played a round of golf. There really wasn't a great deal more.

She drummed her fingers, made a start, deleted it, wrote a bit more and sat back in her chair to contemplate. There was another tap at the door. *What was it now?*

"Yes," she barked. If her mother was disturbing her again to ask what flavour crisps she wanted with her sandwiches, she would be really cross.

Instead a dark curly head peeped round the door.

"Dad!" She smiled.

"All right, love? Still working?"

"Well, an assignment to do, but I'm at a bit of a loss of how to start."

"*Silent Witness* is on!" he goaded. "I'll get your mother to put the kettle on again, shall I? Go on, leave the assignment – you can finish it another time when you haven't had such a long day: you must be exhausted."

Louisa deliberated, looking at the single sentence on the screen in front of her. *My name is Louisa Harrison and I live with my parents in Anweledig and I work in the local bank.* Then she looked at the face at the door, smiling down at her.

"Actually, looking at it, I think I've finished already!" she said, re-tied her dressing gown, pulled on her slippers and followed him downstairs to the lounge.

The porch door of Cwmtwrch Farm banged open and a figure wrapped in an oilskin crashed in. An elderly lady grabbed at the door as it buffeted against the wind. "Come on in, bach," she cried and helped the bundle of layers into the warm.

"Oh, thanks, Nain," puffed the bundle to his grandmother. "Phew, it's cold out there!" The little lady reached up to help him off with his coat and scurried it away to its peg. The hats and scarf were taken from his hand and slung onto the airer above the Rayburn. By the time the young man had propped his wellies on the rack in the corner, a mop had sucked all the rain and sleet from the tiled floor and a brush had swept away the clumps of mud. A fresh mug of tea was poured and reached the old chair by the Rayburn just as Johnny Brechdan himself did.

"There you are, bach," smiled his grandmother with a look of complete love in her eyes.

"Oh, thank you, that's wonderful! Just what I needed," Johnny grinned in return as he stretched out his legs and rested his socked feet on the front of the Rayburn.

"Oi, socks off that!" clipped Nain, "you burn through any more pairs and I'll stop repairing them!"

"No, you won't," he laughed and winked at her.

"You!" she chided. "You've got the cheek of your father, God rest his soul. How were the barns? Any problems?"

"No, no, all fine. That draught seems to have worked on the two ewes that were a bit rough yesterday, so that's good news. So, yes, all fine." Johnny took a long sip of his tea and leant back into his armchair even further, as if it might be possible to get even more comfortable than he already was. "You go on up if you want to – Taid already in bed?"

"Yes, twenty minutes since – told him to get himself ready for me and I would be up as soon as you were safely back indoors."

"Best not keep him waiting then! *Nos da*, Nain, good night."

"Good night, bach, *nos da*," she smiled and walked to the heavy door leading to the stairs, collecting a pile of ironed clothes to take upstairs with her. "Cake in the tin," he heard as the door latch clicked shut.

Johnny stretched again, and then opened the door to the Rayburn's fire. He poked and prodded it about, raddling out the ashes in a way that would have Nain tutting, "*Gently*, boy, *gently*!" A few logs from the broken-down wicker basket were slung in and he leant back into the chair, watching the flames curl around their new prey.

He loved this time of night. He was physically tired, but, barring emergencies, he'd done all he needed to for the day. His grandparents, Nain and Taid, were early to bed and he would be left with the house to himself. Sometimes he would scoot off down the local, or maybe watch a bit of television or go on his computer. Other times he'd just sit in front of the fire, maybe doze or maybe just sit: there was always plenty enough to think about on a farm and far too little time to simply rest.

As he sat and wondered whether he could be bothered to go and get a piece of that cake that his Nain had mentioned, his phone burst into song. Johnny sighed, then rummaged in his back pocket and pulled it out. *Ah, Gina!* Johnny smiled. *What did she want at this time of night? Probably what she usually wanted at this time of night…*

Chapter 2

Cyn flined â draenog – as cross as a hedgehog

It was Thursday evening and Louisa was driving home in a bad mood. She knew that she shouldn't have looked at it at lunchtime, but she had, and her whole afternoon had been foul as a result. She could still see the words in her mind's eye, chatty, welcoming and witty and there for anyone who might come across it. Rachel Dowling's blog. Miss Goody Two-shoes had not only done her homework, but she had made it interesting and fun to read. Whilst she, Louisa, had been wrapped in a blanket on the sofa watching telly, Rachel had been writing up the fun she'd had over the weekend. Louisa wasn't *really* jealous, but Rachel did have a little more than her to write about.

"Hi Everyone! My name is Rachel and welcome to my blog!" it had said. Louisa had tutted at its triteness, but she hadn't been able to help reading on. "I'm 26 years old," and Louisa had frowned at the knowledge – she had assumed that Rachel was much younger than she was, "and I live in a flat with my two great friends Rosie and Samuel." Louisa had been annoyed – of *course* it was easier to have an interesting life if you lived with your two great friends. *She* would probably live with two great friends if she weren't living with her mum and dad. Rachel needn't be so smug about it.

"We're all just recovering from a fantastic weekend in North Wales where we were supposed to go hill walking, but actually didn't manage to leave the pub!" Her immature ramblings had gone on to include a snowball fight with some locals that had resulted in an invite back to their house for an impromptu party. A few of the group were in a band, so they had all ended up jamming and singing the night away.

11

So, Louisa had fumed all afternoon, crashing about the bank, glaring at her customers and making stupid errors. If *she'd* gone to North Wales for a weekend, the same thing would probably have happened to her. Instead, however, she'd trailed around a round of golf with her father and three of her father's friends, followed by a meal at the golfie, followed by a night on the sofa in front of the television. Pretty much the same as every other Saturday night this year – and last.

As her Corsa sped over the common, she beeped her horn angrily at the sheep that had settled in the road, reluctant to leave the warmth of the dark tarmac. Damn sheep; the sooner they fenced the blessed common, the better, she cursed. Those sheep had already caused Mrs Jeffers to end up in the ditch, and she was sure that someone else would follow before winter was out.

As she neared the turning to Anweledig, she thought again about Rachel, Rosie and Samuel all coming home after work. Rachel was a nurse in the local Accident and Emergency Department and Rosie was a speech therapist. She didn't know what Samuel did yet – perhaps tomorrow's blog would enlighten her. He was bound to be a – a stuntman, or an astronaut, she thought, batting the small teddy that hung from her rear view mirror out of the way. They would all settle in the lounge, Rosie would be sat cross-legged on the sofa, Rachel would probably be sat on the floor. All would be chatting and laughing about their day.

What awaited her? Her mum toiling in the kitchen, worrying about what she was cooking and her father trying to get her to sit and watch television with him all evening. No wonder she never did anything. No wonder she never got round to buying her own place or renting a flat with great friends – her father always got her to put things off, so that they could spend time together, sitting on the sofa like an elderly couple whilst her mum was bullied into waiting on them hand and foot.

Mind, it had always been the same really, even when it had been different. In hindsight, it was her moaning one afternoon that she was bored and how she wished they could be more like the Ingalls family that had sparked off the big countryside adventure. Inspired by Laura Ingalls's antics running about the prairies barefoot, Louisa had sulked to her dad that her life would be so much more fun if they lived on the prairies, rather than on their boring housing estate. She guiltily remembered saying to him, "I would love to catch wild animals and weave baskets with grasses, but how can I when we live on Mount Pleasant?"

Looking back it was amazing that he gave it any more credence than simply saying, "Well, take your shoes off and go and collect some grass then. Mind out for dog poo and see you at tea time." Instead, he'd taken it to heart and formulated a plan. Six months later, they were living in Anweledig...

Somehow it had been decided that Esther, then in her early forties, would give up her part-time job in the local bank and spend her days tending a vegetable garden and attending weaving and other countryside classes, so that she could pass on her skills to their daughter. The money that they lost in wages would more than be recouped by cheap veg and giving woven mats away for Christmas presents. However, Esther hadn't approached the role of Ma Ingalls with much enthusiasm.

Louisa remembered the day they had waved goodbye to their friends and neighbours, many of whom she had never seen again, despite only moving seven miles away. They had been plucky adventurers, brave enough to grasp their dreams with both hands. Louisa would become a wild-child, running with foxes and communicating with nature through a series of whistles and clicks. Their neighbours had wished them well and Louisa had sat in the car thinking that her whole life was about to change. Change it did, but not in the way that had been expected...

In some ways it had been lucky that Esther had had her stroke three days after they had moved: it meant that they never had to come to terms with the fact that they might not have lived out their dreams thanks to disinterest alone.

Louisa remembered it as a time of turmoil, being shipped to Grandma's house in the middle of the night and then returning to their new home to find a different mother inhabiting the body of her old one – one with a scrunched up hand, a flailing leg and a dribbling, drooping face. Over time, her speech had improved, but Esther's mobility and dexterity was never fully recovered, although she managed daily chores with a stubborn slowness.

David tried to push Louisa out into the wilds to play, but there was no one else for miles around to play with and she was not used to playing on her own. The guy across the yard became Uncle Bob, but he was in his late fifties and although he told her things about foxes, he never offered to take her to their dens.

Louisa secretly never minded that she was unable to become a fox-child; by now she far preferred watching *The Railway Children* on video in front of a fire on a Saturday afternoon, to tending her own section of the vegetable garden, as had been the initial plan. David sat with her, keeping busy by attending to her needs and Esther pottered around in the background, muttering under her breath as she went. Somehow, even despite the massive change that had occurred within Esther, the life of Louisa and David wasn't really that different to what it had been in Mount Pleasant. None of them seemed to notice that the family wasn't living the dream; it was simply suburbia with a better view.

Louisa had grown up a diligent child and she did well at school with the brains she had been born with, neither stretching nor addling them. When her mother's old job in the bank came up, only now full-time, it seemed fate that she got it, the manager perhaps still feeling guilty that Esther had received no real help after her stroke, despite having left her post of twenty-two years just a week before.

And that had been it: life. Up in the morning, tea brought to her by a muttering – but not complaining, mark you – Esther. Ironed blouses, MOT'd cars, packed lunches, straight back home to help her mother at the end of the day. Supper, sofa, bed. She'd never really questioned it – until now…

Louisa flicked her indicator on and turned towards Anweledig. The turn was down a steep little lane that led into a hamlet of five old cottages clustered around a yard with the Harrison's large modern brick house stuck on the end. It was the council planning department's concession to allowing modernisation in Anweledig and was such an aesthetic disaster, that they would never have to allow such a thing again.

The hamlet of Anweledig had been built to house workers from the big house nearby. The owner at the time, a dusty old lady who was only really thirty, ruled her household with a rod of unpleasantness. She had insisted that her domestic staff lived near enough so as not to be late, yet out of her line of vision so that she didn't have to stare at their miserable little houses and hear their nasty little quarrels: she'd had plenty of her own quarrels to listen to. Anweledig had been the perfect solution. Tucked in a sunken bit of a north-facing hill, it was a quaint little cluster of houses built around a large yard that had a well in the middle.

It was now a sought after location for "drop outs" as Louisa's father called them. People who worked away and came to their houses every six weeks or so to spend the weekend frantically trying to get their second homes warm and aired. One house was awaiting its owners' retirement, another was the dumping ground for stuff that was too bulky to have moved with its owner to her new lover's house and was instead sat getting damp waiting for *that* relationship to finish.

The Dingle was the only house in the hamlet that had a drive, a gate, a well-kempt garden and a security light that kept flickering on and highlighting surreptitious men with torches strolling in the shadows down by the river…

Louisa turned into the gate that her mother would have popped out to open for her ten minutes before and her father would close behind her. Good, her dad wasn't back yet, so there was room for Louisa's car in front of the security light: hers was a newer model, so it made sense that it was the one nearest the house. The light clicked on making the hamlet as bright as day and Louisa frowned when she saw that the old grey snow was still piled at the side of the drive: surely her father could have moved that by now?

What she *should* do tonight should be to go straight upstairs and make a start on that blessed blog. At least it would be done, and then she could start thinking about how to make it a bit more interesting for the next session. With her homework on her mind all the time, it was no wonder she couldn't get stuck in to getting out and about a bit more, finding a few great friends somewhere, starting a couple of clubs or hobbies somewhere else. Yes, she thought, get stuck in to that, then she could begin on the rest of her life…

"Hello," called her mum as she opened the front door, "how was your day?" Louisa grunted: she wasn't in the mood for small talk. "Your dad's just left the office; he'll be home in ten. Cup of tea while you're waiting?"

"Yeah, all right," Louisa muttered, kicking off her shoes. She looked at the stairs with her bedroom door across the landing at the top of them. It was a bit dark and the stairs were quite steep. Perhaps it would be more appropriate to have a bit more of a chat with her mum for a while and then do the blog thing later. She could always look on the Internet for a club – perhaps get to contact a few people from it online before she actually went; that would save her turning up and not knowing anyone.

Therefore, she chucked her keys onto the hall table and watched as they slid across the polished surface to drop quietly onto the carpeted floor: I'll remember that they're there tomorrow morning she thought, and headed for the sofa. The television clicked on all too easily and Louisa found a game show. Slightly different people to yesterday – but only slightly different. A cup appeared on the table next to her end of the sofa and Louisa reached out for it without a response. It looked like she was going to have to put off getting a life for another day…

Louisa sat in the white leather sofa and her dad fetched the pouffe for her feet. He tossed over a chenille blanket and turned up the real-effect fire.

"OK, love?"

"Yeah, thanks, Dad," replied Louisa as she snuggled down into the warmth.

"Did you manage to start your assignment?" called Esther from the computer desk in the corner.

"Aw, leave her be," smiled David, winking at his daughter, "she's been at work all day; let the girl have a break."

"Well, I just thought she said she had to get it started tonight."

"Leave it, Esther. All right?" growled David, the tone in his voice hardening. Esther shuffled in her chair as if a shuffle was somehow the only rebuke she was allowed. David winked again at Louisa and Louisa mouthed her thanks back. She knew her mum meant well, but she didn't half go on.

Silent Witness came on and David passed over the remote control for Louisa to adjust the settings.

"Any chance of another cuppa?" he called over to Esther, sharing a cheeky giggle with Louisa as he did. Esther muttered under her breath but Louisa pretended that she hadn't heard: her mother always muttered. One turned off to it eventually.

Just as the first autopsy was being carried out in all-surround-sound, another cup of tea was plonked on the table at Louisa's side.

"Thanks, Mum," she muttered. David muttered the same and Esther went back to her computer.

The tuttings and the mutterings and the sound of pages of a manual turning back and fore rattled away from the corner as Louisa and David exchanged frowns. "File – save as – let's call it, um, *test page* – save! There – done! Well, that was easy enough!"

Louisa turned the volume up and slammed the remote control down on the table. The sofa pair tittered and settled down once more.

After a bit more muttering there was the sound of a printer whirring into being and an exclamation of triumph from Esther. "At last! I knew it couldn't be that difficult!" and she bumped her head on the computer desk as she reached down to check her printed masterpiece.

"Mu-um, I hope that we're not going to have this *every* night now, are we?"

"No, it's OK, love, I've finished now. I'll come and join you." Esther perched on the armchair perpendicular to the sofa. "Now, what's been happening here then?"

CHAPTER 3

Fel cachu ceffyl mewn dŵr – like horse-dung in water (to peter out, make no impact)

It was a miserable morning as Iestyn rattled along in the ancient Land Rover, grinding up the track that zigzagged its way up the rugged hillside. The feeble wipers smeared the sleet across the windscreen and more piled in through the side window onto his face as a gust of wind managed to sneak its way through the two-inch crack: he'd told his dad that there were problems with the window and not to wind it down – but had he listened? Of course he hadn't.

He'd already checked and fed the beef cows on the lower land and now he had to go up on the open hill to check the ewes due to lamb later and to chuck them a few bales of feed to supplement the grass. Farms surrounded the rough common land and each farm had ancient rights to graze a certain amount of stock on the land. Although in the past, these rights had included cows, sheep, horses and geese and the right to gather, crop and cut, most of the farmers now just used their sheep grazing rights, with the occasional bailing of bracken for bedding.

As Iestyn crawled over the brow, he saw another knackered Land Rover parked at a feed trough – Johnny Brechdan from Cwmtwrch Farm. He drove over to see him, bumping over the heather and scattering a hare as he went, his dog going mad with excitement in the back. Johnny had obviously just filled the trough and had climbed back into his truck and was too cold to get out again. The pair had had a good laugh as their Land Rovers sat side by side – Iestyn shouting out of his two-inch crack and then Johnny having to climb over his passenger seat as his driver's-side door handle had come off on the inside.

Iestyn and Johnny had been friends since they had attended Bwlch y Garreg primary school, both driving themselves down their long tracks each morning, before abandoning whatever vehicle they had been allowed to take and walking the remainder along public roads.

As Iestyn's brother had long since left the farm in the search for a warm office, Iestyn had stayed; the plan being that he would slowly take over the farm, working it under the gaze of his parents. Johnny was the only grandchild and so he was also in the same position, happy to have been primed from an early age for the role.

They would laugh together with only a hint of wryness about their lives and what their elders were willing to hand over to them. Iestyn had boasted that he'd been allowed to move from the bench to a chair with a cushion on it at the kitchen table, whereas Johnny had been asked just the night before whether Nain and Taid might finally be able to retire soon and go and live in a nice warm bungalow somewhere. They wanted to know would he actually work the farm, or would he sell it to pay for his whoring and gambling debts?

They were both large men, toughened by their lifestyle of hard work, outside in all weathers. Johnny's fair hair was stiff as a brush under his floppy sunhat, whereas Iestyn's dark hair was slaked to his head under his black beanie.

After a few grunts about what was new, Johnny shouted his usual question over the biting wind. "How's the hunt for women?"

Iestyn grimaced; there was never any point in trying to evade Johnny's questioning. It was his main interest in life and therefore he felt duty bound to check on everyone else's progress. Johnny Brechdan never had such trouble; women seemed to drop out of the sky and land on his private parts – the woman who delivered the feed bags, the girl in the office at the vets and the German walker he found on the hill with a broken ankle and looked after for a while in a happily-ending *Misery*-type scenario.

"The only thing I find on the hill is a sheep with its throat ripped out by a dog and the bumper that fell off my Landy the other day – it's just not bloody fair!" Iestyn would groan as Johnny regaled yet another success story in the realm of love – or at least superficial love with real sex.

"Oh, nearly sorted," shouted Iestyn. "I think I saw one a week ago in Joyce's shop – *and* she was under fifty. You?"

"Not bad, not bad. Saw Sarah last Friday and then bumped into Lucy in some shop in town and had a rather nice lunch hour with her! Anyway, whatever happened to Jane Hammons? Thought you were nearly in there."

"Nah, not really interested. You know. Anyway, she's got bigger hands than me – would never be any good at lambing. Poor old ewes – would make their bloody eyes water."

"Not really interested? Or just interested in someone else? Come on, Iestyn, you're not still mooning over bloody Menna Edwards are you?"

Iestyn shrugged.

"Well, get over there then. Go. Now! Just ask her out for fuck's sake. Then if – no, *when* – she says 'no, you must be fuckin' joking you ugly old bastard,' you can get over her and start chasing someone who might actually *want* to shag you, rather than just chat to you about lambing. Actually, I think Menna has turned into a bloke somewhere along the way. I reckon when she gets back to that bungalow of hers, she spends her evenings sitting in her pants, scratching and drinking cans of Special Brew."

"Talking of which, fancy another pre-Christmas night out?" asked Iestyn.

"Aye, go on then, needs must I suppose. Eight o'clock? Bull? OK. But, by then, I want to hear that you actually *went* to Glascwm and that you actually *spoke* to Menna about something other than farming and that you ended the conversation with a comment about picking her up at eight o'clock some night this week? OK? Christ, it's like trying to educate pork. Look: do it – or *I'll* do it. I've always reckoned that Menna's been giving me the eye, so…"

"OK, OK, I'll do it. I'll go now."

"Promise?"

"Promise."

"Right, I want a text message about the response by dusk, otherwise, I'll stand you up on the pint and be round there myself for a foot rub over supper, OK?"

Iestyn grinned sheepishly and nodded. Johnny gave him one of his looks and with a great deal of false starts and shuddering, both Land Rovers rattled into life and set off in different directions across the open hills, Iestyn waving a few fingers though his open window and John showing off that he still had a functioning horn.

As Iestyn bounced back across the heather to the track and then set off to his own stock's feeding area, he thought about what Johnny had said. He loved Johnny's zest for life and his enthusiasm for just getting on with it. For Johnny, it was OK as things always worked out in the end – if *he* went and asked Menna Edwards out, he would be almost guaranteed a date by the end of a ten minute conversation, and if Menna *did* say no, he would have shrugged and then shagged her mother before he left the farm. But it was more difficult for Iestyn: he actually only wanted Menna. He didn't want her mother, or the woman who had come to help with the books, or the one that he met in the shop on the way home if he'd been thwarted on all other occasions.

He'd liked Menna since his mid-teens – actually, liked was too wishy-washy. He *loved* her. He loved her smile, her freckled face, her strong arms and, well, everything about her. They'd been friends for years and he knew that she liked him, but probably only in a good pal sort of way.

At school, he'd been too shy to make any approaches. Then, on the day he'd drunk four pints of cider at the local fair, to enable him to even think about plucking up courage to ask her out, bloody Paul the Neuadd had beaten him to it. Word had whipped around the beer tent, as he was slugging down what was intended to be his Dutch courage, that Menna Edwards was going out with Paul Morgan and Iestyn remembered the churn in the pit of his stomach – and it wasn't just the pints of locally brewed Death By Apples on top of a spit roast beef baguette. Years later he still thought, *Damn – if only I'd gotten off my fat arse after two pints, history may have been very different.*

For three years he'd been in a bad mood every time he'd spotted Menna and Paul hacking around in the Neuadd truck, or winning rosettes at shows that his scraggy hill sheep weren't even allowed to watch through the fence. Slowly he'd gotten over it and simply accepted it as one of life's inevitable blows.

Eventually, he'd heard that they'd split up, although no one ever confessed to knowing the real reason and who was the dumper and the dumpee (although many spent plenty of time guessing) and he wondered whether he might step in and fill the gap. However, he'd soon got the message that he'd mucked that up too…

Therefore, being Iestyn, sorting things out had never been an urgent need – it was something he should do something about after he'd finished lambing/hedging/fencing/tailing. Maybe after he'd had a decent haircut or when he was wearing his blue jumper. In addition to this, he was also aware that it seemed that Menna had changed. Perhaps she'd never gotten over Paul the Neuadd. She was more serious, less fun loving and light-hearted. She was always just about to go somewhere or do something and it never seemed to him to be the right time – even in *his* sense of the words 'right' and 'time'.

"She needs to spend a week with me," Johnny Brechdan would say. "I'd cheer her up, look after her, maybe even blow through her pipes…"

"Don't talk shite," Iestyn would say, half worried that Johnny would do as he said – and, knowing Johnny's record, if he'd decided that was where this month's charm quota was going, then it usually had its desired effect. Iestyn was always glad when Johnny was chatting up some other poor cow, as it meant that he was leaving Menna in peace. Give her a bit more time, let her get over Paul the Neuadd and then perhaps he, Iestyn, could try again, maybe ask her if she might like to go out – perhaps they could go to the curry house in Tan-y-Bryn for a meal – or even a little further afield? Abergavenny, maybe, that was supposed to be good for food.

Despite Iestyn's daydreams and on-going watchfulness, he didn't realistically think that Menna would *ever* fancy him. Johnny was right; she now seemed asexual where men were concerned – had done for a few years.

So, until the situation changed, Iestyn pottered along, occasionally getting lucky at a Young Farmers' Club dance or doing the gentlemanly thing for the friend of Johnny Brechdan's latest conquest – and in fairness, Johnny tended to choose so well that even the ugly mate was good company, and Iestyn had many nights out in this way – it was just that he'd be a few moves behind Johnny every time, so that by the time he was getting to really know a girl, Johnny would be pissing off her friend and they would both disappear back to where they came from.

"Johnny m'n," he would say, "can't you be a bit kinder, just for a couple more weeks? We were just beginning to get on well then!"

"Iestyn, you'll have to speed up your tactics, mate" he would reply. "It's the nine and a half weeks thing: they're met, wooed, loved and dropped within that time span. If you're still calling each other Mr Bevan and Miss Brodie at that point, well, no wonder she can't be bothered to come back on her own!"

Menna had been part of the crowd in the Bull for the last couple of years and they always texted her to say that they were going along. She was good fun, but she was also one of the few people of their age who still lived in Bwlch y Garreg and so it made sense to include her in their nights out.

Iestyn loved it when she managed to make a night in the pub. Suddenly the bar seemed shinier, the beer tasted nicer and his jokes were of a higher calibre. Despite this, she was as shy as he was when there were just the two of them, so they never really made it on to subjects that might reveal a little more of her thoughts about him. But times alone never really lasted long. A two-minute chat about what they might be up to at the weekend would soon be interrupted as Johnny would come out of the shitter and give them a graphic account of what had just been happening. If they met on the road, another vehicle would pull up behind and peep its horn and any conversation would have to be cut short.

Johnny was right in a way about Menna having turned into a bloke somewhere along the line. She was always dressed in asexual jeans and rugby or checked lumberjack shirt. She never acted like a female in that he could never say, *Ooh, you look nice*, as she usually didn't; she looked like what she was – hard-working Menna, who'd just spent the day doing something really physical, usually in the rain, and therefore being completely appropriately dressed in coverall oilskins. If he couldn't be bothered to dress up for the sheep, why on earth should Menna?

However, there was something about Menna that Johnny Brechdan hadn't *quite* grasped. She wasn't a bloke, as she *always smelt nice*. Not just "not stinky", but actually positively delicious. He remembered Menna's mother always scrubbing any children in her care's hands with a massive block of dark green soap before meals or snacks were allowed to be touched. The blocks were so big and old that they had sharp corners and were impossible for little hands to grasp. He and Menna used to giggle as the block would shoot out of their grasp and land on the immaculate lino and then they would have to chase it around the floor, needing both pairs of hands to trap it and lift it back to its resting place.

Jean would be shouting at them from the kitchen to hurry up as they rubbed their hands, now red from the harsh soap, dry. No, Jean was not likely to be the kind of person who now bought her daughter Lavender of the Valley, or whatever flavour it was that women had to make them smell nice: therefore, it must be Menna choosing it and *that* was the difference…

He'd spent months, nay, years, trying to manipulate situations, opportunities to meet, but they never really came to anything. He knew he was being a bit pathetic about the whole thing, but he'd invested so much time in the Trying to Bump Into Menna Edwards scenario, that if she turned him down now it would probably be worse than keeping the flicker alive. He was so busy and she was so busy that it wasn't so much a daily obsession, as a niggling itch reminding him that he should really be moving things on a bit.

As he jumped out of the truck and twisted his ankle in a rut that was frozen harder than he'd thought, he hopped about enthused and full of promise. Wouldn't it be great to be able to report to Johnny that night that he'd not only gone to see Menna, but that he was taking her out the following week. Somewhere nice, somewhere like a new restaurant in town. Iestyn split a bag of feed with a knife from his back pocket and emptied it out into the trough. Sheep came running from all around him and nudged and buffeted the backs of his legs. "Oi, you buggers!" he shouted at them as he grabbed another bag from the truck. A couple of bales of hay were dragged out and sprinkled around the feeding area/patch of frozen mud.

He slung the empty bags into the back of the truck and jumped in. Right. He would do it *now*. Right now. No time like the present. Just get on with it. The time was nigh. Ripe for plucking. *Carpe diem*. His Land Rover shuddered into life and Iestyn crawled off, the long way round, to go and seize the day.

Iestyn finally stalled his truck in the yard of Glascwm. It was a vast, clean yard that had all the farm's vehicles parked in a row, as if they were keeping to the allocated parking bays of a busy supermarket. At the Bevan farm, people just abandoned their vehicles wherever they decided to stop, thus cluttering up the yard. The family then spent an inordinate amount of time moving things about so as not to clonk them with a reversing tractor or a feed delivery truck. Iestyn made a mental note to tackle his mother and father about it: perhaps he should do it now and come back and see Menna later?

But the assumed scorn of Johnny Brechdan was stronger than the desire to flee and Johnny was only moaning and swearing at him for his own good. He, Iestyn, did actually *want* a date with Menna, he just wasn't sure that she wanted one with him.

He could see Menna's mother, Jean's head peeping through the kitchen window. Damn: he'd hoped that Menna would have been there on her own, but he'd been spotted now, so there was no going back. He pulled off his beanie hat and took a quick look in the rearview mirror at his reflection. He was horrified. His hair was slaked flat from the hat and in need of a wash, a cut and a style. He popped his hat back on quickly.

His face wasn't much better. His beard was at least five days old and had gone past five o'clock shadow and moved on to the lazy-bastard-can't-be-bothered-to-shave look. His skin was glowing bright red from the wind and his nose had a drip on the end – best watch that indoors, it was always worse when he stepped in from the cold to the warm.

He jumped out into the sleet, called to his dog to "lie down, you bugger" and then reached into the back to tuck an old jacket around her, then pulled his own jacket around himself. *Well, here goes nothing.* Perhaps Johnny was right – if she did laugh in his face and tell him he must be joking, at least he could move on. Trouble was, he knew that he would be moving on knowing that he had turned up with dirty hair and a runny nose: he wasn't really giving it his best shot.

"Hello Iestyn, how are you, love? Come in, come in!" called Jean from the doorway. Iestyn nodded his greetings and jogged the remaining twenty yards with Jean holding the door open, frowning as she let the weather into the farmhouse kitchen in her attempt to be welcoming. Iestyn stumbled into the kitchen and stood on the tiles in his great muddy wellies and his dripping wet coat. There, sitting at the dinner table, were Menna, her father Bill and her aunty, each eating a plate of pie with vegetables.

"Here, love," fussed Jean, "put your coat *there* and your boots can go *there* and hats, yes, hats go over *there*."

Iestyn removed his outer layers as the group at the table watched, chewing their potatoes. Menna was sat in the window, effectively barricaded in by her father and her aunty. Iestyn hauled a great drip back into his nose and then took the tissue proffered by Jean, muttering his thanks. He'd known Jean for years and he still felt like a little boy in her presence as she so definitely ruled the roost once someone stepped over her threshold.

He muttered his greetings to the group at the table and when he had finished sorting himself out, he suddenly felt desperately awkward. "Look, I'm sorry," he said, "I only popped round as I was passing; I had no idea of the time. I don't want to interrupt your lunch…"

"Nonsense, nonsense," cried Jean, "always pleased to see a neighbour – and you'll remember Menna's Aunty Sadie, won't you? Come and sit down, we've plenty for another one!"

"Yes!" called Aunty Sadie. "Come and sit yourself here. How are you, Joe, bach, I've not seen you for years?"

"He's not Joe, he's Iestyn, Aunty," said Menna. "Joe's the one who works in London?"

"Well, *dieu, dieu* Iestyn, you *have* grown! Last time I saw you, well, you were shorter than me! Now look at you! Turn around, turn around!" Iestyn obligingly turned around, his arms stuck out at the side and as he did so, he caught Menna trying to hide a giggle. "Well, well, what a fine figure of a man. Isn't he, Menna?"

"Yeah, Superman – without the clean pants," she smirked, taking the elastic band out of her ponytail and re-fixing it. "Or maybe Batman without the decent car."

"Sit down, lad," said Bill, "make yourself at home."

Iestyn thanked him and gladly walked towards the table, but in doing so, caught a glimpse of himself in the large mirror over the fireplace. His hair was no better than it had been five minutes before in the truck, his over-jumper had last week's breakfast down it and the warmth was making his cheeks glow even more than they usually did. He took his jumper off hoping to get it out of the way before he reached the table. He was then faced with his second jumper, a stripy acrylic number that mother had brought home one day from God only knows where. He stripped that off too, to calls of "And the rest!" from Sadie.

Finally he sat himself at the table, directly opposite to a giggling Menna, in a T-shirt with a ripped neck and a stain of sheep dip across its front. He could smell his own feet, so he tucked them backwards under the chair and hoped that the smell of the chicken pie would overpower them.

"So," said Bill, "what brings you to this neck of the woods?" It was only said in conversation, but Bill knew as well as Iestyn did that

Glascwm was the last farm on a road that led only to a few more cottages and a dead end.

"Oh, just passing, you know, doing a few errands," said Iestyn and he thanked Jean for the large plate of lunch that she put on the table in front of him. He tucked in, finding it easier to eat than to make conversation. Menna had reached her last potato and Aunty had finished hers and having put her cutlery down, she settled to watch the fine figure of a man choke on his chicken pie.

"That was lovely thanks, love," said Bill, "any more?"

"Oh. Sorry. No there isn't, now," said Jean.

Everyone looked at Iestyn's plate, which was already half empty. He looked up. "Oh, I'm so sorry, I've eaten your seconds – look, have that bit of pie, Bill. I haven't touched it."

"No, no. No problem, boy, you keep going," said Bill looking around at the other plates. "You want that potato, Menna?"

"No, you have it, Dad, I'm full," and Menna passed her last potato over to her hungry father who cut slithers from it, as if trying to make it last.

"How's business, Iestyn?" asked Jean.

"Good, good thanks," he replied, his mouth just full of Bill's delicious second helping of pie crust. "Could do with a break in the weather, though."

"Yes, it's foul isn't it?"

There was silence, but for the clock ticking on the mantelpiece and for the creaking that was coming from Iestyn's chair as he squirmed.

"What about you? How's it going?"

"Yes, good thanks, boy, good – apart from the weather, as you said."

Iestyn couldn't eat fast enough. Damn Johnny Brechdan and his stupid ideas. Why had he listened to him? These things should be planned, thought through – you shouldn't turn up at someone's house to ask them for a date when you have BO, smelly feet, bad hair, a red face and then proceed to eat their father's dinner; it was never going to work.

"Oh, you're a good eater," smiled Aunty. "I love a good eater. My Alf, *dieu*, he could eat…"

"Most people can," said Bill. "Keeps them alive."

Iestyn caught Menna's eye, she was nearly purple with the effort of not exploding into laughter. It was as if she were *enjoying* his discomfort. Iestyn crammed his last forkful of carrots into his mouth, just as Bill nibbled his last sliver of potato.

"That was delicious, Jean. Thank you," Iestyn said. "Gosh, is that the time, I really must go now, folks, thank you again."

"You're welcome, lad, you're welcome. Are you sure that you won't join us for some pudding? Spotted dick and custard?"

It was Iestyn's favourite. "No, no, I really must go, but thank you anyway." He nodded at Aunty, who wiggled her fingers back at him. "Oh, and Menna, we're going for a pint in the Bull tonight if you fancy? Only if you're free, like?"

"OK," she said. "Might see you there then. Thanks," and she raised her eyebrows at him, still with that urge to laugh written across her face.

"Go on, Menna, see him out," said Aunty, "it's obvious it's *you* he's come to see!"

"No, no, just passing," Iestyn said as he scrambled to his feet. Please, Aunty, don't make this any worse than it already is…

She did: "Come on, Menna, come past me," said Aunty, making it all worse as she scraped her chair forward and leant into the table. Menna muttered that there was no need and Iestyn pleaded that there was no need, but Aunty insisted and Menna squeezed past her and reached Iestyn at the door just in time to pass him another tissue.

"Sorry about that," muttered Iestyn, as he struggled to keep his balance whilst he pulled his wellies on.

"Wrong foot," said Menna, fidgeting as she untucked her rugby shirt from her jeans and then stuffed it back in again.

"Eh?"

"You've put them on the wrong feet."

"It's OK; this is how I wear them. They're a bit big you see and this makes them fit…" Iestyn knew he was talking rubbish and that Menna knew he was talking rubbish, but he couldn't face being in that kitchen a moment longer.

"Thanks again, folks, and sorry to eat your dinner, Bill."

"Any time, boy, any time," said Bill, waving his hand at him.

Jean walked to the door, her arms laden with plates. "Don't forget your hat," she said and plucked it from the hat hooks. Iestyn dragged it onto his head, pleased to be able to hide at least one of the day's worst features. "Iestyn – aren't those boots on the…"

"Wrong feet," said Menna, "yes, they are. But apparently he likes them like that, don't you, Iestyn?"

"Thanks again," he called and he bolted for the door, skidding in a puddle that his boots had left earlier and having to make a fifteen-stone grab for Menna to stop himself crashing to the ground.

"Oh Christ, Menna, I'm sorry, are you OK?"

Menna giggled. "I'm fine, don't worry! Now are you sure you're in a fit enough state to drive?"

"Just let me out of here…" he groaned, half – but not quite – giggling. "Maybe see you tonight?"

"Oh, actually now I'm thinking about it, I don't think I can. Think I'm going over to Mandy's. Sorry," she said. "See ya."

A text did arrive on Johnny's phone before dusk. It read, "Last time I listen to you, you bastard."

Chapter 4

Fel ci yn llyfu ei ddolur – like a dog licking its wounds

Hi! Rachel here, diligently doing my computer homework. My flatmates, Rosie and Sam and I have just been having a heated debate /blazing row about aerodynamics. Luckily, just as Rosie and Sam were about to come to blows, the doorbell rang and it was our new neighbour from three doors down, come to introduce himself. Turns out, he is an engineer and was able to explain it all to us. Then he took us for a ride in his new BMW convertible to prove the point. How lucky was that!

Louisa felt her stomach roll over in anger and jealousy. She'd called the bloke from three doors away, Uncle Bob, and he'd had a Montego with dog hair in it. She could barely bring herself to skim the next section, but saw that it mentioned swimming, a new swimsuit, fifty lengths and coffee afterwards with the dishy new lifeguard, Jaff.

If she, Louisa, had posted her blog the other day, very little would have changed – what could she blog about apart from Doreen's new blouse that was sent from Head Office being two sizes too big and Barry the golf pro who had told her about his kidney stone investigation.

Rachel ended with a request for advice on how to break the fifty-length barrier, as she was simply unable to do any more and thus invited the interaction that Herbie had desired. Two people had already replied and both messages had lots of exclamation marks and references to their own lengths…

Louisa got up and paced about the room. She noted the dutiful family photo of her and her parents taken on some boring day out. She looked with distaste at the range of glass animal ornaments – why on earth had she decided to collect them?

Her room was immaculate. The cream carpet had only ever had slippers traverse it and her satin bed quilt was removed each night and replaced – for show – each morning: just the same as the one in her parents' bedroom.

She looked in the mirror and saw her round face and her sensible shoulder-length bob. Her work blouse was in the wash basket and she had replaced it with a round-neck t-shirt and comfortable jeans with elastic inserts at the side. Rachel had worn skinny jeans and biker boots at the last session. Rosie had had a woollen dress and tonged curls.

Louisa had always felt a bit awkward around people of her own age. It was as if she wasn't quite on their wavelength. She could be chatty and even flirtatious with the older people at the golf club, but with anyone of less than forty she felt tongue-tied and nervous. However, she also felt resentful. She felt as if she was actually much more interesting with much better conversation skills than they had – if only they'd give her a chance, and shut up and listen for a while. They just never seemed to give her the break that she needed to show off her wit and wackiness.

At school she'd always felt that she should have been in the in-crowd. She should have been at the back chatting and giggling with Sarah Stroud and her cronies, rather than being at the side of the front row, sharing a desk with the near-silent Isabel Roberts. But Sarah

Stroud had never shut up and listened to her for long enough to appreciate her sense of humour and her turn of phrase.

Sadly, it seemed that this was still the case in her adult life. She was sure that she could make Rosie and Rachel laugh out loud as she nudged them and pointed at something, making a little comment about it being surreal or random. Yet, as usual, they hadn't seemed to have even noticed that she was in their class, let alone looked at her as a potential great friend.

Louisa had always assumed that life happened to people and it would be the one that they rightly deserved. She had been well behaved and worked hard at school. Her reward for that was a good job at her local bank. She had a clean car and she showered each morning. Her figure wasn't exciting, but it was reasonable. Surely all these things should add up to being married by now?

She had presumed that she would have met a hard working bloke, a nice chap who also played a bit of golf and liked meals out. They should have got wed, or maybe not – maybe lived in sin for a while. She should actually be enjoying a series of foreign holidays for a few years before starting a family. They would have a boy and a girl, she would work part time and they would alternate Sunday lunches at her parents and his.

Instead, these things seemed to be happening to other people instead of her. She'd kept her side of the bargain, surely it was the rest of the world's turn to keep its side?

There was a tap at the door and a cup of tea with Esther attached loomed. "Here you are, love; a cup to help you get your homework done – and your dad says to tell you that part two of *Silent Witness* starts in ten minutes!"

"Thanks, Mum," said Louisa and accepted the cup and put it on the coaster on her desk.

Esther seemed to want to stop and chat, but didn't have any chat in her. She peeped into the wash basket and removed the work blouse and shuffled off. Louisa was sitting at her desk, left alone in her pink t-shirt and her comfortable jeans with a cup of tea made to her exact requirements within an arm's length.

Just *why* hadn't she gotten round to creating herself a life? An interesting, enviable life that would make an enjoyable blog? Could

31

she really write about her and her dad's reckonings that the murderer was the man in the red coat because of the insurance scam? Would anyone bother to have interactions about *Silent Witness* theories? And if they did, would their thoughts have lots of exclamation marks on?

She shook her head in frustration. *This was* pathetic! She'd allowed herself to become a boring, uninteresting, dull woman who dressed twice her age, yet was scathing about people she secretly thought she deserved to be.

She hated to admit it – but perhaps Rachel and Rosie had *decided* to move out of their parents' homes and get a flat together. Perhaps they'd *invited* Sam to join them. Perhaps it hadn't been financially astute or sensible; perhaps it had just been for – for fun?

Louisa remembered back to the sixth form when she had turned down the offer of a date; she'd known that Pete Blanche would never have been the man she would marry – he was shorter than her for a start and that would never have done, so she turned him down. Shame really – he'd gone out with Cheryl Bainbridge instead and they'd gone to Camp America for the summer. He'd actually been all right really.

Then she'd quite liked that John Hamish who'd come down from St Andrews in Fife to help tend the golf course last summer. He'd brought a little excitement and a few dirty jokes into the dusty environment of the golf club, and he'd even leant on his roller and told her how good she would look in a tam-o'-shanter. Louisa had immediately changed from being a once-every-couple-of-months kind of golfer to a once-a-weeker. She wore red jumpers and bought a better pair of sunglasses. But then she'd overheard him telling Margey Harding the same *and* she'd gotten a wink despite the fact she was pushing fifty. Somehow his rakish Scottish charm had worn a little thin after that and Louisa had felt ashamed to have been taken in by his guile and had seen him for what he really was – a fraud.

As she sat slumped at her desk, Louisa felt a life-changing moment beginning to dawn. She could hear the credits that signalled the end of the snooker echoing up the stairs. Soon she would be listening to the beginning of *Silent Witness*, and then her dad's footsteps would clomp up the stairs. She had about two minutes to make a decision. Was it really time to start kick-starting a life, start being someone who could write an interesting blog or was it time to settle next to her dad, snuggle under some chenille and throw another night at the TV?

Footsteps were heard on the stairs. She had thirteen stair steps to decide.

"Louisa! Are you coming down? I've just popped out for chips!"

Well, it would be rude not to…

CHAPTER 5

Rhwng y cŵn a'r brain – between the dogs and the crows (going to rack and ruin)

It was a cold Christmas Eve with clouds rolling in from the east and Iestyn was out banging his fingers with a claw hammer half way up a hillside, trying to fix the hinges of a knackered old gate. It had been in poor condition for years, tied shut with string and with an old fence post tied, swinging, underneath it to stop the cleverest of the sheep from crawling under it. Last week it had finally collapsed and Iestyn was determined to get it mended before lambing started. Having seen Jean's parking allocations, he was having one of his – usually short-lived – drives towards efficiency: a stitch in time and all that.

He had just re-hung the gate with an air of triumph and was pushing it open and watching in pleasure as it swung gently back until clicking quietly shut on the new latch. Brilliant – only 37 more gates to go: perhaps he'd save the rest of them until he'd marked out the parking bays…

As he gathered up his tools and slung them in the back of the Land Rover, he took a moment to look down the valley to his parents' farm. He could see his father limping across the yard with his familiar but strange gait, holding two buckets and bundled up against the weather. His mother was another pile of coats ducking in and out of the shed that held the sheep dogs and scraping the worst of the muck out of the pen and into the wheelbarrow.

Iestyn knew that he and Johnny joked about their families, but he would never knock them. They were only doing what farming families did. No generation ever felt entitled to sell the family silver, so that meant that someone from each generation had to slog day in, day out, every day of the year. No one ever managed to properly retire, they just did jobs that fitted their current levels of physical strength, passing on the earlier and later shifts to the younger ones and trying hard not to baulk at newer methods.

Pencwmhir was a hill farm of some 150 acres – mainly scrubby pasture with grazing rights over the open hill. As the name, Pencwmhir suggested, their farm was at the head of a long valley and their access track snaked parallel to the stream for a mile until it hit the public road.

Iestyn looked up the valley from his vantage point as the waves of sleet started buffeting across the land. He saw the sheep crouched on the lee side of the hedges in a way that would have his father sucking in the air through his teeth. He squinted through the weather and saw a glinting four-by-four bumping over the first cattle grid.

Iestyn smiled and chuckled as he watched the Grand Cherokee ease itself down the stone track. He remembered how Joe used to drive in his father's Land Rover, crashing through potholes and driving with two wheels up the bank to see how steep he could go before it tipped. He obviously understood his father's irritation now and his careful driving showed that he'd paid for the Jeep himself.

Iestyn watched the Jeep stop at the next gate and waited as Joe got out and stepped into his wellies, opened the gate, went back, put his shoes on, drove through the gate, then repeated the tedious drill to shut it. It seemed as if he was getting more and more anal every time he came home – and obviously Sima wasn't embracing country mud yet, either.

Iestyn rattled down the rest of the track, looking forward to seeing his brother; Joe always lightened up the farm and brought a little fun and frivolity into a relentlessly practical home, and Sima would breathe fresh life into his fantasies for the oncoming dark weeks…

He bumped into the yard at the same time that Joe and Sima did. Tomos had chosen to open Joe's gate and so Iestyn had to get out and do his own. Iestyn could see Sima pointing and telling Joe to park as close to the door as was possible – it seemed that she forgot each time she came just how much mud and shite a farm produced.

Isla was rinsing her wellies in the brook that ran along the back of the house as Joe stepped out and shook his father's hand and attempted to hug him.

"Good to see you, boy," said Tomos as he patted a dirty hand on the shoulder of Joe's designer jacket. "Hello, Sima, how are you, my dear?"

"Very well, Tomos, how are you?" she purred from within the Jeep, pulling on a pair of flowery wellies and zipping her white pumps into a bag.

"Come on in, bach," smiled Tomos, his weathered face softened by the beauty's charm. "Too cold to be outside on a day like this." He was oblivious to his wife dressed in three coats and trying to dislodge a stubborn turd from her wellie treads in the brook.

They all moved into the enormous kitchen, Sima unzipping her pumps once more and Tomos waving them away: Sima's wellies were far cleaner than any of their carpet slippers. She was put into a chair nearest the fire and eventually the chattering of her gleaming teeth began to subside. Joe came in laden with presents, all beautifully gift-wrapped. He placed them under the Christmas tree that Tomos had hacked down from the side of the hill in the Forestry Commission plantation and which had then been decorated by Isla, with Iestyn doing the high bits.

They were the decorations that had adorned the Bevan Christmas tree for decades, many of them crafted at some point by the Bevan boys, but they looked suddenly tatty next to the glorious packaging, all themed with silver ribbons and bows.

Iestyn leant against the Rayburn shifting from side to side as Isla opened the oven door to remove some particularly restrained scones and then returned to fetch the kettle from the hob. The family chattered together as they caught up on the past couple of months' worth of news.

"So, what's with the Cherokee?" laughed Iestyn, "London's roads cutting up a bit?"

"Actually, my road's got more potholes than your track," smiled Joe, never minding the teasing about his soft city existence.

"And brought down any more banks recently?"

"Yeah, ruined two banks and squandered a pension fund just last week actually – that's how I managed to buy the Jeep, you know, with my bonus."

"What about you, Sima, my love," asked Tomos, "how's business with you?"

"Fantastic, thanks, Tomos," she smiled, "fantastic."

Iestyn smirked. He knew what Tomos thought about the people who paid Sima to be their life coach, but he also knew that Tomos admired anyone who worked hard and made money – even if it were for a service that was a pile of bloody nonsense. It just seemed a little unfair to Tomos that Sima made more money than the farming Bevans made put together – and they had far more blisters, crushed fingernails and septic blackthorn splinters to show for theirs. Her two-bedroom flat was worth more than their whole farm – and it was paid for.

"Yes, Iestyn," said Joe, "and she still has a space in her January client list with your name on it, isn't that right, Sima? On the stage one programme teaching you how to brush your teeth and stop wearing 1980s jumpers."

"No, he's already perfect. He would jump straight to the stage five programme – just a bit of tinkering, a little French poetry perhaps."

Iestyn glowed warm inside. Sima always made him feel like that – how on earth had she fallen for an arse like Joe? Tall, dark and exotic, her long black curls looked like they just tumbled wherever they wanted to, but Iestyn now knew enough about Sima to know that every single one had been commanded into position and told to stay right there. Perhaps he needed to move to London or find out whether she had a sister or an ugly mate?

Isla handed out the tea, remembering that Sima didn't have milk, but forgetting that she didn't do carbohydrates as she handed round a plate of her not-quite-so-enormous-as-usual scones. Sima noticed that Joe picked the biggest one. "I thought you were off the carbs for a while, Joe?"

"Well, I have to keep the cold out somehow," he grinned, "and a gut like this doesn't look after itself – needs a lot of maintenance!" Joe wobbled the jelly that hung over his belt. Iestyn laughed – it was a joke between them that Joe's first bonus had bought him a soft belly.

"So, how's the love life, Iestyn?" Iestyn's love life was always a topic of interest to Sima and Iestyn was embarrassed to report that little had changed since the last time.

"Well, you know, bit lean like, being winter and all that…"

"Lean?" laughed Joe. "Since when did *nothing happening* become *lean*?"

"Saw Johnny Brechdan on the tops the other day," said Iestyn changing the subject that to him was well and truly exhausted. "Sends his regards."

"Johnny who?"

"Brechdan," explained Joe to Sima, "means *sandwich* in Welsh. As dry as an old sandwich is Johnny, so he's called Johnny Brechdan – has been since he was about five."

"But why not Johnny Bone or Johnny Desert?"

"Oh, you couldn't call a boy Johnny Bone *or* Johnny Desert," said Tomos incredulously, "wouldn't be right. Anyway, is their Gemma due yet?"

"Gemma?" asked Iestyn.

"You know, Gemma, married to Paul Thomas's son."

"What, Paul Thomas the Pentwyn?"

"No, Paul Thomas the Bryn. You know, Hywel Thomas's lad."

"No, not Hywel Thomas," joined in Isla, "*Arwel* Thomas."

"Arwel? Was he the one with the puncture?"

"Yesss, that's him."

Joe put his head in his hands and groaned. "Sima, take me home – I don't think I can take a whole Christmas with this going on; I'd forgotten what Bevan conversations were like."

Sima laughed and winked at Iestyn, "So, *has* Gemma had hers yet?"

"No," said Isla, "she's not due 'til March, surely? I know it's after Bethan's."

"Bethan? Bethan the Park?"

"No, Bethan Harris, over Fairclough's way…"

"Right! Stop!" shouted Joe. "Change of conversation please. No more Bevan talk whilst Sima is here – she hasn't a hope in knowing who Bethan Harris is…"

"Bethan Harris? Bethan Harris is dead. Must be twenty-five years now…"

Esther Harrison sat at her computer and pressed *print* with a triumphant click of her mouse. To her delight another whirr came from the printer at her feet and it scrolled out a sheet of paper. Esther

Harrison, **ESTHER HARRISON**, *Esther Harrison* it read in different sizes and styles of font. She really was getting the hang of this now.

However, it was no surprise to her when the sound of the printer awakened a tut and a call from the sofa. Those bloody two, she cursed to herself. Sitting there like Lord and Lady Muck, demanding what was it this time – hot chocolate?

"Well, *you* can make it yourself," she began, but backed down to a "Come on, love, she's had a hard day! First day back to work after Christmas is always tough," tirade from her husband. Although Esther couldn't imagine that working in Tan-y-Bryn's only bank then slumping on the sofa could have got *that* difficult since she herself had left, nor could she imagine that David's job in the local paint and building supplies factory was much harder, but she knew that they both thought housework did itself, and that she spent her days lunching with Marjorie and doing crosswords in front of the fire. Therefore, she reluctantly pushed her computer chair backwards and went, muttering, into the kitchen. At least if they stayed on the sofa, she wouldn't have to spend twice as long clearing up after their efforts.

As Esther waited for the kettle to boil, she looked at the piece of paper still in her hand. What she really needed was to be the secretary of something, so that she legitimately had some letters to write. Perhaps she could breathe a bit of life back into a few old plans and start forging a career for herself. She could do that; she had the time and now she had the skills too. Esther was sure that she would make a good secretary – perhaps she'd ask at the golf club to see if they wanted a bit of administrative help?

She warmed the teapot, and then began spooning leaves into it. Damn. Hot chocolate was what they'd wanted. She rinsed out the teapot and reached for the milk instead. As she heated three cups' worth in the small milk pan, she thought back over her day and wondered where she might be able to use her new skills. Marjorie was lucky: she had a part-time job in a double glazing firm's office. She typed and filed all day for two days a week and she loved it.

Yes, Marjorie had loads of contacts in town and plenty of ideas. What had she said just that lunchtime as they'd sat in The Tasty Bite, talking about letters? Esther pondered as she spooned chocolate powder into three cups. Ah, it had been about the menu, the naff decorations, and the service. And the toilets. Oh, and the wobbly tables.

As they'd sat waiting for their desserts, Marjorie had gotten increasingly frustrated with the table and had stuffed a folded napkin under it in annoyance, tutting about how the place had gone so far down hill so quickly.

"Perhaps we should tell them?" Esther had smiled.

"Hmph, write it on a brick and then chuck it through the window," Marjorie had snarled and then proceeded simply to not tip.

Esther poured the last of the milk over the chocolate powder and stirred. Perhaps she *should* tell them. They had one of those signs that said, "If you like what you see, tell others. If you don't, tell us!" stuck on the wall.

She got the mini-whisk out of the cupboard and frothed up the milk in the cups. Maybe if she typed just a short polite note to suggest a few changes and posted it to them, they might appreciate her honesty?

She took a chunk of milk chocolate from Louisa's selection box in the cupboard and absent-mindedly grated it over the tops of the drinks.

Yes, a short, pleasant, constructive note would do the trick. No one could object to that and if it were anonymous, then there would be no need for embarrassment when she next went in.

She put the drinks on a tray, wiped down all the surfaces and went though into the lounge, rolling her eyes at the tirade of comments about whether she'd been milking the cow herself.

Esther could be a little bit cunning when she needed to be. She fussed around asking questions about the programme, what had happened and if the hot chocolate had enough sugar in. She soon got on their nerves and retired to her desk knowing that they would leave her in peace rather than risk having her fuss some more. She reckoned she had about half an hour to carry out her task – nature would probably take its course about then and until that time, it was unlikely that either of them would move. Mind, if they could find out a way that she could do *that* for them, then she would have probably a whole hour's peace...

She slowly started to type. Her address first, then she slowly deleted it, and then put it in italics. Then she deleted it again: such a letter didn't need an address...

Dear whomever it may concern, she began: it was as if the room had grown silent. No one breathed. Even the sipping was being done quietly. She carried on, typing as quietly as the keys would allow and looked again, sure that there would be a projector shining her words onto the screen of the television, instead of it showing *Silent Witness*.

She felt guilty, she felt dirty and she felt a little bit unkind. However, she thought again of that notice – *if you don't like it, tell us* – well, wasn't she doing just that?

My friend and I recently visited your establishment and partook of a... She halted, keen to keep her anonymity from an eagle-eyed waitress... *coffee and a mince pie. Although it was pleasant enough, there were a few points that made our visit less enjoyable than it might have been and, seeing your notice, I thought it might be beneficial to let you know...*

Esther took a breath and ran her hands through her hair and was surprised to find that she was perspiring. She read back through her letter and felt more confident – it was succinct, yet polite. No, it wouldn't offend anyone, and any proper business should be pleased that she'd made the effort to give it some feedback.

Reassured, she rubbed the moisture from her palms onto her jeans and carried on with renewed vigour. She was just signing off as "a well-wisher" when the television credits began to roll. She gave a quick look around and as Louisa began to yawn, and David gave a stretch, she quickly pressed *print*. The noise of the print head zapping slowly back and fore made her jump as it broke the silence.

"What are you printing, Mum?" yawned Louisa.

"Nothing really," said Esther a little bit too quickly, "just practising. There, all done."

She reached down, grabbed the page and tucked it behind her previous practice sheet. "I'll just take the cups out to the kitchen," she said, jumping up. Two cups were dangled over the back of the sofa and Esther was able to grab them and scuttle off without anyone being any the wiser...

It was gone eight when Menna pushed open the door of her bungalow. She was absolutely shattered. She was pleasantly filled with turkey curry, but also soaking wet and cold from the five-minute trot between the big house and her own home. She stood in the hallway and let herself drip onto the mat for a few seconds. She clicked on the lamp in the corner and then removed her wellies and put them into the wire boot stand. Her coat was placed on the ornate hooks that lined the wall over the radiator and she took off her wet trousers and hung them up too, ready to be climbed back into in the morning.

She went into the kitchen and the light shone pink over the room. She pulled the pink curtains to and the room felt snug and warm. She filled the Rayburn with logs from the basket and put the kettle on to boil; she would do the ash and replenish the log basket in the morning. Menna stood in front of the shelf and scanned her CDs, finally picking one out and putting it into the CD player. Soon the room was filled with Aretha Franklin as she wandered off to the shower.

Her bathroom was the archetypal girl's room. The white suite that had had blue paint slapped around (and over) it, was now complemented by a pale peach. She had ripped out the pale blue lino and laid a warm laminate and covered it in rugs. The mirror was heart-shaped with rosebuds round the outside and one wall was hung with a cascade of white plastic flowers. An old shelving unit had been transformed into one of waxed wood and was stocked with ornamental bottles of potions and creams. Her shower was filled with colourful sponges and brushes and her white towels hung from large daisies fixed onto the walls. Throughout, the bathroom was washed with the sound of 'Chain of Fools' that cooed out of the humidity-proofed speaker hanging in the corner.

Menna removed the rest of her clothes and stepped into the shower to wash the remains of the day from her skin and replace the scent with that of white lily shower gel.

Wrapped in a long, embroidered silk dressing gown, Menna wandered into the lounge and stoked the wood burner. She put a pile of kindling onto the embers and watched as they glowed and finally burst into flames. Then she piled in more wood from the basket and walked to the sideboard, a sizeable hunk of dark oak that her mother had dumped in the barn and Menna had lovingly restored by scraping off the old varnish and polishing it until it shone.

She loved her home, her own little domain. Living with her parents had been an experience in pragmatism. Other girls her age had had pink princess bedrooms or funky purple ones with pop stars lining the walls. Hers had always had white paint and she had not been allowed Blu-Tack.

When she'd finally been given the keys for the bungalow, her heart had rejoiced – at last she'd be able to live a bit more like she wanted to. She still ended up at the big house for meals and for her washing, but that was fine, it was practical and she worked hard enough without having piles of washing-up to do.

The bungalow had been lived in for thirty years by Tal, the ancient farmhand, who had eventually gone to live with his sister. Tal hadn't been into interior design and had washed every wall in a pale blue that made the place feel cold and damp, even in the middle of summer. Menna had set about transforming it as soon as he'd moved the last box out.

She'd spent many hours scouring second-hand shops and packages regularly arrived from eBay and over the last couple of years, she'd transformed the blue iceberg into a den of luxurious femininity. She didn't have a lot of money for fripperies, but she had an eye for a bargain and loved retro-chic.

No one had ever really seen the bungalow as it now stood. Her friends and parents had helped her move in and some had helped with a bit of painting, but as their excitement had dwindled, so had their offers of help and that was fine. Menna had enjoyed her foray into domesticity, and she had been happy to shut the doors of an evening and paint or rub down or drill holes in all the doorways so that her speakers filled the whole house with sound.

She saw her parents every day, so all their interaction was at the big house with no need for them to call by. If friends wanted to find her, they went to the house first, as her bungalow was half a mile further up the track, but also she tended to meet them out of an evening – in the pub or at someone else's house, which might have more than just half a pint of milk in the fridge.

Over the months, as her domain became more and more removed from her outer persona, so she felt less comfortable about people coming by. It was a form of embarrassment as they would bound to be amazed by the way that she wanted to live. She knew that people expected that she lived in tasteless disarray. She was so very unlike her mother in personality that everyone therefore assumed that she had to be her opposite. People joked that it must be annoying for her to always have her toilet seat up, even though she lived alone. She was sure that they expected her to be a parody of the archetypal Welsh bloke because that's how she dressed for work: sitting in her pants drinking a can of Special Brew and watching re-runs of *Top Gear* with plates of last night's curry still lying on the floor.

It made her nervous to think how amazed her close friends and family would find it, but she knew that *everyone* would be surprised if they turned up to find her luxuriating in a floor-length dressing gown listening to Shirley Bassey.

It was her intention to "come out" of her closet over time, but first she wanted to enjoy practicing her new expression in a place that was safe from people saying, "Eh? What d'ya want to wear *that* for?" It had been quite telling that she had exchanged Christmas presents with her parents after a rather festivity-free Christmas dinner and none of the gifts that she had received had made her smile anything other than a fake thank you. Did her mum really think that she would actually *want* a pack of navy blue T-shirts or a glass Pyrex flan dish? There were lots of things that a twenty-six-year-old woman who had just moved into her new home might love and none of them involved navy blue or Pyrex.

She sat on a satin floor cushion in front of the sideboard and slid open the door, humming along to 'Respect!' What would it be tonight? What would transport her into her own special world, one where her mother didn't stand and purse her lips and watch what she was doing, or her father didn't keep his head down for an easy life. *Gone With the Wind*? No, *Casablanca*!

She slid out the case and crawled over the deep-pile rug to the television in the corner. After she had set the film to start, she popped back to the kitchen to make herself a cup of tea, turned off Aretha and returned to the sofa draped in a soft throw. She massaged body lotion into her skin as the opening credits rolled. By the time Bergman had spotted Bogart, Menna was sitting in a French café in occupied France, drinking an espresso and drawing on an elegant cigarette holder.

Chapter 6

Natur y cyw yn y cawl – the nature of the chick in the broth (someone who has inherited the family traits)

Louisa was sitting on her bed wanting desperately to be angry with someone else, but finding that her thoughts kept coming back to herself. She had changed into her pyjamas and slung her uniform on the floor: not exactly a big statement of her feelings, Esther would pick them up the next morning with only the smallest of grumbles.

She looked sideways into the winged mirror that sat on her dressing table, alongside her jewellery box with the revolving ballet dancer on it and saw her profile – plump, miserable and dressed for bed at eight p.m. She turned away, knowing that it needed more than a suck in of her stomach and a throwing back of her shoulders to make her feel better.

She'd parked her car a little further away from the office than usual today. Her regular space on the side street fifty yards from the bank was being dug up – *just* in time for the after-Christmas sales – and it had annoyed her as she'd had to drive around looking for somewhere else. Consequently, at the end of the day she had had to walk down the high street, past all the shopkeepers as they swept up after a day of people bargain hunting with wet feet. And there they were. In the window of Tan-y-Bryn's only trendy wine bar: Rosie, Rachel and a group of their greatest friends.

They had all been sitting in a curved sofa around a large table filled with empty glasses. They were laughing and beautiful and trendy and, and beautiful and happy, and beautiful. And she was none of those. It had crashed her down to earth, as before that (save for the parking fiasco) it had been a reasonable day: Doreen had brought in a home-made sponge, the young bloke from the Spar had been in for change and had joked with her *and* she'd managed to read part of the newspaper when it had been quiet in the morning. As Louisa Harrison's days went, that was pretty good.

But then she'd seen them. And realised that actually her day had been shit. Boring, pointless, middle-aged and shit. Why did none of *her* mates pop in to ask if she fancied a cocktail after work? Because she didn't have any. Why couldn't *she* look good curled up on a wine bar sofa chatting to a mate? Because her knee would have seized up from lack of suppleness, stiffness brought on by too little exercise. Why wasn't her hair looking sexy piled up on her head, fixed with a twirl of tinsel and with tendrils hanging around her face? Because she had a bob that was cut by her mother's hairdresser.

On her desk the Internet finally jumped into being, and although she really didn't feel like it, Louisa sat down and typed in the address for her blog. Then she couldn't help herself and typed in the URL for Rachel's blog – hoping to find an explanation of why she had been sitting with her great friends in the bar. Maybe they had been working? Maybe it was a wake of an old aunty – although, if it was, it needn't have looked so much fun.

It was actually worse than Louisa could have hoped for:

Hi, I can't write for long, but I wanted to just do this before I went out! One of the crowd called today and left a message saying that he felt that we should all go out, 'Just Because!' I agree: Just Because is a perfect excuse! Therefore, we'll try for our usual table straight from work – I wonder how many of us will come and whether they'll think Just Because is a good enough reason as well?

Must dash! Bye, Rachel x

Just *because*? One of the *crowd*? Our *usual* table?

She'd never had a usual table – apart from perhaps the kitchen table – and she'd certainly never been part of any crowd. All her life she'd watched the wider world through a double-glazed window. As a child, she'd seen children walking up their path and then the doorbell would ring. Her father would answer it and she would hear him talking to the child and the door would close. She would watch from her place on the sofa with a blanket over her knees as the child skipped back down the path and returned to the others.

Her dad would always dismiss it by saying that he and she were about to do something interesting anyway; they would read a story or start a game and she would feel that perhaps she was better off not going out to play. But later, when the game had stopped and her father had returned to his newspaper and she was plonked back on the sofa watching *Blue Peter*, she would see a gang of children racing up the estate on their bikes or huddled in a group around someone's new toy and she would feel a pang of regret. That stab of jealousy was *exactly* the same feeling she had experienced earlier that afternoon.

Suddenly, it was all too much and with resentment and frustration washing over her, Louisa burst into tears just as there was a gentle knock at the door and her dad's curly head poked in.

David had just popped up to make a little suggestion to his daughter to try and entice her from her room down to the sofa to sit by him. She was his little companion, his partner in crime – far more fun to sit next to than his pious wife, who tended to tut and roll her eyes at his foibles. She would never throw caution to the wind and tuck into a tin of Quality Street in the same naughty, impish way that Louisa did; Esther would comment on his cholesterol level and make him feel a greedy slob. But tins of Quality Street weren't about sustenance and vitamin intake; they were about treating oneself and one's loved ones over the Christmas period.

He was just about to smile at her and make his suggestion when he saw his daughter's despair. "My love, my love, whatever is the matter?" he said as he lurched towards her. He cradled her sobbing head to his chest and felt the tears rise up in his own eyes. "What's the matter, my baby, what is it? You can tell me."

"I can't," she blubbed.

"Yes, you can," he soothed. "Is it work?" She shook her head. "Are you ill?" He wracked his brains; it was so long since Louisa had cried like this. "Have you fallen out with your friends? A boyfriend?" Like many doting parents, David assumed that his beautiful daughter had an active social and love life, despite there being no visible evidence of either; their door had never been knocked by a stranger asking whether Louisa was in.

The sobs changed and her sticky face peered up to his – ah, this was probably the root; Louisa had always been an open child and would always answer questions as long as they were the right ones.

"Friends?" she blubbed. "What friends? And *boyfriend*! That's a laugh." She buried her head again and her sobs went a little quieter.

David felt a barb go through his soul. All he'd ever really wanted was for his family to be happy – Esther and Louisa – he would do anything to make them happier, always had done. But, as he watched Louisa sobbing, his mind couldn't help but drift back to times when perhaps he hadn't done quite everything in his gift to make his family happy – or at least not unless *he* was happy first.

When he and Esther had got married, he'd been proud of her energy and her willingness to help out. Unfortunately for him, her abilities were soon recognised by others and she became first invited, and then completely sucked in by the rounds of good causes that needed people to actually *do* something, rather than just cluck about doing something. So she baked cakes for raffles, delivered shopping to sick people and basically had one hundred reasons why she simply couldn't spend any time seeing to her husband and his needs.

When Louisa had come along, Esther had started working part-time and therefore had even more opportunity – in the eyes of others – to do a little more for her community. It was fine, they said, take the little one along too; the older folks love to see babies!

It wasn't that David was a complete monster, it was just that, well, he had needs and he felt that because he worked as hard as his father had before him, it would have been nice for him to have had a newspaper on the arm of his chair when he came home from work, or a cup of tea proffered. Instead, he usually found a note on the kitchen table: *Gone to see to Mrs Johnson. Back at 6.30, Soup in fridge* and then his wife would return at 7.30, muttering that Mrs J certainly liked to talk.

Esther had worked part-time so that she had more time to spend with *her* family – doing *family* things – surely, not so that she could spend more time dressing peoples' ulcers or feeding mangy cats. It got so that Louisa didn't want to go and play jigsaws whilst her mother spring-cleaned houses the occupants of which were in hospital. David sheepishly recognised that he'd become a bit of a martyr and instead of letting his daughter play outside with her mates, he'd played with her himself.

He would leave games of Cluedo out or pots of paint on the kitchen table. He would take books off Louisa's bookshelf and put them in a pile on the arm of the sofa. He could see that he was making Esther feel guilty, but she obviously felt even more moved by the fact that there was an old guy living in squalor as his marbles slowly rolled away.

So it had continued. He would take Louisa swimming when Esther called bingo numbers at the old folks Saturday get-togethers. He would take her down the park whilst Esther ran the over 60s yoga club. Although he enjoyed his time with Louisa, on the whole, it was actually done with the single aim of having a dig at his wife. To make her feel as if she was missing out – which she was – and to make her feel bad – which she did.

Then on that day when Louisa said she wanted to run wild like Laura Ingalls, a light had gone on in David's brain – just move. Move away from all the needy folks and the well-intentioned people who organised his wife's life and thought that a phone call to her had meant that they had done their bit. If she lived in the middle of bloody nowhere, she *couldn't* keep popping out to feed someone's cat. Even *she* couldn't justify driving seven miles in each direction to mop the piss off some guy's floor. Someone else would have to do it – or the guy would perhaps have to learn not to piss on his floor. Can't feed your cat? Don't have a bloody cat.

David's trump card was to pretend it was for Louisa's benefit when it had actually been *wholly* for his.

Looking at Louisa, he realised that he was now being punished for his selfishness in the worst possible way. Being chuffed off that his wife was leading a working party to scrub graffiti from a bus shelter when she could have been listening to his tale about John Talbot from despatch, and brewing him a cuppa, had meant that he'd insisted on watching *Blue Peter* with his daughter rather than letting her go and play Icky Dicky outside with some mates.

The upshot was that the local children had got out the habit of calling for Louisa Harrison; her dad was always putting them off.

Now, looking down at her red eyes and her runny nose, he felt like he could cry himself.

"Come on, Louisa, you have lots of friends," he said as lightly as he could, but he really needed to hear a positive answer.

"Like who? Uncle Bob? Well, he's dead now, so name another one? Yours and Mum's friends at the golf club? Doreen at work?"

"Yes, why not?" said David, trying to think of other names. "What about Alex?"

"I suppose she chats if I see her in the street, but she never comes round anymore." David thought back to the last time Alex's ginger head had been in their home – probably the time that she and Louisa had fallen out and Alex had trapped Louisa's fingers under the piano lid and Louisa had pushed Alex off the stool. It had been a long time ago. David felt at a loss.

"But, but, we love you."

"I know, Dad, but I'm twenty-six. I'm supposed to have my own friends, my own life. Not just attach myself to yours." She wiped her eyes with a hanky from her sleeve and attempted to smile.

"What's brought this on, love?" asked David. "You seemed fine earlier this evening…" Louisa shrugged and reached for a tissue. Her arm nudged the mouse and the screen saver jolted off, revealing Rachel's blog. David read it.

"I see," he said slowly. "This is your homework, right? Your blog homework? And your life isn't as – as exciting as Rachel's?" Louisa sniffed and nodded, looking a little sheepish. David straightened up and put his hands on his head. He was responsible for this. He was. He wanted to keep her for himself, for his own means; keep her safe and warm, at home, with him. He loved it when they sat together on the sofa, eating marshmallows and bullying Esther to make cups of tea. He felt like they were a little gang and that no one could touch them. Well, now it seemed that no one wanted to. He finally realised that he wasn't supposed to be her gang and she wasn't a line of defence between him and the discussions he needed to have with his wife. He was her dad; he was supposed to be giving her the independence to step out into the world and find her own life – instead he had pushed away her flimsy efforts at attaining things, quietly suggesting that she did them another day and hoping that she'd forget about them. He should have been supporting her activities. Instead, he'd thwarted them at every turn.

Even now he had the habitual urge to say, "Don't worry, we'll find you some friends at the weekend, love. *Taggart* is on; why don't you come down with me now and we can sort the rest out next week?" He knew that she would probably be relieved to hear it and come down and do just that. There was a chocolate orange in the fridge with her name on it and Esther would be hovering somewhere near a kettle –

it could be very simple. But then he saw his beloved daughter's swollen eyes and her runny nose. She was looking to him for guidance and it was his job as her father to provide it – even if it meant that his world would have to change too.

He sat on the bed, struggling with the words. Surely his daughter had to have *some* friends? "OK, so what do we need to do?"

Louisa shrugged.

"What does – Rachel – do of an evening?"

"She lives in a flat with two friends and they go out and they go away for weekends and friends come round and ..."

David laughed and held his hands up, "Hold on, hold on! One change at a time!" Louisa's face fell. "No," he corrected himself, "as many changes as you want... Look, I know it's been tough for you growing up..." David wasn't sure in what way it might have been tough, but it sounded like a good get out clause for both of them, "...but, Louisa, we haven't stopped you doing any of those things, have we? I mean, I know it's not been easy, your, your mother having her stroke an' all, and I know that you have been a tremendous help to her, but it's not that... Well, we haven't demanded you stay, have we? And we could manage without you – we would never *want* to though of course – I would love it if you could live with us until we get buried in the back garden..."

Louisa looked at her father and David felt guilty that he was now trying to make her make *him* feel better. He was still finding it difficult to be the adult in this relationship.

"Dad, Dad, no, of course you've never insisted I stay and I know that Mum can manage most things but..." her voice trailed off, as if she was unsure of what she could get away with saying next.

The truth was that Louisa probably *had* been thinking that she was staying at home for her mother's sake – at least, that is what they tended to tell people if they asked. But what did her mum actually need her to do? She did chop onions and peel potatoes occasionally, but so did her father, and it wasn't an unreasonable thing to expect from a fellow house occupant. She would hang out clothes or fetch them in if she was home, but most of them were hers anyway. In fact, if David added up all the hot drinks and sandwiches she demanded and the extra towels that required picking up, Louisa probably actually caused her mother work, rather than saved her from it.

It was an important moment of realisation. All those years they had been telling themselves, and other people, that Louisa couldn't get on with living in the same way as other people her age did, because she was looking after her sick mother. It was as if, in her mind, she returned home after a long day in the bank to a lump slumped on the sofa wrapped in a blanket that she had to feed, water and wash. Poor little Cinderella would then make the meals, clean the house and read her mother a story before carrying her to bed on her own frail back. Reality, of course, was a mother that struggled in her own life, but the only tangible effect of this on her daughter's existence was that her onions tended to be a little more roughly chopped than she would prefer.

Louisa looked embarrassed and ashamed. "I s'pose I just felt I couldn't leave, in case…things got…worse?" It was lame and limp and everything else that was pathetic. David could see, deep in his heart, that his precious daughter quite simply couldn't be arsed. She'd got used to being mollycoddled in the same way that he'd got used to mollycoddling and it had had repercussions far beyond their initial intentions. He'd turned into a drab old stick who bullied his wife and indulged his daughter and she'd turned into a lazy slob who couldn't make decisions for herself and whose acceptable level of risk-taking was putting her hand into the multi-pack of crisps without looking to see which flavour she was heading for.

In the same way that Louisa couldn't be bothered to choose a job that she might actually enjoy, or make her own sandwiches, she also couldn't be bothered to look for or pay for her own flat. She couldn't be bothered to sit on a second-hand sofa when there was a deluxe corner unit at her disposal at home. Why live with people you were bound to fall out with over abandoned pubic hairs and dirty coffee cups when you could stay with people who'd fought out all the ground rules before you were even born?

"I think," she began, beginning to blush, "I think I need to get a move on…"

"That's my girl," smiled David. "Always the adventurer!" Then they both squirmed, so he collected an abandoned teacup, made his excuses and left.

Chapter 7

Fel twll tin ci ar yr haul – like a dog's arse in the sun (dull, without sparkle)

Iestyn was settled in front of *Animals Do the Funniest Things* when lights flashed across the kitchen ceiling indicating that someone had just driven into the yard.

"Who'll that be?" asked Tomos craning his head around his chair.

"Dunno, Dad, can't tell by just the lights."

"Well, have a look, lad, might be someone important."

Iestyn groaned and dragged himself out of his chair and padded to the window. *Brechdan. What the hell was he after?* Iestyn wasn't sure that he could handle Johnny's enthusiasm for life, tonight. All he wanted to do was to have a long soak in a warm bath and then sit and slob in front of the TV. Unfortunately, the bath was full of Isla's mackintosh which was being re-waterproofed, with one of her ancient remedies that the packet had disintegrated around, and unless he wanted to go and sort that out, he had to make do with being grubby and sitting on the sofa in front of the TV.

By the time Iestyn had reached the door, Brechdan was in the kitchen. "Evening all, how is everyone today?"

"Grand, boy, grand," came the call from the winged chair.

"How's things at Cwmtwrch, Johnny? Had a good Christmas?" called Isla. She had been good friends with Johnny's grandparents since they'd taken Johnny on as a child after the death of his parents, and she always enjoyed the boost in atmosphere that Johnny brought to any room he was in.

"Yes, thanks we've had a lovely time, but tonight I have been thrown out."

"Oh? Why's that, boy?" asked Tomos, knowing it would be something stupid that Johnny was cooking up.

"I've been thrown out to go and take my old friend Iestyn out for a night on the town. A pre-New-Year's-Eve night out. Those were my orders: take him out and cheer the miserable git up."

"Nah, you're all right thanks, Johnny, I'm not really up for—"

"Well, what a lovely idea," said Isla. "Thank you, Johnny; he *is* a bit of a miserable git at the moment, isn't he, Tomos?"

"Yes, yes, you're right, he is."

"Oi, bloody charming that is – if I *am* a miserable git, it's because I live with you two and I get all the shitty jobs and the bath is full of mother's bloody swedeing mac and—"

"All the more reason why you need to come out with me then," chipped Johnny. "That OK with you folks? Can you do without his miserable face for the rest of the night and maybe give him a little lie-in in the morning?"

"Course we can. It would be a pleasure. Thank you, Johnny, for taking him off our hands."

"Absolutely, and look, here's thirty quid to pay some tart to cheer him up good and proper..." said Tomos, taking his wallet from his back pocket and handing the money over to Johnny.

"Tomos!"

"Well, the boy's been single for bloody *years* m'n," he replied. "It'll go black and fall off if he's not careful. It needs to be used, boy, otherwise it'll forget what it's there for."

"My thoughts exactly," smiled Johnny. "Thank you, Tomos, now come on, Iestyn, you have five minutes to douse yourself in enough Christmas aftershave to get rid of your stench and then I want you back down here in your finest togs."

Iestyn grumbled and muttered as he slouched across the floor and crashed through the door at the bottom of the stairs, "...well, as long as you know that I don't actually *want* to go..." he mumbled, whilst Johnny sat down and made himself at home.

Esther pottered in the kitchen, drying the last few bits of cutlery and wiping over the surfaces. She knew that she would be called on for tea and had re-boiled the kettle twice so that it would be near to the boil when they put their request in. Funny really, she could hear that *Taggart* had started – they would be missing the crux of the storyline now if they weren't quick, then there would *really* be trouble.

As she gave the table another wipe over, her eye caught sight of the local newspaper, sitting by David's lunch box, packed ready for the morning. She began to flick through it; usually she knew a few of the local deaths and sometimes a marriage.

She idly turned the pages. *Mayor Plants Tree with Schoolchildren. Bowls Club Buys New Mats* and *Woman Breaks Ankle in Council Pothole.* Then a picture made her look twice: the woman standing outside the café with a piece of paper in her hand looked familiar. Then the headline made her catch her breath: *Anon Letter Turned Out to be Business Turning Point.*

Esther's heart pounded as she scraped out a chair and sat by the table to get a better view – it couldn't be? Surely?

Café owner Pat Marshwood of The Tasty Bite café on King Street, Tan-y-Bryn, was initially upset and angry by a letter that landed on her doormat with no name or address on it, but it eventually became the turning point that her business needed.

Pat, 52, has run The Tasty Bite café for fourteen years with husband, John. "But when John became ill five years ago, more and more of the chores became down to me and, in hindsight, I really haven't been coping," said Pat. "When you are in the service industry, it can be the little things that make the difference, and, unfortunately these were the ones that I had let slip."

Esther blew out a breath and wiped off the sweat that had formed on her face on a sheet of kitchen towel. She sat down again and could barely bring herself to read on – had she, Esther Harrison, really written a spiteful letter to a woman with a sick husband who was struggling to run their business? Yes, she had – and she was rightfully ashamed, nay, appalled by her actions.

She read on, peeping through her fingers as if the barrier would help shield her from her wrongdoing.

"However," said Pat, "after the initial upset, John and I sat down and looked at it again and decided that we needed extra help. My sister has been able to step in and it has made a world of a difference in just three days! I've done a spring clean and John has revamped the menu – oh, and the tables no longer wobble…" laughs Pat.

We asked Pat what she would like to say to the anonymous writer: "Well, if you'd asked me that on the morning I got the letter, you wouldn't be able to print it; it hasn't exactly been the best Christmas present we could have received from one of our customers! However, I now thank that person for their time and honesty, and if they ever want to own up, they can choose lunch from our new menu and sit on a stable table by our clean windows and enjoy themselves!"

So, if you know who the anonymous business advisor is, call the Tan-y-Bryn Gazette on the usual number…

Esther leant back in her chair and released a breath. No one must *ever* know it was her ever, ever, *ever*. Perhaps she'd got away with it this time, but she may not be so lucky again. And she certainly wouldn't fancy *her* name blazed across the front page of the *Tan-y-Bryn Gazette.*

As she stood up, she felt a little shaky and steadied herself on the back of the chair. The shock probably: she didn't tend to have much excitement in her life. She looked up into the mirror that hung between two cupboards on the kitchen wall and saw a red flush creep over her face. She felt her cheeks and then giggled slightly. Hugging her little secret to herself, she set the kettle on to boil again and went to see what was going on in the world of prime time television…

"Right then, Iestyn, what'll it be?"

"Dunno, pint I s'pose."

"Two pints of Best and a double whisky chaser, please, mate," said Johnny to the barman.

"I hope that's not for me," grumbled Iestyn, "I don't fancy whisky tonight."

"Iestyn, we're in the smartest bar in town, it's a Wednesday night, you've got Joe's best clothes on and you don't have to get up in the morning, *plus* the tightest old man in the world has given you thirty quid to get pissed on, so you're going to have a bloody whisky chaser, OK?"

Iestyn shrugged and then took a big slurp out of his pint, then smiled. "Thanks, mate, this *is* nice."

"Course it bloody is, now drink up; I want this on the head."

Iestyn did as he was told and soon a smile started peeping onto his face. He sat on the shining stool and surveyed the room. "Hey, it's bloody nice in here now, they've done something to it I think?"

"Done something to it?" said the guy behind the bar. "Mate, the owner's just spent over fifty grand making this place look good, plus another two grand on bloody Christmas decorations! Surely you can say something better than that!"

"OK then, it's *very nice,*" grinned Iestyn.

"Thank you. Same again, boys?"

"Yes please," said Johnny.

"Hang on, how come I'm getting the chasers and you're only drinking pints?"

"Iestyn, your dad only gave us thirty quid, and anyway, someone has got to look after you and hold your coat whilst you're busy and— Hey, look over there…"

"Where?"

"*There,* you dick,"

"At what?"

"For God's sake, Iestyn, the most beautiful women in the county have just walked into the bar wearing pink bunny ears and you haven't noticed them? For fuck's sake: Tomos was right about you…"

Johnny walked over to where the women were settling themselves down, managed to find that he knew one of them and was quickly offered a seat. He turned and beckoned Iestyn over and so Iestyn picked up his various drinks and mumbling quietly to himself, followed his opportunistic friend to his doom…

Iestyn was feeling drunk. He often had a few pints a couple of times a week, but it was usually whilst sitting in the Bull, and at a measured pace. By the end of a given night out, he would have slugged down the same sort of amount as he usually did, had the same amount of wees and two bags of crisps: one ready salted and one Monster Munch, or *one for the mouth ulcers* as Ed would call them. By the time he had walked home, he would be just about sober enough to drink a pint of tea, eat a pile of cheese sandwiches and fall into bed without any severe repercussions. Mornings after weren't exactly pleasant, but he could stagger through them and by the time he had cadged a lift back for his truck, all would be well.

Tonight, he had a feeling that it wouldn't end that way. Johnny was on sparkling form with the ladies. They were a hen party of eight women, all hell bent on having a good night and letting their hair down. Somehow Johnny and Iestyn had joined the kitty and were drinking whatever it was the person visiting the bar would get for them. Iestyn was sure that amongst the Smirnoff Ices and the Bacardi Rogos, he was also having a few more chasers of his own, courtesy of Johnny. As the night wore on, he was becoming less and less sure of what it was that was going down the hatch, but it wasn't his usual pints of Best, that was for sure. He was finally beginning to enjoy himself. The women were a good laugh and he was getting into the swing of things.

Suzy, a bridesmaid-to-be sitting beside him, was chattering away and he was laughing and chatting back. She'd been given the task of planning the night out and was taking it very seriously, taking novelties out of a bag of tricks at her feet at intervals, all to peals of laughter.

Johnny was sitting across the table from him and already had some rabbit ears on and a pair of comedy Y-fronts over his trousers. Iestyn didn't want to tell the women that the Y-fronts he had on *under* his trousers were actually more vile than Johnny's... A raspberry Mad Dog, tasting suspiciously of whisky, was washed down and then Iestyn had to extract himself to visit the gents. He climbed over the back of the sofa, to prevent everyone else having to get up, and the women either side of him tugged at the legs of his jeans. "Gerrof!" he yelled, still with a measure enough of self-preservation to be concerned that his orange pants might be revealed. The women just laughed and emptied a bag of peanuts down the exposed crack of his arse.

He wove his way through the chairs, clutching on to their backs for stability. There weren't that many people in tonight, just a few tables' worth dotted around, and once out of the reach of the hen party, the atmosphere was more civilised with people chatting together rather than screeching, and sipping rather than necking. He felt a little oafish, but he also felt good; it was good to let your hair down occasionally, and he and Johnny were doing it in style tonight.

He glanced in the mirror as he washed his hands. Joe's last-season clothes were holding up well, especially with a strand of red tinsel draped around the shoulders, but his hair was a little wild and his skin was flushed and open-pored. Never mind, he thought: get back out there into the dimmed lights and he would be fine.

As he stumbled back to the table, he saw that Suzy was by the jukebox.

"Iestyn! Oi, Iestyn, come over here! Come on, you choose one!" she shouted. Over he went and pressed a random collection of numbers.

"Oi, you shit!" Suzy cackled. "You've put on bloody 'Unchained Melody'!"

"Sorry," giggled Iestyn as he headed back for his seat. Someone had plonked a bottle of WKD in front of him and as a decent song ended and 'Unchained Melody' started, the women all grabbed their bottles and started singing, using their new props as microphones. Before Iestyn knew it, he too was standing, singing, his arms draped over his neighbours' shoulders, wearing a hula wreath over his tinsel and his own pair of rabbit ears.

Everyone climbed on the chairs and the sofa, yowling as they tried to reach the high notes. Iestyn was on soft ground as his feet slid about on the sofa's cushions. Suzy was hanging onto his shoulder on one side and Rebecca was tugging at his belt hoops for stability on the other side. It was bound to happen and as the crescendo was reached, they all started to topple backwards. Someone made a grab for Rebecca, giving Iestyn a second to get one leg over the back of the sofa. But, it wasn't enough and the three of them crashed to the floor, Iestyn on the bottom of the pile.

As he lay on the floor pouring WKD over his own face, two women with rabbit ears lying on top of him, he heard someone shout, "*Piley-on!*" and six other women and Johnny Brechdan ran round the side of the sofa and dived on top of them. His head was sticking out and despite his hysterical laughter, he groaned every time another woman landed. He could see feet with stilettos on sticking out of the pile, he could see stocking tops and pink fingernails trying to wriggle skirts down and he could see Johnny's face grinning into his from the top of the pile. "Fuckin' marvellous!" he winked at Iestyn, before rolling off onto the floor.

There was the sound of bar staff coming over, "OK, folks, OK, folks, that's enough I think. Come on, everyone up! Time to go home!" and the hens were hauled to their feet, dusted off and encouraged in the direction of the door. Iestyn was still at the bottom of the heap and was left on the floor, crushed, covered in sticky drinks, his hula wreath squashed flat and peanuts beginning to itch in his backside. No member of the bar staff seemed to want to tackle the fifteen-stone pissed bloke, so they left him there, assuming he would do as his mate had done and follow the women out of the door, like a dog stalking rabbits.

Iestyn woke a while later with someone shaking his shoulders. "Iestyn, Iestyn, time to go home now. They want to close the bar?"

"Wha...?"

"Come on, time to go home. Come on, up you get." The voice seemed familiar, but Iestyn could not place it, what with the fug in his head. "Can someone give me a hand, please!" the voice shouted. "I can't lift him!"

Two strong arms hauled him to a sitting position and then dragged him to the door, his feet bouncing along the carpet. "Are you *sure* you want to take this twat home, love?"

"Not really, but I live nearby, I can tip him out within crawling distance."

"Well, if you're certain. Let me chuck him in your truck for you."

Iestyn remembered being poured into the back of a truck and having a shoe and a wallet thrown in after him. And then a pair of rabbit ears and some Y-fronts (which he kept, shame to waste a good working pair). He remembered a bloke's voice shouting for the truck owner to just throw him out if he misbehaved as drunks tend to have a homing device and that this one was too big to get hypothermia easily.

He heard a woman's voice shouting her thanks and for the other bloke not to worry, as she would be fine. He then remembered a gentle and kindly voice checking that he was OK, then a rougher version shoving him across the seat and telling him to move over, you fat twat, as she dragged a seat belt around him, then the kindness returned as a sweet-smelling coat was draped over him.

He didn't remember being sick over the coat, or over the whole of the back seat. He didn't remember his parents being woken by the crashing about and then his father calling him a drunken prick and dumping him on the sofa.

He sort of remembered a shadow standing over him, looking down at him and laughing gently as she called him a right state. And then doors slammed and he was thrust back into darkness and left to fend for himself until the morning.

He woke with a bucket that his mother must have put next to him, but obviously not in the right place as the spatter of sick on the floor was presumably his as well.

Chapter 8

Fel iâr yn crafu – like a hen scratching (not getting anywhere)

Diane Dawson was standing by her front door on the morning of New Year's Eve. She had her coat over her arm and a bag containing her mid-morning Kit Kat and her tuna sandwich lunch lay at her feet. Where was he? David Harrison had been giving her a lift every Tuesday and Thursday for the past eight years. Probably for ninety-eight per cent of those times, he'd arrived at between 8.21 and 8.24 a.m. Therefore 8.20 was early and 8.26 was late. What reason could there be for him being nearly *eight* minutes late?

Diane worked in the office of the paint and building supplies factory where David was the foreman of Team One. He had an old-fashioned courtesy that Diane adored. Those four rides back and forth to the office were the highlights of her week. Although they rarely progressed beyond the weather and things that their families had been doing, Diane treasured the attention and the gentle pleasure that sitting next to David's overpowering aftershave in the morning and his souring shirts late afternoon gave her.

Her feelings for him could never be described as an attraction; they were more of a mutual ability to pretend at fancying someone who pretended to fancy one back. Neither seemed to want to even consider taking it further, and no kind of affair should ever be staked on discussions about fog. Their respective partners may treat them with disdain and bored familiarity, but their eight-minute drives, plus walks to and from the car park allowed them to be the people they still hoped that they were. Diane was still light-hearted and cheerful, instead of a miserable witch who watched soaps all evening accompanied by a microwaved supper, whilst her husband, Harry, played chess on the computer in the study with a plate of toasted sandwiches at his side.

David, however, was gallant and thoughtful and opened the door for Diane. Of course, he may do the same for Esther, but Diane had an inkling that he may not…

She peeped out again and this time the Mondeo was coming around the corner. Diane checked her hair in the mirror, licked her lips for that glistening first smile and set off down her drive just as he avoided clipping the kerb with his immaculate alloys.

"Sorry, Diane, sorry, my dear," he said as he ran round the car to open her door. "I've just had one of those mornings."

Diane assured him that it was no problem as she settled back into the seat and clicked on the belt. "So, what are the plans for tonight? Where'll you be seeing in the new year?" she began, but then she looked across at him. He looked tired and drawn and had a shaving nick on his cheek. "We thought we might go… David, are you all right? I don't mean to be personal, but you look a little, well, a little, er…"

"I'm fine; just a little insomnia last night. Probably been a bit unsettled because of Christmas, you know."

"Yes, I know what you mean – it's all very nice, but it's good to get back to normal afterwards, isn't it?"

There was silence as David pulled out of the estate, misjudging the speed of an approaching bus and earning himself flashing lights and a crude gesture.

"Sorry," he mumbled again, "if we'd got stuck behind that thing, we'd be stuck behind it all the way in."

They passed the caravan site where they usually moved on from weather to what had happened/would happen at the weekend, depending on whether it was Tuesday or Thursday.

"So," she began, "how was Christmas?"

David stared ahead and Diane wondered whether he had heard her. "David? So, how was your—"

"Have you ever wondered whether you've got it all wrong?"

Diane's heart leapt – perhaps this was the opening that she'd been waiting for all these years? But, did she really want him to be her lover? What about Harry? He was a bit of a miserable old fart these days, but did she really want to leave him?

"I had a talk with Louisa last night…"

Louisa? Oh. Louisa. That sap. The plump child-woman who was the apple of David's eye. The one that the sun shone out of, when her backside wasn't stuck to the sofa. Diane had only met her once, but had heard enough about her to last a lifetime. She didn't want to talk about Louisa, Louisa, every journey. She was sick of hearing about what passed as a young person's escapades. Being told that Louisa had bought a new air freshener for her car on her lunch hour was not a topic of conversation in Diane's book.

She, Diane, wanted to talk about *David and her*, she wanted their flirting to move up a gear, she wanted him to tell her how he was getting fed up with Esther. She wanted hints that his marriage was on the rocks, that he wished he had gone for a woman like her etcetera, etcetera.

Diane's two children had left home in their late teens and although they had popped back for various intervals afterwards, Diane felt that she had done a good job; children weren't supposed to be plumped up every night like another sofa cushion, they should be encouraged to make their own way in the world – ideally just around the corner, but their own way. They should also not be a main topic of conversation between potentially consenting adults.

"How is Louisa? Did she have a good break?" Diane asked graciously, the nails digging into her palms the only giveaway to the irritation that she felt.

"Oh, I think so, but no, this was about something else, something rather disturbing."

"Oh?" Diane really hoped that Louisa was pregnant with triplets by one of a potential five men, most of whom lived in squalor. Then at least they would be talking about something sexual, even if it was still about Louisa.

"Yes, it seems that she has had to do one of those blog things for homework, and she, well, she thinks that there is nothing interesting in her life to write about."

Diane stopped herself from exploding into, "Well, of course there bloody isn't! I could have told you that!" Instead, she managed, "Gosh, that's worrying."

"Yes, she was so upset. Now she wants to get her own place, get some friends, a boyfriend, you know – those kinds of things."

"I suppose life can be quite empty at that age, without, well without these things?" said Diane quietly.

David glared at her across the car – Diane was clearly not supposed to agree with Louisa's state of unhappiness.

"I said I'd ring around; try and find her a flat or something – perhaps a room with someone from work – Natasha has had lodgers in the past, I know. Perhaps she might be willing? I'll ask her."

Diane shook her head. She knew that she'd let her own life slip into a whirl of TV listings and the quest to relax, but she was passionate that her children should have a life that they would be enjoying at all times. She put her sexual frustration on hold for another day.

"David, my love," and she put her hand on his wrist and it felt warm and strong. "No, no, no, no, no. You will *not* ask around at work. You must *not* phone letting agents or pop by the newsagent's board in your lunchtime." David looked as if he'd been struck by a slap to the face.

"I *beg* your pardon?"

"The reason Louisa is…well, in this situation, is because you and Esther do *everything* for her. She's an adult and adults need to make their own decisions and," and she couldn't resist, "their own sandwiches. Otherwise – they – won't – know – how – to."

David looked furious. "Well, I know you mean well, but I'll thank you to allow me to bring up my daughter in my own way."

"David – you've already brought her up! She's twenty-six! She should have left home at eighteen, got a damp bedsit, moved back when she was skint, moved out again, lived with friends, gone out, got drunk, fallen down, decided not to do it again and then done it again…"

"Diane! She's still a child!"

"No, David, she's a grown woman!" Diane raised her eyebrows at him and then turned away to let his comment sink in.

David fumed and raced into the car park. Instead of pulling in near the office door for Diane to walk just a short distance and leaving him

63

to park, he pulled straight into a parking space at an angle that left her a mere crack to squeeze out through.

Diane trotted after him across the car park, desperate to reconcile the tension. The touch of his arm had been electric to her and she'd gone and blown it before it had even had a chance to start.

Iestyn woke to the sounds of his mother banging together what were surely saucepans. His head was pounding, his stomach was churning and his mouth was foul. He groaned. "Oh," she said. "You're awake." Then he knew it must have been bad.

"Drink this, eat those and then get yourself into the shower. You've a *lot* of making up to do." Isla thrust a mug of strong tea at him and a large plate of toast. As he took it, he saw the state of the floor that Isla was trying to avoid with her slippers.

"That's not the worst of it," she clipped. "Try the back seat of Menna Edwards' truck."

Iestyn groaned again and rolled back into the forgiving folds of the sofa. "Trouble is," smiled Isla, "we can't be too cross, as we sent you out there! You feeling OK, love?"

"Not really."

"I didn't think you would be. Come on, get yourself sorted and then we'll get you to Glascwm to clean out the truck."

Menna? The gentle voice? Oh, why did it have to have been Menna? Where the hell had Johnny Brechdan gone? And how on earth had Menna found him?

Isla seemed to be able to see into his mind. "Apparently Menna was sitting with a friend in the same bar, but she didn't think you or Johnny saw her. She saw you crash over the back of the sofa or something, and assumed that you had left with the others. But then she nearly fell over you when she went to the loo as the bar was closing. Apparently you were asleep on the carpet with rabbit ears on, or something..."

"Did she bring me home?"

"Yes, and you thanked her by being sick over her coat and all over her truck. How the hell she got you in here, I'll never know; strong as an ox that girl."

Iestyn groaned again. As he shifted his head, the little men in jackboots jumping up and down inside it sucked the last of the moisture from his brain cells and his eyes winced shut involuntarily. It was all coming back to him. The hens, the rabbit ears and, as he shifted his position on the sofa, the peanuts down his backside. Menna had seen all that? She'd seen him standing on a sofa draped in women, yowling 'Unchained Melody' into a bottle of WKD, found him asleep on the carpet. *Well done, Bevan – classy. Really classy.*

It was hacking down with rain by the time Iestyn was dropped at Menna's bungalow. Luckily there had not been anyone about as they drove through Glascwm's yard on the way to her bungalow; he didn't feel much like greeting his neighbours after such a disastrous night and he could imagine Jean's look of revulsion as she scented his breath over that of the cows.

Menna's truck was parked by her bungalow with both back doors open to the elements. Iestyn was dropped off unceremoniously, clutching a bucket filled with cleaning products including a pair of rubber gloves that would about cover the end of his fingertips, donated to him by Isla. He also had a large carrier bag to put Menna's coat into.

"Menna said can you drive it to the farm when you've finished; she's got the bloke from the Ministry there, so she can't be here with you now, but will give you a lift back – or if she can't, Jean or Bill will."

Iestyn groaned again – facing Menna would be bad enough, but Bill or Jean? That would be too much to bear. He'd been hoping to cut across the fields and call for a lift from that bastard Brechdan when he got to the road; he was owed a favour for being abandoned the night before – most of this was actually Brechdan's fault anyway.

As he wondered if Menna had an outside toilet, he filled the bucket with water from the garage tap, added a generous portion of cleaning fluids, and set about scrubbing the yuck from the back seat, retching as he went. Every time he bent over to reach something from the floor, nausea engulfed him and he had to sit still until it passed. Whole peanuts had to be scooped out of the crevices and a dirty pair of rabbit ears rescued from under the seat. It was retribution of the worst kind…

It was a wet and pathetic Iestyn with a slight tang of something antiseptic that drove into Glascwm's yard later that morning. Menna was just coming out of a barn with a man with a pile of paperwork and she acknowledged him, then turned back to her companion. Iestyn was motioned by Jean towards the vehicle line-up and guided in as if he were boarding a cross-channel car ferry. He managed a little wave and then squeezed out of the door, desperate not to scratch the adjacent vehicle with the ripped zip that was hanging from his jacket.

He walked over towards Menna, clutching his bucket and carrier bag and hovered around, feeling awkward, but not wanting to interrupt.

"Well, thank you very much," said Menna to the man from the Ministry, "I'll get on with that then and we'll see you again in, what, three months?"

"Yes, three months. That'll take us to, end of March?"

They shook hands and then turned to Iestyn and his bucket. "Hello," said the man, "Iestyn Bevan isn't it? Pencwmhir?"

"Yes, yes, hello," he said quietly.

"I'm just giving Iestyn a lift back now," said Menna, "he's been kind enough to, er, valet my truck!"

"No, no, it's fine," started Iestyn, "I'll walk… It's not far…"

"Oh, do car valeting as well do you? Good for you, boy: farmers need to diversify these days, don't they? Good lad." Iestyn nodded as he caught Menna's raised eyebrow out of the corner of his eye. "Look, I'm actually going near your place now, on my way back to Bwlch y Garreg – I can drop you off if you want? I'm aware I've just given Menna an awful lot of work to do, and it's no problem. You'll probably be wanting to get ready to celebrate the new year?"

Iestyn went green. "Well…" Iestyn looked at Menna who was skimming through the paperwork that she'd been given. In one way, he would love to get a chance to talk to Menna, to explain why he'd been such a cock and to thank her for sort of looking after him and to say sorry for being sick in her truck and to, and to ask – could it really be true that she draped a coat over him in such a gentle way last night? In another way, he just wanted to go home, scrub the smell of vomit from his hands, go back to bed and groan for a little bit longer and deal with the apologies some other time. Anyhow, she didn't really look as if she wanted to have much to do with him – and why would she? She'd scraped a pissed friend off the floor of a bar in order to get him home, rather than to a police cell, and he'd repaid her by throwing up all over her truck and her possessions: not really a defining moment in the start of a new sort of relationship...

"Thank you, that would be very helpful," he mumbled. "And, Menna, thank you so much for your help last night..."

"I would say, any time, but I don't actually mean it as such."

Iestyn grinned sheepishly, "Well, *I* mean it, I don't know where I'd be if you hadn't been there to help..."

"Probably still in the same position." She reached over to him and he mistook the move for one of sympathy and smiled. Instead, she removed something from his back and, with a bewildered expression on her face, held out a crumpled Smirnoff Ice label.

Iestyn took it, mumbled his thanks again and followed the man to his truck and they set off down the track, each bump making his stomach churn and his head throb, as he answered endless worthy questions about his new car-valeting business...

CHAPTER 9

Hen genawes – an old vixen (an unpleasant woman, old bitch)

It was Esther's favourite time of the day although, frankly, that didn't need to amount to a great deal. She would be up before David and Louisa, popping them a cup of tea and then having a shower herself. Even though they were adults, they both seemed to require her presence in the morning, finding ties to match shirts, digging out lost car keys and generally passing them things just before they were about to moan that they couldn't find them.

She knew that she was being a bit of a doormat, but it actually made her life easier. Both David and Louisa had the knack of making it feel as if it were her fault if they'd lost their scarf/mislaid office keys/had dog shit on their shoe. She would have to do everything anyway, so she was better off pre-empting things and making sure they were done before the frantic "Mu-um/Es-ther, have you seen my keys? I left them on the hook and now they're not there – where have you moved them to?" that had her scuttling around, only to find them in a coat pocket where they'd been left.

So, she put keys back on the hook, rescued packed-lunch boxes from cars, cleaned shoes and double-checked sandwich flavour preferences. It was a thankless task, but her main mission in this household was to save herself from being driven to wasted tears of anger and resentment.

It wasn't that she didn't *love* Louisa and David; it was more that she saw her mission of support being a precursor to her love and enjoyment of them. She took her role as housewife very seriously; she had been taught to clean by a stickler of a grandmother and the rest could come only after her chores were done. The trouble was, there was almost *always* something else to do. They would play games as a family at some point, but it was not proper and therefore possible before the floors were clean and all the clothes were ironed and put away.

Since her stroke, it had become much harder to carry out her chores, and it became a matter of pride not to ask for help. Therefore although she could probably have legitimately asked her growing daughter to do a little bit more for herself, to do so would have meant that she, Esther, wasn't coping – and she could – even if it meant that things took her the whole day.

Therefore it often took until mid-afternoon before she had not only cleared up their clutter and anticipated the next flux of disasters, but had also done the washing, the ironing, the cleaning and the peeling of potatoes for tea. The hour before she needed to get up and start preparing for them to come home, exhausted from their toil, was now officially *her* time. Time she felt she could legitimately spend lounging on the sofa watching daytime television if she wanted to, or to read a book with her feet up. More recently, she had had more pressing business to occupy her…

Esther sat at her computer and spread her clenched hand over the mouse with her other one. She opened the file, now named *ANON,* that had a different font to her usual one – in case a recipient might trace the use of Times New Roman to her.

This time, there was little consideration or debate about the morality of what she was about to do; it was more of a question of which words she was going to use.

Dear Mrs Mathews,

I am a well-wisher who uses your hairdresser's occasionally and I enjoy its ambience and the quality of my cut. My reason for writing this is therefore neither spite nor malevolence, but a goodwill gesture for the benefit of your business.

Friends often compliment me on my haircut, and ask me where I had it done. However, when I mention the name of your establishment, some have groaned and said that they would go there too, but for one thing – unfortunately, it is your body odour.

Women of our age do tend to perspire more than we used to and I am afraid to say that, enhanced by your nylon overalls, it can be rather unpleasant.

Might I suggest a shower each morning, followed by the application of a quality anti-perspirant deodorant? A fresh blouse each day made from natural fibres will ensure that the result will last the whole shift.

Please do not be offended by this observation, as it is meant well. There is no need to try and guess who I am as I only sporadically patronise your salon and I will never mention this to anyone else, so your secret is safe with me.

Kind regards,
A Well-wishing Customer

Esther read the letter through only once for grammatical errors, then banged *print*. If she were quick, she could catch the five o'clock post. Mrs Mathews would get it in the morning, buy deodorant in her lunch break and wash the sour pinny by the time Esther arrived for her appointment on the Friday.

Esther wrote the address on the envelope in elaborate copperplate writing, completely different to her usual, economical style. She wanted it to look important, but also a standard design. She fished in her purse for a stamp then took her coat from the rack – the postbox was only two hundred yards away, but her speed of movement meant that she would quickly get cold. She grabbed her stick and hobbled down the drive.

As the only person in Anweledig during a weekday, she was surprised to see the door of The Old Laundry open and a man in a suit step out.

He had a file in his hand and a mobile phone in a pouch on his belt. Ha! she thought, as she watched him finger it, there's no signal for that thing here, far too much of a hollow!

The smile snapped back onto the man's face as a woman followed him out. She was tall and had a bright red coat pulled tightly in at the waist. Her crocheted beret was the same black as her hair, but her lips matched her coat.

"It's perfect," Esther heard her tell the man that she assumed to be an estate agent. "Just what I've been looking for."

Typical, thought Esther, just what Anweledig needs, another executive who works away all week, then comes home for weekends behind closed doors. Of the five houses in the hamlet, theirs was the only one that had normal people in since dear old Uncle Bob of The Old Laundry died two months ago. She'd known it would go on the market, but there hadn't even been time for any signs to be erected, yet someone seemed interested already!

She and Bob had got on well. He was in his late seventies, but they'd enjoyed each other's company in a bland kind of way – coffee every Tuesday and Thursday morning at eleven, at alternate houses. He'd brought the Harrisons produce from his lush garden and David had cut his hedges in return. Without Uncle Bob, Anweledig had been a sad little place midweek – David and Louisa at work and the four other little cottages being either holiday homes, or homes to those that worked away so often that they might as well be holiday homes.

The agent nodded respectfully to Esther, then returned to his client who had mouthed hello and waved at Esther, presumably in case they might need to be friends one day.

The postbox at the top of the lane leading from Anweledig was a difficult walk for Esther. For some reason the camber got to her, as did the roughness of the broken-up road surface. Her rehabilitation had been to make it to the postbox each day and, at first, it had been tortuous. She still made sure that she walked at least that far on a daily basis and so it was a point of principle that she never gave any letters to David to post – not that she would let this letter out of sight until it reached the confines of the postbox: David was not a suspicious character, but he might have expressed a vague interest as to why she was writing a letter to her hairdresser when she was going to see her later that week…

As she neared the postbox, leaning heavily on her stick, she saw the postman Tommy Brand's van screeching to a halt beside it. He scrambled out and trotted round the van to the box. She saw him see her and wince: the posties at the Tan-y-Bryn branch seemed to compete in every aspect of their work – who got back to the depot first, who could wear shorts longest into the winter, who could wear out their van the quickest. It grated on Tommy to have to wait for Esther to reach the postbox, but he knew better than to trot to meet her – he'd been told off for that before.

"Hi, Esther, how are you today?" he called, hopping from one foot to another in the cold.

"Very well thanks, Tommy – surely you can get your long trousers on in this weather and not lose face? Your legs are blue!"

"Nope, still two boys in them – I lost last year as I copped out for a ten below, so I'm determined not to this year, even if my van ices over."

"Well, here's another letter for you. I suppose you can always put a spare sack over your knees if it gets really cold?"

Esther saw Tommy's confused look and felt silly – fit young postmen don't put things over their knees to help keep them warm, unless those things breathed heavily and were called something like Lolita – and even then, warmth wouldn't be the overriding factor.

Tommy grabbed the letter and darted back into his van and sped off in a sprinkling of little stones, leaving Esther facing the long totter back down the hill. She was forced into the hedge twice, first by the estate agent and then the black-haired lady – hers was the silver Boxter. Great, thought Esther, hopefully that would mean that she would pester the Council about the state of the roads too.

Louisa felt pleased with herself as she drove to her computer class that Thursday. Not only had she done her homework, she'd bought herself a new pair of jeans and some funky boots. She'd nearly veered back to her elasticated-waist ones that came in at a third of the price but the assistant in Tan-y-Bryn's only vaguely trendy clothes shop, assured her that the more expensive ones looked great and were well worth the extra investment. They had been a slightly larger size than Louisa had imagined that they would need to be, but the girl had said that comparing them to her previous style would not be an accurate comparison.

71

"That's why fat people wear elasticated-waisters," she'd said, nearly blowing her only lunchtime sale. "It's because they can get away with two sizes smaller!"

As Louisa parked outside the college, she was pleased to see Rachel's Beetle already there. Good, she thought, now I can make an entrance.

Herbie seemed very pleased to see her and welcomed her into class. "I got your email regarding your blog, Louisa – or *Lulu* should I say – thank you. Sounds like you've got a really exciting life going on at the moment, yeah?"

Louisa nodded guiltily and scuttled to her seat, darting a quick look at Rosie and Rachel who were sat in their usual spot, chatting. Damn, Rachel had tracksuit bottoms on and trainers – surely jeans weren't going out of fashion, meaning she would have to buy a pair of those towelling trackies next?

She slipped in next to Moira, who smiled warmly at her. "Hi," Louisa smiled back, practicing being friendly, "how has your week been?"

"Not as exciting as yours by the look of things! I got here early and Herbie showed me your blog – all go for you at the moment, isn't it? I'm surprised you made it here with life so hectic!"

Louisa cringed and settled into her chair – perhaps she'd been a little over the top? She'd decided that her blog would be the start of the new her. She had decided that her new identity needed a more exciting name – Lulu: still Louisa in many ways, but just a little more interesting. And, boy, was Lulu already having adventures! Louisa had reckoned that the things that were happening in her blog were things that would bound to be taking place over the next few months, but as she only had a month that she needed to blog about to complete the course, she felt it prudent to stuff all the news into it now – and the actual happenings could follow later…

However, as she saw Moira's look requiring her to expand on her adventures, perhaps in hindsight it would have been enough to have just visited the estate agent without having claimed to have looked at five flats – and gone out for a drink with a potential flat share?

"Right then, everybody," said Herbie, calling the class to attention, "I thought tonight we'd do a bit of a round up, y'know? Have a bit of a rap after our holiday break, yeah? Find out how we're all getting on with our blogs and seeing what we've learnt from using them. I want to hear how you're all *interacting* with strangers in cyberspace, yeah?"

The class jumped at the thought of sitting in a circle chatting, rather than being taught something and so shuffled their chairs to the front of the room. Louisa was still feeling confident about her exciting new boots and jeans and so scraped her chair across the floorboards as if it were turbo-charged. To her delight, she made it next to Rosie, just as the circle closed in on itself.

"Hiya," said Rosie.

"Hi," said Louisa, feeling like she had in school when she'd managed to wangle it to stand next to one of the in-crowd in the dinner hall queue. She sensed that Rosie didn't think it such a big deal as she was leaning forward in her chair humming to herself. Louisa took a risk and stuck her boots out in front of them both.

"Nice boots," Rosie said, "I saw some like that in the shoe shop in town."

"Yeah, I spotted them too and *had* to have them!" said Louisa. Then she felt bad in case she had made herself sound spoilt and indulgent.

Luckily, Rosie laughed. "I know what you mean – I felt I just had to have these ones – mind, that was a few years ago; I've only just finished paying for them!" and she stuck out her biker boots. "See, look the heel is coming away again; I've mended them three times, but they keep coming unstuck."

"Oh, that's a pain," replied Louisa. She was feeling almost thrilled with herself; she was actually having a conversation with someone that she had been completely in awe of and, to be fair to her, it wasn't her that was being too boring this time, it was the other person who was talking about mending boots with glue. "Have you tried Stuck to Glue? I've mended loads of shoes with that." It was only half a lie; her dad had mended loads of shoes with that.

"Really? Hang on, let me write that down…" and Rosie scribbled *Lulu – Stuck to Glue* on the inside cover of her file. Louisa beamed as Herbie rolled up his shirt sleeves revealing his pale wiry arms and clapped his hands for attention.

*

73

Iestyn, Joe, Sima and Johnny Brechdan shouldered open the door to the Bull and walked up to the bar. It was a Thursday evening and therefore Darts' Night. The Christmas decorations were still up, but then they'd probably be up for months yet if previous years were anything to go by.

"It's so quaint," whispered Sima looking around and the others nodded, thinking she must be talking about the flagstone floor, the horse brasses tarnished and covered in ash from the fire, and nicotine still staining the ceiling. "You still have old farts in your pubs here – those old boys would be in a glass case in our bars."

She nodded at the elderly men in the corner, shirts buttoned up to their scrawny necks and tank tops on to keep out the draughts. The men wilted and beamed back at her.

"For God's sake, don't encourage them. You do *not* want to smell that guy's breath," muttered Iestyn, who called over, "All right, Ken? All right, Derri?"

"All right, boy," the men replied and turned back to their warm halves.

"Well, well, Iestyn. Joe, welcome back, lad – been skiing for new year, I hear? Very nice. Johnny, you here again? Haven't you got a home to go to?" The landlord worked his bar and was pleased to see the group on a dull midweek night. "And, who is this lovely lady that you've brought with you to be sacrificed for the benefit of the darts' team?"

"Ed, this is Sima. Sima, Ed." Sima shook his hand over the bar and Ed melted. "What will it be then, boys? And one on the house for the lady."

"Christ!" laughed Joe. "That'll be the first time that those words have ever been uttered in this place! Usually, Sima, I get told to stop hogging the fire like a namby-pamby office boy and start flashing some of my city wealth."

"Now, I'll have to warn you, Joe," said Ed, hurriedly polishing a couple of glasses and only just stopping himself from breathing on them to improve the shine, "we don't have any champagne on ice, no fancy cocktail shakers and definitely no umbrellas – well, there is that one in the porch that no one's claimed, but I don't think anyone would want that in their drink. And Johnny – no banana milkshakes for you today either, I'm afraid."

They gave their order and the fact that Sima asked for something that wasn't behind the bar didn't faze Ed and he said – another first – that he would go and look in the cellar and then bring the drinks over.

"Bloody hell!" laughed Johnny, "normally he puts a deposit on the glasses so that I have to bring them back to the bar at the end of the night – says that it saves him getting off his fat arse."

Ed eventually returned with the four drinks on a tray. He saved Sima's until last and then sat beside her.

"So, Sima, what brings you here to us then – surely to God it's not Joe Bevan?"

"Of course it's Joe – but if it weren't for Joe, then I would travel this far just to sample a night of your fine hospitality!"

Ed flushed; he was used to banter and spent his evenings batting witticisms across the bar, but Sima's hooded charm wrong-footed him. "So, Sima, what do you do for a living then, bach?"

"Life coach, Ed."

"Life coach, eh? Is that how Joe met you – he must be first in the queue for needing a life coach – well, not now, and perhaps not in front of young Brechdan here, but, well, well… So, what advice can you give me then?" Ed stood up, threw his arms to his side, "Fine specimen that I am!"

Joe smirked and winked at Iestyn. Iestyn cringed, knowing that Sima took her profession far too seriously to fob him off with some cheap remark. Instead, she pushed her chair back and assessed him and his surroundings. Ed was beginning to look uncomfortable. She walked a few paces back and looked again at the package that was the middle-aged landlord of the Bull.

"Come here," she signalled. He trotted over, now beginning to regret the request. Sima leant over and Ed put his ear up to her. She cupped her hands so that no one else could hear and whispered to him. The others watched, giggling, as he flushed, looked confused, then cross, then embarrassed. Then he started to nod. Sima pulled away and held his shoulders and looked into his eyes and smiled. "OK, Ed? You understand what I just said? You'll be OK with that? Here's my card, so if you need to chat it over at all, just phone me, OK? Good." She hugged him and the man that hadn't been hugged in years drank in her advice and her perfume and her beautiful softness. He

75

immediately stood six inches taller and walked back to the bar, trousers hiked up to lift his stomach.

Once back behind the bar, he looked at Sima, received her wink and looked at his next customer. "Yes, sir, now what can I get for you?"

"Another satisfied customer, Sima?" asked Iestyn, laughing at Joe who was sitting with his head in his hands.

"She just can't help herself," he groaned, "mind, Ed could probably use a bit of direction!" Joe looked around the pub. "So, nothing's changed here then has it? See that cobweb, Sima, that's been there since I had my first half of cider at fourteen!"

"No," said Johnny, "that cobweb *there* was the early one. *That* one was made during our Hooch phase."

"So, Johnny," said Joe, "how's the farm going?"

"Not too good I'm afraid – so bloody cold this winter..."

"Don't tell me!" interjected Iestyn. "So bloody cold that lambs will be born stunted as their mothers spent so much time hunched up. Come on, Johnny, please don't turn into my dad!"

The door ground open once more and a gust of wind wrapped around the table.

"Menna!" called Johnny, "you're late!"

The windswept woman in lumberjack shirt and jeans slammed the door behind her and ran her hand through her tangled curls.

"Phew, bloody cold out there. All right, Ed?" her voice rang out through the pub and all its occupants grunted their greetings to her. "And it's bloody hot in here, Ed, have you been pinching Dai's oil again? Drink anyone?" she called over to Iestyn's table as she dragged off her shirt and rolled up the sleeves of the rugby top beneath. Iestyn cringed as he hadn't seen Menna yet since the morning after the rabbit ears night, and he really hadn't worked out how he should play it. Ed passed Menna a pint and she strode over to Iestyn's table, turned a chair around and sat astride it.

"Hi all," she breezed, "how's it going? Poured any bottles of WKD on your face recently, Iestyn?"

"Ah, yes, sorry about that, Menna, and thanks again. How's the truck? Did I get all the bits out?"

"Well, most of them. I put the dog in there in the end, she did a better job; five-day-old puke is no joke when you can't keep the windows open. It's OK until I put the heaters on full, and then it still smells a bit of…*raspberry* funnily enough."

Johnny laughed. "Excellent! The raspberry: now that was *Hannah's* round, unless I am mistaken!" Menna gave a quick glance towards Iestyn and then looked back down at the table and pretended to inspect her pint.

Iestyn saw that it was definitely time to move the conversation on: something about that night was simply not funny to Menna, and not just in a way that having a bloke throw up in your truck *per se* isn't funny.

"OK, enough now, Johnny. Menna, I don't think you've met Sima before? Sima, this is Menna. Menna, this is Sima, Joe's girlfriend."

Menna blushed awkwardly as she took in the immaculate Sima and then shook her hand, wiping her own first on a denim-clad thigh. "Sorry, just been out checking the sheep. Had to drag a few of them round."

"Never mind," smiled Sima, "lanolin's good for my skin!"

Menna looked at her beautifully-manicured hands and then held out her own stubby chapped ones that were still swollen from the earlier cold. "Lanolin's never done mine any good," she laughed and sat on them, as if they were better hidden out of the way so that they couldn't be compared to Sima's.

Joe laughed, "How are you going to drink your pint now, Menna?"

"Oh, I'll find a way, I usually do."

Sima picked up the glass and held it to her lips and Menna took a healthy slurp.

Sima laughed; she loved coming to Joe's farm and the village in which he grew up. She loved the simple pleasures of a family that got on and enjoyed each other's company. The people seemed real with real work to do, the weather was real and the mud was really real. It was no bad thing to be reminded sometimes that you shouldn't wear white jeans and pumps in mid-winter.

In Pencwmhir, they didn't have a thermostat that allowed them to wear satin camisoles and shorties to relax of an evening all year round: it just got bloody cold. Slippers, dressing gowns and five layers were needed. You simply got dressed and undressed as quickly as possible and it was a good idea to leave your three tops inside your jumper so that they could all be put on as one.

Pencwmhir's shower was feeble and lukewarm, even the bath was too cold to luxuriate in – Sima found that her breasts stuck out the water and became chilled, much to Joe's delight. The product that scoured Tomos' grime from it played havoc with her skin and her feet would get so dusty and hairy from the bathroom floor when she got out, that she never felt properly cleansed anyway.

However, Sima would use her visits as grounding ones. She knew that her lifestyle in London was beginning to become a parody of what she preached to her clients. She'd begun doing affirmations and writing down her goals and they'd started coming true. At the beginning of her career as a self-employed life coach, she'd worked out a good hourly rate, incorporating all her business costs, then felt cheeky one day so doubled it. Twice as many clients started ringing.

She went to the gym three times a week and her body became a temple of fitness and health. She didn't drink eight glasses of water a day, she drank nine, and her skin glowed. She didn't bother with the one about jelly cubes for her hair and nails, thinking it scientifically flawed – but her talons and locks grew at a rate that allowed constant restyling, keeping her one step ahead of her peers.

However, Sima was beginning to feel that she was likely to implode in a frenzy of perfection and success. Joe said that the only reason he was allowed to enter her flat was to give her cleaner something to clean up after and the only reason he was allowed in her bed was to stop her disappearing up her own backside. And that, too, was why she liked Pencwmhir. After the initial shocks that the indoor wildlife gave her, she began to enjoy the experiences – mushrooms under things that had dropped onto the bathroom floor, mice lying in traps in the cupboards that the cornflakes were in and Tomos drenching his chips in vinegar that had pickled fruit flies in.

She also never met women like Menna in her circle of friends in London. Menna Edwards was only a few years younger than her, but seemed wise and strong as an ox. Joe had told her about Menna, how she would wear unisex clothes just because they were there and they kept her warm. Her hair was a tangled mess of reddish curls that ended up in a ponytail secured by an elastic band that looked like it had come into her possession wrapped around a wad of post.

Sima was concerned for the condition of the girl's skin, as tonight it looked as if it had been buffed with a scouring pad, obviously chapped by the wind, and she desperately wanted to suggest a daily application of sunblock as a barrier. Yet her blue eyes had a twinkle which suggested that perhaps Menna wasn't bothered. However, there was obviously something a little uncomfortable for Menna about that recent evening – of which she'd heard a little from Isla and Tomos. Sima made it her business to try and find out what was *really* going on...

Menna smiled at Sima and then turned back to the table. "What's the Jeep like on rough ground, Joe?" she asked. "I'm assuming that that highly-polished beast out in the car park is yours? Unless Iestyn and Johnny have sold their souls to the devil and clubbed together, of course."

Sima quietly got to her feet and muttered about getting the next round, knowing that she wouldn't be missed, nor would she miss out.

Ed was not his usual self. He was standing upright, polishing glasses with a *clean* cloth and his own glass held water.

"Sima," he said, slightly self-consciously, "same again?"

"Thank you, Ed," and Ed glowed once more at her smile. "Although I think that Menna's just started hers." He raised an eyebrow, and Sima turned to see the last drop of ale trickle into Menna's mouth. "Bloody needed that," Sima heard. "Perhaps another one for her, too, please..."

As Ed pottered behind the bar, lining up the drinks, Sima eyed her new gaggle of friends. Menna was a kind of woman that she rarely met. Not asexual in a deliberate way, but undeveloped. Like an eight-year-old out with a group of older girls.

Then Sima saw a shine in Menna's eyes. A loud laugh at Iestyn's comment about the mouse in Isla's wellie, and a glance that settled on him just a little too long while he was looking elsewhere. Iestyn? Did Menna really want to drive *Iestyn's* tractor? Surely not: they'd been friends for years! Perhaps *that* was what the discomfort was about? To Sima, it all started to make a bit more sense – Menna looking down into her pint when Johnny had talked about the other women in the bar, actually being bothered to drive a drunk Iestyn home in the first place and now sitting smiling at him and laughing at his jokes. Sima loved her work: the untangling of things to find out what was *really* going on in someone's life was a mission to her and here was as good a place to start as any...

"Hey, Ed," she beckoned as she passed him a new twenty-pound note. "What's the story with Menna? Single? Boyfriend? Gay? What's the score?"

Ed shrugged. "Dunno really, just Menna I s'pose. Never really thought about it. Hard worker though, *dieu, dieu*. Not gay though – been with blokes in her time – more a case of not got round to it much lately, I think." He took the crisp note and handed her back a pile of sticky fifty-pence pieces. Sima debated putting them in her purse, decided against it and stuck them in the Sooty charity tin.

"Thanks," said Ed, "that's probably more than we've had all year in that bloody thing. People are more than happy to draw breasts on poor old Sooty there, but are they willing to put more than a few coppers into him? Are they bollocks."

Sima smiled, took the tray and walked back to the table just in time to hear the end of Johnny's alternator tale – apparently it was a classic.

CHAPTER 10

Mae brân i frân yn rhywle – there's a crow for a crow somewhere (there's a partner for everyone somewhere)

Iestyn loved this time of the evening on Joe's visits. Joe would accompany their father on his rounds of checking the animals as his years away from the farm had turned it into a novelty for him. Isla was in the draughty little office catching up on paperwork and Iestyn was assigned the role of keeping Sima company: it was the best job of the farming year.

It wasn't that Iestyn coveted his brother's girlfriend; it was just that there was no one else like Sima – apart from the occasional film star. She was nearly six foot tall with a fit hourglass figure. Her hair was exotically tousled, and was never messy, even after coming in from the token trip around the yard. Her skin was like warm cocoa, soft and inviting and was enhanced by impeccable make-up.

Iestyn simply liked to be in her presence and enjoyed just looking at her. She must to be used to it, as she never seemed to mind. To compare her to the local women he knew would be like comparing a Rolls Royce to a mountain bike with a shopping basket on the front; there was no point, they had different purposes. Sima's role was to light up the Bevan's kitchen, whereas the local women were great to help unload a trailer of feed sacks or to herd a bullock into a clamp. They were great fun to pass an evening with over a pint in the local, but it wouldn't be right to harry Sima into getting her round in, to send her walking over a sticky carpet, to rest her arms in a puddle on the bar next to Boring Bob or Bad Breath Ken. Sima should be sat at the best table in the house, being waited on by the *maître d'* himself.

Yet, there she would sit in Tomos' battered wing chair, resting the sleeves of her white shirt on the arms that usually held a dribbling teacup, a pile of biscuits or a bitten-off fingernail. Her feet nestled amongst ash and the grit that had fallen from the treads of Tomos' slippers. She seemed oblivious to all the dust, the woodlice and the howling draughts.

Iestyn knew that Sima's flat was immaculate. Her kitchen had only cooked salads, or heated up fresh ready-meals purchased from the deli. Her windows never opened to the noise and fumes of the city and her immense wardrobes were shrines to order and the dry cleaner's packaging. Iestyn could only think that in coming to Pencwmhir, she steeled herself in the way that she taught her clients to when they had a speech to make or an interview to attend. He passed her a chipped mug and threw a few more logs into the Rayburn.

"Thank you, Iestyn, a lovely cup of tea. So, tell me, how is life going for you?" Sima was the only person who spoke to Iestyn in such a personal way. She wasn't nosy; she was just interested. Johnny Brechdan would ask, "So, what's news?" and his father would occasionally ask, "All right, boy?" but they never really meant any more than an opening to a conversation and would be very uncomfortable if he poured out any of the things he talked about with Sima.

"Well, not a great deal different to when you asked last, to be honest!" He sat down opposite her and took a sip from his own

81

chipped cup – one stating *Frankie Says Relax*. "The cattle are doing well this winter and we got a good price for that young bull that you saw when you came last time."

Sima nodded, as if she were genuinely interested, "And, what of your personal goals? What of your love life?"

Iestyn winced a little, "Ah, not doing as well as the bullocks I'm afraid. Bit bleak there still, I'm sorry to say."

"You said you wanted to get out more – have you been able to do that?" It was as if he was one of her clients and she couldn't help slipping into her counselling role; he half expected her to move to a kitchen chair behind him and start taking notes.

"Well, I did go down the local a bit more often at first, but I kept getting nobbled by Bad Breath Ken, so there was little point really. He put me off the beer that I couldn't afford anyway, so it all became a bit of a waste of time. *And* they all took the piss out of me as I wore Joe's old shirts – calling me the Chelsea Farmer – occasionally Menna comes along too, but well, she's not interested in anything apart from farming really, so there's no point in trying to cultivate anything there…"

"Are you sure? She seemed really nice the other night."

"Oh, Menna's great," Iestyn shrugged, "good laugh, *great* farmer, really knows her engines too – always good in a crisis is Menna. She'd make someone a lovely husband one day…"

"What about Johnny, how does he fare?"

"Johnny? Well, Johnny has the knack of having beautiful women falling out of space and landing on his todger, but when things get thin, he goes and tupps Tanya Dan-y-Coed."

"Tupps?"

"You know, what a ram does to a ewe."

"Tanya Dan-y-Coed?"

"Yes, she's got a great new trailer and her bull is good stock – but it does help that no one can lay hedges like Johnny Brechdan…"

"Hedges? A proper hedge, or a family of women called Hedge?" Sima smiled. She always laughed at the way that the Bevans talked, their mutterings that were completely obvious to one another and anyone else in their world, but nonsensical to an outsider such as her.

"Iestyn, we've got to change this mind set – you and your friends can't go on shagging neighbours whenever you want to borrow a piece of equipment; it's not right. Plus this strategy falls down when the ram you need is owned by Bad Breath Ken. No, you need to become a bit more adventurous, or we'll be having the same conversation in six months time. Why not, well, why not look a little closer at what's around you? You know, see what's closer to home – with new eyes?" Sima looked to Iestyn as if she was trying to put a plan into action, but he didn't know what she was talking about. "You might be surprised as to what's on your doorstep? Other than that, I'll have to ask Joe to set you up with one of his London floozies, but you're too good for them and they can't mend tractor engines to save their lives…"

The door blew open and Joe and his father came in. Joe stamped his feet and rubbed his gloved hands together. He was muffled up in an arctic-quality down coat, a woollen cap with ears and a pair of waterproof trousers over his fleece leggings, but still shuddered from the biting cold. Tomos removed his body warmer and rolled up his shirtsleeves. "You're getting soft, boy; it's not even proper winter yet. Too used to central heating and hot chocolate, that's your trouble."

"He'd never survive back here now, would he, Tomos?" called Sima from her spot next to the fire. "We've sucked him into city life and made him good for nothing else!"

Tomos laughed and went to collect the kettle to make them a drink. "Here, Dad," said Iestyn, getting out of his chair and motioning for his father to take his seat, "I'll get it. Another cup for you, Sima?"

"Gosh, no, I've already had three today!"

"Only three?" said Tomos, "I had that many for breakfast…"

Iestyn smiled as he wandered over to the kitchen cupboards. What had Sima been getting at? Closer to home? What did she mean? Tan-y-Bryn? That was close to home. Perhaps she meant for him to look there? Perhaps he'd type Tan-y-Bryn into the Internet later and see what he came up with; it would be nice to have his own Sima sat by the fire next to him one day…

Esther sat in the hairdresser's chair and breathed in the fragrant scent around her. Her hair was wet and scraped back from her face revealing her age blotches and the wrinkles around her eyes, but she felt good.

She looked in the mirror and saw Mona Mathews eyeing her up

from the other side of the salon and then slowly walk over. She was wearing a white cotton blouse and a new apron. In fact, all the stylists had new overalls and it gave the salon a lift; those frayed royal-blue nylon ones really had seen better days.

"Hello, Esther," said Mona, running her fingers through Esther's hair. "What will it be today?"

Esther felt elated as she chattered away about nothing much. Mona Mathews was clean and fresh and it was a pleasure to be in her company. Normally Esther would be nervous as Mona moved around her and would keep her coffee near to her face, dreading it if Mona fumbled across her to untangle the wires of the dryer, the smell of stale sweat making her gurn.

However, today there was none of that. It looked as if the nylon three-day blouses had been banished, with fresh cotton being worn in their place. As Mona moved from side to side, dabbing on the dye and wiping stray dribbles with her clean cloth, Esther got a little more adventurous, even turning slightly to sniff the air. No, no more sour curry smell, no perspired fish, only the smell of freshly-cut flowers.

As the dye was given time to take, Esther was passed a drink and a copy of the local paper. She flicked through it, reading a story about a children's play here and some vandalism there. Then her stomach churned as she turned a page and saw a particular headline and she looked around her to see if anyone was watching her reaction. No one was looking at her, they were all going about their business, sweeping up hair and asking about holiday plans. No, it wasn't a trap after all. She allowed herself a breath before reading the article.

Tan-y-Bryn seems to be in the grip of an anonymous letter writer! A second anonymous letter has been received, this time Jocelyn's Greengrocer's has been the one to receive the opinions of a person who does not have the courage to convey their opinions face to face.

Hang on a minute, thought Esther, putting the paper down and watching colour flood to her cheeks in the mirror in front of her. That's a bit unfair – it wasn't that she didn't have the courage, she had courage galore, it was just that she thought it was fairer to be more direct. It could take months of hint dropping to get things changed. Just look at The Tasty Bite – one discreet letter and the whole business had improved. Everyone's a winner!

"I feel so angry…" stated Jocelyn who has run the greengrocer's for thirty-five years, "talking about tattiness, mud on the floor and dated fittings. Well, what do potatoes really need to show them off? Gold shelves? If people want me to refurbish my shop every year with new fittings, my customers will have to pay for it – and I am sure that the majority know that potatoes come with a certain amount of mud on them."

Esther felt a little uncomfortable. Perhaps Jocelyn had a point – carrot trays maybe didn't need to be Bauhaus. She had anticipated another Thank You, like the one from The Tasty Bite. She hadn't really wanted this.

"Nasty business that." The voice came from behind her and made her jump. Mona had come to check on her colour.

"What? This?" Esther tapped the paper. "Yes – why don't people just, well, talk? A quiet word is usually enough, isn't it? And anyway, carrot and potato displays needing new fittings! I ask you!"

Mona smiled and held Esther's shoulders in an affectionate embrace. "Yes, that's all people need. Anyway, another five minutes should do it, Esther, love. Everything OK, here? Do you need another coffee?"

"I'm fine thanks, Mona," said Esther, grasping Mona's hand with her good hand. "It's just so nice to sit and soak up the atmosphere here – I always love coming here, just to feel like I've really relaxed, you know?"

Mona smiled and walked away. Esther let out her breath, hoping that she hadn't overplayed it. She didn't really think so and as she saw Mona discretely blow her breath into her cupped hand and sniff it, she felt redeemed and dived into the Deaths and Marriages page with gusto.

CHAPTER 11

Yn byw lle mae'r brain yn marw – living where the crows die (living frugally or meanly)

Iestyn was sitting on his bed putting his socks on when there was a tap at the door. "Hello," he called, assuming it was Isla with a pile of washing to be put on the chair next to the other pile of washing. Instead, it was Sima.

"Hi," she said, peeping round the door with a large holdall in her hand. "Can I come in? Joe's out with your dad doing the rounds, so I thought I'd bring you these." Iestyn looked at the bag with interest. "It's just a few things I thought you might like; I've got a friend who has – put on weight – so was chucking them out. I said I would ask if you want them – you know, for work clothes perhaps?"

Iestyn laughed, he knew that she knew that he would only wear such things for work clothes in about twenty years' time when they were nearing rags. He wasn't sure where she'd really got them, but his pride wasn't offended.

"Thanks, Sima, you trying to tidy me up? Surely I can't get much more up to the minute than this?" Iestyn laughed as he thrust his chest out displaying his acrylic grey work jumper with purple diamonds across the chest. It had ragged cuffs, and holes and stains galore.

Sima looked at it with her arms folded. "Actually, take that bloody thing off. It's revolting. Come on, off." Iestyn reluctantly removed it and gave it to her outstretched hand. The action revealed a turquoise polo shirt underneath. "OK, and that, come on, it's fifteen years old."

"Maybe, but the cows don't notice."

"Well, they should. Come on, off."

Iestyn sat self-consciously with his naked chest white against his tanned neck, face and forearms. "Well, what *can* I wear? Come on, I'm bloody freezing." The curtains blew across the room at that moment as if to make a point. Sima glanced at them.

"And your curtains are vile too; rooms like this should have unbleached Egyptian cotton. Right. Let's sort this lot out." She yanked open his wardrobe and found a string of empty coat hangers. Iestyn cringed and pointed at the piles on the chair and the ancient trunk.

"No problem. Nice clean slate to start off with then. Here – put this on." Sima unzipped the bag and threw a navy T-shirt at him. "Cotton. Will wash like a dream, even if it goes in with Tomos' wellies." She ignored Iestyn's protestations about it being too good for work. "Iestyn, if you keep it for best, it'll be as unfashionable as that horrible jumper before you even wear it – T-shirts need more use than just one outing per six weeks – and anyway, there are a few here, so you needn't worry. OK?"

"OK." Iestyn put it on and had to admit it felt good.

"Right, an overshirt." She threw a shirt at him and then a casual jacket. "Now, trousers. Get those bloody things off too – come on, Iestyn, is there any of the original jeans left?"

"I've, er, actually got two pairs on," he confessed. "The under-pair have holes in different places."

"*Off!* Go on, I won't look I promise – I don't think I could bear to see your underpants if this is the state of things you show to the world. I'll just hang these up."

Within ten minutes Sima had emptied his chest of drawers and replenished them with an array of folded, quality clothes. The pile by the door was just about fit for a slaughterman's ragbag. She used a couple of the least stained T-shirts and a container of strong cleaner that she produced from her bag to whip around the surfaces and replaced the clutter of empty aerosol cans and dried-up aftershave bottles on the dressing table with a matching set of toiletries that Joe had apparently received for Christmas but would never wear. "Now you won't smell like Ed from the pub."

Iestyn stood up and looked at himself in his newly visible mirror. He smiled and turned around and smiled again. "Thanks, Sima!"

"You're very welcome. Now you have an arse rather than a pile of ripped pockets and a six pack, rather than a gathering of stains." She looked at him and softened, "You look great! Makes you feel good too, huh? Wear them everyday, OK? No saving for best as soon as my back is turned, all right? There are plenty more around if you need them. Now, can you help me put this lot into these bags and straight into the boot of the Jeep; I know you Bevans, you'll be hooking them out of the bin as soon as I'm out of the gate – there's still plenty of wear in that faded shapeless T-shirt if you look closely, isn't there?"

Iestyn laughed, knowing it was true. He met Joe in the kitchen as he walked through with the three bin bags that contained his old wardrobe.

"Oh God, you've been well and truly Sima'd haven't you? Is there no one left? Oi, and that's my old T-shirt, you bastard! I wondered where that had gone. My favourite too…"

"Hush," clipped Sima, as she walked behind Iestyn with a bag full of rubbish. "You've got two new ones to replace it." Joe conceded, remembering how he'd given it up when Sima showed him in a mirror how it pulled across his stomach.

"OK," he muttered, "but keep it for best: don't you dare wear it to muck out those bloody cows…"

Louisa was walking down the high street. It was the start of her lunch hour and she had felt like a little fresh air. Their staff room was pleasant enough, but she was beginning to think that she needed to get out and about a bit more. Sitting on a slightly different chair than the one she'd been sat on downstairs all morning and nibbling at her sandwiches whilst she read through the pile of magazines that Doreen brought to work with her each week no longer felt enough. If she was going to broaden her horizons, she needed to start actually doing it – and what better way to broaden your horizons than take a walk down your local high street of a lunchtime?

It was cold and so she stopped to rearrange the scarf around her neck and to pull her mittens on. There was a knock from the window at the side of the pavement next to her. She ignored it, assuming that it was from kids taking the mickey out of her. The knock happened again and then again. She took a breath and turned to look. Instead of kids leering out of the window at her and puffing out their cheeks as if to mock her BMI, there were Rosie and Rachel sat at a table, smiling at her and waving at her to come on in.

She checked behind her to make sure that they were not motioning to someone else and then smiled back at them and hurried round to the café door.

"Hi," Rosie called over, "we saw you looking a bit cold, so we thought that you'd be better off in here with us drinking hot chocolate! Want one?" and they held out ridiculously large mugs topped with whipped cream, marshmallows and shakings of cocoa powder.

"Thanks, actually I would," she grinned and self-consciously slipped into a chair beside Rachel.

The waiter came over and Rosie giggled at him, "I think our friend wants one too – I think we need to be on commission! Perhaps I should get mine for free?"

"No," replied Rachel, "it was *my* suggestion. I'll get *mine* for free and maybe Rosie can have another marshmallow or something…"

The waiter laughed. "Perhaps I can stretch to a free marshmallow all round. What colour would you like? Pink or white? I'll just run it past my boss…"

The girls laughed and Louisa laughed too. She soon struggled out of her coat and all her wrappings and enjoyed the humid warmth of the café. It was somewhere she'd never been before, thinking it was a bit of a ham, egg and chips with a mug of tea kind of place – and although she loved ham, egg and chips served with a mug of tea, her parents pretended not to, so she had taken on their thoughts on the subject.

She beamed at the words, *our friend*, and hugely enjoyed sitting at a table with Rosie and Rachel. In the corner, the waiter made her hot chocolate and then brought it over with a small saucer of extra marshmallows. "Ooh, thank you," she smiled, "that looks good."

"Best hot chocolate in town," grinned the waiter.

"Only bloody hot chocolate in town," said Rachel.

The girls carried on chattering about nothing in particular and Louisa laughed with them and smiled and was even able to join in occasionally.

Sometimes she felt gauche; she wasn't as good at flirting with the waiter as they were and she was unable to demand a further marshmallow as compensation for her chocolate being a bit cold, but Rosie and Rachel laughed at the prospect and she felt welcome as their guest.

She sat for ten minutes or so chatting about the course and answering their questions about what she did and did she like it and why the hell did she live *there* and such like. She remembered what she had read about in one of Doreen's magazines about if you are feeling shy in company to ask questions back.

She was halfway down her hot chocolate when Rachel looked at her watch. "Shit! I'm gonna be late; Rosie, we'd better go." Warning bells rang in Louisa's mind – they had seen her coming and were going to leave her with the bill…

"Sorry, Lulu, we've got to go; I've got to get Rachel back for half past. Shit, we'll have to dash – look, nice to see you again and we'll catch up with you again soon, yeah?"

Louisa felt sick; it was back to being taken for a fool. "Er, OK," she stammered, "no problem." Should she ask whether they'd paid? Should she offer to pay anyway and thus dispel any embarrassment or should she jump up and say that she had to rush too and therefore the waiter would have to collect the money when they were all on the premises.

She looked into the remains of her hot chocolate to try and take hold of herself whilst she decided how to make a stand. Just as she had decided that the best thing might be to pretend she was in a rush too as she had some more mates to call on, Rachel called over the waiter, her voice muffled through her scarf.

"Off ladies?" he asked as he arrived at their table.

"Just us two I think," replied Rosie, "are you staying here to finish your hot chocolate, Lulu?"

Louisa's heart leapt. "Only if I can have another marshmallow…" she smiled and the others all laughed.

"Here," said Rosie, handing the waiter a ten-pound note, "my shout – for all three. I was paid on Friday, so you might as well have it whilst it's there – next week, I'll be back to climbing out of the toilet window."

"Thanks," replied Rachel.

"No, no, I can't possibly let you pay for mine," began Louisa, "here, how much was it?" and she fumbled in her coat for her purse.

"Don't worry about it," said Rosie, "my treat – you can get the next one!"

"Thank you! I will, yes, I'll get the next one." They waved to her and scuttled out of the door and the waiter chattered as he gathered their mugs and wiped their spillages from the table.

"Take your time," he smiled, "the bottom half of a hot chocolate is always the best…" and off he went to the kitchen, collecting a few stray teaspoons and a mug from another table as he went.

Louisa glowed. She sat at her table watching the townspeople scurrying by along the pavement outside and she finally felt as if she were one of them.

All her life she had felt on the outside of any group activity. As a child, she had assumed that she must be more fragile, a bit more poorly a bit more often than the other children. She was the one who would have to forgo birthday parties as she had a bit of a temperature, when other children would have made any fever better through the medium of jelly and screaming games.

She was never allowed out after dark, or when it was too cold. She must have been more delicate as cold apparently went to *her* chest, yet didn't bother going to the other kids' chests. Saying that, she had rarely been taken to the doctors.

She had never really been bullied, more just ignored as the sap in the corner who wasn't much fun.

As an adult it was easier. You made your own choices about what you did and you didn't need to give a flimsy note to a teacher who would raise her eyebrow and look over her glasses at her and say things like, "*Louisa can't do the sponsored walk because she has a sore foot*, eh? Which foot is sore, Louisa? I haven't seen you limping?"

"My dad thinks it's too far, Miss."

"Does he indeed…"

As an adult you just didn't put your name on the list in the first place.

She'd never really been pestered by a bloke – well, maybe Overbearing Charles occasionally at the golfie, but he was more of a bore than a letch. She wouldn't be confident enough to tell someone that they were boring her now and could they move on to the next poor soul please, as Rosie had apparently done on Friday night. Instead, she would be the one being chatted to all night about football knowing inside that the bloke was so pissed he wouldn't remember if she were rude to him or not by the morning.

Her warm glow began to slip and she started to feel – what? Angry? No, perhaps not that strongly. Cross? Yes, cross. She instinctively knew that her father's limitations for her had been something to do with getting one over on her mother, rather than it being simply for her safety and well-being, but she had never understood the reason. So, was it her *dad's* fault that she had no social skills? Or maybe it was her *mum's* fault? Was all that rushing around with no thought for her family really such a bad thing? Louisa had always assumed that it was, but actually was helping a few neighbours in need really so terrible?

The sad thing was, that regardless of any initial unhelpfulness, Louisa was very aware that, as an adult, it was now officially *her* problem. *Her* responsibility, *her* loss if she didn't get it sorted. She felt as if she were at the beginning of a mammoth task, with a sofa waiting comfortably at her side in case she stumbled and fell.

CHAPTER 12

Blingo hwch â chyllell bren – to skin a sow with a wooden knife (to attempt the impossible)

Sima pulled her office chair to her desk and lifted the lid from the Carrot and Orange Sunrise that she had just bought from the juice bar on the corner. She checked her schedule on her Blackberry®, already knowing that she had fifteen minutes before her next appointment arrived. Sophia Barnard was fifty, recently left by her husband and in need of re-invention. Well, she'd be coming to the right place.

Sima had so many recently-divorced fifty-somethings on her books that she had devised a programme especially for them: weight loss, new haircut, move from family home to riverside flat, shopping and researching the viability of running their own business in something completely different to their previous job. Twenty sessions for starters, plus ten per cent of any personal shopping done through her recommended outlet, her personal trainer or her hairdresser.

The phone rang out just as she was trying to determine one of the lesser flavours in her juice.

"Good morning, Sima Arshad."

"Oh, hello. Sima?" came a nervous little voice.

"Yes, good morning?"

"My name is Menna Edwards; you may not remember me, I'm a friend of Joe's – we met at the pub that time? In Bwlch y Garreg?" The

Welsh accent brought a red-faced woman with a rugby shirt tucked into her jeans to Sima's mind.

"Hello, Menna – yes, of course I remember you! How are you?"

"Very well, thanks, very well. I hope you don't mind me ringing – I got your number from Ed behind the bar. Do you have a spare five minutes please?"

"Of course, I don't mind – I've got a client at eleven, but until then, I'm all yours."

There was silence. Sima was used to this – for many people, it had taken so much courage to phone her that, when they were actually speaking to her, they realised that they didn't know what they were going to say.

"Well, it's, well, I'm just – well…" Menna ground to a halt.

"Are you phoning for a bit of advice perhaps? A talk over about where you'd like to be heading? That kind of thing?"

"Yes." Menna's voice sounded relieved. "I'm sort of in a rut and haven't thought about how I look or changed anything for years and, although I love my work and the farm is my life and, well, I know what I like at home, but then as I go to step out the door, well it all feels a bit uncomfortable, a bit pointless…" Menna tailed off.

"You just want to portray a slightly different image, is that it? To show that there is a little bit more to Menna Edwards than, well, lumberjack shirts and wellie boots?" Sima suggested gently. "That's quite common; sometimes we have the main bits of life right, but other parts need a bit of tinkering." Sima stood and walked to her window. She loved her view of the centre of London: the Houses of Parliament in the distance, the dome of St Paul's, the slow grace of the London Eye.

She imagined Menna in some back bedroom, with sleet spitting against the window. She'd be dressed in jeans and a T-shirt, rugby shirt and fleece. Her feet would be in broken-down trainers with, yes, socks with Disney animals on. Sima guessed that Menna would probably be speaking as quietly as she could in order for her mother to not be able to overhear.

"That's exactly it," Menna laughed, embarrassed that she needed to do this. "Well, I mean, you saw the state of me the other night. It's just that I've become Good Old Menna, good at humping sacks and mending tractors – and although I am happy with that, it's just that people see no further. You know what I mean?"

She means *Iestyn* doesn't see any further, thought Sima. "I know exactly what you mean; it's very common…"

"And you have done so much for Ed with just a two-minute conversation, I just wondered whether you might have, well, a little bit of advice for me…" Menna tailed off, awkward again at what she was asking.

"I'd be delighted – but first, tell me about Ed. I'm intrigued!"

"Well, people are thinking that they've come into the wrong pub!" Menna was back on easy ground and could laugh again. "'A task a day, a task a day,' is all he says to people now – one day he dusted the ceiling, another day he washed the curtains – we couldn't believe it! They all shrunk of course, but they're a completely different colour. And, no more snacks or alcoholic drinks behind the bar for him or any staff – he says he must have lost a stone already. Oh, and he stands up straight too – well, when he remembers."

"Fantastic," laughed Sima, "I am glad. I knew he just needed a prod. As for you, Menna, I'd be delighted to prod you as well, and you do so much for Joe's family – and his tractors – that it would be my pleasure. Let me have a think and I'll phone you back. You can make a start – and we'll talk properly in a week or two – we're back down in a fortnight I think? It's not this coming weekend, but the next one, OK?"

Menna gushed her thanks, left her bungalow's phone number, a request for discretion and slammed the phone down. Sima could imagine her standing shaking with relief that she'd done something that she'd been thinking about every day for three weeks.

Sima's phone rang again. It was the receptionist who manned the lobby of the suite of offices. "Send her up, thank you," said Sima, keen to get old roly-poly Sophia in and then out of the office so that she could concentrate on dabbling in Menna Edwards' life. How to reconcile rough, dirty work, long hours, little ready cash and a scouring-pad-red face with a modern woman with feminine charms enough to win the heart of her childhood friend and fellow tractor enthusiast Iestyn Bevan. It was a dream case for a professional dabbler, a dream case that she couldn't wait to get started on.

Menna stood in the back bedroom of her parents' house looking out into the sleet to watch for her mother scuttling back across the yard, wrapped up in her waterproofs. The plastic windows squeezed into the lopsided openings of the old farmhouse stopped the noise of the wind, but she knew how cold it would be out there.

Well, she'd done it. Phoned Sima. The person she realised that she was pinning her hopes on. She looked into the mirror on the polished dressing table and frowned; she was just a bundle of clothes on a body. She had no real idea even of whether she could be considered attractive. Her body was fit and strong, but sported supportive bras and large dark-coloured pants. Her hair was a mop in an elastic band-held ponytail: it couldn't really be said to have a style. She tended to cut the tangles out and she had so many split ends that the length usually took care of itself. The Powys Farmer's shop jeans were not intended to be stylish or flattering. They were just jeans that people wore for practical reasons. They didn't go in much at the waist or sit nicely on the hips, they had extra rivets and were double-stitched on the inner thigh seams.

She had her silk dressing gowns and her faux fur throws at home, but she hadn't got round to buying any daywear yet and had drawn a blank at what style she should aim for. She couldn't pop to the village shop in Marilyn Monroe white silk, and she couldn't really work out anything suitable in between that and her National Farmers' Union T-shirt.

She used to be a little more trendy, perhaps not as experimental as her friends had been, but she'd been happy in her own style and had made an effort most days. However, over the past few years she'd retreated into work and her outside-of-work persona had taken not just a back seat, but had gone for a snooze in the lobby and she had no way of trying to call it back.

She'd found that it seemed to be impossible to reconcile any kind of style and the kind of hard work that a farm required. And actually, muddy smartly-heeled boots looked awful: muddy wellies looked OK. It was impossible to stay clean when you had to walk across a yard that has had sheep on it and go anywhere in a truck that you sat in earlier in your muddy waterproofs. Also, farming didn't have a cut-off time – you simply worked until you didn't *have* to do some more – and as soon as you did, day or night, you just got out and carried on.

Yes, she could go back to wearing make-up, but an afternoon dragging hay about on a storming hillside would have her back being Alice Cooper – the same as when her new mascara ran in the queue of a Young Farmers' Club dance when she was fourteen. Hairdressers made her feel uncomfortable, being unable to think or state what she actually wanted. She would always walk out ruffling her hair and looking forward to having a shower when she got home and slowly those experiences had been phased out too.

Many of Menna's friends managed both farming and femininity, but perhaps they chose their own clothes, and didn't put most of them on account at Powys Farmer's. Menna didn't have much ready cash at her disposal – her mother had given her a lump sum to be put towards setting up her house, but had expected more in the way of ranges of saucepans and less of a range of bathroom accessories for her money. Bills were paid directly by the farm and her wages were paltry, based on the premise that the farm would be hers in due course.

Therefore she had few resources to fritter on experimentation. She couldn't go on a shopping spree and buy things designed for one wear or even one year's wear only. Nor could she go and spend an afternoon having a head full of highlights if it wasn't *exactly* what she wanted. She'd never get another eighty quid *and* an afternoon off to put any mistakes right. Manicures – pointless. Pedicures? Waste of money. And anyway, there was something quite practical about having feet as hard as hooves when they kicked about in wellies all day.

Menna slipped out of the bedroom and went back down the stairs. Best to get away from the office before Mother came up, else she would start asking casual questions that one was *obliged* to answer as to who she might have been ringing. As she entered the warm kitchen, she felt energised and excited: what would Sima come up with for her? What would her game plan be? Whatever it was, she knew that she had to give it a real try.

Iestyn sat at the computer and typed in *Tan-y-Bryn*. As he scrolled down the list of business directories and descriptions of the town's historic nature, he munched on a massive cheese sandwich: supper was still a little way off and he was starving.

He clicked onto a list of clubs in the area, but quickly dismissed them as not for him: squash, running groups, water volleyball and rambling sounded like too much hard work, even if Sima would beam if he told her he'd joined one of them. At the ends of his days, he was knackered: the last thing he needed was more exercise. No, even if it meant playing squash against the woman of his dreams, it really wasn't going to happen.

What was it again that Sima had lectured him on this time? He thought back to her conversation – it was always *her* conversation, never *their* conversation. When she suggested that he needed to get stuck in to some different interests locally, somewhere where he might have a chance of meeting someone new. What she really meant of course was someone female – volleyball against Johnny Brechdan was a bit pointless; they would be better just talking about it in the pub once a week…

The online community was a possibility, but he didn't have time for endless chat rooms. Mother tended to hog the computer after supper for the farm paperwork and he knew that he would never be a sad git tapping away into the small hours – he'd be asleep by then and miss all the good stuff!

Iestyn stuffed the last of the sandwich into his mouth, cramming it so full that he had to push the bread around with his fingers. It had been a habit since he was young and used to earn him a clip at the table, but now it was his guilty secret that he could indulge when he was on his own.

His search brought up "*…work in nearby Tan-y-Bryn…*" Who was this then? Someone he knew? Iestyn clicked on what turned out to be a blog:

"*Hi, my name is Lulu and…*"

He washed down the last of his mouthful with a swig of tea and groaned slightly as it eased itself down his throat. He wished Mother would hurry up with supper, otherwise he'd have to make himself another sandwich in the meantime.

Sounds interesting, Iestyn thought. Lulu? Lives near Tan-y-Bryn? Who would that be then? He read down, his attention momentarily sparked.

"So if anyone has any thoughts about what to look for in a flat or a flatmate, I would be interested to know – I've never rented a place of my own before and don't want to end up living in a damp dump with a nerd who keeps pet snakes in the bathroom!"

Without really thinking, Iestyn signed up and replied. A last mouthful of tea had him pressing "Post". Good: he could now legitimately tell Sima that he'd done his homework. With perfect timing a shout was heard from downstairs. Iestyn gathered up his plates, blew the worst of the crumbs off the keyboard and headed down for supper.

Louisa sat in her chair in a state of shock. Someone – had – replied – to – her – blog! Rachel probably had tens of interactive replies, but it was the kind of thing that *never* happened to Louisa. In the same way she had never got picked for rounders, a dance, or to be sat next to on a school trip, so she never expected anyone to reply to her blog. And he sounded quite nice – not much to go on so far perhaps, but he sounded pleasant and fun – probably a really nice bloke! Good looking too, she suspected!

Now, how to answer? She took a sip of her tea. How would Rachel answer such a statement? No doubt with confidence and wit, ensuring another response without question. Perhaps she'd go and have a bath. Go and mull it over.

She could hear her mother climbing the stairs, that tortuous sound of a fellow human being struggling in order to bring her a cup of tea. She wished that instead of being irritated by her mother, she had a mother that she could chat with; it would be great to be able to have another opinion about this new bloke – even if it were just a giggle and a bit of understanding that it might be interesting to her. Rosie had said that she told her mother most things – even when she'd woken up and forgotten that she'd allowed four blokes to sleep on their living room floor as they were caught in the pub by the snow!

Rosie's comments had made Louisa realise that she had never really understood her own mother, never moved on from having her as someone who told her what she should be doing or reminded her to eat her greens – even though she probably did neither.

Louisa realised that she didn't know what made her mother tick;

she knew what annoyed her, but had never really bothered to find out what made her happy. Maybe she should – in her new phase – take a fresh look at things, make more of an effort to understand. Perhaps in time she and Esther could cultivate a relationship like Rosie and her mother's: Louisa wouldn't be telling her that she had four strangers sleeping on her floor, but maybe they could go shopping together or swap clothes – or perhaps just jewellery, thought Louisa as she pictured herself struggling to get her thighs into a pair of her mother's trousers…

Esther tapped the door and a mug of tea was pushed around the corner. "Thanks, Mum," said Louisa, "thanks for bringing that up. Hey, you know my blog thing? I've had a response!"

"That's interesting! Is it from someone you know?" Esther's head peered round the door and she leant against the door frame.

"Don't think so, someone must have done a search for something I had mentioned and found it. Amazing really, hey? I've only done a few entries."

"I suppose some people have their whole social life online don't they? I don't know whether that's healthy, but I suppose if it stops some people feeling lonely – especially if they don't manage to get out much, it can't be a bad thing."

The two women chatted back and forth for a while and then the conversation came to a natural end. "Right, I'll leave you to your reply!" smiled Esther and pottered off back towards the stairs.

"Yeah, thanks again for the tea," called Louisa and she turned back to her blog. That was quite nice, she thought. Chatting with her mum like that; perhaps – perhaps she wasn't always a miserable old trout after all. Louisa took a slurp of her tea and smacked her lips. Maybe it was time she started pulling her weight around the house a little? But, saying all that, there was something bloody nice about someone else bringing you up a nice cup of tea after you'd had a hard day at work…

She read the comment on her blog again so that she could memorise it, then gathered up the plump bath sheet that sat on the shelf by her door and padded off to the bathroom to immerse herself in creamy suds, to drip puddles all over the floor and to leave a smattering of dead skin around the top of the tub. That would be another downside to sharing a flat, she thought, as she selected her products: having to get in after some other dirty slob had used the bath and left all their mess everywhere...

CHAPTER 13

Tarw potel – bottled bull (artificial insemination)

Sima stood in her hall with the phone to her ear and one of her heels resting on top of the elaborate umbrella stand. "Iestyn! How are you? Lovely to hear from you. Sorry if I'm a bit out of puff, I've just come back from a run." She swapped legs and put the other foot up and stretched out her hamstring. "Oh, not far – just four miles tonight. Your brother's still out there. Wanted to do the extra loop; he's on a bit of an intensive fitness regime at the moment – the one I put my overweight ladies on!"

She looked into the mirror and pushed her hair back from her face; as usual a few dark tendrils had escaped from her headband. "*Iestyn!*" she giggled. "How cruel! He's not overweight; he's just a little, well, flabby!"

Iestyn's laugh rang out from her receiver as she walked into the kitchen and took an isotonic drink from the fridge, pressing the button for the speaker phone and putting the handset down.

"So, how's everything with you?" she asked, dropping into a squat. "How's the...er...?"

"Love life?" Iestyn filled in the gap. "That's what you usually ask, after all?"

"Well, why not! Iestyn – how is the love life?" Sima dropped onto the floor and started counting her stomach crunches.

"Well," started Iestyn a little sheepishly, "not a *great* deal different to when you last interrogated me about it. But, I *have* found someone online and I believe that she is female!"

"Online? Oh. OK, so what makes you think that she's female? *Nineteen... twenty...*"

"She talks about paint in her hair and the colour her lounge walls will be."

"Yes, definitely female then. What are you talking about with her?"

"Mainly giving advice on leaving home."

"You! Advice on leaving home? How exactly are you qualified for that?" Sima jumped up and prepared for forty lunges.

"Not sure really… Perhaps it's more advice on why you shouldn't stay at home. But she sounds sort of fun."

"Sort of?"

"Well, it's hard to tell isn't it – you need to see someone don't you, to see if you like them. You know, see the size of their…"

"Farm?"

"Yes, their farm! Johnny Brechdan thinks he recognises her turn of phrase. He says that she's maybe the one who gave him head in the taxi on the way back from Denligh's? On that Tuesday? You know, Davie's Tuesday?"

Sima shook her head and swapped legs and started the recount. When you had a conversation with a Bevan, you really had to concentrate; there was no way that you could multitask *and* understand a Bevan conversation.

"Well, you know what you need to do now?" she said picking up the receiver and walking down the hall to the bathroom. "Flirt a bit, you know – add a smiley or even an X after a comment. See what happens."

"I can't do that!"

"Course you can," she said, reaching into the shower cubicle and setting the water running. "Just test the water! Remember, she has no idea who you are really, so take a risk! Did Johnny Brechdan get where he gets without sticking his neck out occasionally?"

"It's not his neck that he sticks out, unfortunately. Anyway, did I tell you that he shagged a cousin last week? Yeah, they got chatting afterwards and started tracing back and… Uh Oh! Little baby two-heads could be on its way…"

Sima laughed, "OK, I've got to go now; I need to have a shower. I'll tell Joe that you called, but we'll be seeing you soon anyway. Good luck though and I'll look forward to hearing how it went!"

Iestyn heard the phone click off and he groaned. Sima – been for a run – needing a shower. *Having* a shower. Oh, wonderful! Joe was such a lucky bastard.

He put the phone back down into its cradle, sat amongst a pile of papers in the "office", and got to his feet. Good God, he thought as he caught a glimpse of himself in the dusty oval mirror, hanging from a rusting chain on the wall. He'd managed to find another acrylic jumper from somewhere and had teamed it with an out-of-shape red polo shirt with one half of its collar pointing out the top. Joe had been right; he hadn't been able to bring himself to wear his "new" clothes to work in for long. There was really no point in ruining them for the sake of admiring glances from a miserable old sheepdog.

He ruffled his hair and it stood up in tufts where it was put. Sima had said that she needed a shower, but he *really* needed a shower. She'd probably be quietly glowing after her beautiful body had gracefully loped through a park: if Joe had any idea of how lucky he was, he should be *licking* her clean. The difference was that he, Iestyn, hadn't had a proper wash for days. He'd been sitting in a fusty old Land Rover, stood, knelt and sat in muck and generally been a bit of a bloke. Thank God they didn't have a video phone, he thought as he pressed the computer's On button – perhaps he really needed to add a kiss to his messages to the virtual female. Even if it were Brechdan's earlier benefactor: he desperately required a reason to get himself back on track a little. At least he still changed his underpants each day – even *his* standards had a baseline – well, most days they did…

As the computer ground away, he imagined Sima in her power shower; everything white or chrome and the whole thing gleaming. When Iestyn had gone to stay with Joe, he'd had a shower at Sima's flat and loved the fact that at arm's reach there were shelves full of shower products so fruity and luxurious that Iestyn had felt that he could eat them. Joe had said that he smelt like a smoothie when he'd finally come out of the bathroom, but Sima swore by her natural ingredients-only products, all with a hint of something in them that justified costing an absolute fortune.

The last one to use the Pencwmhir shower had been Mabel the sheepdog, as Mother had insisted that she should be washed before being taken to the vet. Therefore the tray was strewn with mud, grit and dog hair. Then Father had hung his coat up in it and thrown in his wellies after the river had washed over their tops when he wasn't concentrating.

That was the trouble in the Bevan household; nothing was straightforward. If Iestyn wanted a shower, he first had to hang the coat somewhere else, find a place to stand the wellies upside down to dry, rinse away the mud and dog hair, unblock the plughole of the resulting yuck, only to get in and find that there was no shampoo left, the soap covered in hair – animal and human, public and private – and there would be no dry towel to hand, either.

Alternatively, there was the bathroom upstairs. The water would be boiling in the tank from the Rayburn, but it would trickle out of the ancient tap at a dribble meaning that the bath would be lukewarm at best by the time it was filled. One would then lie in it, with a wind whistling through the rattling window so fiercely that it would make waves on the surface of the water and threaten his manhood should it be so foolish as to surface.

Sima's towels were huge, luxurious and sat, folded on a heated chrome shelf in reach of the shower. Bevan towels were small, ragged and God knows where…

Iestyn knew that both of his parents worked their fingers to the bone. He knew that they really couldn't fit anything else into their days, or stretch their tight budget, but sometimes he felt it would be wonderful to come in one cold night and have a hot bath next to a heated chrome towel rail and afterwards stand on a rag rug that didn't make your feet dirty again. Sima would somehow prioritise it and make it all happen. It was no wonder that he continued to wear decades-old acrylic.

It was the same with women, really. He wasn't a snob, but he knew that to bring a woman back to Pencwmhir would dissolve any sense of romance clocked up at a party or in a pub. First the lucky lady would have to open five badly-maintained gates in the pitch black, on a muddy lane. Then she'd have to share a bed with not just Iestyn but four scratchy blankets and a draught, and in the morning she'd have to listen to Mr Bevan clearing his throat in the bathroom eight un-soundproofed inches from Iestyn's headboard. Any shower to wash away the hopefully sticky activity of the night before would have to be taken in the company of a pair of size eleven wellie boots and a bar of household soap. It was never going to be the precursor for a second date.

Iestyn felt it was a chicken and egg thing. If he had a girlfriend, then he'd try a bit harder and make more of an effort to scrub up a bit more often and to get his own place. Yet, without a girlfriend, there seemed little point. He got on well with his parents, he didn't have to commute to work and there was no need to do any different than wear what was warm and available.

In fact, the only woman who ever really came to the house to see him was Menna – and that was only occasionally and purely on business. After his recent debacles, he was still keen to get things moving. He cringed when he thought of the "lunch" at her house and groaned when he thought of her dragging him away from the hen night like a stunned pig. Perhaps it was fate's way of telling him that they, too, were actually distant cousins and that they shouldn't procreate.

Maybe he'd just do as Sima seemed to be advising and take a punt on Lulu? Maybe it would be better to have a fresh start; someone who didn't have it in the back of their mind that Iestyn Bevan forgot to wear pants on his second day of school.

So, as Iestyn clicked onto Lulu's blog, he did so with trepidation and a little spark of excitement at a potential new beginning.

And so, for a range of convoluted reasons, Iestyn wrote, "Don't worry about it! All you need is a cupboard for your tomato sauce, a saucepan for your beans, and a toaster and you will be fine ☺," in response to Lulu's lengthy ramble about not realising that there were so many things that one needed when one was establishing one's first home.

CHAPTER 14

Cic i'r post i'r fuwch gael clywed – kicking the post for the cow to feel it (broad hint)

Menna was on the top of the hill. The rain flailed horizontally into the side of her truck. Whereas Iestyn's vehicle would have been flooded out by now, hers was perfectly sealed and the heaters were keeping her warm. She took a sip from the flask that she'd grabbed from the counter as she'd left her parents' house that morning. There were always two ready-prepared each day, alongside two little parcels of food.

Menna unwrapped today's second parcel and found a slab of fruitcake – *great, fruitcake and hot sweet tea!* Perfect after wading around in the mud for half an hour, in and out of the truck, opening gates and unloading bags of feed for the stock. Her coat lay steaming on the seat next to her as she dabbed up the stray currants with a wet finger. She'd been thinking about what Sima might have planned for her, but what had seemed both sensible and possible when talking to a woman wearing a white trouser suit in a warm office, suddenly seemed a ridiculous waste of effort.

She wiped her nose on her cuff, rather than rummage through wet pockets for a damp hanky, and in doing so dislodged a pool of water that must have settled on the collar of her jumper. She shuddered as it ran down her neck.

Cursing, she leant forward and wiped the steam off the inside of the window with her sleeve and muttered at the snot now smeared across the glass in its place. She peered out into the gloom and then looked harder at something wriggling in the distance. *Damn*, it looked like a sheep caught in the fence. She groaned as the rain turned to hail. She stuffed the last of the cake into her mouth and sluiced it down with the remaining tea. She wiped her hands on her waterproof trousers, wrestled herself into her coat and battled back out into the weather.

Menna jogged down the steep slope towards the fence, skidding the last few yards and landing in a pile near the sheep. The sheep's eyes rolled in fright and pain as it battled to free itself from the wire and escape this new threat of a muddy human being. Menna could see from the markings on its back that it was one of the Bevans' – why were Iestyn's sheep always the thickest ones doing the stupidest things? This one seemed to have its head and a leg stuck in the mesh; a section had been patched and so had smaller holes than the rest.

Menna wrestled with the beast, trying to set it free. She swore at it as it scraped a sharp foot down her hand and arm. She soon got the ewe out, but could see that it was hurt, as it lay on the ground struggling to stand and then falling over again.

A quick check made Menna think that it had probably damaged a leg – possibly a dislocation. She saw her truck twenty-five yards away, at the top of a slippery slope and cursed again. Then she dragged the sheep onto her thighs and then as gently as she could, she bumped herself and it up the hill. At least the sheep wasn't struggling anymore – perhaps even Iestyn's sheep had the sense to know that it would hurt more if it struggled.

Somehow, she got it to her truck and, then, with a disc-slipping effort, hauled it and the five gallons of water in its laden fleece into the back and shut the door.

She stood for a couple of seconds to catch her breath and then noticed that blood was running off her hand, diluted by the pouring rain. Suddenly she felt the pain and dabbed at it with her other hand – it didn't seem too bad, but would need some kind of dressing. Better get rid of Iestyn's stupid sheep first and then get it sorted.

Menna started the truck, turned the heaters up full and pulled away, testing the terrain slowly as she made sure that she wasn't going to slide sideways down the slaked grass. She got back onto the track and then bounced back over the tops to Iestyn's side of the hill – damn, their gates were always knackered. Dropped hinges and lots of sodden knotted ropes: the gates leading down to Glascwm were hung perfectly and the catches and hinges were greased every year. Her mum's calendars of jobs were irritating at times, but she had to admit that they had a purpose.

By the time Menna had lurched down the steep track, she had been spotted and Tomos shouldered the final gate open for her. She showed him the sheep in the back of her truck and he was just shouldering it off to the barn for a proper look, when Iestyn appeared.

"Sort her hand out will you, boy? Nasty cut," grunted Tomos as he slipped and slid off across the yard.

"Hi-ya, Menna, you OK?" called Iestyn, a little sheepishly, still shamefaced about the night of the rabbit ears.

"Yeah, OK, just cut my hand and arm here a bit. Found your sheep stuck in a fence – funny how they all keep trying to top themselves rather than live under your care…"

"Ah, they love me really – know I'm just trying to toughen them up; it's for their own good. Nothing wrong with being stuck in a fence for a few days when— Hey, that's nasty – come on in, let's have a look at it."

Iestyn led her quickly to the house and took her coat. They kicked their wellies off in the porch in a way that would never have been allowed at Glascwm and padded into the warm kitchen, each with socks flapping at the front of their feet. Menna's thick and warm; Iestyn's unmatched and full of holes.

Iestyn grimaced. "Come on, that's a nasty gash you have there. Here, let's wash it." Iestyn ran the hot tap and carefully rinsed the grit and mud from the wound. "There, once the shite is off it, we can have a good look."

Menna smiled as he turned her hand this way and that, as if he were a brain surgeon, rather than a sausage-fingered farmer whose only usual medical aids were a dose of Terramycin and a slap on the rump.

He seemed to be quite enjoying holding her strong but slender forearm, as if he hadn't noticed before that it was peppered in freckles. Menna found herself wishing that it was a bigger wound so that this could go on for longer. She didn't have much physical affection in her life, what with a mother who was a cold island of agricultural efficiency and a father who was always working. She couldn't remember the last time someone had spent time with her like this, and it was lovely. Like a massage with fragrant oils, like stepping from a soft towel and slipping into a hot bath... Iestyn turned suddenly and it was as if he'd caught her gazing with a soppy smile at his dark hair, and the spell was broken.

"Look, Menna," he started, "about the other night…"

"Oh, Iestyn, don't worry about it! What are mates for if not to carry their pissed friends home!"

"Well, it's more about what was going on in the bar. I, well, Johnny made me go out and, we just bumped into those women, and—"

"Iestyn! I said don't worry about it! Everyone is entitled to have a bit of fun! You don't *have* to sit in the Bull and talk about crankshafts, you know. I know that I certainly don't!"

"Oh?"

"Well, it's nice to go out somewhere different sometimes, yeah? You know, meet a few new people, have a laugh? It's not all Bwlch y Garreg, Bwlch y Garreg?"

"Yeah, yeah, I s'pose. But…"

"That's much better, thanks," Menna found herself saying, looking at her arm. "You'd make a lovely nurse!"

107

Iestyn looked like he was going to say something else, but instead turned off the tap and patted her arm dry with a dirty towel.

"Let me get a bandage – Mother has a stash somewhere. Yep, in this old biscuit tin up here." Iestyn reached up high to the top of the cupboard to fetch the dusty old Quality Street tin and Menna managed a quick peep at the strong waist that was revealed in the gap between his trouser waistband and his shirt. She felt herself tingle inside and she had an urge to reach out and touch it, to fold her arms around it and nestle her face into his back.

But she didn't. Menna didn't do things like that.

Instead, she laughed as he blew the dust off the lid and pulled it open. Inside were a selection of ripped-up strips of bed sheet, each folded neatly and popped into a plastic bag.

"Ah," said Iestyn, "this is about the limit of our first aid kit. All apparently sterile – boiled to buggery and sealed for your convenience back in 1975. I'm hoping that they're not Joe's old sheets, but I have a horrible feeling that they might just be…"

"Never mind," said Menna, "what doesn't kill me will make me stronger."

"Maybe, but let's just hope that this isn't the start of septicaemia, otherwise you might regret saying that!"

The gentleness flowed back as Menna submitted to being wrapped up very slowly in three different strips of bed sheet, one being a little more discoloured than the others and Iestyn surmised that that was probably the bit in the middle of the bed and the others from nearer the hems.

By the time he'd wrapped and unwrapped and then secured the bandage with a series of massive knots, Menna felt quite light-headed. She'd never seen this side of Iestyn before – a gentle, tender side that seemed to be enjoying looking after her. Surely he wouldn't bandage Johnny Brechdan up in this manner? So, it must be because she was female and thus he had recognised she was female and therefore…

"Come on, sit down now, I'll make you a nice cuppa – if you've lost a lot of blood in the quest to save one of our delightful pedigree sheep, the least I can do is make you a drink."

He pottered a bit more and then passed her a large mug and one of Isla's scones and just as Menna was about to say, "Christ, she doesn't still make those bloody things does she?" there was the sound of a gunshot from outside. They both winced.

"Oh well," said Iestyn, as he took back her scone and drink, "I'll have that back then if you didn't manage to save the damn thing after all. See – if you'd been a bit more careful, you'd have earned this!"

Menna smiled up at him as she received her goodies back and Iestyn sat down in the seat opposite her. Then he got up and fiddled with the fire. Then he sat down and looked at her again. Menna felt the silence was companionable, but Iestyn broke it first each time, fiddling with logs, topping up her tea, and then topping up his.

He wriggled, making some small talk about borrowing her trailer and then shut up again.

Iestyn looked different somehow. It wasn't just the trendier clothes that made him suddenly seem taller and with a perfect V physique – he'd always looked good to Menna, even if his acrylic had sparked a little too much with static in the past. It was something about his face: it just looked different. More alive somehow. His eyes were nearly black as they looked into hers, as if he was mulling something over. Something important.

The door burst open and Iestyn jumped to his feet. It was Tomos wrestling with his oilskin. "All right, boy? Bloody thing had had it. Sorry Menna, love, thank you for trying, but, well, bloody thing had a broken thigh – must have fallen or got caught in a bloody rabbit hole, *then* got caught in the fence afterwards. Would have cost a bloody fortune with the vet, so, well, I shot it.

"Isla's just wrapping you up the other leg now – take it home with you as thanks for your efforts. Pointless burying the bloody thing – not being ill or anything like that. The Ministry will just have to call it 'lost'. A *run off to the coast*, perhaps! Anyway, sorted your arm has he? Good boy. Nasty cut that – have you had your tetanus jab?"

Tomos's chatter muffled Iestyn's awkward shuffling and Menna was soon busy with TB, badgers and rabbit holes, as if the past half hour had never happened.

But as she left the warmth of the kitchen, her bandaged arm clutching a leg of lamb wrapped in a council recycling bag, her eyes caught Iestyn's stare, deep from the corner of the room and although she still couldn't quite comprehend its origin, it renewed the pre-

Tomos glow in her loins and she closed the door behind her with a step that would have had a spring in it had it not been encumbered by a heavy lump of raw meat…

Esther sat on the torn seat of the dirty blue bus as it revved itself up to climb the hill. The gears crunched and the driver ground his foot to the floor, the concentration of his face in the mirror reflecting how well he knew the bus and how carefully he was listening to the engine before he went for broke. He timed it perfectly and the gearbox crashed and the bus shot forward, causing Esther to make a grab for the handrail on the back of the seat in front of her. She pulled her hand away in disgust as she felt the not-yet-hardened slime of chewing gum that some unpleasant so-and-so had stuck to the underside.

For goodness' sake she cursed to herself, *this bus just gets worse!* The smell of disturbed spearmint mingled with the exhaust fumes that had been pumped through the draughty windows: Daphne Rogers' Buses had obviously not taken *their* letter to heart…

She'd wondered about the tone of her note and it had actually been the first that she'd rewritten – her assumption being that Daphne Rogers would probably get so many letters of complaint that a gentle one in her usual style would be water off a duck's back.

She'd mentioned cleanliness – or the lack of it – torn seats, jammed windows and the state of the driver's fingernails. She hated the fact that he would occasionally stop in a quiet lay-by and duck into the woods, coming out twenty seconds later whistling and wiping his hands on his uniform trousers. That is why she never got on the bus unless she had *exactly* the right money – everyone knew that coins were dirty, but there was no need to experience the dirtying process in action.

As the bus glided to a halt outside Tŷ Bryn, a large house perched on the top of a bleak section of hill, Esther broke into a grin of satisfaction. Whilst two women climbed onto the bus, wheezing with the effort, Esther noted the net curtains hanging in all four windows of the house facing the road. The job had obviously been hastily done as the curtains dipped in the middle and rose on each corner, as if someone had just tacked them up as quickly as they could.

But that was so much better than the previous situation – she was sick of seeing that man in his underpants, particularly when he'd had his hand down the front for warmth, which was often. The woman was as bad: on her weekly bus journeys into town, Esther had witnessed her plucking her bikini line, doing yoga in her nightie and cupping and smelling a fart.

Her letter to Tŷ Bryn had been succinct, brief and on an "it might be helpful for you to know" basis. She had mentioned that she didn't go on the bus herself, but had overheard a woman in a shop talking about it. She was careful not to narrow her identity down to one of the forty or so people who regularly used this particular bus route – only five of which at most were likely to be computer literate.

The two old women dragged themselves to the rear of the bus and, as the driver got bored with waiting for them to settle and revved away, they lurched into the seat in front of Esther. She nodded to them and they grunted in reply; the three women recognised each other due to travelling regularly together, but did not know each others' names.

Esther yawned inwardly as they waffled their way through grocery prices, Doctor Mathis being marvellous and the more whiskery one's Ken being such a miserable old goat recently that she didn't know what to do with him. *Leave that coat on the bus and wash your hair occasionally*, Esther muttered to herself. She considered a letter, but decided that the case wasn't worthy enough.

Then a new track of conversation caught her attention. Geography teacher? Tan-y-Bryn High School?

"Well, our Sian is really fed up – it's her A level year and the damn woman has gone off on the sick! Probably *stress* or something." This was said and received in a way that suggested that the two women didn't believe in stress: it was an ailment invented by shysters, by those who simply weren't up to the job.

"Good God, the woman has been teaching for twenty-five years – why does she suddenly find it *stressful*?"

Esther leant forward, desperate to hear what was being said, but finding it difficult what with the constant revving.

Could that really be Mrs Hardy? Mrs Taught-Louisa-Geography Hardy? Esther's heart fluttered and she could feel her face flush once more. She'd only meant to give the woman a bit of a friendly nudge; she'd never meant to make her sick.

111

It had always been unfinished business as far as Esther had been concerned. Mrs Hardy had been Louisa's sixth form geography teacher and under her, Louisa had turned from a grade A student to one that had scraped a D. Mrs Hardy had been lazy and inconsistent. She apparently never planned lessons, just waffled through a chapter in a textbook, getting her pupils to take it in turns to read a page. Louisa's favourite subject under Mr Jeffers had turned into something she struggled with and no longer enjoyed. Esther had wanted to complain at the time, but Louisa, then Louisa *and* David, hadn't allowed it.

She had taken the opportunity of her new found computer composition skills to rectify things: a few home truths, but perhaps a couple too many digs. Esther bit her lip and leant forward again, the bus now cruising sedately along a flat section.

"So, poor Sian has a mixture of supply and non-specialist teachers to take her through the most important part of her course! I ask you! She was really enjoying it before this. I'd like to shake that bloody woman – I'd show her what *stress* really is!"

Whiskers agreed and rambled off about her Ken's stress, with which they were both hypocritically sympathetic.

Esther leant back into the dusty seat, washed over with the now familiar feeling of nausea coupled with exhilaration. Her hands gripped the arm until the crusted velour made her flesh creep. Was it a victory or a failure? Had it achieved its aim and been of benefit to the community, or had it been a spiteful, cowardly act that did no good to anyone but had made her feel slightly less impotent?

What if Mrs Hardy had changed her ways say, five years ago? What if she were now a fantastic teacher? What if she, Esther, had just ruined another woman's health? Getting the guy at Tŷ Bryn to scratch his bollocks behind opaque curtains was a benefit to mankind, but this?

Esther got out at her stop, bid everyone on the bus goodbye and thanked the driver. He grunted at her in return, revolving his false teeth around his mouth. Miserable man, she thought. *Someone should teach him not to be so rude…*

Chapter 15

Yn bigog fel draenog – prickly like a hedgehog (a cross person)

Menna walked back along the track to her bungalow. The wind was whipping the sleet sideways and she had to hold the side of her hood to stop it stinging her face. She had just ploughed through a roast lamb dinner, made with the leg that Tomos had cut for her and that Jean had made Bill check thoroughly to make sure it wouldn't poison them all due to former neglect.

"For goodness' sake, Jean, just because their gates aren't swinging perfectly, doesn't mean that their animals are bad; you can't get a better hill stockman than Tomos Bevan," Bill mumbled as he checked over the pink meat.

"Maybe, but I bet his slaughter knife is as dirty as his truck," she'd snapped in return. However, they'd all sat down to a wonderful plate of roast potatoes, swede, and sweet, succulent lamb rubbed with rosemary. *Mum was a fantastic cook, you had to give her that.* But Menna, her mood darkening, also recognised that her mum had to ruin every pleasant experience with a dig or a jibe to make someone else feel that they had failed – probably with the good intention of spurring them on to doing something that would correct that failure, but a dig no less. And tonight, it had been Menna's turn.

They had been sitting at the table and had just finished eating the tasty meal. Bill had leant back in his chair, thanked his wife and said that he couldn't remember when they had a roast as good as that one. The obvious thing would have been to say, "No, you are right; that was delicious."

Instead, her mother had said, "It would have been when Paul used to come round for Sunday lunches. Oh, now *they* were good roasts! It was such a shame that you let him slip away, Menna, a really nice man and *such* a good farm. It could all have been so different if you'd managed to keep hold of him. Look at you now, single and stuck in that soulless little bungalow, when you could have been living in the Neuadd by now! What a waste…"

Menna had looked at her mother in amazement. "Thank you, Mother," she had said, "but I didn't let him *slip away*, I didn't *want* to be with him. And I am not going to base my life's decisions on how you like to spend your Sunday lunchtimes…"

"Calm down, I was only saying that I used to enjoy the roasts," said Jean, getting up and clearing the dishes away. Then she did what she always did when she had offended someone, which was get on with the next chore, humming happily as if nothing had happened, leaving the other person fuming with rage.

Bill had tutted and shaken his head and muttered, "Take no notice," to Menna, but it had left Menna angry and upset and it had been a while since she had felt like that. A while since she'd felt like much at all concerning Paul Morgan…

Paul the Neuadd. Big family within the farming community. Big farm, big reputation. Big kudos in dating Paul the Neuadd. Iestyn and Johnny Brechdan used to tease her that they'd heard that Paul the Neuadd had an *enormous* tractor, but they'd been in their late teens and so that kind of thing was thought to be hilariously funny.

To Menna and her friends, Paul the Neuadd was a legend. He would turn up late at functions, dark and imposing, from his big farm, and people would gravitate to him, and he would know everyone in the room, be distantly related to half of them and would give them a few minutes each. He would then retreat, off in his big truck to – *no one knew where*…

The boys all wanted to be like him, to *be* him. The girls all wanted to go out with him. Menna wanted to go out with him too, but she didn't know why. Then, one day, after a day at the local trotting races, he had walked up to Menna who had been laughing with a few mates in the beer tent and he had asked her out. Surprised and very flattered she had said yes.

"I'll pick you up at 7.30, Thursday?" he'd asked.

"OK," she'd replied. No courtship, no chatting up, no nothing. And so it was that she had a date with Paul the Neuadd, quite an accomplishment for one from Bwlch y Garreg.

Jean had been beside herself with excitement. "Paul the Neuadd! Menna, just think, you'll be going for Sunday lunch at the Neuadd!"

"Mum, I'm going for a drink on a Thursday, not lunch on a Sunday."

"But, you *will* do, Menna, you *will* do! Just think, Sunday lunch at the Neuadd!" Menna had tutted and walked away, muttering at her mother to calm down.

However, in time, she did indeed go to Sunday lunch at the Neuadd, and eventually one Saturday night leading on to, ultimately, Sunday tea.

Theirs was a strange courtship, built mainly on being with other people or going about on farming business, but doing it together. They would duck in to see Harry Begwyn about some clippers or chat through open car windows with other neighbours until someone pulled up behind them in the lane.

It was as if the community was glad that they were together and that was enough in itself. Paul was pleasant enough company, but was never a chatterer. Menna came to learn that the reason he would have ten-minute conversations with people was because that was all he had in him – for anyone, including her.

Sunday lunches had seemed desperately important to Jean, and for some reason to Paul's mother, Anwen, too. Paul liked roasts, so he went along with them and Menna knew no different, so she did too. That's what couples did, wasn't it? Go for Sunday roasts at each other's parents' houses?

Their sex life was reasonable considering Menna's lack of years and Paul's alleged, but unconfirmed, experience, him being twelve years her senior, and it became a Thursday and Saturday night thing. On Thursday they went out for a curry and on Saturday they went out to the local pub or a Young Farmers' dance or some other function on the farming calendar – and always on to somewhere else, even if it were just home to bed. (So, *that's* where he used to go! she'd realised.)

Menna had known that she should feel excited and flattered and proud, but she hadn't really known why she didn't. She did enjoy Paul's company and she enjoyed the things that they did together, even if it were mending a tractor, as she learned a lot from him and it was a companionable pairing even if it was lacking in a few fireworks.

Jean had had it all worked out: "You'll probably run the Neuadd, as Paul's parents would really want to build a bungalow and live in that at their age. Perhaps we can swap ground – use a bit of their low ground and maybe borrow their bull – he's a good 'un, but expensive to hire, see Menna. Have a chat with Paul and see if he can let us borrow him will you?"

Menna would tut and mutter "Mother," every now and then, but she almost believed it too…

Then one day, it had all changed. She'd realised that her period was late. Bang: pregnant. Menna felt that she should feel excitement – they'd been together for about three years now and this is what couples that had been together for three years did.

She told him over their Thursday night chicken tikka masala, pilau rice and vegetable naan at the local curry house and she waited for his reaction; although a man of few words, she'd expected a bit of joy, a bit of emotion. He would have given other people in her position lots of congratulations on hearing their good news.

"Oh. Oh dear. Pregnant, eh?"

"I think I'm about two weeks late. I did a test yesterday."

"Oh. Pregnant. How's this going to work then?"

"Well," said Menna, more than a little taken aback, "I have been thinking, although it's still a bit of a shock. Perhaps we could, well, move in together somewhere? You know, as we are going to be a, well, a family?"

"Yes. I suppose so." Paul nodded. Then he blew out and took a swig of Tiger beer. "No, I hadn't expected that."

"Hey! George mate! How's it going? Yeah, good thanks!"

And that had been that.

Menna had sat in silence chewing on her naan bread. She'd nodded at George, who they'd often met on their Thursday curry nights, and that was all she'd needed to do in acknowledgement of him monopolising the rest of their night's conversation. George had no concept that he might be interrupting, but then as far as Paul was concerned, he obviously wasn't.

In the truck on the way home, the silence weighed heavily. Instead of taking the broad track up to the Neuadd, Paul had driven on towards Bwlch y Garreg.

"Oh," said Menna in surprise, "are we staying at mine tonight?"

"Well," said Paul with his eyes fixed onto the road ahead, his hairy knuckles gripping the wheel, "we can't, well, you know…with a baby in there, can we? So, I might as well drop you back at yours. Then I can make an early start in the morning. Got to be at market by eight at the latest."

"Paul – I've just found out that I'm pregnant, not HIV positive. People all over the world are having sex whilst pregnant. And, for God's sake – your cock's not *that* big you know!" Trying to make light of it didn't work. "And anyway, Paul, we don't have to, you know, have sex – we could just *sleep* together. Maybe even chat?"

Paul muttered again about having to be up early and Menna, thinking that maybe he needed a little time to come to terms with impending fatherhood, allowed him to drive her home. The kiss goodnight had been hygienic to say the least...

Jean had been equally surprised to see Menna home on a Thursday night, the first since six weeks into seeing Paul the Neuadd. "You haven't argued have you?"

"No, Mum."

"Well, you need to be careful there, Menna. The Morgans are a big family, you know. Paul's a good catch. Neuadd's a good farm. You treat him well, my girl, you hear?"

"Mum, we haven't argued all right? And anyway, even if we had, I'm not a prostitute."

Jean hadn't been convinced – about the argument or the prostitution – as Menna looked as if she was about to burst into tears as she walked out of the door.

"That bloody girl," Menna had heard her mother say to her father, "being so fickle. Well, I hope she's not gone and upset the Neuadd."

As the freezing rain slashed against her face, Menna's torch flickered and then sputtered out. *Bloody thing, was the charger not working, or what?* Now she had to walk the rest of the way home in the pitch black. With no moon and no street lights for two miles, Menna couldn't see her hand in front of her face, literally. She couldn't walk quickly and keep warm, she had to shuffle otherwise she would fall headlong. She stumbled along, splashing through puddles and tripping over rocks jutting out of the track. It did nothing to improve her mood. By the time she reached her bungalow, she was cold, wet, fed up and miserable. Not even the promise of Mrs Miniver could revive her mood, so Menna dumped her clothes in the hall, dried her hair with a towel and stomped off to bed.

Chapter 16

Cyw gwaelod y nyth – the chick at the bottom of the nest (the last chick to leave the nest)

Louisa stood at the doorway of number 40 Market Street and smiled again at the estate agent who was rocking back and forth on his shiny shoes. "I really am sorry," she said again. "He's never usually late and I did say 12.20 sharp."

"It's fine, no problem at all," clipped the man, checking his watch, although his face suggested that it was becoming a bit of a bore. Louisa cursed her father under her breath and then felt cross with herself. She should be able to pass the time with just a *little* small talk surely?

"So, do you have er, many flats up for rent in Tan-y-Bryn?"

"Five. Three two-beds and two one-beds."

"Oh."

She looked into the window of the Pound Shop below the flat and thought how handy it would be to have such a place so near when she was setting up her new home. Although she had assumed that she would just pinch a few of her parents' clothes pegs and scouring pads, it might actually be nice to have a few of her own things new.

Come on, come on, make an effort. This was supposed to be a new start: keep trying, girl!

"Is there – is there much difference in price?"

"Between what?"

"The flats – one-beds and two-beds?" She smiled engagingly as he dived for his ringing phone and turned away from her. To her relief she saw her father's car pull up and David jumped out, grabbing his coat from the passenger seat.

"Sorry I'm late, love, got Market Road and Market Street mixed up."

"Da-ad," she frowned, "I *told* you it was Street."

"Ah, Mr Harrison, how are you, sir? No, no problem at all. Shall we go on in? After you!" The estate agent clicked on his salesman's charm and followed David into the hall, asking about his journey and had he looked at anything else. Louisa was left to trail in behind them, neither of whom noticed her scowl.

"Er, excuse me," she felt like saying, "it's going to be *my* flat," but then she realised that she'd allowed her dad to make the phone call and book the appointment – in hindsight, perhaps she *could* have done it herself.

She climbed the stairs with a wrinkle across her nose: it smelt a bit musty and that swirly green carpet must have been there for years. But standing at the door at the top of the stairs declaring Flat 40B in only slightly grimy white plastic, gave her a tremor of excitement – the first flat she'd ever looked at and it happened to be her bra size! How was that for fate?

She stepped inside, anticipating a large airy flat with a shiny new kitchen with a central island and marble surfaces. She'd hoped for stripped floors and off-white walls. She'd not quite decided between a freestanding bath fed from above or a power shower, but ideally the tiles would be Welsh slate.

Instead, she was confronted by a dingy little hall with five yellowed doors leading from it, which the agent opened to show Louisa and David a galley kitchen, an internal bathroom, two small bedrooms and a reasonable sitting room housing a gas fire with a "condemned" sticker across it.

"The landlord's going to replace it before the flat's let," the estate agent promised, in response to David's raised eyebrow.

"Well, Louisa," asked David, "what do you think?"

"Well, it's OK I s'pose..." she started.

"I remember my first flat!" David turned to the agent. "No heating, no hot water, outdoor privy – horrible place!"

"Yeah, and mine – ours came with a cat and we soon found out why: we never had to feed it once ourselves!" laughed the agent. "Yes, your first flat should be a bit on the, well, the *less salubrious* side shall we say! Got to create some memories haven't you!"

David suddenly looked sharp. "Yes, but actually, young people today, perhaps they expect more..."

"I'll take it!" said Louisa. "It's the only one I can afford on my own at the moment and it's fine." She looked around again – a lick of paint, a few scented candles and it would soon be OK. Her dad could help her paint it – and he could buy the paint cheap from work. Yes, she needed a bit of a kick-start to her adventure, a grotty flat to moan about with her new friends – no point in having it all luxurious, otherwise she might as well stay at home.

The look on the agent's face showed how surprised he was that the squishy marshmallow girl that he had ignored outside actually had an opinion. However, he strode forward and shook her hand. "Well, congratulations! Welcome to your new home!" He turned to David. "I'll need a month's rent in advance, a reference from her employer and if there is none available from a previous landlord, then I'll need a parental guarantor? OK with you?"

David nodded and though Louisa was slightly put out, it would be good if her dad sorted the nitty gritty – and, ideally, put up the deposit. He would get his money back afterwards, so it didn't really matter.

As the agent painstakingly typed their details into his electric notebook, Louisa had another look around – yes, it would be OK. Also, at that price, she didn't *need* a flatmate to share with, so if it took a while to find someone suitable, she could still manage. She wondered if Esther would run her up some new curtains. Some nice velvet ones to keep in the warmth – maybe the same cream as those that they had at home? Perhaps they could chat together about colour schemes as she sewed – her mum would like that…

Chapter 17

Mor oer â llyffant – as cold as a toad (very cold person)

"I've bought the tickets for the annual sheep breeders dinner for this year," said Menna's mother, Jean, as Menna was eating her breakfast. "February second."

"Great," said Menna, her mouth full of toast, "where is it this year?"

"Lamp Hotel," clipped her mother who had finished her own breakfast over an hour ago and was ironing frantically in the corner. "The Stag didn't have enough potatoes," she said, as if that was reason enough.

"I remember," nodded Menna, smiling at the outrage of the previous year as hungry farmers near inhaled their main courses and had to fill up on crisps. She, Iestyn and Johnny had crept out for chips during the speeches, giggling like naughty children as they sat in the car park in her truck and tried not to get grease on their smart clothes.

"You all right with what you wore last year?"

Menna knew that Jean was sharp and knew that if she asked the question early enough, she would not really think about it and then by the time she did realise, it would be too late – no chance of wheedling money out of Mother if she'd already agreed to wearing last year's outfit just a few weeks before.

Menna thought back to the tailored black trousers and white blouse that she'd worn to what was known as the last big blow out before lambing started. "Yeah, s'pose so." People had kept stopping her and asking for more gravy, but at least she'd been comfortable. Most of the other women wore dresses – some beautiful, others dated and too tight, but no one really minded; everyone knew each other and so it didn't really matter what anyone wore. Iestyn had worn one of Joe's suits and had looked uncomfortable, but hunky. He hadn't seemed to notice what she was wearing and probably wouldn't again this year, he'd just been glad that she hadn't been drinking so that she could drive them to the chippy and back.

Perhaps she'd speak to Sima and see what she thought. She might be able to pop into town and buy something new with the leftovers from her bungalow decorating fund; it could be her chance to show a different side to Menna Edwards, one without tracksuit bottoms.

"Actually, Mum, maybe I could do with something different – you know, a dress or something? I could go to Cardiff, maybe? Get something nice?"

"Cardiff? Phooey!" blew Jean. "Well, it's possible I suppose. A dress might not be *such* a good idea – you know, with your ankles? Dresses can make lower legs look quite puffy: you're probably better off with a nice pair of trousers? Why not look in the catalogue and get yourself a new blouse instead?"

Menna shrugged, losing the will to fight for a corner that she knew very little about. Her mate, Jan, always wore trousers and she looked really good in them. Menna finished her breakfast as her mother whipped through the rest of the ironing.

"Right," she said, getting to her feet, "I'll get back out and carry on with the mucking out," pushing her chair away from the table and heading towards the porch.

She didn't notice her mother put down the iron before the last tea towel had been steamed into submission and put into a pile – a thing she had never done before. She didn't notice her mother biting her lips as a little flutter of self-doubt flickered across her face. And she certainly didn't notice her mother's face flash with pain as she remembered a beautiful red dress that had been a punctuation mark in her own youth…

Louisa sidestepped her mother's excitement about the flat and popped upstairs to her computer – no way could she wait until after supper to see if *he* had replied! How had her comment been received? Would there be a snappy comment back? Would he have left maybe a more sincere message – no, of course he wouldn't have. Replying, "Somewhere near a chippy that doesn't have your parents sleeping in the spare bedroom is a good start!" to her leading question about what to look for in getting a flat had not been the lead in to a romantic tryst – it had probably been a bloke with five minutes on his hands before his mother called him for his tea.

And what about her comment about preferring Chinese? It had taken her forty-five minutes to think of that and first she'd had a proper tussle with the instinct to reply that she would not wish to live next door to a chip shop, what with the noise and the smells and the late night disruption, thank you very much. Yet, it was a worthy consideration for someone in her situation. Not to mention possible damage to her car parked outside – the thought of having to remove grease that had been smeared on her windscreen by some drunken fool, or a sauce portion shoved up her exhaust pipe was off-putting to say the least.

Louisa was almost shaking as the PC whirred back into life, she was too impatient to change into her civvies, as her dad called them, and instead had spent the boot up re-arranging her Whimsy and glass dog collections.

She rattled the mouse – *come on*! The Internet leapt into being just as she heard her dad's car snaking down the lane into Anweledig and her irritation grew – he was bound to call her down or come straight upstairs to discuss the flat. She'd sort of moved on from the needing a new flat phase. Indeed, if she were honest with herself, it had been adventure enough just to go and see one and to say yes to renting it. Perhaps she could now stay with her folks; maybe until she'd seen somewhere that she might like to buy? Perhaps see how things panned out with this bloke first? No point signing up for a year's tenancy, if she were going to be engaged within six months.

Her blog jumped up and there were *two* messages! Irritatingly, one from Herbie saying, "Hi, Lulu, keep up the good work, yeah?", but a much better one – from – *him*!

"Lou-ee-sa! Lou-EE-sa! Are you up there? Are you coming down? I've got some news!"

Louisa snarled in fury – she so *desperately* wanted to be left in peace. However, she called, "Yes – I'm on my way down now," instead and wrenched open her door just as her mind processed the comment: *Glad you prefer Chinese – I do too! Perhaps we could meet and compare notes over noodles one night?* ☺

"Lou-ee-sa! Are you there? Come down – oh, there you are love."

Louisa stomped down the stairs; the last thing she needed was her dad coming up and sniffing about, reading her messages over her shoulder. How appropriate for her blog to be at the "Well, I just couldn't handle living with my folks any longer! You know, needed my own space, yeah?" stage.

Mr Harrison was nearly brimming over with excitement as he stood in the kitchen with Esther buzzing around in the background, trying to turn sausages without missing out on any of the news; it would never be re-told for her benefit, so she had to listen carefully.

"All right, love?" said David, resisting the urge to hop from foot to foot, "I've got some news!" He was disappointed to see Louisa's scowl. It had been said in the past, by some of the less kind people at the golf club, that his daughter had a face like a smacked arse, but he never liked to acknowledge that side of her: we all have our moments…

"I went down to the estate agents after work, love – that's why I'm a bit late back – and have paid your deposit and a month's rent in advance and guaranteed the remaining six month's rent *and* given a reference from my employer, and therefore – it's yours! From Wednesday!" He threw open his arms and his eyebrows mingled with the middle of his forehead and he waited for his daughter to squeal in excitement and dance him round the kitchen. Her first flat! They were going to have such fun!

He'd been cross with Diane in the car earlier when he'd asked if she'd minded waiting for five minutes whilst he popped in and completed the paperwork. He'd rather hoped that she'd have just walked home – it would have been quicker. Instead, she'd sat there, coat and bag on her lap and her lips pursed.

"Shouldn't Louisa be doing this bit, David?" was all that she'd asked, not seeming convinced by the answer that his daughter was busy. He could have sworn that he heard her mutter, "Busy having her tea made for her…" under her breath, but Diane had sworn that she had just coughed and so he'd let it lie…

However, it so happened that Louisa *had* been busy having her tea made for her and out of the corner of his eye he could see his wife struggling to mash the potato without the saucepan swinging round in circles and he felt disappointed. *Come on, girl; show a little enthusiasm will you?*

"Great," said Louisa, in a voice that said, "Really?"

"Mum, it's going to fall," she added, looking past her father to where her mother was struggling, but without making a move to go and help. Esther butted the saucepan further back on the side with her hip and gripped the work surface harder with her weaker hand.

David felt unable to leave it at that, despite the slur, and opened himself up for a greater fall. "I thought that the deposit and the first month's rent could be our housewarming gift?" he tailed off, seeing Esther's eyebrow rise in a way that shouted, "And what of our conservatory?" But he didn't ask for much, all he really wanted was a warm hug and a sharing of his excitement.

"Thanks, Dad," said Louisa, pinching a sausage from under the grill and walking past him. "I'll be back in a sec'," she said, "I've just got to check something," and he saw his daughter run back upstairs, chomping on her sausage, blissfully unaware of the amount of hours that he would have to work to earn the money he'd just gifted her.

Money that wasn't solely his to make decisions about. Money that he'd sworn would go towards a conservatory to keep his wife warm on a spring afternoon.

"That was *your* sausage she pinched," Esther snarled, rolling her eyes, and turned back to pound her mash.

"Oh, don't be so miserly, Esther – the girl only gets her first flat once in a lifetime. Don't spoil things for her now, for goodness sake!" It was easy to snap at Esther: he'd had years of practice…

CHAPTER 18

Fel gafr ar daranau – like a goat in a thunderstorm (agitated, nervous)

Menna was sitting in her bungalow after work when the phone rang. She had been expecting the call and had a pad of paper and a pen at the ready and had pulled the little coffee table over to the sofa.

"Menna? Hello, it's Sima here, how are you?"

"Sima! Hello, I'm very well thanks, and you?"

"Fantastic. Is it a convenient moment to have a chat?"

It certainly is, thought Menna; she had been waiting for this for days.

"I've been having a think about what you said, but run through it again with me, I want to make sure I've got the scenario right."

Menna chattered in a way that would have surprised her, if she'd stopped to think about it. She had perfect clarity in her own mind about what the problems were and possibly even why; strange really that she couldn't just sort herself out. Sima yep-yep-I-see'd from the other end of the line and, when Menna was done, she clarified things a little more before launching into her own thoughts.

Menna wrote a list of notes on her pad; trying to write it down exactly as Sima said it so that she could make sense of it afterwards.

"Now, do you think you can do those things?" asked Sima at the end.

Menna scanned her list. "Um, yes, I think that they are fine. Yes, I can do those."

"OK, but start at the beginning. The actions at the end might be a lot more uncomfortable if you haven't taken the smaller steps first."

"Yes, I can imagine!" Menna laughed. She was excited, nervous and keen to get moving.

"What I also need you to do – and this is a little bit harder – is to try and have a think about where all this has come from? I know that we all have our hang ups, and this is just the way we human beings are, but if you understand a bit about *why* you find it hard to be anything more than *good old Menna,* you might be able to tackle it a bit better?

"Now, Joe and I are coming down again in a week or two, but until then, get stuck in and have a think about it all and then we can talk properly – maybe we'll go out for lunch or something? It might be quite nice to escape the indoor slugs and the scones for an hour or two! Love Pencwmhir as I do, sometimes it would be nice to have something to eat that didn't come with mountains of mash…"

Menna laughed, "I know what you mean. I'm sure I can think of somewhere that we can sit down without having to drink an urnfull of tea before we are allowed to get up again!"

They said their goodbyes and Menna thanked Sima again for her time and her thoughts. She would add *find a nice café* to her list of things to do.

Menna sat back into the sofa, pulling the opulent throw around her and hugging its warmth with joy. She felt like she was at the beginning of a journey; one that could take her who knows where! She read through her notes again and added a few more points in the margins. The checking out styles and looking at what other people wore and she thought looked good should be easy enough (if she bought a few magazines and watched a bit of telly – she was unlikely to run into Trinny and Susannah down the Bull or up on the hills); it was the *understanding it* bit that might be a little more painful…

She could blame a lot of things on her mother – and in many of the cases that would be blame enough – but she knew deep down that the *real* reason that she was a person who just worked and got on with things was something that neither her mother nor anyone else knew anything about…

Menna had found that Paul Morgan had become suddenly busy after her announcement about the pregnancy. Their Thursday night curry was now unpalatable to him, despite their having had one each week for the past three years. How did someone go off a chicken tikka masala on their 156th time of eating it, she wondered.

Instead they ate with either Menna's or Paul's parents. Paul became very much in demand by other people. The early mornings that were part of a farmer's life became something that needed a solitary night's sleep in preparation. Saturday nights at the pub started later and later so that they missed their previous conversations on their own before the others turned up. Paul started giving lifts to people in a way that Paul the Neuadd would never have bothered to do before. Menna could simply never catch him alone. There was no chance of a serious conversation about anything.

She would snatch ten minutes in the car and suggest that perhaps they speak to his parents – see if they could separate part of the vast house off for them, or maybe build something of their own on the Neuadd's acres? Alternatively, there was her parents' farm, Glascwm. There were plenty of options, but they all required them to *get a move on*! Seven months wasn't long.

"Yeah," Paul would say. "Let's just wait until we're sure. You know, things happen."

"Do you *want* something to happen?" Menna would shout. "Is *that* what you're stalling for? Are you going to feed me a bottle of gin and pop me in a hot bath? Hide behind the barn and jump out at me?" Paul would give her a pitiful glance and Menna would shut up.

She was used to being in the shadow of Paul the Neuadd, or at least what everyone thought was Paul the Neuadd. So she allowed him more time to get used to the idea. To allow him to pick a moment to tell of the plans he had been thinking through. But how could there be a right moment, when George was always popping round or Paul was giving Samson a lift into town?

Menna was getting desperate. She was doing her bit; she had cut back on her coffee intake and had stepped up on veg. She ate no pâté, blue cheese or nuts – she didn't like nuts anyway, but she made sure that she ate no nuts. Yet Paul did nothing. He wouldn't even allow her to contact a midwife as one of his many cousins worked on reception at the surgery and the secret would be out in no time.

"But they are sworn to confidentiality!" raged Menna.

Paul raised an eyebrow – *confidentiality? Gayle Thomas? Come on...* And he was right. Everyone in Tan-y-Bryn and its surrounding villages knew everything about their neighbours' health – usually before the neighbour did, and it was all down to Gayle Thomas. In fact, she felt it was part of the service: secrets being no good for a person's well-being...

So Menna worried her way through weeks six, seven and eight. She devoured the book that she'd bought and then hidden under her bed. Ridiculous, a woman of twenty-two hiding books under her bed, but she wrapped it in a towel every night as the baby graduated from blastocyst to embryo to foetus.

Louisa was back in her bedroom. She was creeping around it due to guilt, well, half guilt, half lack of interest...

She knew that her father was, at that very moment, whitewashing the ceiling in her new flat covering his face in flecks of paint, in a way that would make his shoulders ache for the next two weeks. She knew because she had popped by on the way home and seen him at it.

He'd taken his overalls with him in a bag that morning. Louisa had managed to "forget" hers and it hadn't been long before she'd been given permission to go home – no point in ruining her work clothes was there? She'd feigned disappointment, but had reluctantly agreed having made sure that she fingered a paintbrush for long enough to have paint on her hands and a tiny little dab in her hair for authenticity.

Her father had seemed to be enjoying himself, so she'd thanked him and left him to it. Neither seemed to feel it appropriate to mention that her overalls were only a fifteen-minute drive away and the job was at least four hours from being finished.

It was completely obvious to Louisa that there was no way that she could muck about painting a ceiling, new flat or no new flat, when there were more important matters on the boil. Three times during the past week she'd had a message from *him* – Iestyn, he'd said his name was – which must mean that he was awfully keen! He'd repeated the comment about going for a Chinese meal – this time claiming he'd be able to show off his skill with chopsticks. She had cleverly sidestepped the previous invite, just in case he was only joking. Now it seemed that it was a formal request for a date – and that deserved an answer and she had been thinking about it, and discussing it with Doreen, and thinking about it and discussing it again with Doreen, all day.

It didn't seem strange to Louisa that someone who she had shared only about 1,000 characters with might, on the strength of that, wish to spend an evening with her. She had always believed that once given an outing, her wit and personality would shine through – and this was obviously the medium it was shining through. She also had no apprehension about meeting a stranger found on the Internet; bad things that happened on blind dates didn't happen to people like her – only silly people who took risks. She knew his name and that he was a farmer near Tan-y-Bryn and that was reference enough, it wasn't an area renowned for its serial killers.

She heard her mum rustling around downstairs and felt another pang of guilt. I'll get on with my - *homework* - tonight and then I'll get stuck into the flat tomorrow night, she thought as she changed into her silk pyjamas. Perhaps her mum could just bring her a sandwich up for tea – rather than her feeling like she had to cook a full roast. She'd not liked the look on her mum's face when she'd walked through the door that evening: she had certainly not been convinced by the paint in Louisa's hair…

She attacked the keyboard with verve, now that she actually had something legitimate to blog about. It would be great to post this, sort out a reply to Iestyn and maybe get another response from him again by the morning – and even Rosie or Rachel too? Maybe she should post something on one of theirs – something witty about marshmallows again?

Hi, Everyone! Me back again – this time with paint on my hands and in my hair! Why is it that paint gets just everywhere especially when you try and be careful? It's so exciting to have my own place and I can't wait to move in, but the flat sure needs a coat of paint to hide the nicotine ceilings and something to cover the swirly green carpet! Why is it that the only places that are affordable come with wall to wall stains of dubious provenance…

"Lou-*i*-sa! Tea!" came the call from downstairs. Louisa groaned in frustration – would they *ever* let her get on with her own life?

"Uh, could you bring it up here please? I'll just have a sandwich if it's easier," she called back, pushing her luck a little.

Esther was obviously feeling brave as David was out of the house. "Louisa, it may have escaped your notice, but it takes me five minutes to get up the stairs *without* a plate of chicken with mushroom sauce in my hand. I imagine that you would find it just a *little* bit easier to come down? Also, if you think I am binning an hour and a half's effort in the kitchen to make you a sandwich instead, you can forget it."

Louisa grunted, posted her new blog and sulked down the stairs. She put her and her mother's plates on a tray and took them into the sitting room, plonked them onto the coffee table and clicked the television on. If her mum was going to be in such a foul mood, then at least she could have the television on to drown it out. Great, *Springwatch* adverts. Now her mother would be on about the bloody blue tits again…

David had just finished the sitting room ceiling and was settling down on the floor to do a bit of skirting board undercoating. He'd felt cold, so had turned on the heating – it was OK, he'd give Louisa a bit of cash for it to cover the bill.

He was quite enjoying himself, having a bit of an adventure. Their modern house in Anweledig was great in that it needed little apart from routine maintenance, but you couldn't beat the feeling of standing back and seeing the creation of a bright new room from what had been a dirty, dingy dive. The only problem was, it showed just how dated and grotty the carpet was; perhaps he could get an offcut and fit it for Louisa as a treat?

He'd been disappointed that Louisa hadn't seemed to want to stay and get stuck in. She'd been paying for the flat since Wednesday and hadn't spent any time in it so far. There was plenty of work needed before she moved in, granted, but the only way to get things done was to do them and she hadn't really seemed to grasp that yet. Maybe she'd be a little more excited when she came the following night with her overalls. Diane had been a bit scathing about Louisa's eagerness to leave home and, annoyingly, it seemed that she might be right if tonight's apathetic attempt at decorating was anything to go by.

He'd tried to hide the paint from Diane when he'd given her a lift home, but her eagle eyes had seen him lugging it to the car park and secreting it in the boot earlier. "For Louisa's flat?" she'd asked when he'd returned to the office.

"Well, I thought I'd just help her out – it's a lot of work for her, especially when she's not done it before. Expensive too – I just thought I'd, you know, give her a hand, you know, until she's settled."

He'd squirmed under Diane's gaze and knew what she was thinking. "Well," she had said slowly, "just make sure you don't take over. You know – let her lead it. We all have to learn by doing, remember – we don't learn by sitting back and watching our dads…"

David had mumbled a reply and had been glad to be called away for a phone call.

However, tonight it seemed that Diane had been right, but she was his *only daughter* and if he couldn't do odd jobs to make her happy, what could he do?

David had just masking-taped the carpet when there was a bang on the door. *Great! She'd come back after all!* He'd known deep down that she wouldn't let him do it all by himself. *Perhaps she'd been so long because she'd been making him a sandwich – good, he was starving!*

He put down his brush and checked his hands for paint – he didn't want to get gloss on the door handles – and clomped down the stairs. To his surprise, he didn't open the door to an overalled Louisa with a smile and a club sandwich, instead he opened it to a beaming Diane, wearing old clothes and clutching two packets from the fish and chip shop in her hands.

"Hello! I thought I'd come by and help with the great adventure!"

David feigned a smile and waved her through. He was embarrassed that she would find out that, as predicted, he was doing all the work whilst Louisa was sitting at home on her plump behind, quite possibly just finishing off a plate of Esther's chicken with mushroom sauce. He waited for the smug question or the "On your own?" comment, with that raised eyebrow of hers.

Instead, Diane accepted the guided tour with excitement and enthusiasm, glossing over the damp patches in the way that David had just glossed over a few spiders. "Lovely big room," she said about the sitting room. "There'll be a nice view here I expect" she muttered about the kitchen.

It wasn't long before he felt relaxed and glad that she had come. It was as if he could now share his excitement about the transformation from dingy dive to deluxe des res with someone who appreciated it. "Hungry?" she asked at last, holding up the two paper-wrapped parcels.

"Not half!" he laughed and thanked her as she tossed him one. They opened them out on the work surface in the galley kitchen and the room filled with the scent of hot vinegar, finally something that could overpower the smell of the damp under the lino. They stood side by side eating their fish and chips, looking out the window at the potentially nice view.

"You've got to have chips when you're decorating," said Diane, "it's the rules!"

"I agree; it's the real reason I'm doing the painting!" said David and they started tucking into them with gusto. David felt almost joyous at being with a woman who enjoyed her food. Esther was naturally lean but was a miserable, self-denying person about food and was slightly obsessed by fibre. She didn't ever think, "Ooh, that looks nice," about something and then just eat it. In fact it would be hard to think, "Ooh, that looks nice," about anything she ate.

She would grind her way through home-made muesli of a morning and wash it down with a cup of nettle tea. Snacks were rice cakes or oatmeal biscuits. Liquid refreshment was usually hot water – and bucket loads of the stuff was needed to make all the bran she ate swell sufficiently to cleanse her colon.

Her bowels were super efficient and she would sneer if she spotted David sneaking into the downstairs toilet with a newspaper, "See you in an hour then," she would smirk. Although he appreciated that his varicose veins were as much to do with his constipation as the elastane in his socks, he sometimes wished that he had a partner who was easy to treat. Perhaps that was why he'd always spoiled Louisa so, in order to have someone to enjoy the simple pleasures with.

He looked again at Diane as she licked her fingers. "Delicious!" she said and broke off a bit more fish, smiling at David as she wiped a bit of batter from her chin.

He started chatting as if she weren't the same occasionally acid-tongued Diane he sat next to four times a week discussing the weather. He told her about his plans for the place, as if it were his own first flat. He thought he'd take up the lino in the kitchen – it would only be thirty quid or so for an offcut and also Louisa could choose a blind for the window – or perhaps he'd get one of those blue ones for her from the shop window of Chives?

He'd asked the landlord if he could swap the electric strip light for one of those rails with spotlights on and whether he could put up a few shelves, as there wasn't a great deal of cupboard space.

Diane laughed at him and said that he was like a boy with a new toy! She bet that the landlord was extremely pleased to have Louisa as her new tenant – "...does the place up as well as paying the rent!"

Diane rolled up her chip wrapper and went to squeeze past David to wash her hands. As she tried to walk past him through the narrow galley kitchen, face to face, paunch to rather large bust, they got wedged.

They both laughed, embarrassed at first, not knowing whether the other was more embarrassed at being a bit fatter than they ought. They, however, were just, well, nicely covered.

Should Diane go back the way she'd come or should she push on through? Should David suck his paunch in that was nestling so nicely beneath Diane's sturdy bosom or did he stay and enjoy the warmth for a few more minutes?

He chose the warmth. And it was obviously fine by her.

She wriggled this way and that, but it was more like a cat finding the best place to be stroked, rather than one trying to move away from a dog with a nasty streak.

After thirty seconds of this strange dance, some spell took hold of them both. Diane looked up into David's eyes and reached her chubby little arms up to caress his hair.

David gazed back and swept his glossy, chippy hands around Diane's back and they kissed. And they sucked. And they slurped. They both felt so warm and soft and so moulded together. Her fat points poured nicely into his leaner parts. Her breasts rested on his stomach and her belly snuggled under his straining belt.

David had never intended to have a fling with anyone, and he *knew* that he shouldn't be doing this, as when his wife's face flashed before his eyes, it had that disapproving glare on it. Since the opportunity for flirtation so rarely came his way, he decided that for the good of his life-excitement ratings, he should embrace it. And – it felt so good! Kissing a fleshy mouth that tasted of chips. He compared it to Esther's pursed dog's arse of a mouth, usually with a bit of oatmeal floating around in it, and Diane's won hands down. He moved on to her ears, where her perfume engulfed his senses.

He felt himself stirring below and Diane must have too as she ground her tracksuited hips into him. He dropped his hands down her back and grabbed her buttocks, great substantial wedges of fat, cruelly cut into by a nylon panty line, but deliciously generous to a man starved on the lean rations of Esther's barely-covered bones and white, ironed underwear.

That was all the encouragement Diane needed and she dived into his trousers…

Afterwards, they lay on the kitchen floor, sticking to the foul-smelling lino and giggled with each other. Their trousers were pulled down over their shoes and therefore their feet were joined together. Slowly and without embarrassment their clothes were retrieved and put back on and again David relished Diane's unselfish pleasures. Her great breasts would have been easy to be self-conscious about, but she lay there with them wobbling and flopping about as she moved, talked and laughed. David felt in seventh heaven; she had neither washed her hands nor wiped up any spillages and he felt fantastically squelchy and alive.

The cold eventually drove them on to work and they retreated to the lounge and by the end of the night they had painted it all, with only a coat of gloss needed on the woodwork. They cleaned the brushes together, chatting easily about previous decorating projects they had known, and the night came to a natural close.

There didn't seem to be a need to discuss what had happened earlier, or what might become of it; that would somehow make it furtive and wrong.

Instead, David drew her into his arms and kissed the top of her head. "Thank you for a wonderful evening, and thank you for helping, and thank you for the chips too!"

"You're very welcome," she replied, nestling her hand under his shirt, "I had a great time: those chips were marvellous!" Then she pinched his backside, winked at him and walked away. "You never know," she said looking over her shoulder at him, "I might even come back and help you again! I'm good at stripping…wallpaper."

David lit up, "Do!" he called, "I'd, er, love the help!" He closed the door behind her and leant back against it and blew out a satisfied puff. The smile on his face was enormous and he sang as he cleared away the rest of the mess.

He felt neither guilt nor remorse. It had been a fantastic evening – just a fantastic evening that had included sex. It hadn't been sordid or wanton, just pleasurable and fun. It didn't feel like a betrayal of his marriage vows, more like an extra curricular activity that wouldn't affect his main studies.

As he turned off the lights and walked down the stairs with a spring in his step and a stain on his trousers, he felt very glad that his daughter's flat was in such a pitiful state…the more he needed to be there, the better!

CHAPTER 19

Byw fel ci a hwch – living like dog and sow (fighting all the time)

The following afternoon, Esther crashed the gammon slices onto the board, grabbed a knife and stabbed open the shrink-wrapped plastic covering. The meat burst out as the pressure was released and sprayed her in a shower of juices. The cool liquid on her face did nothing to calm her temper.

David had just phoned her from the golf course, asking if she were going to make parsley sauce as it was Louisa's favourite. Of *course* she was going to make parsley sauce. She *always* made parsley sauce with gammon and mashed potato; it was just what she did. Did he not think that the reason she made parsley sauce was because she knew that Louisa loved it so?

Most of the things she did in the house were because that's what the occupants wanted and, because she cared so much about them, that is

135

what she did. He might have the time to sit and chatter to Louisa and to wrap her in chenille throws – that was how he showed her *his* love – but she, Esther didn't have time to make parsley sauce *and* sit and chat on the sofa to her daughter. Otherwise, Louisa would never have parsley sauce and that would make her sad. Someone had to look after the practical side of nurturing and, it seemed that the job fell to her.

Her husband's comments made her so *angry*. Everyone thought David was wonderful. Their friends always looked past her to welcome *him* into their houses. His work colleagues idolised him as their firm but fair gaffer and, oh, wasn't he just *marvellous* with Louisa...

Maybe everyone had just a bad side and maybe only she, Esther, got to see his. She was just *sick* of being asked to do things that she was about to do anyway. It made it seem that she was incapable of making her own decisions – *I mean, parsley sauce? Come on!*

She slammed the meat into the oven and then dragged herself up the stairs in frustrated speed to change and put her spattered blouse on to soak. She cursed David again – if he'd not made her so exasperated, she wouldn't have been so careless with those blasted gammon slices. It was as if she had no opinions, no mind of her own to make decisions with.

Well, she *did* have a mind, and she *did* have an opinion – just like the opinion she had about the woman on the desk in the library – was there *really* such a need to dress like a tart and wear so much make-up? It was a library for goodness sake: there was no need to show so much cleavage just to dole out books and shush at teenagers. Esther felt that she could probably get that across in a card – no need for a formal letter.

By the time she had rinsed her blouse, David was just getting out of the car. She could hear him as he put his golf clubs into the garage – *they* always got put into the right place. *They* never got dumped in a corner, *far too bloody precious.*

She reached the kitchen in a bad mood: bloody gammon, bloody golf clubs and bloody David. She could hear him as he sauntered in and threw his keys onto the table (instead of putting them on the hook where he would expect to find them when he next needed to go out). She could hear him hum as he took his coat off and slung it over the newel post when he *knew* it should be hung on the coat rack. Then she heard his shoes getting removed one by one, with the laces still done up, and then hoofed against the skirting board. It was like living with a bloody teenager, she fumed, as she disappeared into the utility room to calm down.

On her return, David was sitting down at the kitchen table looking around in surprise. Esther made a pot of tea and then poured him one. She passed him a cup. "Thanks," he said. "I was wondering where that was!"

"I've only just made it!" Esther began, trying hard not to shriek. "You've only been back two minutes. Do you want me to make a cup every minute from the moment you leave the golf club so that it's always available?"

"Esther, love, calm down! I was only joking!" David shook out his paper with a little chuckle and a shake of his head. Esther felt like crowning him. He had a knack of making her jump to his will and then belittling any small rebellion with that patronising, "Esther, love!" and then his chuckle. She just found herself getting more and more worked up as he seemed to settle down and get more relaxed. However, she decided against crowning him or storming out and instead returned to her pastry making.

David took a loud slug of tea, "Ooh, lovely cup, Esther, love, thanks."

She didn't know whether to scream, "Well of course it bloody is! It's tea and I make several cups of it for you each day: it's not that difficult to get it right, is it?" Instead, she counted to three and said, as light-heartedly as she could muster, "You're welcome."

"Nasty business this." He said.

"What?" she replied, putting down her pastry knife. That irritated her too – him, saying something that she was supposed to answer, when she had no idea what he was talking about. *What the bloody hell are you on about now? Do you expect me to sit next to you, reading the same thing in case you wish to discuss it?* One, two, three... "What's that, love?"

"This – this letter writing thing going on in town."

Esther put her knife down. Then picked it up again. "Yes, I've read a bit before about that. Been more has there?" She was surprised that he couldn't hear her heart pounding, sending flour dust in puffs from her pinny.

"The women in work were saying that there's been two dozen or more."

"Two dozen!" she exclaimed, then checked herself. "As many as that?"

"Well, the Inspector, here, in the paper…" David took an infuriatingly long sip of tea, "says they've had three reported, you know, as complaints…offences."

"I thought people had been pleased to have received them – you know, when they'd had time to think about what had been said. Like in the Tasty Bite café?"

"The Tasty Bite café? What was that then?"

"Oh, can't remember really – just that the owner had said that what had been said was actually accurate and putting it right had turned her business around. Something like that anyway…"

David shrugged, "Don't remember reading that. But, here: *The Inspector says that the letters are petty and malicious, referring to people's hygiene and one woman's weight problem.* Tsch, some people, eh? Nothing better to do…" David turned the page.

"Weight problem?" started Esther, "What do they mean, *one woman's weight problem*?"

"Dunno," he replied vaguely, clearly no longer interested, "Hey, looks like our old estate might finally be getting their play area! Typical, eh? Only fifteen years too late for our Louisa to play out in!"

"But, but – *weight problem?*" Esther was now thinking aloud and knew that it had to stop. She'd never mentioned anyone's *weight problem*. Could have done of course, Natalie Phillips could do with a reminder for starters, but she hadn't, *yet*. The Inspector must have been generalising or maybe just got it wrong. Unless…unless – unless someone else was doing it too?

Esther's apple pie was thrown into the oven, the pastry leaves that were usually carefully feathered, were instead two sausages splattered with beaten egg and porcupined with hairs from the pastry brush. *Surely no one else would do such a thing?* She checked the temperature and set the timer.

She, Esther, was writing those letters in a constructive, positive manner, aiming to help and to turn businesses around. It sounded like this other person – or God forbid, persons – who had jumped on the bandwagon, was being underhand and spiteful. What had the Inspector said? Malicious?

Perhaps the Inspector needed a little one, from her, to explain that she – anonymously of course – was the original letter writer and was a positive, constructive person, not a spiteful malicious one – just so as he understood.

As she walked to the sink to wash the flour from her hands, she peeped over David's shoulder at the picture of the Inspector on the inside page. Perhaps whilst she was at it, she could mention to him that a more modern haircut wouldn't go amiss; such thick grey hair didn't wear a fringe well...

Chapter 20

Mynd ar drot cadno – going at a fox trot (without a care in the world)

Johnny Brechdan hated Chinese food – nasty slimy noodley things, he would moan, but he was leant against the counter in the local takeaway on a Thursday evening giving it his all.

He'd chosen his timing carefully: nine-thirty in the evening. Too late for sober ordering of an evening meal and too early for drunken chicken ball cramming. It had been a good call as he'd been the only customer in there for the whole ten minutes.

"So," he said finally, "you recommend – remembering that I don't like chicken, but I do like noodles – beef chow mein and a portion of Chinese vegetables to start with, yes?"

The girl laughed, flicking her hair over her shoulders, "Yes! I can't believe I've ever met *anyone* who's taken so long to choose!"

"Ah, well there is no one else like me, you see!" he smiled, making sure that his eyes twinkled in his special little way.

"That's not what I said, but, yes, I suppose you are quite unique," she laughed. "Now, is that what you want to order?"

"Yep."

"You sure?"

"Yep."

"You're really, really sure?"

"Yes. But – actually, can I ask for just one more thing?" The girl feigned exasperation, but gave the game away as she blushed. "Could I have your phone number, please?"

"Would you like fries with that, sir?" she retorted, as she flounced into the kitchen with the order ticket.

Johnny pulled up triumphantly in the car park of the Bull and splashed his truck through a puddle, showering dirty water over the window of the snug. He was pleased to see Joe's Cherokee parked as near to the entrance as was possible; good, that meant that the others were already in.

He marched into the pub and saw them all sat round a table in the corner, trying to sit out of the draught, as near to the fire as possible without being in sensory range of Bad Breath Ken. He dumped a white carrier bag in the middle of the table.

"Present for you," he said, as seriously as he could muster. Joe looked confused and peered into the bag and started unloading it.

"What on earth is this for? A lukewarm Chinese takeaway for a night in the pub – you been robbin' again? Number forty-seven, what's that?"

"Beef chow mein probably."

"Prawn crackers?"

"Bloody horrible things," dismissed Johnny. "What else?"

"Well, you ordered it – or maybe that bloke you knocked over the head ordered it?" said Joe, putting his hand back into the bag, much to Sima's disgust.

"Number 815372? How big is their menu?" asked Iestyn, reaching over and stuffing a few prawn crackers into his mouth.

"Ah, that one's mine," smiled Johnny and took the lid off a foil dish with a load of Chinese vegetables staring up at him. "There, Joe, eat that, Fat Boy: I just need this." He took the lid, wiped the grease off the underside with a serviette from inside the bag and popped it into his pocket with a wink at Iestyn and a smile.

"Oh, I get it now: you're after Sue – Noodle Soodle who works at the Chinese?"

"Not *after* mate, in conversation with …"

"Conversation, my arse," said landlord Ed coming over. "Brechdan, get that stinking slop out of my pub. No picnics in here please. We do serve a fine selection of crisps, scampi fries *and* peanuts: really no need to bring in your own."

"It's OK, Ed, I've got all I need now – you can chuck the rest in your bin."

"Oh. Going free is it?"

"Yep, all yours, mate."

"In which case, I'll take it off your hands – I can treat myself to a decent breakfast tomorrow now. Nothing beats cold chow mein for brekkie of a morning."

Sima looked on in amazement as Ed packed up the goodies and headed off back to the bar. "So, this Noodle Soodle," asked Sima, "is she related to Bacon Sandwich Lil?" The others laughed.

Johnny squirmed and held his hands up, "OK, OK, so Bacon Sandwich Lil was not my finest hour…"

"Finest hour?" crowed Iestyn, "Finest five minutes – and all to escape having to queue for a bacon sandwich: shame on you, Brechdan, shame on you!"

"Anyway," said Sima, not finished with him yet, "back to Noodle Soodle – nice girl is she?"

"Gorgeous."

"Been after her long have you?"

"Yep. Saw her yesterday unloading frozen chicken from a van. Been thinking about her all night."

CHAPTER 21

Cnoi cil – to chew the cud

Sima met Menna in a wholefood café in town. Menna was nervous about her choice of venue. "It was the only place I could think of that didn't automatically have a pile of white sliced next to the salt and vinegar…"

"No, this is wonderful," said Sima, "although anything would seem

141

like nouvelle cuisine after the plate of swede and gravy that I watched Iestyn devour while he was waiting for the chicken to be carved last night…"

"That explains quite a lot about Iestyn," laughed Menna.

"Yes, I'll have to give it to the boy, he's not a picky eater! But, he is wonderful; he hitched a lift to the metalled road with me this morning on the pretence of checking something, but I am sure that it was only because he wanted to spare me from having to drag those gates open through the mud!"

"Probably feels guilty that they're in such a state – he's been promising Isla that he'll mend that end one since *last* winter, and it was pretty knackered then!" Menna was enjoying talking about Iestyn, glad that Sima seemed to like him. In fact, she'd much rather chat with Sima about anything, than what was actually on the agenda: her. Menna Edwards.

She had her jeans on again and a navy sweatshirt. Mother had been worried about the weather forecast, so as Menna had been going into town anyway she'd had not wanted to miss an opportunity for stockpiling supplies and getting a few jobs done. Therefore, en route to her life coaching appointment, Menna had collected some tablets from the vets, some dog meal and gate latches from the farmers' merchant's, a pile of meat for the freezer from the butcher as well as returning the library books, paying bills, querying bills and racking up a few more in various outlets around town. She'd been out since half past nine, and hadn't given much thought to her lunching attire. Luckily Sima, who was wearing elegant jeans, heeled boots and an unproofed leather jacket, didn't seem to have noticed.

They ordered their lunches and then Sima reached into her bag for a notebook. "I just brought this one, as I didn't want Joe to suspect that I was 'working'," she explained, as if by way of an apology that she didn't have a leather-bound A4 Smythson and a gold-plated pen. Then Sima took out a gold pen from her bag: ah, she did have one of those after all…

"Right then," she said and Menna leaned forward to drink in her words. "I've started by just cutting a few suggestions out of magazines for outfits that I think would probably suit you… I know that some of these cost a fortune, but it's more the *style* I'm thinking of. The look, not the actual pieces, OK?" Menna craned in further, expecting to see Zandra Rhodes in a sequined mermaid's outfit. Instead, she was pleasantly surprised to see relatively simple outfits that were just funked up enough to make them interesting. Sima pointed out how Menna's shape was similar to one particular celebrity and, well *that* length top would work, especially with *that* style of trousers – and she could wear *those* type of boots with either a dress or trousers.

It was the first time that anyone had ever spent such exclusive time with Menna, giving her advice in a non-patronising way. Menna soon felt at ease and as their meals arrived, she was feeling confident enough to point out that she liked that one, but wasn't so keen on this one. "I wondered about that one too," said Sima, "Yes, I think you're right." Sima treated her like an adult who was of course *bound* to have opinions on what she might like to wear.

Menna was less aware that Sima was slipping in more pertinent questions about her life and what she thought about this or that as they flicked through the glossies. If there was an uncomfortable silence, she would point again at a necklace, saying it would look a completely different outfit if she wore something like that, or maybe a less chunky version.

"What these kind of blockages usually go back to," said Sima, "is maybe just one comment or action that someone said or did that made you lose your confidence in your abilities to decide for yourself and be happy with that decision. We all make bad style choices occasionally – yes, even me," she smiled as she saw Menna's raised eyebrows, "in fact, *especially* me – but the difference is that they are just a bad day, not a change in outlook. It goes back to thinking about some defining point in your life and acknowledging it, and then moving forward. Easier said than done, I know, but maybe just make a start by thinking about it? Now, where is the Ladies'?"

Menna pointed to a door with two cauliflowers painted on the front of it, as opposed to the one with a bunch of wilting carrots, and Sima left her alone with her thoughts. Menna looked around the café and picked at the last of the coleslaw on her plate. She realised now what Sima had done, but she wasn't sure whether she wanted to open the floodgates right now.

It wasn't difficult for Menna to guess when her defining moment

143

was; in fact it had a large label on it in her memory bank saying just that…

It had been a Tuesday afternoon and Menna had been clearing out the stock shed. She had dredged most of the muck up with the tractor, but was now clearing round the edges with a spade and a wheelbarrow. With her pregnancy at around nine weeks, she was feeling sick and fed up. She retched as she uncovered a knot of rancid faeces. She shuddered as she disturbed a nest of rats and one ran over her foot. She felt a tiredness that was alien to one usually so fit and strong and Paul's unwillingness to discuss her pregnancy didn't help, he didn't even permit her to tell anyone about it. She felt that she couldn't enjoy the experience properly, let alone look forward to the baby due at the end of it. Even thinking about making plans was impossible, as the person that so much relied upon was carrying on as if it didn't exist.

Oh, this is ridiculous, she seethed to herself. Anyone else in the same position would be being mollycoddled – or at least looked out for. *Weren't office workers entitled to a lie down in the afternoon if they were tired? Surely someone should be making her a cup of tea? Or rubbing her back – or was that later?*

She knew that her hormones would be raging and that it would be acceptable to feel highly emotional, but her feelings weren't being brought on by oestrogen or progesterone changes, what she was suffering from was plain useless boyfriend-ness.

Her spade caught on a lump on the floor and the jar swung her arm around and she scraped her knuckles on the concrete wall. Although the pain was an irritant rather than an agony, it was the final straw for Menna. After a moment's hesitation, she decided against bursting into tears and lying down on a pile of straw to cry herself to sleep and instead she threw her spade at a scuttling rat and stormed off to her truck. Her mother would go mad if she knew that Menna were leaving a job unfinished, but no one should be treated like this, Paul the Neuadd, or no effin' Neuadd.

She reached the farm in fifteen minutes, rather than the usual twenty-five and this included a slow down to allow her to undo the button on her jeans which were pressing heavily against her blossoming belly.

She found him in the barn, doing much the same job that she had been doing, but on a grander scale.

"Paul!" she called from the huge doorway. "We have to talk."

Paul looked as if he'd been expecting this. The tractor was duly silenced and he climbed slowly down. His pursed mouth suggested that he would give her five minutes tops.

She was amazed that he stood and listened to her ranting – no, *took* it – for so long. She told him how they needed to live together, and sooner rather than later, so that they could be settled when the baby came, how they were going to be a family whether it was planned or not, how she *had* to see a midwife. How they just needed to *get moving* on whatever plans they were going to make.

He listened patiently to her tirade, standing with his arms and legs crossed, staring at her wellies, his face hardening into a black stare. He waited until she was spent, holding on to his reply a couple of times while she flushed out another sentence. Eventually she was quiet and she nodded at his raised eyebrows: *OK, you can speak now; your turn.*

"Menna. This – er – situation, is difficult for me. You see, I don't intend to be a farmer. Well, I know that I am one at the moment, but I really don't want to be. I'm just helping my parents out for a while. What I really want to be is an estate agent. I've been planning to go to college, to do estate management, and I've just been accepted. I applied to Newcastle University as a mature student and I start in September." He tailed off and shrugged, as if he'd finished now and that was all she really needed to know. It was as if he'd told her that he preferred red to blue and that he was sorry that she'd bought him a blue shirt for Christmas but it just wouldn't do...

Menna realised with a jolt that she knew the Paul the Neuadd that joshed with his friends, worked with his animals and she was familiar with his public persona, but that she'd had no inkling as to what went on inside Paul Morgan's head when he wasn't out and about or what he really wanted from life.

Menna exploded, "But, but *Paul!*" she said, thinking that she couldn't have heard him correctly. "Everything you do, everything you talk about is farming, farming, farming!"

"Now maybe, but what it means in practical terms, is that I won't be living at the farm from, well, September. I'll be in college digs – halls I suppose."

145

Menna turned around, her world falling down around her. She'd never wanted the big farm. Her mother may have wanted her re-christened Menna the Neuadd, but that had never been her master plan. Nothing at all had been her master plan. But being a single parent wouldn't have been her wish either if she had had one. She'd never really thought about having children – she'd assumed that she would one day when she met the man she wanted to be with, but – and this came as a bit of a surprise, too – it wasn't necessarily Paul Morgan.

She'd been going out with Paul the Neuadd without a great deal of thought as to why or for how long. She knew that she was still young and a bit inexperienced in the ways of love and it just seemed to be an acceptable way of passing the time. Because everyone else had been so happy at their pairing, she'd not given the quality of the relationship as much consideration as she should have, absorbing everyone else's opinion (i.e. that she got quite a catch, and to everyone's surprise and congratulations) rather than analysing her own feelings on the matter.

She looked around at the farm: all the land she could see belonged to the Neuadd. The three tractors, the three 4x4s, the two trailers, the five barns – all aspirational in the eyes of her parents, but they meant nothing to Menna – and now it was apparent that they meant nothing to Paul either.

"Anyway, Menna, I've got to crack on, I've got to get this cleared as Dad's bringing some sheep in for their jabs." He climbed back on the tractor and pulled his hat back on.

"But, but the baby – it'll be born sometime around then – October probably?"

At which point, Paul brought the conversation to a close, the same way that he did with his friends when they'd had their ten minutes at the roadside. The tractor engine kicked into life and Paul started revving, cocking his head as if he were concentrating on the engine noise. In the Landy on a lane, Paul would then draw away so that his interlocutor could no longer be heard, even if they did still have something to say, and they would be left at the side of the road seeing a hand raise in their rear-view mirror to bid them farewell.

However, this time, it wasn't an acquaintance who wanted to chat for too long about the weather, it was his pregnant girlfriend. The wave was an *It's OK, we'll sort the nitty gritty out later, don't panic, it's all in hand* kind of a wave.

"See you Thursday? Pick you up at 7.30?" he shouted, and then slammed the door of the cab and crashed the gears into reverse. He looked over his shoulder to check how far he had to go back and nodded to Menna as if she'd popped by to borrow some sheep nuts. He slammed the tractor back and then took a run up at a great pile of shite.

Menna had walked away feeling numb and confused. Had she really just heard all that? Had she really just heard that Paul the Neuadd wanted to be an estate agent? Was she the only one who had never guessed? It was no problem that he didn't want to farm, but if he'd just *said so* at some point, any point, well, she might have thought a little harder about what she really wanted to do. She'd drifted into farming because it had always been her way of life. She'd never actually made the decision, she'd just taken on more at the farm as her schooling had slowed into revision sessions and then stopped after her first set of exams.

She'd never questioned it until now and she was kicking herself that she'd let herself slip into this situation. Twenty-two years old, farming, in a relationship with Paul the Neuadd, pregnant and now her baby's father wanted to change everything and go and be an estate agent. How had she allowed this to happen? What a mess.

In addition, what had that conversation actually meant in relationship to her and their future? Had he meant, "What a shame, I'll have to give up my dream of estate agency and we'll stay here and make a life together," or "Come with me! It'll be fine!" or was it more of a "Sorry, darling, but you're on your own." Her head was spinning and she didn't know which direction the spin was going in…

She had climbed into her truck and started the engine, wincing at the cramps in her stomach – stretching pains they'd be, she'd read about them, her body stretching in readiness to accommodate the baby's growth.

Sima came back from the Ladies' looking fresh and rejuvenated with newly-brushed hair and some re-applied lipstick. Menna felt emotional, as well as a scruffy mess. She was suddenly aware of the dried animal feed ingrained on the thighs of her jeans and the dirt in the stitching of her trainers. She just wanted to go.

"I've asked for the bill, Sima. I'm sorry, but I really need to get going now. Thanks for all that you've done, you've given me some real food for thought."

"You're very welcome, Menna, I've really enjoyed our lunch! We'll have to do it again sometime. Actually I did promise I wouldn't be late back either, Tomos says that the weather is coming in; there'll be feet of snow by the morning he tells me!"

The waitress came, and Menna took the bill and rummaged in her coat pocket for her purse. "Oh, hang on," said Sima, producing hers from her bag, "this one is on Joe – keep the change – it is apparently for something you did to help his dad out that Joe is very appreciative of, so – his treat!"

"There's no need—" started Menna.

"Maybe, but Joe doesn't know that!" smiled Sima, "and, if it makes him feel better to know that he's thanked you for doing something that perhaps he should have done when he was down – rather than spending his time sleeping off Isla's scones –then everyone's a winner. Come on, I'll walk back with you – Joe's truck is almost next to yours."

She popped the magazine pages into a plastic sleeve and then put them in a plain brown envelope, as if she understood Menna's need to keep the process quiet for the time being, and they walked out, Sima now chatting about Joe's plans to try and hang a few gates with Iestyn later: "Although I am pretty much expecting to find him lying sleeping on the sofa in front of *Star Wars*, and Iestyn out in the rain working…"

As they stood beside Joe's Cherokee, Sima gave Menna a hug. "Don't be surprised if you feel a little emotional after we've spoken, OK? Sometimes these things are quite difficult to think about and acknowledge, but once you have, you'll feel much more positive about, well, everything, if my other clients are anything to go by! So, give yourself an easy time for the next few days and then get stuck into it all, OK? If you really dive in, get a few things out of your system and make some changes, it tends to all be a lot easier than dragging it out for longer; it dilutes the effort."

Menna nodded, feeling close to tears. Then she quickly hugged Sima back, and felt bad as she'd left feed dust on Sima's jacket, then she dived into her truck. She just wanted to be on her own, get back before the snow hit and get a little clarity about what she really thought about all the Paul the Neuadd stuff.

CHAPTER 22

Cadno o ddiwrnod – a fox-like day (a day when weather is unsettled and changes suddenly)

Nain opened the oven door of the Rayburn and propped it open with her slippered foot. She pulled out a pie with her patchwork oven gloves and set it on the side to cool. She returned and retrieved two trays of fairy cakes and a small tin pot with some kidneys in.

She dabbed her fingers on the cakes to check that they were cooked and then moved a chair to prop open the oven door to let the rest of the hot air out to help heat the giant kitchen.

She turned as the door banged open and a figure huddled up in two coats and waterproof trousers swept in amongst a swirl of snow and a blast of freezing cold air. Nain scuttled over and took the door from the figure and slammed it against the blizzard. "All right, *bach*?" she said, taking one of his coats from him and pushing his slippers towards him from the rack in the corner.

"Phew, it's wild out there; freezing cold *and* blowing a gale. The snow's all piled up against the barn door; I could hardly get it open! We'll be digging our way out tomorrow!"

"Well," replied Nain, whipping a mop across the tiled floor to soak up the melting snow from her grandson's wellies, "you sit down by the fire and I'll fetch you a brew to warm you through."

"Thanks, Nain," said Johnny, rubbing his hands together to try and get some feeling back into them.

Suddenly, everything went black and the television that had been chattering away quietly in the corner flicked off. Both Johnny and Nain groaned. "Oh, not again," said Nain. "Hang on, let me get the matches." Soon there was a little glow on the mantelpiece and then another two on the table. "Hope it comes on again soon, I've still got half that pig in the freezer. Oh well, I'm off to bed. Your taid's up there

149

already, best not keep him waiting! Blow them out when you're done, OK?"

"OK, sleep well."

"And you, *bach*. Cakes are on the side. *Nos da*, goodnight," and the small figure carrying a candle and a hot water bottle went out of the door.

Johnny sat back in the chair and stretched his feet out and rested his socks on the front of the Rayburn. There was something about a power cut – they'd had loads up at the farm when he was a lad and his grandparents had always made them fun. They had played cards at the kitchen table, by candlelight, and toasted muffins over the fire (even though they usually used the Rayburn to cook and that chugged away power cuts or not).

Johnny hummed to himself as he wolfed a couple of fairy cakes and washed them down with a slug of tea from the massive mug that his nain always kept washed and ready for his next brew. He checked his mobile, but no reception. What could he do with the rest of his evening? He couldn't go to the pub – even in a four-by-four it would be madness. He had walked to the pub in a snowstorm once before and had been amazed to find all his neighbours had done the same and they'd all sat in the candlelight with their boots drying around the roaring fire and it had been one of the best nights ever. But tonight, he couldn't be bothered to take the risk: he was too knackered to chance walking five miles in a blizzard, just to find that Ed had shut up shop and gone to bed with a torch and a magazine for an early night.

He drummed his fingers.

He ate another cake.

He drained the teapot into his mug and grimaced at its stewed luke-warmness.

He managed another cake. And half of a fifth.

He was about to get up and head for bed when he heard the dogs barking over the howling wind. He turned his head to hear better and willed them to stop. He listened for a while; if it were a fox or a badger, the noise would usually die down pretty quickly. Yet this time it didn't, in fact it was getting louder and more frantic. Who the hell could be round the yard at this time? A cold January night – even Iestyn Bevan wasn't *that* desperate for company, surely?

A second bout of yelping drove him from his chair – much more and Taid would be out there wandering around the sheds in his pyjamas checking to see what was upsetting them.

He cursed and wrestled himself back into his waterproofs, which were now damp and cold. After hearing one more tirade, he grabbed the torch off the hook and plunged back into the darkness.

The wind and the cold hit him and the horizontal snow slapped him in the face. "Shutupyoustupidfuckindogs!" he yelled, but the noise continued. Head down he crossed the yard – perhaps he hadn't managed to fasten that barn door properly because of the snow and it was banging: that would make the dogs bark.

He trudged to the barn, but found it closed and just as it should be. "F'fuck's sake," he mumbled – he could wander round all night like this and only to find that a mouse had been blowing raspberries through the mesh of the kennels.

The dogs quietened slightly at his presence and after a token prod round the smaller barn, he waded back through the snow to the house, his previous footsteps already partially muffled by the downfall.

Feeling fed up, he leant against the door and fumbled for the door-knob with his massive gloves. Sod it, he thought, they'd just have to bark if they thought they heard something. He was about to push the door open when the dogs set off again, just after Johnny thought he'd heard a feeble little voice calling, "*Is someone there? Help me! Please, help me!*"

Esther wouldn't have noticed, dozing as she was, but when the power went off in Anweledig, both David and Louisa looked to her indignantly for action. Where were the candles? Surely they should be lit pretty quickly? How were they going to manage for nine p.m. cuppas? Who was going to sort out recording *Silent Witness* for them; they *had* to find out the killer's identity?

"I think," said Esther, "that there are some candles under the sink? In that plastic tub?"

"Oh."

"Right."

There was silence in the darkness.

"OK: *I'll* get them then, shall I?"

151

"Can you manage, love? Mind you don't trip over that hall mat."

"Can you get some crisps when you're in the kitchen, Mum, I'm still a bit peckish. Not cheese and onion though. Salt and vinegar or...beef."

"Louisa? How the hell am I going find some crisps, let alone see what flavour they are? It's pitch black!"

"Sor-ree! I thought you were going in for candles that's all."

Esther got slowly to her feet and walked with her hands held straight out in front of her until she found the door. David rapped a beat on his knees with his hands and Louisa said that she hoped that it wouldn't last for long, as it would muck up some of the systems at work.

"If it does last, you won't be able to go in," David said.

"Oh, yeah! Well, let's hope it lasts then!"

"And even if we do get the power back, with this snow, we'll probably be stuck in Anweledig anyway! We'll all have to stay at home and play Monopoly!" said David, "it'll be just like the old times!"

"Great. I hate Monopoly."

"Chess then."

"No, I hate chess too; I always lose."

"Well, what *do* you want to play?"

"Dunno."

Esther decided to stay a bit longer in the kitchen and rummage a bit deeper for the candles...

Johnny stood still and strained to listen through the howling of the blizzard. The cold bit at his face and he pulled his multiple collars up further around his neck. All he could hear were those bloody dogs. "Bloodydogsshutupyoubastards," he roared at the rattling shed, and then cocked his ear again in the lull that followed.

"Over here!"

Surely that was a voice? "Help me, please, help me!" it called from the corner of the yard. Johnny swung round, beaming his torch in the direction that he thought it came from. Damn Taid for buying the feeblest torch on the market: it was like trying to find someone with a ten-pence-piece's worth of tunnel vision. The voice set the dogs off again, this time more excitedly than before.

He stalked across the yard, the snow crunching under his wellies as he called, "Hello? Where are you?" in the direction of the voice. He wasn't scared – just intrigued: surely anyone with bad intentions would not be bothered to venture out on a night like this to a place like this? Surely there would be easier pickings somewhere else?

Eventually his torch's beam swung across a shape bent nearly double in the corner of the yard. Johnny stopped – it looked like there was something wrong. Did they have a gun? Was it a scorned woman hell-bent on revenge? Or maybe a jealous boyfriend who had got wind of something? Did he have a gun concealed under that coat? It could be the perfect time for an "accident": it could take days to find him in this snow and by the time he was discovered, having "fallen" into the icy river, the estranged couple would have made up and be sat drinking tea and watching the story unfold on the news.

Then the shape gave a large animal groan, like a cow searching for her calf and Johnny Brechdan ran the rest of the way towards it. *It* became a woman and it sounded as if she were in terrible pain.

"It's OK," he shouted, "I've got you now – what on earth's the matter?"

White from cold and crumpled with pain and fright, a woman's face looked around at him. Her hands were blue, and they were wrapped around a large bump on her front. Shit. Pregnant. Hugely pregnant and in his yard.

"OK, OK, I've got you," he said as reassuringly as he could. He took her by the shoulders and she leaned towards him, barely acknowledging his presence. She had on a coat that Taid would call "a bloody fashion thing, only good for sitting by a fire in" and she was obviously freezing. Her suede boots were soaked right through and her jeans were sodden from the snow.

The woman groaned again then grunted at Johnny, "My car – in a ditch. I crashed. The baby's early – I thought I could get there on my own – oh God, oh God, here it comes again…" She doubled over and screamed in pain, gripping onto Johnny's arms, her head buried in his coat.

"OK, I've got you, I've got you, it'll be OK," he said, knowing full well that it wouldn't.

After half a minute or so, the woman managed to stand almost

153

upright, "OK, now," she whispered, nodding her head at him, "the contractions, they're coming every few minutes."

"Right. In." said Johnny and he marched her as quickly as he could to the door, him crunching through the snow in his wellies and her slip sliding in those stupid-bloody-fashion-boots, good for walking on carpets.

"Nain! Taid! Get here!" he shouted as soon as he kicked the door open. One candle flame managed to survive the draught howling through the gap and even that flickered dangerously as he booted it shut again.

"Right, get by that fire. Nain! Taid! Get down here!" he shouted again and ushered the woman forward, chattering in what he hoped was a soothing way. "I'm Johnny and I'll look after you, Nain'll come down now and she'll know what to do. Don't worry. It'll be fine. Now, what's your name?"

"Tansy," the woman whispered as she leant forward once more, "Oh God, not again…" Johnny gripped her and she gripped him and Tansy cried out in pain. A bewildered Nain and Taid appeared at the door of the kitchen, each with a candle.

"Johnny, what on earth is going on?" started Nain and then her candle picked up the scene. "Oh, good God, where did you find her?"

"In the yard. Car's crashed. Her name's Tansy."

Tansy stopped her groans and looked up, obviously latching on to someone who might have a clue about what might be happening next.

"All right, *bach*," Nain stepped in and clutched the girl's hands. "She's freezing. Tomos – fire. Johnny – I want the bedding from your room, your mattress, everything. She'll be warmer here. Tomos – I want sheets, towels, anything. And something clean and soft to wrap the baby in, OK? Right, *bach* – Tansy – you're going to be fine. Phones are down and I think you're too far gone for us to drive you anywhere. First we need to get your wet clothes off. Tomos – a clean nightie. No – she's too tall. Johnny, get one of your biggest t-shirts and a sweatshirt and some socks – long woolly socks – and a dressing gown; the thick blue one?"

Johnny dragged the mattress and bedding in to lay it by the Rayburn and then scuttled back upstairs for the clothes. Taid had stoked the fire and re-filled the kettles and a saucepan for extra hot water and was rummaging under the sink for more candles. Johnny raced back in with an armful of his clothes and put them on the chair beside Tansy just as another set of contractions came. She looked for him and then grabbed his arms as she howled in pain, her head now buried in his stomach. Nain stood beside her, rubbing her back and muttering, "It's OK, *bach*, shout as loud as you want; them sheep don't mind a bit of noise!"

The groans subsided and Tansy managed to stand upright and Johnny stared into eyes that were squinting with pain. She had bobbed silvery-blonde hair and a full face that would probably usually be attractive in a strong, rosy kind of way.

Nain and Johnny quickly took her wet boots and clothes off her and popped her into Johnny's long T-shirt with a sweatshirt on top, claiming *Todd's Stag Tour, 2009: Committed to Educating the Masses in the Art of Love.* Her feet were white and wrinkled from being wet and cold for so long and Tansy managed a smile as Johnny wriggled on a pair of his woollen socks and then rubbed them to get the circulation moving again. Throughout it all, Nain kept up a chatter of what they were doing and how it would soon be over, whilst ordering Taid and Johnny around with her eyebrows and nods of her head.

Johnny was roped in to support Tansy and they started walking back and fore, back and fore down the long kitchen. As the contractions took her breath away, she would grab his arms and then shriek in pain; Johnny had to stop himself squealing in tandem as her strong fingers dug into his flesh.

After a while the tempo changed and Tansy dropped onto the duvet. She screamed in agony and leant back into Nain who had knelt down behind her. For what seemed an age, Johnny alternated between walking back and fore by himself and then hovering around, looking over Nain's shoulder.

Eventually, Johnny found himself at the business end and was suddenly exhilarated. He'd been involved with lambing since he was a toddler, but here he was with a real live woman! He caught Taid's eye and nearly giggled. Nain took control of the situation.

"Johnny, now, can you see the head?"

Johnny felt a bit like a naughty schoolboy as he moved a candle to look. He felt like he was in a ridiculous dream. A short while ago he'd been sat in front of the fire debating whether to go to bed or wait for ten minutes and *then* go to bed, and now he was about to watch a baby being born. He looked up at Tansy. Her face was clenched in pain, but to him she looked absolutely beautiful: the personification of glorious motherhood. He felt overwhelmed by her strength and her resolve. He was sure that he would be whimpering by now, pleading to be knocked out or to have an *epidombell* or whatever they were called. Yet here was Tansy, in agony, but listening intently to what Nain was saying quietly to her between contractions.

He now felt that all the females he had known – and he had known quite a few, quite well – were just girls. Girls having a bit of fun in the way that he'd been just a boy having a bit of fun. Noodle Soodle, Bacon Sandwich Lil, Tessa Top Field – all just girls enjoying a bit of flirtation, sucking up a bit of romancing and giving as good as they got in lay-bys or in four-poster beds, but Tansy was real. Beautiful, strong, animal almost. So now it was *his* turn to step up to the plate: to be a man at last, rather than a boy mucking about and telling his mates about some floozy's tits.

So, instead of swallowing a giggle about it being his favourite position to spend an evening in, he looked up at this fine woman wrapped in his sweatshirt and whispered, "Go on, Tansy, I can see its head! Go on; you're nearly there!"

Obligingly Tansy gave a massive scream and the baby shot out in one go. Johnny dived down and managed to catch it as it spilled out onto the pile of bedding. He felt like cheering – and so he did.

"It's a girl!" he screamed. "A lovely little girl!" He held it in his hands and looked into the baby's eyes that, for a short moment, stared back at him in the candlelight. Johnny felt an emotion that he'd never known before wash over him. He felt as if it was just him and this baby in the whole world and it was his job to protect and look after it for ever more.

Taid silently handed him a soft towel and he wrapped the baby as carefully as he could and held it out to Tansy, who was still slumped against his nain.

"A girl?" she whispered weakly. Her face different now – worn out instead of in pain. "Oh, look, a little girl!"

Nain rubbed her shoulders from behind her and kissed her hair, wiping her own tears from her smiling cheeks. "Well done, *bach*, clever girl," she said over and over again. "Oh, she's so beautiful!" She gestured to Taid to push the armchair over and a duvet was laid over it and Tansy was helped up from the floor. Johnny checked the baby was breathing and that her mouth was clear, just as he would a lamb.

When Tansy was settled and covered by a blanket, he passed her bundle and just sat on the floor beside her chair and watched as the new mother inspected her baby. Johnny patted Tansy's arm through the blanket. "You were wonderful," he whispered, still in a bit of a trance.

"So were you," she smiled, "so were you..."

Within the hour, Nain had got things a little more organised. Everyone had drunk at least three cups of tea – Tansy's with extra sugar in – and had eaten a couple more fairy cakes. The Rayburn was pumping out heat and all the soiled bedding had been removed. Nain had cut the cord and delivered the placenta and she'd cleaned Tansy up as best she could.

Tansy was sitting on the sofa with the baby feeding at her breast. Although it had taken several attempts, the baby seemed to know what she had to do and had forgiven all the re-positioning and fumbling around. Johnny peered at his watch, thinking that it must be nearly midnight and was amazed to find it was half past four...

As baby sucked at her first meal, Tansy looked up. "I've just realised, you've no idea who I am or how I got to be here, have you?"

Johnny smiled and shook his head. He wanted to say, *None of that matters. What matters is that you and the baby are here with us and we're going to keep you safe. Safe forever.*

"I'm Tansy Shackles and I live over at Cefn Mawr." Johnny nodded: he knew the village as his great aunt lived there. He thought Tansy was vaguely familiar, now he'd time to think about it, he filled up in the garage there too, occasionally – perhaps that's where he'd seen her before.

"I'm not due yet for another few weeks, really – and my friend who was going to be with me had gone away. I slipped on the ice yesterday morning and fell on my backside, so I sort of wasn't surprised when it started. I knew the weather was getting worse, but I just wanted to be in hospital – bit stupid to drive myself I suppose – but to be honest, I thought I'd be fine – I thought other people just made a bit of a fuss! In hindsight, I didn't realise that there was pain like *that* in life! Even more stupid still to drive myself in a blizzard, but I thought at least the roads would be quiet if I needed to stop every few minutes for a contraction! Then as I was coming down your pitch, the snow had gotten worse and I couldn't see where the road ended and the ditch began. I must have hit some ice and I skidded and then – bang – front wheel down in the ditch!"

Johnny looked at Tansy – poor thing, she must have been terrified. Yet, after all she'd been through she was sitting there, feeding her baby, gently stroking her head with the tip of her finger: the image of maternal tranquillity.

"Anyway, it was soon obvious that I wasn't going to get out of there, so I knew it was either get out and walk or have the baby in the car. I saw your turning and for about thirty seconds I saw your lights, then they all switched off at once..."

"That must have been the power cut," said Nain, quietly rinsing through some soiled bedding at the sink, "at, ooh, just before nine?"

"I don't know what I would have done if I hadn't seen them for that short time, but I knew that there had to be people here, and so I set off. Your lane winds a bit though, doesn't it? The lights seemed to be only a couple of hundred yards away, but the track seemed to go on forever!"

"You poor thing," said Johnny, still in awe of the strength of the woman sat in front of him. To do all that and then to be sat quite peacefully in a chair feeding a baby – her whole world had changed in less than twelve hours and there she was, taking it all in her stride.

Never mind Tansy's life changing, he knew that his had too. The love he felt for the baby was overwhelming. He wanted to hold her and stroke her head, just like Tansy was. He wanted to protect them both, keep them near to him, protect Tansy from ever having to go through anything bad again.

He felt that his life up until this point had been a trial run, a tease until the real one started. It was as if a switch in his head had been turned from "flirtation" to "devotion" as the unfamiliar feelings oozed from him. It was probably the tiredness, but he actually felt elated and far from sleep.

"What about people to contact, Tansy, *bach*," asked Nain as her strong arms wrung nearly every drop of moisture from an old towel. "A husband, or partner as you call them today? Your parents? Who shall we call – when we get the phones back on that is."

A shadow fluttered across Tansy's brow, as if she were remembering something painful. "No one really," she muttered, trying to be matter-of-fact. "I've not got parents – alive that is – anymore; I'll need to contact Kathy, my friend, but there's no rush. And, well, I've got no husband to speak of anymore. The baby's father," she whispered, and struggled to find the words, "well, he left about three months ago. Said he…said he couldn't cope."

Nain shook her head and signed. "Oh, I am sorry to hear that, *bach*, but don't you worry…"

"No! Don't worry about anything!" interjected Johnny. "We'll look after you! Here! Yes, won't we, Nain?" His eyes were bright and his face full of excitement.

"Of course we will, of course we will. Tansy and the little one can stay as long as they like. As long as they like!"

Tansy smiled with gratitude as she caught Johnny's eye. "Thank you," she muttered, tiredness now sweeping over her, "thank you so much."

"Just one more thing, lovely," said Nain, wiping her hands dry on a towel, "and then you must get some sleep – any names?"

"I've not decided yet," Tansy replied. "I thought I'd wait until I saw it – her. What's your name, Nain?"

"Me? Oh, I'm Gwen. Means white or fair in Welsh."

"Perfect," smiled Tansy. "Well, Gwen, meet Gwen Shackles. Gwen – *Gwennie* Elizabeth Shackles."

That was it for Johnny. He burst into tears and slumped into the pile of blankets, sitting on his heels with his face hidden in a cushion.

"Don't mind him," he heard Gwen senior say, "he's a bit sentimental this one. Takes after his grandfather!"

Johnny heard a chuckle from the back of the kitchen. "Christ, in my seventy-two years I don't think I've ever been called *sentimental*! A stubborn old bastard, perhaps. Pig-headed and ignorant maybe, but never *sentimental!*"

But, far better than that, Johnny felt a hand reach down to stroke his hair. "You'll be OK," crooned a gentle voice, "you'll be OK."

As the storm continued to rage outside, Johnny spent the most wonderful twenty minutes tucked up in the armchair with baby Gwennie snuggled onto his chest whilst Gwen senior helped Tansy have a shower in his en-suite bathroom – and for the right reasons he was glad it was as clean and neat as it could be. He'd heard Nain speak of "skin to skin" contact between the baby and its parent that helps the baby feel settled and content, so he soon had Gwennie lying on his bare chest snuffling and staring at him. Tansy had laughed as Gwen had wrapped a blanket around them both. "I've been at – ooh, probably ten deliveries," she smiled, "and I don't think I've ever seen this before!" And then she whispered to Johnny as Tansy walked gingerly towards the bathroom, "Don't you go getting too attached, Johnny, love, they'll be off back to their own world soon."

"Nain, m'n," he'd replied, pretending to be indignant, "I'm just holding the little thing; don't you worry about me."

Yet when Tansy returned, now in a pair of his boxer shorts and a different T-shirt and dressing gown, he told her to get herself comfortable and take her time before he reluctantly handed Gwennie over. He'd had many cuddles from many women – and many women had wanted more cuddles that he'd felt willing to give – but none yet had been so precious as that from Gwennie Shackles as her little fingers gripped his one large one: she'd gotten right under his skin and she was only two hours old.

Taid had found a small wooden crate that their fruit and vegetables had been delivered in earlier that week and he'd lined it with a blanket and then a clean sheet. Tansy fed Gwennie again, still struggling to find a comfortable position and then when Gwennie, swaddled in a sheet, dropped off her breast, milk-drunk, she was laid carefully into the little box and covered by another sheet and a blanket. The box was laid beside Tansy on the double mattress now dragged back in front of the Rayburn and Tansy was finally able to sleep.

Because Johnny no longer had a mattress on his bed, he made a makeshift bed out of the sofa at the far end of the kitchen. "Wake me if you need anything," he said to Tansy and he really, really meant it. Finally the household fell into a deep slumber as the snow continued to fall outside and the wind continued to howl and the temperature went on dropping.

CHAPTER 23

Mor llon â brithyll – as happy as a trout

The snow had meant that the residents of Anweledig were also trapped in their houses. Louisa had checked with a quick peep out of the window the next morning and, satisfied that there was absolutely *no way* she'd get to town, she had gleefully left a message on the bank's answering machine to explain her unfortunate absence and then bounced back into bed. How quickly she forgot her promise to start digging out her car straight away...

David, however, was made of sterner stuff. He was slightly disappointed that their power had been returned during the night; he had rather relished the adventure of having to brave the cold, cook on a camping stove and to prove how much metal he really had in him.

Esther was pottering round the kitchen, clearing away the breakfast dishes when the front door burst open.

"Esther! Esther?"

"Yes, love?" she called, walking out to the hall with a tea towel and a wet cup in her hand.

"Snowed in. Can't get out – I'll have to dig my way through. Need to phone work first. Now – where's the phone?"

"Probably in the lounge...on the stand?"

David looked expectantly, as if she'd probably hidden it, so she walked slowly into the lounge to check. Yes, there it was on the stand. "Here you are," she said, passing it to him and shuddering from the cold air that was blasting through the open door. "Oo, shut that will you, love, it's freezing."

"Esther, I'm *trying* to ring work. Now, what's happened to this phone?"

"Well, you can ring from inside as well as from the doorway – and what do you mean? What's happened to the phone?"

"It's broken," he said, handing it back to her with a frown.

"Oh, the battery's dead; it mustn't have been on the stand properly."

"Well, is there another one fully charged, or not?"

Esther now had a cup, a tea towel and a phone in her strong hand as she headed for the kitchen. Good – the other phone was on its stand and fully charged. She put down her belongings and swapped the phones.

"Esther! I do actually *need* to phone work. I don't want them to think I'm late for no reason."

Eventually she passed him the phone. "Well, it is *slightly* easier for you to fetch these things than me…"

"Yes, but I've got my coat on…"

"…and *please* can you shut that door!"

"Gosh, Esther, you are in a bit of a bad mood this morning: what's up?"

Esther clenched her teeth and managed to squeak out a, "Nothing," as she returned to her chores. Was she in a bad mood? She was sure that she was quite happy five minutes before. Perhaps she *was* getting tetchier these days? David seemed to think she was anyway – perhaps she should see the doctor and get her hormone levels checked. She wiped the cup and put it on the shelf.

"Esther! They said it was OK, but to try and get in as soon as I can," came the shout from the doorway. "Now, I need the spade. If I can dig the car out of Anweledig, the top road may be a bit clearer. Esther, where did you put the spade?"

"What do you mean? I would think it's probably in the garage?"

"No, don't think so. *Where* in the garage?"

"It's usually hanging up next to the rakes?" Nothing and nobody moved. "Oh, hang on, *I'll* find it." Esther put her coat on and struggled into her boots. The path to the garage was treacherous for her as her weaker side was the house side and she needed to hold on to steady her balance. David opened the garage door.

"*There* it is," she said, pointing to the hook next to the rakes.

"Oh yes, so it is." David fetched the shovel and set off on his journey to battle with tigers in the snow. "Tell Louisa that if I can get mine out, she can follow – probably in about an hour or so?"

"OK," said Esther, exhausted through exasperation and effort and she set off back to the house. "Louisa!" she called up the stairs. Silence. "Louisa – Dad says he'll be able to clear the drive in an hour or so. Perhaps you could help him?" More silence. Esther sighed and started pulling herself up the stairs. She knocked on Louisa's door.

"Yes?"

"Louisa, Dad says he'll be…"

"Yes, I heard – an hour. Tell him I'll be out to help him in a minute; I'm just finishing this." Louisa pointed at her computer: it looked like she was writing out a comment from her blog onto a piece of paper.

Esther rolled her eyes, shut the door and took a few seconds to rest before setting off back down the stairs. She went to the front door to put her boots on, then stood back up and muttered, "Actually, tell him your bloody self," and returned to her drying up in the kitchen.

Johnny dragged himself away from the breastfeeding baby to go and have a look at Tansy's car and fetch their belongings. He wrapped up warmly, stuffed his double-socked feet into his wellies and headed out into the whiteness. The snow had finally stopped falling and the sun was weakly trying to warm things up, but was failing miserably.

He grabbed a spade and headed off down the track, accompanied by three dogs. He could see Tansy's footprints, blurred by more snow, which she'd made as she walked up the lane the night before. He shuddered with concern as he saw them stumble from side to side and then spotted an area trampled down, presumably as she stopped for a contraction. He felt amazed by what she'd been through and his respect grew. As he walked he began to get warmer. The dogs were rushing about, sniffing from side to side and enjoying being out of their shed. Johnny had always loved the snow and it simply enhanced his feelings of a clean new start to his life.

The electricity was still off and he was in no hurry for it to come back on. Until it did and the roads were clear, Tansy couldn't realistically go anywhere: she'd have to stay at the farm – with him…

He eventually came out onto the council road and saw what must be her Fiesta stuck in a hedge. A quick inspection showed that it was stuck in a snowdrift, rather than having crashed or dropped into the ditch. He spent a pleasant half hour scraping the snow from around it and clearing a route to their farm track. It felt good to be labouring, although he still felt tired from the lack of sleep, and he was pleased to be able to show Tansy how useful he could be. Johnny finally started the car and with a little skidding and revving, he drove it along the road and parked it on their track out of the way of other vehicles that might come sliding round the corner looking for a nice soft Fiesta to act as their buffer.

Realising that he'd not get it any further up the track until the snow melted, he loaded himself up with all Tansy's bags and set off like a pack horse, laden with the stacks of nappies and bags of clutter that a first-time mother has been told she needs.

As he lumbered towards the house and crashed his bags against the door frame, something felt different. Ah, electricity. The radio was on and the fridge in the corner was whirring away, trying to make up for lost time.

"All right, love?" Nain asked as he looked around trying to see Tansy and baby Gwen. "They're both sleeping." Johnny followed her eyes and saw them tucked up on the sofa with a blanket thrown over them. "If Tansy can have as much sleep as possible, it'll do her good," said Nain. "The phone's back on now too, so I've phoned the hospital and spoken to a midwife and I've a few things to check when Tansy wakes. How was the road? Anything been through?"

"No, nothing yet. I think you'd struggle even with a four by four; it's drifted high in places. Tractor'd be OK."

"That's what I thought. Midwife said she'll hold off 'til later – unless there are any problems and then they'll have to send a helicopter!"

Johnny felt a little disappointed; he wanted the best for Tansy, but he didn't want anyone from the outside world interfering. Part of him wanted the snow to go on and on: they'd be fine on their own.

He heard a noise and looked over to see Tansy shifting position trying to get comfortable without waking the baby.

"Hello," she smiled.

"Hello," he whispered back, "how are you?"

"Knackered and a *little* bit sore!" Her face was still puffy with exhaustion, but she had a colour in her cheeks that hadn't been there the night before and her eyes were brighter.

"Well, you don't have to do anything except sit there and get better," clucked Nain, bringing over another cup of tea and a glass of water. She dragged a little table over with her foot and put the drinks on it so that Tansy could reach them without having to stretch. She told Tansy about her conversation with the midwife and asked Johnny to take Gwennie for a while so that she could run through the list of things she had to check.

Johnny dived at the chance for a cuddle and gently lifted a waking Gwennie from Tansy and wrapped her in another blanket. Cooing to her softly, he took her into his bedroom and went to the window. Everything outside was white: the hills, the fields, the track and even the trees had great globs of snow clinging to their branches.

"Look, little Gwennie, this is snow!" he whispered. "It's very cold outside but I'll keep you warm. I'll look after you; I'll *always* look after you, you and your mummy if she'll allow me. Would you like that?" Gwennie obliged by staring up at him, her big blue eyes gazing, unfocussed, into his. With a gentle finger, he stroked her wisps of white hair, shiny against her red scalp and he felt love pour from him and flow over the tiny baby.

He looked around his bedroom, a haven for seducing women. Tidy and clean without being sterile, it had been honed for enticing women. The chair was wedged into a far corner, so the bed had to be sat on instead. Lamps lit both sides of the bed and the main light was on a dimmer switch. CD number two was always ready to promote lovemaking and only required the press of a single button on the remote control.

Yet, now the carefully chosen duvet cover looked childish, as if a fifteen-year-old boy had chosen it, rather than a twenty-six-year-old man. Who cared whether checks were more appealing to the female eye than stripes? The whole room would look much better if there were a stuffed rabbit thrown onto the bed, or if there were a little crib on the floor at its side. He'd be happy to have Gwen on his side of the bed; he could lift her up if she cried and let Tansy sleep on.

Johnny sat on the bed and leant carefully against the headboard, crooning quietly to Gwennie. Eventually she started making hungry noises and he peeped through the door to check it was OK for him to come back into the kitchen. Tansy had the telephone in her hand and a big smile on her face.

"Hello? Kathy? It's me, Tansy. Can you hear me OK? I've had it – her – a baby girl! Gwennie. Gwennie Elizabeth. I know! And you'll not believe this – I'm in a farmhouse in the middle of nowhere! Snow's two foot deep outside and we're snowed in!"

Johnny cradled Gwennie and sang to her to give her mother a little more time. The conversation ended with, "Well, OK, you can just leave him a message. Not that he'll care anyway. Best tell him though, yeah? OK, thanks, bye. Bye."

"All right, *bach*? Everything OK?" Nain had rummaged through Tansy's bags, run a bowl of warm water and was cleaning up Gwennie, showing Johnny how to pat her dry and then put her in a nappy and some proper baby clothes.

By the time a clean, clothed Gwennie was brought back to her, Tansy seemed quite glum. "Oh, it's just reality now, isn't it? And the reality is that my husband has gone and I'm a single parent and I have a baby. How on *earth* am I going to cope? House is a state, my job's rubbish and – well – *everything…*"

"Don't worry about anything," said Johnny immediately. "We'll help; you'll be fine! Stay as long as you need!"

Nain frowned a warning at him. "Do you want to phone your husband yourself, love? Take the phone into the other room; perhaps if you told him that Gwennie had been born, he might come back?"

"Not that simple, I'm afraid," whispered Tansy, "not that simple."

"OK, love." Nain became all practical again. "It can all be sorted later. Look, here she is, all clean and hungry again too! You can give her another feed and we'll get out of your way and give you a little peace. Come on, Johnny, haven't you got some jobs to do?"

Johnny took the hint and reluctantly climbed back into his wellies and headed for the barns.

CHAPTER 24

Mor dwt â nyth dryw – as neat as a wren's nest

Sima pressed the button on the brushed-chrome juicer and counted to fifteen. She opened the overhead cupboard and reached for two glasses and poured the green-grey liquid into them. Joe came into the kitchen still doing up his tie. "Oh, thanks," he muttered as she passed him a glass. "What's this? A puddle?"

"Don't be puerile; it's a potassium drink recipe. It'll rev up your immune system and make you feel full until lunchtime."

"You're joking aren't you?" Joe said and he downed the drink in one go and then wiped his mouth on the back of his hand. He grimaced, and then he shuddered. "Maybe it'll keep me full until the bacon sarnie trolley comes round. Aside from that, it'll probably just give me the shits."

"Better perhaps than your usual constipation, though? Come on, Joe, your body needn't be a temple, but your dad pays more attention to his chickens' diets than you do your own…"

Joe shrugged, "Spoke to Dad last night by the way, they've got snow – two foot in places! Keep getting power cuts – Mother lost the candles apparently – had to wait until the lights came back on to find them!"

"Torches?"

"No, lost them too! All a bit of a disaster! Funny, I miss it really."

"What losing things and living in the dark?"

"No, weather. Real weather – you know, when you get snowed in. When you have to wear lots of layers. Come on, you must have loved it as a kid, when the bus couldn't get through or when school was shut and the pipes froze?"

"No, not really. Come on, I've got to get going." Sima quickly emptied the juicer caddy into the bin, then whipped the chopping board, knife, glasses and juicer washables into the dishwasher and slammed the door shut. She grabbed a disposable cloth and slicked it over the surface, removing any hint that food may ever have been prepared in such a temple to hygiene. She tossed the cloth into the bin and the lid shut silently behind her.

"There," she said, all smiles, "done. Now, can we go?"

"Yeah, s'pose," said Joe, picking up his briefcase and taking his keys off the hook. "Somehow all that stuff just seems a bit more, well, *real*."

"What now? The juicer?"

"No, the weather, losing torches, having to worry about what your chickens are eating – all that *unreliable* stuff. I mean," he said as he pulled the door of the flat to and they waited by the lift, "all this – it's lovely, don't get me wrong…"

"Good, or you can stay in your own flat."

"…but it's so far removed from what is *real*. I mean, what am I doing today?"

"Well, if you don't know, I *certainly* don't. Go on, enlighten me – you're going to buy things? Sell things? Make some money?"

"Exactly. Now, what about you?" The door of the lift slid shut behind them and Sima rolled her eyes as she reached for the underground car park button.

"Joe, what is this? You having an early mid-life crisis or something, just because your mother lost her torch?"

"No, but all I am saying is, well, maybe I'm saying that sometimes we should all think about being a bit more real, you know?"

"Joe. I have a client at nine who needs a life laundry. Another at eleven who is having a divorce and I'm having a full bikini wax at one. How much more reality do you need?" Sima pointed her key fob at her car and popped it open. "Hey, come here," she said and pulled him towards her. "Don't be sad just because we've got a shower that actually washes us and we don't wear ten-year-old acrylic jumpers. It's life! If you want chickens and wellies, well, you'll have to move back home – they've got plenty to go round there – mainly in your parents' utility room. Look, we'll talk later, OK? Bye, lover!" and she ducked into her BMW and purred away, leaving Joe to walk in the opposite direction to the tube station – in the drizzle.

He waved her goodbye as he walked out of the complex. "You know," he said to the back of her car, "I might just do that…"

Sima sat in a traffic jam and groaned in frustration. It wasn't as if she was in threat of being late – she always left plenty of time for traffic – it was just the inefficiency of being sat inside a car in a queue. It wasn't as if she could *do* anything; if she got her Blackberry® out, the car in front would shuffle forwards three foot and she'd feel obliged to put everything down and do the same.

She thought back to what Joe had said that morning; he'd been talking like that quite a bit lately. Not saying, *I want to go and be a farmer in Bwlch y Garreg*, but more voicing little dissatisfactions about his – or their – life in London.

She could *sort of* see his point. Everything in their life worked. It was organised and efficient; even in a traffic jam she could clench and unclench her buttocks and do a seated mini-workout. Both of them were good at their jobs, money was rarely an issue, as there was so much floating around, and her flat, where he pretty much lived at the moment, worked like clockwork – and if it didn't, having someone else to make sure that it did so pretty quickly was only a phone call away.

Clothes were washed and ironed and then returned to the wardrobes. Any clutter was put away by a mystery housemaid, bathrooms were cleaned and carpets vacuumed. Shopping was ordered online and delivered when they weren't there, so that the mystery housemaid put it away in all the right places. All they had to do in the flat was exist.

Their friends were mostly the same: successful, attractive and hell-bent on enjoying life with no responsibilities apart from to themselves. None of them had children or even pets to muddy the waters and they met for drinks after work or dinner at a restaurant on a Saturday night, all looking beautiful and they would chatter, laugh, drink fine wines, and then disappear home in easily afforded taxis.

Joe was right: snow never scuppered their plans, neither did sick cows or hobbling sheep. Their coats really were just bloody fashion items, they didn't need them to do anything else but look great as they did nothing but hop from heated flat to climate-controlled car to heated office spaces. But then, thought Sima as she joined a different queue at a junction, there is no actual *pleasure* in having a crap shower or mice in your sofa cushions – otherwise she could arrange for it to happen. It was the kind of romantic notion that people yearned for, and yet they all moaned like hell when their bus was late or they tripped over a loose paving slab, then stepped in a puddle.

Joe might think he missed the farming life, but he also liked good restaurants and the office camaraderie. She couldn't imagine Isla welcoming him home at the end of a long day with a glass of champagne on a balcony: just the ubiquitous cup of tea and one of those bloody scones.

Maybe she, Sima, should bake Joe a few humungous scones and pop them in a rusty biscuit tin and then store it in a place where no one

169

could reach it without standing on a rickety chair. Maybe when he gets home tonight, I could just pass him a cracked plate with an enormous curranted offering, she thought, slathered in an inch of butter and then ask him about cows.

First though, I'll have to find a decent recipe for scones. And buy a baking tray and a set of scales, she thought. Actually, sod it: I'll just text the housekeeping company and ask them to bring some over.

Sima turned into the underground car park at her office building and drove into her space. She reached for her bag and slung her jacket over her arm. Within thirty paces, she was in the lift and zipping her way up to her fifth floor office. Bloody Joe and his need for reality in life. Let Isla and Tomos do an hour and a half of weight-bearing stretches with Work It Bob, then go for a full Hollywood wax. *Then* they'd understand that there was pain and authenticity in city life too.

CHAPTER 25

Mor wlyb â llygoden ddŵr – as wet as a water rat

When Gwennie Elizabeth was four days old, her mother said that it was time to thank their hosts for their wonderful hospitality and move back home. Tansy had been seen by a midwife who had said that mother and daughter were doing wonderfully well and who had praised Nain for doing everything right.

Johnny reckoned that Tansy didn't actually *want* to go home, rather that she felt that she *should*. "You can stay as long as you want, you know," he'd repeated to her just that morning.

"I know, and thank you, it's just, well, we're in your way and we need to get home and get started."

"You're not in the way, not in the slightest. I – we – love having you here." Tansy had smiled again and thanked him, but she had been resolute that they should at least try to survive on their own.

Johnny had offered to drive them home in Taid's four-by-four as the roads still had snow in places, and his own truck wasn't in a fit state to drive a lady and a baby *anywhere*, let alone on their maiden voyage.

He would then collect them again in two days time if there were no further snow, and bring them back to the farm so that Tansy could drive her car back.

At Nain's suggestion, he had driven up and down the track a couple of times to make sure a clear route was in place. His usual impulse would be to skid and slide his way along it, relishing the action; even at twenty-six, it was still great fun to be driving a 4 x 4 in the snow! This time, however, he had driven sensibly and made sure that a good rut was worn through.

He loaded all of Tansy and Gwennie's things into the truck, plus a whole lot more. There was enough food for two days, so all that Tansy had to do was to take foil off plates and put them into the microwave. Gwennie's new car seat was assembled and installed and eventually she was installed too. Nain gave them a hug goodbye and then she and Taid waved them out of the yard.

Tansy seemed a bit nervous about heading for home and kept checking for her keys and faffing about with Gwen's car seat.

They passed her car sat plonked at the end of the track, now looking a little abandoned as the worst of the snow had melted from around it – it looked as if it had just been dropped from space.

They drove in silence for most of the journey, both seemed to be deep in thought. Johnny had hoped to use the journey to clinch his relationship with Tansy, to find out her exact marital status and to shoot off a few of his best charm bullets. The trouble was, he didn't feel like bullshitting her and he didn't think it would be very well-received; he was on virgin territory and wasn't sure which way to turn.

Telling a four-day mum that she was looking great when she really wasn't, would probably make her cry. Talking about a favourite restaurant in the hope that he could turn an interest into an invitation was tactless as she probably wouldn't be going anywhere for some time, what with the breastfeeding on demand. Anyway, Tansy seemed quite sad and low: it must be the four-day blues. Nain had mentioned something about those – or was it three-day? Whatever it was, he was probably best just to shut up and let her feel sad about returning to a cold empty house, which would mean that she would miss him and his big warm one…

*

Once in the village of Cefn Mawr, Tansy directed Johnny towards her house. He was intrigued to see what it would be like as he realised that he actually knew very little about Tansy, despite which he felt that he knew all that he needed.

Eventually they pulled up outside an end of terrace cottage. It was built of dark stone and had a varnished wooden door. It was a nondescript little house, the same as the others in the row – apart from the fact that running out from under the door was a little trickle of water...

"Shit – Tansy, give me your keys!" Johnny cried and dived at the front door. He opened it quickly and went in, squelching on a wet hall carpet and seeing water gently seeping down the beige-covered stairs.

He heard a cry from behind him and he rushed back to Tansy who was now standing in the doorway with her hands over her face. "Quick, where's the stopcock?"

"The what?" she wailed. "Oh, I don't know. Greg always did things like that."

Johnny rushed off, he pulled all the half-empty bottles of cleaner out from under the sink – nothing. "Where could it be?" he yelled from inside the pantry. Tansy burst into tears.

"I don't know – try the shower room?"

He ran into the shower room under the stairs and clattered more half-empty bottles of bleach out of the way and to his relief found the stopcock. He turned it slowly and ran the tap until it stopped.

He gave a huge sigh of relief and stood up from a puddle on the lino, brushing the worst of the water from his knees. He looked around him; *everywhere* was sodden. Water was dripping through the ceiling, down light fittings, and pooling on the floor. Anything that came into contact with the carpets was sodden; Tansy's cream macintosh had been hung on a lower peg and the end of the belt *just* brushed the carpet and had soaked up a foot of grey water. Johnny went to find Tansy, squelching over wet carpet as he walked. She was sitting on a kitchen chair groaning. The kitchen looked like it might have been smart and cosmopolitan in a bland kind of way once. Someone had taken a great deal of care with the décor and the fittings at some point, but these had been covered over by someone who didn't seem to have the same time or energy as that DIY expert.

The chrome vegetable rack was full of rotting fruit, there were piles of newspapers on the floor in the corner that were doing their best to suck up the water. Bags of shopping had been slung next to the storage heater and Johnny could see milk and frozen items popping out over the top that would be ruined now – would have been ruined not long after they'd been put there. The bin was overflowing and was smelling pretty rank, dishes filled in the sink and a breakfast bowl still half-filled with milk and cornflakes was sat on the table next to a half-eaten sandwich and an empty ready meal tub that looked a bit like it might once have held cauliflower cheese. The whole mess was indicative of someone who hadn't been coping very well for a while.

Tansy was sitting with her head in her hands. "Oh, just look at it," she sobbed, "what am I going to do? I can't sort this lot out *and* look after a baby. Oh, why did it have to happen *now,* of all times?"

She got up and walked towards the lounge, taking care not to slip on the wet lino. "Look!" she cried. "All ruined." The lounge had a similar feel to the kitchen; it too had been someone's pride and joy once, but had been taken over by someone who obviously didn't have the same priorities in life. The spotlights, which had water dripping from them, and the flat-screen plasma television that dominated one wall had the ring of a bloke who liked his drill and shopping at Homebase of a weekend.

The baskets of ironing, the clothes horse in the middle of the floor and the empty coffee cups on the glass-topped coffee table however, had an inescapable aura of "I'll do it later…"

Johnny took a quick look around, "OK… Look, it's not too bad; just the carpets and anything that's touching them."

"*Everything's* touching the carpets," groaned Tansy, her head still buried in her hands.

"No, look, the sofa's got feet, so that should be fine." He grabbed a pile of sodden magazines from the corner and placed a pile under each foot of the sofa. "There, up another few inches, that'll be fine now. Right, let's get these DVDs out of danger," and he threw all but the bottom few onto the coffee table and then put the wet ones on their sides to drain. He jacked up the armchair with some more newspapers and tied up the curtains, which were slowly sucking up the water from the carpet, into knots.

Johnny sat next to Tansy on the now-wobbly sofa. He put his arm around her and pulled her towards him, trying so hard not to show his excitement at what had happened. "It'll be OK," he crooned, enjoying the warmth of her next to him, "it's only cosmetic stuff. You insured…? Good, all sorted then. It'll just have been because of the power cut; your trip switch must have popped at the same time as the electricity – and the heating – went off. It would have got pretty cold in the attic pretty quickly and then, crack – pipes split. It'll be happening all over. Now, I know that that's no consolation whatsoever, but what I mean is: don't worry. It's all fixable!

"Right, what is going to happen is this: you check that Gwennie's still asleep and is warm enough in the truck. Then go and find your insurance documents. Get a load of stuff for yourself and Gwennie to last a week or so and then you can come back to the farm. We'll sort you a proper room and you can just live with me – with us – until this place gets sorted, OK?"

Tansy snuffled a *thank you* and he helped her off the sofa and then trundled round the rest of the house, trying to minimise damage wherever possible, albeit a little after the horse had bolted and floated off down a sizeable stream. However, it felt good to be proactive – even lifting the corner of the duvet off the carpet might make the difference between a ruined duvet and one that could do with a trip to the launderette when someone had the strength to get round to it.

He lifted the wicker wash basket into the bath and chucked a bundle of dirty washing that had overflowed from it into a pillowcase to take back to wash at the farm. He threw a pile of stuff from the floor in the bedroom into the sink in the corner and then walked around the far side of the bed, but the carpet was wet but clear of further discarded stuff.

He went into what was obviously intended to be Gwennie's room and found her crib and a load of clothes in a small chest of drawers; all were untouched by the flood and so he piled every item of clothing into the Moses basket and took it down to the truck. Tansy was just checking Gwennie, "She's OK," she said, smiling through her tears.

"Good. Look, I've got all Gwennie's stuff. Just get a load of your own and that insurance document and we'll be off. We can always come back if you forget anything."

Tansy sniffed and wiped her nose on the back of her hand. "Thanks, Johnny, I really appreciate this," and she gave his hand a squeeze that made him feel he could carry her, Gwennie and all their stuff over the mountain to the farm if that was what was required.

He followed her back in and popped into the third bedroom to see if he could rescue anything in there.

It was a small room, painted in silver-grey with black wooden blinds at the window. It was a very male room with racks of CDs all over one of the walls. Shelves neatly lined with technical books sat within reach of a computer desk, with an empty space where a computer probably once sat. Everything about the room was neat, catalogued and expensive, in stark contrast to the rest of the house.

However, because everything was so neatly installed on its correct shelving unit, Johnny didn't need to do anything: the carpet was ruined already, as would be the freestanding lamp unit that bent over the table, but at least there were no *personal* personal possessions. As he was about to turn and leave, he saw a box file labelled *Household Utilities – current* and he took it down and leafed through it. Perfect: there behind a divider marked *Insurance* were letters and documents for up-to-date insurance. He turned to see Tansy behind him.

"Don't bother with anything in here," she scowled, "this was Greg's domain. If he hadn't spent so many hours a day in here, farting about with his computer, we probably wouldn't be in this predicament."

"I've got the insurance details."

"Good," Tansy said wearily, "let's shut the door on this room, even with Greg gone, it's still not *mine*, y'know?"

"Greg? That your husband?"

"Yeah. Was – is – whatever. Come on, let's just go."

Tansy had a holdall and a stuffed bin bag at her feet. Johnny gave her the file and took the bags from her.

Iestyn walked into the Bull and stamped his feet on the mat.

"Shut the door!" came cries from several directions. He fumbled for the door handle, but his cold hands slipped off it.

"Shut the fuckin' door, you prick!" shouted an old guy from the corner. Iestyn realised that Grumpy Drunk looked even colder than he, Iestyn, felt after a journey in a truck with the window wound down;

alcohol must be thinning Grumpy's blood. Iestyn muttered his apologies and shut it quickly.

"All right?" he muttered to Johnny who was already sat at the bar, listening to Ed debating the merits of reverse-arm push ups as opposed to straight forward press-ups.

"Evenin' Iestyn," Ed said. "Good to see you. What do you think of the welcoming committee, tonight?"

"Very nice, Ed. I'd not seen Grumpy Drunk for a while: I had been thinking of calling round to his house just to check that he was OK. All right, Johnny?" Johnny looked agitated and was wriggling on his bar stool.

"Yeah, yeah, great. Ed here's been telling me about press-ups – is that right? Ed, mate, all I can say is that if you did some proper work, rather than just talking shit for a living, you wouldn't need to do any press-ups."

"Talking shit is an art, Johnny; it's something I've had to work at. It's just that now I can talk shit whilst wearing a belt two holes tighter than I wore three weeks ago – thanks to that lovely Sima. How is she, Iestyn? Still perfect? Does she talk about how she's priming me for being the next great love of her life? Oh, she'd look wonderful standing next to me behind this bar, both of us doing squats as we greeted our new customers – not you bloody two, mind, we'd get rid of this shower straight away, and have a new cosmopolitan crowd. We'd rename it too. Oh, I don't know, The Ivy or Numero Yuno or something classy like that…"

"Christ, Ed, you *do* talk some shit. Can I have a pint please?"

"And he'll top this one up too," Johnny said, "and— F'fuck's sake, Ed, have you farted?"

"Oh, sorry, yeah. Sima wouldn't like that would she…"

"No she bloody wouldn't – I think we'll take them over there. Put one behind the bar for Menna will you? She said she might come over, too."

Iestyn and Johnny took their pints and went and sat round a table in the corner. Iestyn took a big slurp of his pint and smacked his lips, "So, much snow by your place? We've had—"

"You'll never guess what?" Johnny cut in, gripping the sides of the table in excitement.

"What?"

176

"I've got a baby! Well, not *me* exactly, but in our house! Tansy Shackles she's called – the mother that is. I found her in the yard and the baby's *so* beautiful. She's called Gwen after Nain who helped me deliver her, and, and—"

"Whoa! Slow down! What on earth are you talking about? Nearly as much shit as Ed."

Johnny launched in again, explaining a little more comprehensively this time.

"Bloody hell!" Iestyn struggled to understand the light in Johnny's eyes. "That's a bit of a bummer, you know, if she's in your room and you're in the spare next to Nain and Taid; that'll curtail your...activities!" Iestyn had considered Johnny's grandparents to be his own as well, ever since he had first met them and given them a name. Isla had started by saying, "No, they're not *your* nain and taid, they're *Johnny's*," but had eventually given up. Now Iestyn had Nain and Taid, and then a secondary Nain and Taid Bevan, but Isla had suspected that Nain and Taid Brechdan had always been secretly pleased.

"No, no, you don't understand, it's fantastic! Gwennie's *so* beautiful. She's only six pound two, even now at a week old!"

The door opened again and Menna walked in. Iestyn and Johnny joined in the *Shut the Door!* chorus as the wind licked the warm air that had nearly settled around them. "Sorry!" called Menna and caught Ed's signal that she were to join her friends and he would bring her drink over.

"All right, folks?" she said, as she sat herself down at the table. "How's it going?"

"Don't sit too near Brechdan, he's gone broody!"

"Broody? Brechdan? Cold weather got to your knackers or what? Thanks Ed," she said as a pint was plonked in front of her and she took a large sip. "What's happened? Been presented with twenty love-children or finally realised what that spotty willy of yours is really meant for?"

Johnny explained again, this time prompted by Iestyn when he wasn't quite making sense.

"Wow! Tansy Shackles, eh? I know her – five-ten-ish? Blonde? Lives over at Cefn Mawr? You know," she nudged Iestyn, "she was the one with the pigeon in her grill, *you* know – at Robot Charlie's?"

"Ah, *her!* I know now. Hey, good catch, Brechdan, good catch for a change!"

"No, no," he said, "you don't understand. She's not *with* me, she just turned up, out of the blue. I'd never met her before – anyway, she wasn't at Robot Charlie's. I'd have recognised her."

"So, you had your wicked way with her yet?"

"Iestyn! She only gave birth five days ago!"

"Ah, tell her to get back on the horse…"

"Anyway, it's different. It's not like that."

"Oh, come on. Don't tell me you have a five-foot ten blonde snowed into your house and you haven't tried it on yet!"

"No, you don't understand…" Johnny was getting peeved, but Iestyn and Menna were smirking at each other, enjoying that he was getting so wound up, "…she's beautiful and, well, I love her."

Iestyn blew his mouthful of beer back into his glass and Menna put her drink down. Both were stunned.

"Oh, I know, take the piss, but, well, something's come over me…"

"*That* makes a change…"

"…and I feel so different. She's beautiful, so strong, and I just want to look after her and little Gwennie. I've never felt so, well, so caring and emotional."

"Bloody hell, Johnny," Menna said, "you've got it bad. But, where's the baby's father – surely he'll be back on the scene soon enough when he hears that the baby's been born? Be careful: she'll be all over the place just after having a baby – she may not know what to do and it could all change so quickly."

"I know, but her husband left her a few months ago – he seems a bit of a tosser. Fancy leaving a woman just because she's pregnant?"

"Oh, believe me, it's more common than you think," Menna said, dryly.

"Well you should have seen her – it was wonderful to watch the birth, I feel privileged to have been there… Anyway, I need a piss."

After he'd left the table, Menna and Iestyn looked up at each other, a little wary now they had been left alone.

"Bloody hell, he's got it bad," Iestyn said.

"It'll be good for him. Good for him to think with his heart rather than his cock for a change. Anyway, how are you? Any six-foot women turned up to give birth on your carpet during the snow?"

"No chance. Father pushed the glass out of the kitchen window when he was trying to open it to let some smoke out – he'd left the bacon on – so the house is bloody freezing, or at least even colder than it usually is. A bin bag is *not* a good replacement for glass, even one of those thick ones... How about you?"

"Oh, usual. Mother's in a fret about vet's bills and Father's determined that the barn will get painted before lambing. Been up on a ladder all week in the ice and snow – I ask you! But, I've been all nice and snug in my little bungie, trying to read the paper and ignore the pair of them! I just wish they'd sit still occasionally – or at least let me!"

"Oh, hang on, here's daddy..."

Johnny sat down and reached for his pint. "Oh, and by the way, Tansy's house has been flooded, so she'll have to stay with us until it's fixed!"

"*Surely* you're not supposed to be pleased about that?" Menna said.

"Well, insurance jobs take weeks, don't they?"

"What about her husband? Greg Shackles, isn't it? He's a dab hand at DIY, perhaps he'll help out?" said Iestyn.

"Who is he?" asked Johnny, "I don't think I know him?"

"Bit of a boring bastard, Greg. Works at the builder's yard as a sort of quantity surveyor. I only know him 'cause when we were doing the back room, he helped me with what we needed – spot on he was too. Boring though. Always rattling on about his plasma TV brackets. Didn't mention a five-foot ten blonde wife, though."

"Probably keeping that for his best customers; you don't get that information when you keep asking to split a pack of twenty nails... Well, if you see him again, tell him that his plasma TV will never be working again and that his fancy new brackets are probably rusty." Johnny took a large sip of bitter and smacked his lips together. "God, I must have done something good in a previous life: this feels like Christmas all over again, only a hundred times better!"

179

CHAPTER 26

Stori asgwrn pen llo – calf's skull bone story (an unlikely story)

Johnny and Tansy started getting themselves into a routine. Johnny would get up early to see to the stock, then would bring Tansy a cup of tea in bed and sit on the chair beside her and chat as she fed Gwennie. He would change Gwennie's nappy and pyjamas and then disappear back outside. On his return they would eat breakfast together, then he'd put Gwennie in a sling made from a sheet by Nain and take her outside with him and let Tansy go back upstairs for a sleep.

Gwennie would snuggle up against him with his big coat zipped round the outside of her sling and he would do a few gentle jobs, checking on the cows or chucking a bit of straw around for the dogs.

Sometimes he would take her for a walk down the track, singing *I don't share your greed, the only card I need is the Ace of Spades, the Ace of Spades* or *We Plough the Fields and Scatter*, these being the only two songs he knew nearly all the words to, or he would talk nonsense to her in a silly voice, all in a very un-Johnny-like way. He loved those times, when Gwennie was his sole responsibility and there was no one else but the two of them. He would watch her peeping up at him out of the top of his coat, or he'd sway her gently and share those few special seconds as she couldn't help herself and drifted off to sleep.

Johnny reached the end of the track one morning just in time to see a cloud of smoke coming round the corner. *HONK! HONK! HO—!* Johnny laughed: that was obviously the last of Iestyn's horn again. He could hear Iestyn swearing under his muffled scarf through the stuck-open window.

"This fuckin' truck! That'll be *another* day I have to spend with my head under the fuckin' bonnet!"

Johnny sauntered over, unzipping his coat slightly so that Gwennie's head poked out. "Gwennie, welcome to the world of shit trucks and swearing. All right, mate?"

"This bloody truck – always something falling off or arsing up or… Hey, is that your baby? I'd get out, but I have to climb through the back door at the moment…"

180

"Yes, this is Gwen. Cute, eh?"

"Yeah, she certainly is! And they let you out on your own with her? Make sure you don't leave her somewhere whilst you pop off to service one of your ladies, will you!"

Johnny looked hurt. "Those days are over. I told you that the other night."

"Yeah, but you *always* say that. *This is it! This is the big one! I am a changed man!*"

"Well, this time I mean it."

"You always say that, too. Anyway, how's it going?"

"Great. Tansy's really well, very tired though as this little monkey wakes her mummy up at least three or four times a night, don't you! Yes you do! Your poor mummy, eh Gwennie!" Iestyn looked concerned: it was as if his friend had been possessed by the spirit of Mrs Doubtfire. "But, apart from that, all well. The insurance company is going to fast-track Tansy's house, so I'll go and meet the bloke there tomorrow and then maybe we can start clearing it up. Couple of days' labouring if you want it? Help me clear all the carpets etc out and into a skip? I'll even pay you, how's that?"

"Great, I could do with a bit of cash at the moment; I've got, er, a young lady preparing herself to come on a date with me… I'm amazed really – I dropped some clumsy hint about eating Chinese and she said yes!" Iestyn braced himself for a torrent of laughter, incredulity and then abuse. At least a *Christ, she must be desperate!*

"Hey, that's great news! Is that the woman from the Internet? Fifi or whatever she was called?"

"Lulu."

"Yeah, Lulu. Great. Good for you! About time you settled down, saw someone nice."

"Hang on, I thought you said that you thought she was the one who gave you a blow job in some taxi? And aren't you supposed to tell me that it'd have to be a blind date as I'm so fuckin' ugly that no one who knew me would go anywhere near me, etcetera?"

"Well, probably – to both of those. But, good for you, Iestyn; that sounds really nice."

"Fuck me: I'm off. You've turned Stepford Man on me and I can't cope."

"OK, but come here at nine tomorrow then and we'll go to Tansy's? Good. Right, I need to get madam here home; she'll be needing a feed in about ten minutes. See you tomorrow!"

"Yep, t'da," and Iestyn politely waited until Gwennie was safely out of the way before he started his truck again, otherwise he'd have engulfed her in black fumes: not good for little lungs...

Iestyn watched as his friend swung gently up the track, his arms enclosing the bundle strapped to his chest, protecting her as he crunched through the remaining snow. It just looked so strange. His mate, who usually only ever looked at babies if they were attached to a lactating woman's breast, had been chirping and *caring* about someone else's child. Perhaps it *was* different? Perhaps he really was in love with this Tansy woman? Whatever had happened had happened completely. He hadn't used his phone *once* in Iestyn's presence. Normally he would be constantly checking it, texting, making and receiving the tens of calls a week that were required to juggle his complex social life in the simple quest for lots of sex.

Iestyn had always thought that Johnny would be a serial conqueror of women throughout his life. He didn't seem to have a settling down bone in his penis and that was the only organ he used to plan his life. Yet, here he was declaring his love for someone, looking after their baby while they slept and giving up his seduction pad for their comfort: he'd be wearing slippers next and *then* where would they all be...

Iestyn chugged away along the lane until he reached the village shop. He abandoned his truck alongside three others parked equally haphazardly, paying no attention whatsoever to the parking allocations, considered and marked out carefully at great expense by a man from the council.

He pushed open the door that was covered in posters about events that had happened weeks ago and a little bell signalled his presence. Everything stopped as he entered and the woman behind the till stood with her mouth open. "Perfect timing," she said with a smile. "Now, Iestyn: what is happening with young Brechdan? We need to know." The two other women and the one old farmer clutching a cardboard box full of groceries that effectively wedged him between the narrow

182

shelves nodded. "Is it true that a woman has turned up bearing his love children and that he's getting married next Saturday, otherwise he'll lose the farm? Oh, and how's your mother?"

Iestyn took a deep breath – he should have known that popping quickly into the village shop at a time like this would have been an impossibility…

CHAPTER 27

Y gwyddau yn y ceirch – the geese in the oats (the cat amongst the pigeons)

The afternoon sun had peered in through the windows at Cwmtwrch Farm to a great enough extent to entice Tansy out for a walk. Apart from the distressing visit to her own home, she hadn't been out much. After the initial excitement of the birth, the realities of being a new mother were taking their toll: tiredness, secretions from *everywhere* and a tortuous pain barrier in breastfeeding that wasn't going away. She felt fat, floppy and in need of a haircut.

On the whole, she had felt simple gratitude at staying with Nain, Taid and Johnny. She felt an easy welcome that she didn't seem to be outstaying. They all buzzed around her with their busy daily lives and she slotted in quite happily amongst it all. Gwen senior had a way of absorbing all the work that was in her path and making it look effortless. She was continuously on the move, and even when she was standing and chatting, she would still be doing something: a sticky chair would be wiped, babygrows would be re-arranged on the airer or a pile of something would be moved a stage closer to its eventual destination.

Tansy thought about how her own house would be if she were there at the moment and felt a twinkle of gladness that it was flooded. Such an act of God could never be her fault, so she could happily make the best of it and staying with these wonderful people was certainly the best she could make of anything.

The last few months since Greg had left had been hard. Having a full-time job to do, plus a house and a garden to run had compounded the tiredness of pregnancy. Greg had been a very practical man and his liking had been for everything to be tidied neatly away somewhere – or he would damn well erect another storage solution to solve it.

His garage was a man-shed of fanatic, high-testosterone proportions. Nails peppered the walls, each holding their own tool, and as if drawing around each tool to ensure it wasn't hung on the wrong nail wasn't enough, little labels had been made to fit in the centre of each drawing.

Tansy had spent a miserable afternoon trudging around the shops with him looking for a suitable label printer, and had then been a label widow for two Saturday afternoons on the trot as "lump hammer, wooden handle" had followed on from "claw hammer, metal handle" (which had followed "claw hammer, metal *hnadle*")...

Tansy had always hated those weekend afternoons. It would be a dilemma between storming into the garage, whitewashing all the walls and screaming at him to spend some time with her instead of with his tools, or enjoying the fact that he was out of the way and she could laze around watching Oprah and Trisha on Sky. She knew that the first would probably be better for her marriage in the long run, but the second was actually quite nice in a guilty secret kind of way.

Her feminist side would suggest that she get up and do something exciting herself, follow her own passions. However, her lazy, slovenly side would say, "sod it, I've had a hard week, so I'll just sit and watch people arguing and blame my husband for being dull and boring and not doing something interesting with me at the weekend."

Somehow, after Greg left, although she did the same things that she'd done before on those Saturday afternoons, they were no longer relaxing and a bit cheeky. They were lazy and depressing. Greg's presence in the house had kept the piles of washing at bay, but when he was no longer there to moan about the wet clothes condensating his hallway or grumble about the coats hanging on the newel post at the bottom of the banister – when he'd put up a perfectly functional rack that ensured that every single coat had its own hook (Tansy had sneered and asked whether he wanted to draw round his leather jacket to make sure it went in the right place), things had just slipped and she hadn't the will or the energy to tidy them back up again.

I'm pregnant and my husband has left me, she told herself, *I'm bound to be tired and depressed.* Actually, *I can't be bothered and now it's too much effort to right it all, so I won't do anything*, spoke another more truthful voice. Therefore their neat little end of terrace that had been a place which people would enter and say, "Wow – what a great little house, you've done *so* much!" had now turned into a bit of a pit that people would grimace about and then ask whether she was coping or not.

Therefore, her stay at Cwmtwrch meant that she could leapfrog all that intermediate tidying and sorting and just start again, living like she now intended to: putting things away and keeping on top of the clutter. Hopefully someone would chuck most of her things in a bin bag and then help her to put away new stuff when it arrived courtesy of the insurance company.

Tansy was just starting to pull on her thickest socks when there was a noise from outside in the yard and a bit of giggling. Then Johnny came into the kitchen to fetch her and Gwennie. "Hang on, hang on," clucked Nain as she arrived on the scene with a pile of old sheets and some towels.

"What are you up to now?" smiled Tansy. She loved Johnny's exuberance and his general enjoyment of life; it felt in such contrast to her sluggishness and currently bleak outlook. Perhaps she needed to get a hold of herself a little, show these people that she had a sunnier, more light-hearted side? She didn't want them to think that she was a miserable old bag that moaned about everything and anything, maybe she needed to try a bit harder and show them a bit of the old Tansy: the Tansy that was lively and fun, before getting herself bogged down, marrying the wrong man and getting pregnant with a baby that she would struggle to look after.

She heard a little more rustling and good-natured arguing from outside and then the door was flung open.

"Ta da!" sang Johnny, and Tansy was shocked to see a massive Silver Cross pram standing on the doorstep, up to its rusty axles in the snow.

"Where did you get that?" she laughed.

"*This* was Johnny's when he was a baby," said Nain proudly, running her cloth over the handle. "I knew we should keep it; these things always come in handy eventually!"

Tansy peered inside, not sure that she wanted her beautiful baby to be driven around in something that was probably full of bird shit and had been home to a family of mice for twenty thousand (mouse) generations. However, although a bit rusty here and there, and with a perished hood, it had been thoroughly cleaned and was now lined with a thick pile of bedding. Any hint of decay would be well out of Gwennie's reach.

"Look, I've even oiled the suspension!" Johnny said proudly bouncing it up and down.

"You wouldn't believe the amount of times this was very nearly a go-cart," said Taid quietly from the shadows. Tansy looked at him and could see that he was emotional about the effect that she and Gwennie were having on the apple of his eye.

"Thank you," said Tansy softly, touching Taid's forearm, "thank you so much for all you're doing; I *so* appreciate it!"

"You're welcome, *bach*, you're very welcome," he replied, smiling now with his eyes twinkling at her. "Go on then, get the little lady in her new chariot and take her for her first walk with her mam. It's going to snow again later, so don't be too long."

"Right," said Johnny, clapping his hands together, "let's get going!" He fetched Gwennie from the house and carefully laid her in the pram, making sure that she was all bundled up.

"She'll be fine," said Nain, "these old prams were great at keeping the weather out."

"Watch for mud though," called Taid, heading back towards the barn, "you don't want to get it dirty on its maiden voyage!"

Johnny and Tansy set off across the yard and down the track. Johnny pushed the pram as proud as any biological father would be and the wheels crunched over the snow, its suspension doing a grand job in keeping the worst of the bumps away from Gwennie.

"Are you warm enough?" Johnny asked Tansy, who was shuffling along a little gingerly in Taid's old wellies with one of Johnny's coats pulled over her own.

"Yes, thanks," she smiled, "still a bit sore though, so don't go too fast!"

"We'll go as slow as you like!"

They rounded a corner and stopped as a break in the trees opened onto a beautiful vista of snow-clad mountains with tiny little dark patches dotted across them, signifying other farms.

Johnny felt overwhelmed. He was seeing the beauty of the place with fresh eyes. The view that so often was overlooked and taken for granted, coupled with the fact that he was walking next to the woman he loved and her baby, that *he* was pushing in a pram, made him feel like skipping, like declaring his happiness to the whole world with a loud cry.

His feelings were different from lust. Usually he would take advantage of such a break in proceedings, to perhaps take his lady of the moment by the shoulders as he stood behind her to point out something – anything – on the horizon. His lady would more often than not lean back into him and then he would enclose her in his arms, kiss her on the cheek and then her mouth, then a gentle squeeze of her breast would ensure her becoming putty in his hands.

The more adventurous ones would then go with it, sometimes then grabbing his hand and leading him into the woods, or the field, or the barn or, unfortunately, sometimes behind a burger van. He would let them feel as if they were being a bit cheeky and had taken him by surprise, protesting a bit and saying things like, "Here? Are you mad? Someone'll see us!" and then allow himself to led away. They would do the business, he'd be all overwhelmed as if he'd been enlightened by a powerful seductress, and the door would be left open for inexperienced little Johnny to be given another time he wouldn't forget on a different occasion.

The less-adventurous ones would wriggle away, usually giggling a little protestation and he would have to bide his time, be a little more inventive.

Other times he misjudged it completely and would get a "Gerroff me," snarled at him and occasionally even a slap. Then he would act a little wounded, apologise profusely and change the subject.

However, to pull a stunt like that on Tansy seemed preposterous. It would be crass and sleazy. Tansy should be wooed, looked after and loved. One day, surely, the inevitable would happen, but it would be in a field of flowers or on a goose down quilt in front of a log fire and it would be beautiful and…

Suddenly he was aware that Tansy was standing behind him. She had her head resting gently on his shoulder as she pointed at something across the valley. Johnny froze, not sure what was going on.

"What's that?" she asked, her voice husky in his ear and her breath soft on his skin.

"What?"

"That little brown barn thing over there."

"It's a barn..." he replied and as he turned his head to gauge whether that was what she meant, she wrapped her arms around him, swung herself round and planted a big snogger of a kiss on his lips, grabbed his crotch and squeezed.

"Whoa! Whoa – hang on," Johnny fought for air and wriggled his groin away from the kneading. "Hang on a minute – just – I'll just check Gwennie – what was – hang on – phew."

He didn't know what to think. It had been wonderful, but no, he wasn't ready for this; it wasn't supposed to happen this way! How could she have just grabbed his cock like that? What was she thinking of? Did it mean that she loved him? Was *that* what that had been about?

Tansy looked at him and laughed. "Sorry, got a bit carried away by the moment – you know. Actually, don't know what I was thinking – my bits are like chopped liver still; I'd be hospitalised if I tried anything now! Anyway, is Gwennie warm enough? Perhaps we'd better go back, yeah?"

"Er, yeah, it *is* a bit cold," he stammered.

"Here, let me push for a while. It's a nice pram isn't it? I'd not gotten around to buying one yet – *so* expensive you know. Thought I'd wait and see what sort I could get away with, but, yeah, this one's nice – fill my house though! I'd have to park it in the lounge!"

Johnny stood and watched as Tansy walked, still a little cautiously, up the track. His mouth was wide open. She might have well have jumped up into the air, turned into an overripe tomato, squished herself all over her face, then bounced away laughing for all the sense it had made.

"Tansy – hang on..." he trotted after her and soon caught up. "Tansy," he puffed, out of breath from the exertion of such a shock, "what happened then...it was..."

"Oh, sorry, Johnny," she laughed, dismissing it as if she'd made a small *faux pas* by pointing out a stain on his wellie boot instead. "Got a bit carried away! It happens sometimes, doesn't it? Well, it does to me anyway! Anyway, d'ya know, I'm *starving*! Even this little walk has made me *so* hungry!"

Johnny had been brushed off, plain and simple and he didn't know what to do. He'd played games with people before and it had all been *fun*, hadn't it? This wasn't fun. He was in love and when people are in love, others shouldn't toy with their emotions.

Had it meant that Tansy…loved him? Would an "in love" person grab at someone's crotch like that? No, an in love person would stroke his hair and whisper sweet things to him. So, she wasn't in love with him then. Surely that wasn't just *lust*? It couldn't have been, could it? Just a poorly executed attempt to pull, to have a fumble on the track, a rummage in the snow? But it couldn't have been – because he loved her and therefore it shouldn't work like that…

They arrived back, Tansy still three paces in front of Johnny and chattering about some snowman she'd made as a child. Nain came running out to meet them from the barn. "Oh good, you're back. Johnny, love, can you go in and help Taid – he's got a bullock that's cut his leg on a sheet of corrugated. He can't get to look at it as the beggar won't keep still. Can you help him – just hold his head?"

"Course," he grunted and headed off for the barn, relieved to have an excuse to get out of the way.

"How was your walk, *bach*?" he heard Nain say as she walked back into the house with Tansy and little Gwen.

"Lovely thanks – just so nice to be up and about, and *such* a beautiful day!"

CHAPTER 28

Chwilen yn ei ben – a beetle in his head (obsessed with some matter or a bee in his bonnet)

Iestyn arrived at Johnny's farm at nine o'clock, as agreed. "Morning!" he shouted as he clomped straight into the kitchen, taking off his wellie boots and slinging them into the corner. "Mornin', Nain, mornin', Taid. How are you?"

"Good thanks, boy. You?"

"Yes, good thanks. And this must be Tansy?" he said as he settled himself at the table and reached for some toast.

"Hello," she smiled.

"And Gwennie, we meet again!" The others laughed as Gwennie stared blankly at him.

"She's sure she recognises you," said Tansy, "come on, Gwen, say good morning!"

A mug of tea was pushed towards Iestyn and he took it gratefully in his large chapped hands. "Thank you, oh, it's good to be warm again. That bloody truck of mine and its *bloody* window!"

"Still stuck?" asked Taid.

"Well, I did take the door apart and got it to go up, but then Dad took the bloody thing out again, met John the Cwm, wound it down for a chat and – bang – stuck *again*. And only the coldest winter for about forty years…"

"Yes, since 1947," Nain muttered.

"No, 1987 was colder," Taid replied.

"No, it was on the news, 1947."

"Shall we go?" Johnny stood up and his chair pushed back with a scrape.

"Oh," Iestyn said, still buttering some toast, "er, OK." He raised his eyebrows at Nain, slurped at his tea and quickly slopped some marmalade onto his toast. Johnny grabbed his jacket from behind the door and shrugged himself into it.

"Have you got the keys?" said Tansy, half getting to her feet, "they're in my bag…"

Johnny found her bag on a peg and brought it to her in silence. "Just get them out," she said, "I don't mind," but instead Johnny handed her the bag and waited for her to find them.

"Thanks, Johnny, I really appreciate this. You too, Iestyn." Tansy seemed unsure of herself, as if she had asked one favour too many for Johnny's liking.

"You're welcome," Iestyn said, "no problem at all."

"Yep, but we'd better get going; bloke's coming at ten." Johnny took the keys and headed for the door.

Iestyn followed his friend marching out into the yard, "Oi, slow down!" he called with a mouthful of toast. "What's up?"

"We'll go in my truck; it'll be warmer."

"Johnny, m'n, what's goin' on?"

"Forget it. Let's just go, can we?"

They drove in silence for a few minutes, Johnny staring straight ahead, his eyebrows knitted together. Iestyn faffed about in the passenger seat, removed his rigger boot and adjusted his ruffled sock, drummed a rhythm on his knee and then started fiddling with the stereo. Eventually he couldn't bear it any longer.

"What's up, mate?"

"She kissed me." They spoke together.

"Oh." Iestyn was confused. "Isn't that a – a good thing from someone you're supposed to be in love with?"

"She kissed me – on a whim. On an impulse. In a sleazy, chancer kind of way. As if, well, as if she got a good response it would be a bonus and if she didn't, well, who cares..." He turned to Iestyn, who was still struggling to understand Brechdan's reaction, "Don't you get it?" he said, his face full of angst, "that's the kind of thing that *I* would do, if *I* felt it might be worth a try and wasn't that bothered if it went wrong. Can't you see why that makes it mean *nothing*?"

Iestyn digested this for a few seconds, then burst into laughter, slapping the dashboard in delight. "Johnny Brechdan! At last you've met your match! Your soulmate: that's fantastic!"

At last Johnny managed a smile, "Well, not really. It's made me realise what a cock I've been! Oh God, I'd have been chuffed as buns if this had happened with *anyone* else, but just this once, I'd wanted it to be special, y' know?"

Iestyn was pleased to see that the frown was now gone, but he knew that his friend was still in turmoil. "Look, mate, just because *you* do these things in that way, it doesn't mean that Tansy does." Johnny looked interested, so he carried on. "She might have desperately wanted to kiss you, but didn't know how to or just got carried away by the moment and then when it didn't work, got all embarrassed. I think the moral here is not to judge everyone else by *your* dodgy standards!"

"Yeah," Johnny said, looking brighter and nodding in agreement. "Perhaps she did want to, but didn't know how to, so she did it badly."

"That'll be it. Have a chat with her when you get back; she'll probably be feeling sick at the response you gave her this morning. Put her out of her misery and let her know you're cool about it."

Johnny nodded again. "Cheers, mate, I will. Anyway – did you hear about Olwen Richards turning her truck over? On her way home from Daniel Hargreaves' place apparently? John Richards has gone *mad*. Said that the truck was his favourite…"

Iestyn laughed and they chattered away as they normally would until they pulled up outside Tansy's end of terrace cottage. "OK, here we are," Johnny said, and they jumped out and headed for the door.

Tansy was sitting in an old rocking chair by the fire. It had been brought down from Nain and Taid's bedroom for her. "Johnny's mother used to feed Johnny sat in this chair," Nain had said as she whipped a duster around the base of the rails, "said it was good for her back."

Tansy had thanked her gratefully and rocked gently back and fore using her socked toe propped against the Rayburn door.

She felt sick to her stomach. She'd gone and arsed it all up *again*. *Why* did she do it? She couldn't just sit back and gauge a situation like other people did, she always jumped in, did something silly, and then had to regret it later. And now she'd upset Johnny. The poor bloke was only being kind because she'd given birth right in front of him. What on earth would a bright bloke like him want with her – recently separated from her husband and with a baby that would never be his?

She'd been ridiculous – and now he was offended and although he had still gone to help with her house, it would be only because he couldn't wait for her to get out of his bed – and his house. He'd been so kind and wonderful, he and his lovely family, and then she'd gone and thrown it all back in his face with a naff grope that was better-suited to the back of a rugby club, rather than a walk with her new baby on a crisp afternoon. All she'd been trying to do was to look all light-hearted and fun, but instead had been crass and immature, like a teenager overcome with feelings of excitement that they didn't yet know how to contain.

What would happen now? She wouldn't be able to stay if he were trying to avoid her – and he couldn't have left the house any quicker that morning – it would be unfair on him and on Nain and Taid. She'd have to go home – perhaps if she could get the heating fixed, the rest could be sorted around her? It wasn't what she had had in mind when she and Greg had first talked about starting a family. She should've been sat next to him on a sofa, not sat on her own in a damp house with no carpets.

A tear slid down her cheek, then another one. She wiped it from Gwennie's sleeping face and felt in her pocket for a tissue.

"All right, lovely?" came a gentle voice from beside her and a cup of tea was placed on the edge of the Rayburn. Tansy looked up and gave a watery smile. "Thanks, Gwen. I'm sorry, I'm just a bit weepy today."

"That's OK, love, being a mum takes its toll on you." Gwen senior sat on the sofa next to her and sipped at her own drink. She never did this and Tansy knew that she'd come to listen if she wanted to talk.

"Oh, Gwen," she sobbed, "I've really messed up."

"Come on, love, it can't be that bad?"

"It is – you see, the baby, it – she – isn't my husband's, she isn't Greg's – that's why he left me. We'd been trying for years, but nothing. I announced that I was pregnant just as he was about to read me his letter from the clinic that told him that he had no active sperm. He knew straight away, and I knew that he knew, but we carried on with the charade for a bit, but it couldn't work and he left me a few months later. Said that he couldn't bring up another man's child and that…" Tansy started to sob, "…I was a whore and he could never trust me again…"

Gwen took her round the shoulders and hugged her tight. "Oh, my poor girl, you're not the first and you certainly won't be the last…"

"And now," said Tansy, wiping her nose on her sleeve, "just when it all starts to look up and I'm staying with you wonderful people and Johnny's so kind and, and lovely, I go and make a silly pass at him and mess that up too! I just can't seem to help myself!" She buried her face in her free hand and sobbed.

"Oh dear, I thought Johnny was a little quiet today. Don't worry, you can sort these things out. Talk to him; Johnny's a straightforward boy, he'll understand. And to be perfectly honest with you, I am sure that young Johnny will know *exactly* where you are coming from if you see what I mean... Now, dry your eyes and how about helping me peel a few potatoes for lunch?"

"Of course," Tansy sniffed and she took a deep breath. She wasn't so sure that Nain would think it all quite so harmless if she knew that yesterday she'd grabbed her grandson's cock uninvited and nine months previously, well, best not to even think about that...

Iestyn came in from the garage at the side of the house with a handful of tools. "Hey, it's bloody marvellous out there – tools to die for and all so neatly hung up. I'm going to have to get that Greg bloke to come and sort our end barn – we've reached the stand-at-the-door-and-throw stage!"

"Bloody Bevans... Now, what have you got?"

"I've got two claw hammers, one medium and one large, to pull up carpets with, a chisel in case the lino's stuck down and one of those electronic measuring things – just because I wanted to see how it works... Look, if I point it at you, right? Now move – see? Different measurement! The ceiling to the floor is...two-metres ten and in the hallway to the upstairs is..."

The sound of a key being turned in the front door made Iestyn jump. "Shit," he said and stuffed the measurer in the hall dresser's drawer.

"That's the wrong place," sniggered Johnny, "it's supposed to go on hook 9B!" They were giggling like schoolboys when the door was pushed open and a tall pale man with short brown hair peered in, frowning as soon as he saw them.

"Hello?" he said suspiciously. "Are you the men from the insurance company? Sorry I'm late, I got delayed by an accident on the roads. I'm Greg Shackles, I part-own the house..."

194

"No, no," Johnny said, sobering up as sincerely as he could, "you've just missed him. I'm Johnny Harris and this is Iestyn Bevan. We've been looking after Tansy and came here on her behalf to let the insurance man in? I'm sorry, I didn't know you were coming, otherwise I'd have told him to wait and let you deal with him."

The man looked peeved, but that was probably his look, anyway, he certainly looked comfortable with it. "Well, actually, I knew nothing about any of this, but the insurance company phoned my mobile to check some details – I am still the policyholder after all – and that's how I knew that *my* property had been flooded."

"Well," started Johnny, "in fairness to Tansy, I think she's been a bit overwhelmed with everything – you know she's had the baby now, don't you? She meant to tell you about the flood, I expect it slipped her mind."

"Yes, I am sure that it did," Greg said as he walked past Iestyn and Johnny and went to look in the lounge. "But there tends to be a lot of things that happen to slip our Tansy's mind…" He peered quickly into the kitchen and tutted at the sight of all the rubbish in bin bags on the floor.

Iestyn could see that Johnny was about to rise to the bait and pulled at his arm with a warning glance. Johnny made do with mouthing *wanker* behind Greg's back as he walked back past them and started up the stairs.

"Bit of a mess isn't it?" said Iestyn, following him up, "but not *too* bad, the insurance guy said. It'll need new electrics and all that, but luckily, as the water was clean and wasn't sitting for too long, it shouldn't need a complete re-furb of joists etc." Greg grunted again, clearly not happy with Iestyn's prattling. He made a derisory check of his old bedroom, the nursery and the bathroom.

Then he opened the door to the study and gave a cry of despair. "Bloody Tansy! I see she managed to put all *her* stuff up out of the way, but *my* stuff – oh no – let's leave it in a puddle until it ruins!"

Iestyn was moved to one side by Johnny to see Greg standing with a pile of *Practical DIY* magazines in his hands that he had gathered from behind the door.

"Look, *mate*," Johnny said, clearly struggling to keep his cool. "Tansy came back here four days after giving birth – in our kitchen, actually – to find her home was flooded. I don't think the first thing on her mind was to save your wank mags…"

"They're not wank mags, they're …"

"She was knackered and sore and trying to make a home for her new baby – *your* new baby – and…"

"*My* new baby?"

"Yes, your…"

"Oh no. Not *mine*. Is that what she told you? That I abandoned her, pregnant with my child, because what? Because she couldn't cook my eggs properly?"

Iestyn could see it was all getting a bit heated and moved between the two men. "OK both, let's calm down shall we? Greg – Johnny didn't mean to interfere in your and Tansy's business, and Johnny – Greg wasn't criticising you, now…"

However, Greg wasn't listening to Iestyn. His pale blue eyes were fastened on Johnny and his lips had been pressed into a thin line. "No, I'm not having this," he said. "I don't care who you are – Tansy's new boyfriend is it? Probably. That would be about right: I'm long gone as far as Tansy is concerned, bloody long gone."

"OK, OK, that's enough," Iestyn put his arms out to keep them from making any move towards each other.

Greg butted his hands away, "It's fine, I'm going; there's nothing for me here any more," he snorted and then pushed past them both. At the top of the stairs he stopped and turned. "But I'll ask you this – if you went to a dance, against your better judgment maybe, with your wife, the woman you loved, and while you were getting her a fuckin' burger at the end, she was off shagging some bloke behind the burger van, what would *you* do? Would *you* bring up Burger Boy's baby? No! Well, nor would I…" and he stormed off down the stairs leaving Iestyn and Johnny staring at each other open-mouthed.

Iestyn felt the penny drop in his own mind and he could then see the *exact* moment on Johnny's face when his did too.

"Burger Boy?"

"Bacon Sandwich Lil?"

"Fuck me: I'm a dad."

They ripped up a few carpets and dumped them in the skip outside. The work was half-hearted and quiet. They decided to return and finish the upstairs another day. Then they drove home in silence, Iestyn at the wheel. Every now and then Johnny shook his head and said, "Fuck me." Iestyn's face was a picture. Stony, stony blank and then a little snigger would creep to the corner of his mouth, his nostrils would twitch with the effort of not bursting and then he would recover himself and carry on looking straight ahead, trying to be there for his friend if he were needed, but to keep his comments to himself if he weren't.

As they approached Johnny's track, Iestyn turned to his friend. "What'ya going to do?"

"Dunno. Go to bed I'spect."

"What, forever?"

"Maybe."

Iestyn wracked his brains. "Perhaps – perhaps it's fate, you know, the woman you've fallen in love with and the baby you've fallen in love with, well, perhaps…"

"Iestyn?"

"Yeah?"

"Shut the fuck up, will you?"

"OK."

"Actually, drop me here on the track can you? If anyone asks, say I'm just checking something, yeah?"

"OK."

"Oh, and Iestyn?"

"Yeah?"

"Keep it to yourself will you? This is serious stuff; it won't do anyone any good if this gets out – me, Tansy, Gwennie, *anyone*."

"'Course, mate. Just between you and me."

"See you."

"Yeah, see you. And shout if you need anything – you know, a chat or something."

"Iestyn, I shagged a woman behind a burger van. She was pissed, I was pissed. There's a baby. What is there to chat about?"

Johnny climbed out and jumped into the slush, sending a pile of it shooting up the inside of each leg. Iestyn ground the truck off up the track, parping the feeble horn as he went. Johnny put his hand up in salute to the disappearing vehicle and then sank into the snow on the bank. He put his head into his hands and burst into tears.

He was still sitting there when Iestyn drove back past in his own truck.

"All right?" he called from the already-open window.

Johnny's hand went up, but his head remained down. Iestyn would probably have managed a beep of his horn as he rumbled past, but there was instead the sound of a curse and the air stayed silent.

Eventually Johnny hauled himself to his feet, wiped the snow from his behind and started plodding home.

What was he going to say to her?

Dunno.

If Gwennie was his, should he tell her he knew?

Dunno.

Should he say nothing, let Tansy take Gwennie home and let things develop in their own way?

Dunno.

Should he propose to Tansy, formally adopt Gwennie and all live happily ever after?

Don't-bloody-know.

As he shuffled slowly through the slushy snow, Johnny Brechdan thought back to that seemingly fateful night. It had been a good day at the Cefn Mawr Show. He, Iestyn and another lad, Dai, had been in the beer tent early then had watched the trotting races in the afternoon. They had put twenty quid on an outsider and won nearly £500 in return: it had been a *fantastic* day!

As the night approached, they had joined the throngs of youngsters heading to the adjoining farm and to the dance in the large barn. There, they'd drunk beer in plastic cups, danced, drunk a line of shots, danced some more and fallen over in the puddles of beer on the floor as a line of drunk young farmers shimmied across the RSJs above them. It had been the best sort of night that blokes could have. There were women around them, but not *with* them and they had stayed a group of lads, laughing, joking and necking drinks, all won by a twenty-pound bet.

There had been this woman near them: that much he remembered. She was tallish and wore a Viking helmet with two blonde plaits sticking out of each side, and she had been looking at him. She had been dancing with another man, but she'd been looking at him. Her face had been painted with a Welsh flag on each cheek, and she had been looking at him... Apparently, that had been the bit when he'd started doing the can-can...

The details of the rest of Johnny's night had been filled in, with great hilarity, by the others. The band finished playing and the lights went on, huge spotlights lighting up the fact that the barn was no longer a suave night club, but was instead a big old barn, its dance floor being a concrete slab, stained by animal piss and covered in stamped on plastic glasses. Red, sweaty, shiny people stood and chanted, "More! More! More!" but the band stuck to their guns and left the stage – now recognisable as a large flatbed trailer.

Apparently the Viking had been standing next to Johnny and had tickled his pink shiny face with her plait as her companion shouted for the band to return.

Then she had pinched a sip of his drink. Then she had apparently pinched his bum. So he had pinched hers.

According to Iestyn, they had then held hands, the Viking walking in front of Johnny all the way through the crowd. She had been talking to her partner who was in front of her, whilst doing the conga with Johnny, as subtly as pissed people can do anything amongst a crowd of a thousand other hot, sweaty, drunk, horny youngsters who were also teetering on the edge of fucking their lives up.

"I wanna burger!" the Viking had shouted and her companion had grumbled something back and headed off as quickly as he could so as to beat hundreds of other hungry people to the one burger van.

As the man had disappeared into the throng, the Viking had turned and kissed Johnny, a passionate, no holds barred type of a kiss that rendered him helpless, his arms flailing behind him as he was tipped backwards.

Apparently Iestyn and Dai had then left him and his new friend and headed off in the quest for food themselves – bacon sandwiches. Out of the kindness of their hearts, they had also bought one for him and then had hunted for him, eventually stumbling across him and the

Viking, courtesy of someone's head lamps, rutting in the wet grass behind the burger van. His buttocks were apparently brilliant white and going far too fast. Her breasts were apparently magnificent. The small crowd that stood round them were cheering them on, as being sixteen-year-old drunks with little sexual finesse, they had no thoughts about quality, but were just pleased that the agricultural show was continuing even further into the night.

Iestyn and Dai had thoughtfully held onto Brechdan's bacon sandwich until he surfaced.

The Viking disappeared quickly after the finale, and Johnny sorted his trousers out, told the crowd to fuck off or he'd kill them and then came to claim his prize. He had not been well in the back of the truck that they'd hitched a lift in that night and Iestyn said that they had made the right choice by sticking his head out of the rear door all the way. As it was often said: it had not been his finest hour.

However, it had now become clear that that particular hour had had repercussions. It had caused him embarrassment and a great deal of ribbing: *that* he'd known about. But far more than that, it had caused Gwennie – beautiful, innocent, tiny Gwennie. He'd been so drawn to her, *so* much more so than any rational explanation could have reasoned. The reason was now clear – of *course* he was drawn to her: Mother Nature had made it that way.

As her biological father, Mother Nature needed him to be drawn to her, to love her and protect her. It was his duty. No child would ever ask to be brought into the world thanks to two drunks shagging in the spotlights of a beat-up old Subaru. When she came to know about such things – and aside from the "Yuck, my mum had sex?" phase, she would prefer to know that she had been a planned for, much wanted baby, conceived by two people who loved each other. Not as a time-filler for two drunks as an harassed eighteen-year-old flipped cheap burgers and burned water-filled bacon.

A text message bleeped and Johnny instinctively reached for his phone. Hannah: what did she want? *Hi, I'm rd yr parts later and wd love 2 b round yr parts* ☺. He clicked it off, annoyed at the distraction – yet, this was the life that he'd be giving up. The happy life of a single man, looked after at home, self-employed, good friends and women, women everywhere!

He *could* simply take Tansy and Gwen home, tell Iestyn that Tansy said her dates meant Gwen belonged to a guy she'd been having an affair with for years and quietly shut the door on the responsibility of it all. Then he could text Hannah and get her back round his parts and return to the easy, uncomplicated, orgasmic existence that had been so simple before Tansy Shackles had shouted across his yard on that cold dark night.

He looked up and could see the farm in the distance – only a field and a half's worth of track to go: he needed to slow down…

Right. Tansy, what of Tansy?

Two days ago, he'd been telling everyone how much he loved Tansy. He loved her strength, her beautiful blue eyes, her uninhibited laugh and the way her face lit up when he walked into the room. He loved to sit next to her and just absorb her contentment when she was feeding Gwennie and playing with her tiny fingers. Need that change simply because of what he knew?

Her kiss the day before had rocked him, but only because it wasn't exactly how he wanted it and precisely the time of his choosing; he considered that he did know best when it came to timing in seduction, and that had been a poor choice. However, he felt he was over that. Iestyn had actually been right for once. It may not have happened with a beautiful sun setting over a distant hill, or as a precursor to making delicious love in fields of wild flowers on a summer's day, but he was fine with it: he was a big boy now and had to accept that women did these things when they wanted to too.

So, it was back to the love that was Burger Boy and Bacon Sandwich Lil. There was no doubt that it was karma for all the times that he had planned, chivvied and manipulated situations to give his happy-go-lucky penis a good work-out. Any one of those women might well have the right to feel a bit miffed to know how they had been primed and moulded until spontaneous things happened.

When they had gotten a bit keen, they would have been upset to know that he hadn't really been busy, or that his truck hadn't been off the road. Then, when they were called back for a final curtain call, it hadn't been because Johnny still loved them after all, it would have been because he felt enough water had gone under the bridge for them to have mainly gotten over him – and he fancied another shag.

It was therefore right and proper that the woman he actually had fallen for was the kind of woman whom he hadn't needed to manipulate and indeed, if anything, she had grabbed his bottom first. Yes, he had spent his whole adult life yearning for tall Vikings to drag him off into the night, and now that it had happened, it couldn't be right to claim the twisted moral high ground and object.

However, he thought, if he did the decent thing, the possibility of future dalliances behind burger vans, in wild flower meadows, whatever, were over. On cue, his phone bleeped again, *Hey! Bob's away & I need someone to lay my carpet – fancy?* Ah, Harri, beautiful, beautiful Harri, short, round and *full* of surprises!

Nain and Taid were always on at him to find a nice girl and settle down. "You're missing out, love," Nain would say. "Your cock'll go septic and fall off," Taid would warn. He knew that they would be more than happy to move out of the farmhouse and into a nice new bungalow somewhere on the land and let him run the farm, but he didn't feel ready for such responsibility yet; he was too busy enjoying himself, wasn't he?

He smiled at a few memories and his step perked up as he reached the farm gate. He knew what to do. He'd made his decision and as he wriggled with the catch on the gate and shouldered it open, he knew that, for him, it was the right one.

Louisa climbed the stairs proudly holding the keys, attached to a shiny new key ring, to her flat. However, she was a bit worried that she wouldn't know which door to go through. Esther had insisted on seeing the place that her daughter was now supposedly "living" in, but in which she'd only ever spent about half an hour. Louisa, in a fit of trying to improve her relationship with her mother, had offered to give her a tour.

Louisa put her key into the door of 40B and gave it a twist. And then another one. She gave the door a shove. She could feel her father behind her itching to get involved, but that made her more determined to get it right herself. After another couple of attempts, she gave up in frustration. "Oh, this is ridiculous. The agents must have given me the wrong key."

"Well it's always let me in," said David and took the keys from her and reached past her scowling face to open it smoothly and with only a hint of smugness.

"Right," said Louisa, trying to regain control of the tour, "we'll start in the lounge, I think," and she motioned her mother to the lounge door.

"Very nice, Louisa," said her mother, peering in, "very nice."

"What? It's horrible! Needs a good lick of paint before anyone could say that about it!" Louisa laughed, still in the hallway.

"Well, it looks lovely to me," said Esther.

"Yes, well, I think that this wall here will probably need another coat, but the rest have had two and I think it's made a real difference," David said as he walked past his daughter. "Look here, Esther, it's got those curtain rails that we used to have – you remember? In our first flat?"

"Oh yes, so it does! And, I do like that fireplace – you said that the landlord will put a new fire in there didn't you?"

"Yes, it's going in next Thursday; I've asked for one of those real-flame effect ones? And look, these shelves will be really handy; I've firmed them up a bit – some of them were a bit ropey, but they're nice and strong now…"

Louisa, slightly confused, followed them in and was amazed by the transformation. "Yes, yes they are, aren't they? That's what I thought it would be best to do," she said, trying to get back into the action, "anyway, come and look out here, Mum."

"Hang on, let me see the view from your lounge. Oh, look, David, you can see the park from here; it's nice isn't it?"

"Yes, and the market place – that'll be nice to watch on market day?"

"What, cows?" said Louisa, obviously now bored, "lovely." She left the room and called her mother after her to see the bedrooms. "It's a bit cold in here," she said, rubbing her arms with her gloved hands, "shall we go and get that coffee we were talking about?"

"Hold on!" Esther said. "Let me see the kitchen; it'll be where you'll be spending most of your time, believe me!"

Louisa rolled her eyes. She doubted it.

"Well, this is nice enough, isn't it, Louisa? Bit small, but plenty big enough for one, or for a couple?"

Louisa shrugged. "Dunno really, bit of a state still. Look at the cupboard doors – they're all on the gimp, and see, they didn't even bother to clean up after the last person – chips all over the floor! It looks like someone was rolling round in their chips, rather than eating them. Urgh!"

David dropped to his knees and gathered them up. "Sorry, they were mine. I had some the other night when I was painting – hungry work!" He scuttled to the bin and dropped them in, sheepishly wiping his hands on his jeans to a frown from Esther. "But, anyway, Louisa," he said, "never mind a few chips, *surely* you're pleased with the work that I've done? Surely it looks a hundred times better than it did at first?"

Louisa could feel them both looking at her. Her father had spent night after night in the place and she *was* grateful, but she just, well, she just wasn't that interested. However, she knew that a wrong move at this point could mean the work grinding to a close. She smiled. "Course it is! Thanks, Dad, you've done a great job. Come on, let me say thank you by treating you to that coffee…"

Johnny walked into the kitchen with a big smile on his face. However, it was soon replaced with concern as Nain came scuttling across the room with a pile of washing in her arms, to meet him.

"Have you seen her?" she said, puffing with the exertion of her trot.

"Who?"

"Tansy, of course. She's gone home!"

"Home? What home?"

"Hers. I hoped that she'd found you still there, or that you'd pass her on the way. I saw Iestyn drop the truck off and assumed that she was with you?"

"No, we had to detour via the shop for more pasties for Iestyn; she must have passed us then. How can she go home – there's no water or heating?"

Nain was looking close to tears, "Oh, I know, I know. I tried to stop her, but she wouldn't have it…"

"Greg?"

"Yes, he phoned and she got all upset and said that she would leave straightaway and that it would all be fine – apparently she told him that they would start again and be a *proper* family – that's what she said, a proper family."

Johnny opened the door and started running towards his truck, "Open the gate, Nain, I'll go and get her!"

"Good boy, love, you bring her back. She can't last without clean water with a baby, they'll get ill, if they don't freeze first…"

Johnny crunched the truck into reverse and with a frown of concentration, he bumped through the gate held open by his waving grandmother. He looked in the rear-view mirror and saw her wiping a tear from her eye with her cuff; poor Nain, she'd grown so fond of Tansy and Gwennie, it'd be awful if it ended like this.

For the second time that day, he pulled up outside Tansy's house. Good, her car was there – she was still in the house. He saw a very clean Focus parked perfectly parallel to the pavement – that must be Greg's. Damn, what should he do? Be calm? Forceful? Reasonable?

He knocked tentatively at the door: there was no answer.

He could hear raised voices inside, then the sound of Gwennie crying. He knocked again, louder this time. Still nothing.

He ran to the window and peered in, the curtains still being tied in a knot. He could see Gwennie sitting, howling, in her car seat on the sitting room floor, but there was no sign of Tansy or Greg.

Panic rose within him – that was *his* baby. If no one else was going to protect her, then *he* must. He tried the door, but it was locked. Johnny searched for something to smash through the pane of glass next to the Yale lock when he remembered – he had a key!

He grabbed it from his jacket pocket in the truck and crashed in through the door. "Tansy!" he cried, "Tansy, it's me!"

The shouting stopped and two faces peered, confused, out of the kitchen door. Tansy's was swollen with crying and Greg's was white with rage. "What the hell are you doing back here?" he roared. "Get out of my house!"

"Johnny?" shouted Tansy, then she made a break and ran to get Gwennie from the lounge.

"Tansy, you can't stay here – come home with me!" He walked towards Tansy, who now stood by the lounge door, swinging Gwen gently in her car seat to soothe her.

205

"Whoa – hang on," shouted Greg, his face now contorted with anger, but neither Johnny nor Tansy were paying any attention.

"Come home," Johnny said as gently as he could, "come and live with us… Come on, we'll take care of you – you and Gwennie…"

"Now, hang on, hang on," Greg stormed between them. "What's Lover Boy doing here – in my house? Geddout you tosser!" He strode towards Johnny and started pushing him towards the door, but the eleven-stone quantity surveyor wasn't a match for the fifteen-stone farmer. Big cows sometimes tried to shove Johnny, but never if he didn't want them to…

Johnny was being inconvenienced by the man, but was looking over Greg's shoulder at Tansy, standing sobbing with the baby. "Please, Tansy, come home; we miss you, we want you back. *I* want you back!"

Greg gave up on Johnny as his daps were sliding about on the damp chipboard floor and he turned back to Tansy.

"Tell him, Tansy, tell him to get lost! I thought *we* were going to be a family – that's what we said, wasn't it? Tell Lover Boy to fuck off back to the shit-hole that he came from…"

Johnny took a deep breath – shit-hole? Lover Boy? He could feel his fist beginning to clench. He hadn't hit anyone properly since fifth form when Del Roberts had called him a sheepshagger with a small cock, but he was beginning to feel that it might happen pretty soon.

However, then he saw Tansy's eyes, desperately trying to decide what to do, looking from man to man, as if clocking them both and weighing up the situation. Some wisdom inside Johnny's guts which had never really made an appearance before, told him that if he laid out Greg, then he, Johnny, would become the bad guy and Tansy would have to choose Greg, if only to stop the bleeding.

Instead, he took a deep breath and tried to calm down. "OK, OK, this has all gotten a bit out of hand, yeah?" Greg turned to him – he'd obviously been expecting a punch rather than a chat. "I think we need to hear what Tansy has to say?" Tansy looked up, she'd taken Gwennie out of the car seat and the crying had stopped as she cuddled her to her shoulder as if for a buffer between her own sanity and the insanity that had erupted around her. Johnny could see that she was in no state to be making such decisions or sorting anything out.

"Tansy," barked Greg, "can we just get this twat out of here? He comes barging into our house, shouting the odds – and for your information, Lover Boy, she *is* at home. Look, it was very good of you to help her, but we're OK now – we can sort ourselves out, we don't need you sticking your oar, or your penis, in."

Johnny saw Tansy looking a little miffed at what Greg had just said, and so he took his chance. "Tansy," he said as gently as he could, "I came here this afternoon to take you back to us – to me. We miss you, *I* miss you and little Gwennie…"

"*Gwennie?* That'll be changing, that's for sure…" snorted Greg.

"…you see, I love you, I have done since I first clapped eyes on you – you're so strong, so beautiful and little Gwennie – *and she's fuckin' staying Gwennie*," Johnny spat as an aside to Greg – "well, I'll treat her as my own. I don't care who the father really is, or how she was conceived, if you'll let me, I'll treat her as my own – I love her as if she was mine already…"

"Oh, for God's sake!" Greg cried, his hands up in the air. "What the hell is going on? What's this, bloody Jerry Springer? What – you give birth on this bloke's carpet to God only knows whose child, and three weeks later he loves you and wants to bring up baby as his own? Give me strength!" Greg laughed slightly manically, as if it were all getting a bit much for him. "Go home, Lover Boy, save yourself the worry – by the weekend, you'll be back out drinking with your silly friend and breathing a sigh of relief that no one believed you. Go on, do yourself and everyone else a favour and fuck off…"

Johnny stared at Tansy and Tansy stared at Johnny.

"Well," he said quietly, "what do *you* want to do? I meant what I said, I promise. If you want me to, I can go now and leave you in peace, but all you have to do is get in my truck with Gwen and I'll sort everything else out, I promise. You won't owe me anything – you can come back here when everything is fixed up and you won't ever need to see me again, or, well, we can live happily ever after – you, me and Gwennie. It would be up to you."

Greg dropped to his knees and groaned. "I can't *believe* this is happening! Happily ever after? What the fuck is going on – *Cinderella*? Did Cinderella get up the duff by a big bad wolf or something and I haven't realised?" He took his hands from over his

207

head and then looked at something on the floor beside the hall dresser. "Hang on, isn't that my claw hammer? Yes, it bloody is, *and* my chisel! Tansy – did *you* get these out of the garage and not put them away again?"

"What? What *are* you going on about?"

"This hammer and this chisel – they're supposed to be on hooks in the garage, not scattered about the place willy-nilly. I left these here because I had no place to store them. I trusted you to look after them, Tansy, I *trusted* you. And besides, what were you doing with a hammer and a chisel anyway? You use a *mallet* with a chisel, a *mallet* – stops it denting the handle…"

Suddenly, Tansy seemed to make a decision and from the look on her face it was as easy as choosing to have the tea and not the coffee, thanks. She picked up Gwennie's car seat, swept her bag off the door handle, hitched Gwen up a little higher on her shoulder and walked past Greg, still on his knees holding his tools up at her with an incredulous look on his face.

She planted a kiss on Johnny's cheek. "Thank you, Johnny, thank you for coming to rescue me – us," she smiled. "Come on, let's go home." She swung the door open, turning at the last minute to address Greg. "Greg, I'm really sorry that it's worked out the way it has. I never meant to be a crap wife and I'm sorry for what I did, but, well – I think if you have another relationship with another woman at *any* point in your life, make sure she builds dolls' houses or makes matchstick boats or something, otherwise she'll be ignored and bored shitless as well… Y'know, I think the mistake we made was buying a house that needed work, and a garage. If we'd just stayed in the flat, we could have been happy. We used to have fun, me and you: lately it was as if Jewson's was the third person in our marriage – no wonder it was crowded… Come on, Johnny, let's get out of here."

Johnny held the door open for her, and then looked back towards Greg. A little malicious thing inside him made him whisper, "Oh, and I took the lid off your wood glue and didn't put it back – sorry!"

Tansy was shaking by the time she was sitting in the passenger seat of the truck and Johnny had to sort the straps of Gwennie's seat, aware that Greg was standing in the doorway, looking shell-shocked, but also slightly menacing, with two hammers and a chisel in his hand. What *would* he do when he discovered that when Iestyn had stuffed the measuring device into the drawer, he had left it on…the battery wouldn't half have run low.

The truck pulled away, Tansy looking straight ahead and Johnny staring blackly at Greg. As soon as they got around the corner, Tansy burst into tears. "It's OK, it's OK," said Johnny, patting her arm, "let's just get a bit further away and then we can stop, yeah?"

Johnny was aware that for Tansy, it wasn't all about coming to him, she was also leaving her husband at the same time. He'd left her, now she'd been the decisive one and was leaving him. Also, she'd just had a baby, so everything hurt, her hormones were running riot, her house was a damp shit-hole, her hair was greasy and her backside was huge – yep, perhaps they'd better drive a bit further away than round the corner before they stopped and chatted…

Eventually, Tansy's sobs subsided and she gathered her composure and blew her nose on an old scrap of tissue from her pocket. "I'm sorry, Johnny, I really am. I've caused nothing but trouble since the moment you met me and I'm so sorry. I used to think that I was quite an uncomplicated person who had a straightforward life, but these last few months – Jesus! They've taken their toll and you've had the brunt! And, sorry also – you shouldn't have had to see that…"

"Tansy, don't worry, really. You're not trouble, and you're a pleasure to have around. It's just tough for you that these things all came together."

Tansy sniffed again. "Actually, can we stop a moment? I just need to sort a few more things out with you before we get back to the farm and then we'll have a clean slate."

Johnny pulled over into a gateway and turned the engine off. They were facing out over a spectacular view of the fields coated in snow, with bare trees poking up through. The sun was setting over the far hill, a glorious red orange ball sitting on top of the crest. For a while, they both just sat and watched, Gwennie sleeping soundly in her seat between them. Tansy seemed nervous, Johnny was content and at ease.

"Johnny," she began, "about all that you said earlier…"

"I meant it."

"Well, even if you did, perhaps you need to know a few things about me, about Gwennie…"

"I don't think so."

"If you are even remotely considering taking Gwennie on as your own, you probably need to know who the father is and how it – happened? She's not Greg's you know."

"Tansy…" Johnny grabbed her hand, leaning over Gwennie. "Actually, get out a minute – perhaps Gwen shouldn't hear this!"

They both jumped out into the snow and met again at the front of the truck. Johnny held out his hand and Tansy took it and they trampled over to the field gate, Johnny rejoicing in how soft and gentle her hand was against his own rough skin, and they looked out across the valley, neither seeming keen to break the spell.

Tansy shivered, so Johnny stood behind her and wrapped his arms around her, his chin gently resting on her shoulder. "Tansy, I don't need to know about Gwennie's father or how it happened or why it happened – unless you want him to be a proper dad? I do know *how* these things happen, believe me! Since meeting you, I've thought a lot about what I used to do and it wasn't always pleasant, to say the least! So, I don't need to know and it wouldn't help me to know and it wouldn't help you if I knew and it wouldn't help Gwennie. But, you need to know that I meant what I said. I love you, Tansy; I've never felt as strongly about anything and I know that I will feel like this forever," and he leant around and kissed her gently on the cheek, then she turned her face and their lips met.

There was no grabbing of crotches, no squeezing of breasts. No teenagers watching and no smell of burgers. Neither grabbed the other's hand and leapt into the field to finish the job, nor did they feel the need to act the innocent, nervous about being corrupted. It was just a beautiful first kiss on top of a mountain with the sun going down and their daughter sleeping contentedly a few feet away from them.

As they traipsed back to the truck, Johnny did wonder whether he was being fair by not confessing that he knew the truth about Gwennie's conception, and Tansy questioned whether she'd been fair selling Greg's chop saw to pay for an electricity bill…

It was just getting dark when they returned to Cwmtwrch. Nain gave Tansy a kiss and a quick, "All right, *bach*? Good to have you back," and Gwennie got carried around in a very non-Nain way. Taid squeezed Tansy's shoulder and smiled at her as he walked past her chair. Nain and Taid feigned tiredness just after nine o'clock and the younger couple were left to make their own arrangements.

There were no spoken debates, but Johnny and Tansy had an early night too and slept together with a lot of hugs, giggles and kisses, but nothing else. Gwennie woke them both up three times, but neither really minded: it was just another excuse to fall asleep in each other's arms again.

CHAPTER 29

Fel cacynen mewn bys coch – like a wasp in a foxglove (continually grumbling)

The door slammed and Esther breathed a sigh of relief as she heard Louisa's car start up and reverse down the short drive. She felt like she might be able to relax for a while and recover from the whirlwind of uselessness that was her daughter and her husband leaving for work. Just *why* was it so complicated? She'd worked for years, even when Louisa was young and needed getting ready for school and she hadn't crashed about demanding that someone else found her car keys or assumed that another person had hidden her shoes.

As she reached to put the kettle on, a draught whipped round her hand: bloody Louisa, how did she manage to slam the door so hard and yet not actually shut it? Because she didn't give a monkey's, that's how. She just knew that her mother was there to double-check on everything that she did and therefore, there was simply no need.

For the same reason her curtains would still be shut, the light in her bedroom would probably be on, her bed unmade and her pyjamas scattered across the floor or slung onto the back of a chair. The shower would still be on at the switch and, in fact, thought Esther, it wouldn't surprise her in the least to find Louisa's hairdryer buzzing away, quietly burning out its motor.

"Mum! I need a new hairdryer: my old one is rubbish and you forgot to turn it off and its motor burnt out. Would you be able to get me that new one, the one with the really expensive attachments?"

As Esther walked slowly to the front door, she felt like crying. Where had she gone so wrong over the years? She had friends whose children were pleasant and respectful and actually did things around the house from time to time. They had left home at a reasonable age, and they popped back occasionally to cut the hedge or to bring the children to play.

She used to pride herself that her daughter was having a *real* childhood, not one bogged down with domestic chores, but one spent playing in the woods or making models out of cardboard boxes. In hindsight, although she'd given her daughter the time and space to run wildly in the woods, her daughter had actually used it to watch more videos. Making your daughter's bed so that she could play fox and hounds was one thing. Making it so that she could watch *Snow White* for the hundredth time was possibly another.

On the way back from the front door, Esther tripped over one of David's shoes lying on the hall carpet. She stumbled and fell against the bottom of the banister, just managing to cling onto it and stop herself falling headlong onto the carpet.

And he was the bloody same! Yes, she was a housewife and knew that her role included keeping house, but it was the lack of respect that upset her so. It was knowing that David just kicked his shoes off and thought, *Sod it, Esther will tidy them away,* that hurt.

She'd read lots of marital psychology books over the years and had agreed that, yes, men *were* from Mars and women were definitely from Venus. She had allowed him to retreat into his cave now and then and had made sure that she hadn't stood at the entrance screeching at him to come and take his turn with the washing-up. However, he hadn't reciprocated and seemed not to notice that she might be at the foot of her particular wave at that moment, but would instead call from his cave for more wood for the fire, and could she cut it a little bit smaller in future? She sometimes felt that she was struggling so hard to be the perfect wife and mother, in order to allow her lover and her offspring to reach their full potentials, but instead of celebrating their successes with her and returning the favour, they just expected more of the same.

By the time she'd returned to the kitchen, the kettle had boiled, but she'd lost the moment. The was no point in sitting and saying, *ooh, that's nice* over a relaxing cup of tea when she felt like screaming, *You lazy, ungrateful, lazy bastards!* at the pair of them.

As she wearily started the washing-up, she noticed that David's toothbrush was on the windowsill and the toothpaste lay beside it – cap off of course. Brushing his teeth *after* breakfast? David always brushed his teeth *before* breakfast: what was going on there?

In fact, there had been quite a few ever so slightly unsettling things happening lately. David usually wore a shirt to work for two days running: for the last week or so he'd been putting them in the wash (chucking them in the corner of the room) after one wear.

He'd gone to a hair stylist, rather than the barber's that he'd been going to for twenty-five years, explaining it away by saying he was sick of the man's ridiculous conversation. He'd come back with a slightly different *style* rather than a simple cutting off of excess centimetres. What was going on? Her marriage books would probably tell her that he was having an affair, but David wasn't the sort to have an affair. He was a bit of a fuddy-duddy and very stuck in his ways. In fact, thought Esther with a smile, if he *was* having an affair, he would more than likely ask her if she could buy him some condoms or some lingerie for his new lady!

Perhaps – perhaps the tide was beginning to turn – perhaps he was actually making more of an effort for *her*? Maybe he'd read something that told him to be sure to make the biggest effort for his own wife, to treat her like he did on their first date? Maybe he just hadn't got to the page about picking up your own shoes yet…

David sat in the car and ran his tongue around his minty-fresh teeth. His heart was beating fast and his perspiring was making his after-shave smell stronger. Diane's door opened and a smile leapt to his face as he saw her come out. She hadn't looked at him yet, but her smile was beaming as she called goodbye to her husband.

She looked different. She had a glow to her face – was it extra make-up or was it good loving? Her hair was more coiffured than normal and she had on slightly higher heels than she usually wore. David scrambled from the car and raced around to her side to open the door. "Thank you, good sir," she said saucily, with a little wink. He almost groaned in return. He dived back into his seat and re-started the engine. As was their way, they both looked blandly ahead in case her husband, Harry, was looking out of the window.

"How are you, my lover?" purred Diane as she checked in her bag for something.

"All the better for seeing you," oozed David as he turned the car around and headed out of the estate towards the main road.

As soon as they were past the door of the nosy neighbours in number thirty-seven, they looked at each other with lust and bright-eyed love. David reached for her knee and hitched up her skirt slightly until he felt nylon. She placed her hand on the back of his neck and caressed his newly shaved smoothness. David rolled his head back, enjoying the closeness.

"Oh, Diane," he groaned as he took his hand off her knee and put the car into first gear to pull out of the estate. When his hand snapped back, he found that her legs had parted slightly and he could caress a bit deeper and eventually he found stocking tops. "Oh my God!" he gasped and dived off left into a flagship industrial estate that was now a collection of empty buildings with ash trees sprouting from their gutters. As soon as they rounded the corner away from the gaze of other road users, he stopped the car and they fell on each other, his hand roving around the hot and slightly sweaty flesh that was her upper thighs, and hers kneading away at his legs and very soon his crotch.

Their kisses were hungry and all consuming. He tugged her blouse free from her waistband and raced his hand round her soft back. He had one eye on the clock as he felt for her breast and she also as she tugged down his flies. They satisfied each other quickly and joyously within five wonderful minutes and David was back driving along the main road within six.

"Traffic's slow today, isn't it, Diane?"

"Certainly is, David, perhaps there are roadworks ahead."

"Seems to be just every day recently; perhaps I'd better start picking you up earlier – we don't want to get a reputation at work for being late…"

"No, not for being late…"

It had become their little game, the pretence of normal conversation with just a hint of flirtation. As they were in a car by themselves, they

214

could have talked about piercing each other's genitals over the lunch table for all the difference it would have made, but they preferred their own little rituals.

David felt as if he were coming alive after years of being cocooned in a shell, muffled from the sounds and scents of the world around him. Diane excited him in a way that was reminiscent of the back rows of cinemas and late buses home. The smell of her scent was enough to make his heart flutter and that grope of soft flesh was heavenly to him – and the hotter and stickier, the better.

What made it all even more delightful, was the fact that she apparently felt the same. He saw the light of love in her eyes – it was obvious as soon as she walked out of her front door. The way she reached for him, hungry to open his flies and dive in, made him feel invincible.

He knew they had to be careful: factory gossip was always on its toes, always guessing – usually wrongly, but occasionally bang on the nail, and he knew that it wouldn't take much lipstick on his collar for it to be interpreted as being something worthy of notice.

He recognised that it was not right so far as Esther and Harry were concerned, but how could such excitement, passion and sheer *joie de vivre* possibly be wrong? Surely it would be more wrong to put a lid on the feelings coursing through him? Affairs could be discreet and go on for years, *that* would be the best solution and perfectly possible. They could meet just once a week for proper full-baked sex and chips – maybe at the flat on the nights that Louisa went to college? He could pretend to have lots of DIY to do for Louisa and then he and Diane would have two, maybe two and a half hours to do as they wished and clean up after themselves before returning to their dull and dutiful homes.

He could just imagine it: Diane turning up in just a fur coat and heels, clutching a white carrier bag full of Chinese takeaway. They would eat it, picnic style whilst sitting cross-legged on the carpet in the middle of the floor before Diane pretended it was too hot and removed her coat… Or, he would be painting a ceiling in just his (new) boxer shorts, as he'd forgotten to bring a change of clothes, and Diane would be holding the ladder… Such idle thoughts made his team lose their place at the top of production and Diane's equivalent distractions earned her a ticking off as she sent a scathing email to a colleague, rather than Personnel.

They pulled into their usual space in the works' car park and gave each other their pre-work check: any make-up smudged on Diane, or any make-up at all on David? Check. Clothes tucked in and buttons and zips in the fastened position? Check. Any bodily fluids mopped up to the best of their ability? Yes, check.

"Well, Diane, have a good day at the office, my sweet," smiled David, looking straight ahead as he caressed her knee.

"And you, David," cooed Diane as she cheekily put her hand on his crotch.

David groaned. "Don't do that, Mrs Dawson, else you may find that I'll have to take you over the bonnet and hang whoever might be watching!"

Diane stepped out of the car and then leaned back in to fetch her bag. "I look forward to it, Mr Harrison!" with which she sashayed away across the car park, leaving David with flushed skin and the dilated pupils of a man in lust.

David was distracted all morning. He went for a walk at lunchtime to try and clear his head. He *had* to get a grip on himself; things were beginning to slip. Just make it through the day, he thought, and then tomorrow can be a clean slate.

As the afternoon shift got underway, he stood at the door of the storeroom: now, what on *earth* had he come here for? He shook his head in frustration: he was acting like a teenager smitten for the first time in his life. *Come on, David, sort it out!*

Right, retrace his steps in his mind – he'd been…. Yeah, about to fix that mixing machine and, ah, yes, therefore he needed a pair of mole-grips. David clicked on the light and headed for the shelf with mole-grips on.

Just as he was standing on the small step to reach for a pair, he heard footsteps and then the light went off and the door clicked shut.

"Hello again, big boy," whispered a husky voice, "lost something?"

"Diane? Is that you?"

"I don't know – is it?"

Hands stroked his leg and he sighed, "Diane, oh, that's wonderful, but, well, I really must get this fixed…"

"Fix what, big boy? Ooh and you *are* a big boy, aren't you…"

"Oh, Jesus, the thingy, you know, the machine, oh my God…"

And, of course, that is how their humble affair exploded into the public domain.

Little Gemma Tibsley went to fetch a tube of mastic and got more than she bargained for. Her scream of shock sent three people running from the workshop and two more from admin. Therefore, six people stood at the door and watched the spectacle of Mr Harrison relaxing his grip on Mrs Dawson's pendulous breasts and then pulling her skirt back down to cover her naked backside. He tried to hide behind her as he pulled up his trousers and then rummaged within them for ages trying to get his pants straight.

Mrs Dawson, who was naked from the waist up, was still in shock. She got slowly up from her hands and knees and put her blouse on inside out. She finally realised that her knickers were round her ankles when she wasn't able to shuffle away very fast, and then she pulled them up too – not an easy job with such a tight pencil skirt. She walked from the room in a daze with her pull-up stockings flapping around over her shoes and left the building, still with her bra, coat and handbag hanging on various hooks inside.

The crowd was left watching David Harrison. The men by now were beginning to laugh and catcall him and the women were sniggering, exchanging shocked, but still delighted, glances.

"OK, show's over," mumbled David and he fetched the mole-grips from the shelf and walked slowly out of the door, returning to the workshop, knowing that there were six people watching his every move, fascinated, rejoicing in what they'd just seen and only too ready to recount it to their colleagues.

David felt sick as he set about the machine, his whole body burning with shock and humiliation. He could hear the others going silent and work stopping as one by one they passed round the fantastic news. Damn, he'd brought the wrong mole-grips, but there was *no way* he was going back into that cupboard. So, he carried on pretending to tinker for the whole afternoon.

Ten minutes before the end of the shift, David had decided what he must do. His reputation was already ruined; he might as well just get it over and done with. For nearly two hours he'd mulled over what he might say and now he had to say it.

"OK, boys, stop a minute can you? Can you come here, I've something to say." He watched as all the boys left their machines, winking and raising their eyebrows at each other and walked over to him.

"Gentlemen," he said as they all stood in an arc around him, some not being able to look at him without sniggering, others openly laughing. "You all know by now what happened earlier this afternoon and I just want you to know that it was a – a moment of madness…"

"Why? Were you looking for your dog in there?"

"No, no, a moment of *stupidity* – it hasn't happened before and it won't be happening again. I'm sorry that it did happen…"

"What exactly did happen? I didn't see anything. Can you explain?"

"… and that people had to see it."

"I didn't see it – can you do it again somewhere that *I* can see it?"

"Yeah, and me."

"An' me!"

"Yes, very good," David continued, trying to retain some element of dignity about the situation. "Right, I need to speak to the ladies now, but I am assuming that we can put this behind us…"

"What, like you put something behind Di?"

"… behind us and start again tomorrow…"

"Start what again? Not more shagging in the store cupboard, *surely*!"

David walked from the room, the sweat pouring from his brow. He wiped it with his handkerchief then realised that it was the one he'd wiped himself on earlier and he groaned: God, it was getting worse.

He took a deep breath and entered the administration office. The four women sitting talking earnestly round a desk stopped immediately. Two went red, one giggled and the other "humphed" at him and walked to the window to stand with her back to him.

"Ladies," he said, "I've come to apologise."

"What for?"

"Yeah, why on earth would that be, David?"

"For, well, you know what for."

"He gave Di what for!"

"Look, I'm trying to say I'm really sorry…"

"What – for doing it, or getting caught?"

218

"Well, doing it of course, but, well, I suppose getting caught too. Look, the thing is…"

"I thought there was something going on," said Patricia.

"Yeah, and me – Di Dawson and high heels? With her corns? Definitely something going on."

"No, no, wait…" David felt he was losing control.

"Yes, *and* lipstick; she normally only wore lipgloss."

"Look, I…"

"Well, I hope she's all right; it's a long walk home."

"Especially with no coat, no bag and no bra on!"

"Oh, and no house keys!"

"No phone for a taxi…"

David was getting exasperated: this was worse than the men. "Ladies, all I wanted to say was that I, well, hope that we can draw a line under this and all return to normal tomorrow?" He could see the incredulous look on their faces, but felt that he was nearing the finish line, even if the egg had fallen off his spoon ages ago.

At this point, Brenda Jeffers turned back from the window to face him, her arms folded and her mouth doing a reasonable impression of a dog's arse. "All return to normal? *All return to normal?* David, are you actually aware of what some of us witnessed earlier today – in our place of work?"

"Yes, but…"

"Then you'll know that it's not something that we can all just forget about."

"Brenda, look, I'm so very sorry, but…"

"It's all very well being sorry, but you'll know that it can't just stop here? Mr Brennan will have to be informed."

David could feel his temper beginning to rise; Brenda Jeffers was a sourpuss who would truly be delighting in the drama that had unfolded on that otherwise dull Tuesday afternoon. Just because she'd never been enticing enough to be taken roughly from behind in a workplace store cupboard…

"OK, Brenda," Debra stepped forward, she was the office manager and the oldest of the women there. David breathed a sigh of relief: *she'd* put a stop to Brenda's stirring and the others messing about. "David – obviously seeing that was a shock to us all and I will be

219

speaking to Diane on her return. We do *not* want a repeat performance – especially in a cupboard that we keep our stash of biscuits in – isn't that right, girls?" The women started tittering, Brenda rolled her eyes. "But, yes, let's draw a line under it; we've wasted enough time today."

"Thank you, Debra, thank you." David mumbled goodnight and turned to leave the office.

"Oh, but, David?"

"Yes?"

"Just one more thing…"

"Yes?"

"Surely it wasn't very gallant of you to let Diane go underneath? The state of her knees and on that dirty concrete floor? I mean – come on!"

David fled, hearing the room erupt into cackles behind him. How was he *ever* going to be able to go back in there? By the time he'd reached the main exit door, the sweat was pouring from him, his head was thumping and his heart felt like it was about to grind to a halt. He loosened his upper button on his shirt and flung his jacket off, screwing it into a ball under his arm in a most un-David like way. He knew that there'd be faces lining the windows, finally able to chat and laugh freely at his and Diane's expense. He just couldn't wait to get away.

He approached his car, wishing that he'd parked it facing out in order to gain a few valuable seconds.

"David! Psst!" a strong whisper came from somewhere near his car and then a brown-haired head popped up over the bonnet.

"Diane?"

"Just open the bloody door and let me get in."

He pipped it open and climbed into the driver's seat whilst Diane crawled into the footwell of the passenger seat. "What are you doing still here?" he asked, in no mood for a romantic reunion.

"What do you *bastard*-well think? Start the car: I'm bloody freezing," she spat and it was only then that he looked at her properly. Her thin blouse was still inside out and she was clearly bra-less, but her face was nearly unrecognisable: it was blue with cold, yet somehow also red with crying. Her eyes were so puffy that she looked like she had myxomatosis and her skin had a mottle similar to granite.

David was blank: surely she didn't have to wait all afternoon just to see him?

Diane obviously sensed his confusion. "David – I have no bag, no keys, no coat, and no phone. I cannot walk home with an inside-out blouse and no bra, and I cannot turn my blouse the right way round without a bra on, as I think that people have seen enough of my wares for one day." She was getting animated and her voice was rising in pitch. It was giving David a headache.

"And even if I had walked home, I have no keys, so I would have to sit on the doorstep and wait until my husband got home and then tell him how it was that I left my bra, my bag and my keys in the office."

"So – what are you going to do then?" David wasn't looking for solutions that might involve him.

"What am I going to do?" screeched Diane. "If *I* were going to have to do something, I would have done it hours ago and saved myself getting bloody hypothermia!" David must have still been looking vague. "David – will you please go back to the office and get my things." Diane was now sat in as low a position as possible with her arms clamped firmly over her bust and was looking straight ahead.

"Oh, don't make me go back in there," he groaned, "I've had a hell of a day…"

"What? And me crawling about with my boobs out and then waiting in the cold for two hours was a *good* day at the office?"

David slammed the steering wheel with the palm of his hand and wrenched the door open. He stormed back, under general observation, into the office, just as the women were standing about in the foyer, chatting about him as they put their coats on.

"Where would I find Diane's coat and bag, please?" he snarled.

"There and there," pointed Gemma helpfully to a desk drawer and a coat rack.

"Oh, *now* she wants them, does she?" sneered Brenda.

"Piss off, Brenda," he snapped and stormed past her to collect them. Damn, she'd want her bra too. He checked that no one was watching and then quickly ducked into the store cupboard and clicked on the light. A table had been dragged into the middle of the room and on it was Diane's bra, supporting two five-litre tins of paint. David swore and pulled the tins out and tried to stuff the bra into his pocket.

However, he hadn't bargained on the underwire and there was no way it would fit, so instead he left the building wrestling with the enormous white contraption as it popped out of the various places he tried to stuff it.

Diane took her possessions without a word and clutched them to her. They drove to her house in silence. The bubble had burst. What had just that morning been an exciting, passionate new relationship built on mutual understanding and a zest for life had now been exposed for what it was: two middle-aged people (who had a lot to lose and really should have known better) who had tickled each others fancies and found the jackpot.

They'd had a few weeks of a fantasy life that shouldn't have really been theirs. They'd both had the colour return to their cheeks, had changed their hairstyles, lost a little weight and re-discovered a love of life that didn't need to include soap operas and tutting at *Crimewatch*. They'd realised that they were above *Coronation Street* as they'd rediscovered themselves, their verve and their sexiness.

They'd told each other as they'd lain sticky in each other's arms that they'd never return to being a sloth that didn't look after themselves and fancied a roast dinner rather than a stroll on the beach and love in the dunes. They would be people, from now on, who bothered to sit outside on a clear night and look at the stars, rather than watch the ten o'clock news and shuffle off to bed.

Even if they did it in their separate homes, they'd shun comfy underwear, going instead for more daring or exotic stuff – for themselves as much as for each other.

Yet, somehow, David found himself sitting in the driving seat wondering what the hell was wrong with *her*: his day had been even more shit than hers possibly could have. At least she'd not had to face the others yet. And the miserable bitch had sent him – not asked him, mind, *sent* him – back into the building to get her things, as she couldn't be bothered to get them herself.

Diane unclipped the seatbelt and wriggled into her jacket.

"Your blouse is still inside out."

"Don't you think I might know that? Don't you think it might have dawned on me when I was sitting in the cold for two hours that my blouse wouldn't do up properly and I've got labels on the outside?

222

Tell me, David, should I have taken it off in the car park to turn it the right way, or maybe as we were driving through town…"

"I was only saying."

"Well, don't. Anyway, I'm off. I'll see you." She picked up her bag from the footwell and checked that her stay-ups were actually up this time. David noticed with distaste that she had a hole in one knee with a ladder running up *and* down: God, she looked a state. Harry's car was home – David hoped that he didn't hover inside the door waiting for her.

"See you," she said as she opened the door.

"See you." However, as she moved, he caught a whiff of her perfume and suddenly that scent leaving his car was indicative of the only excitement in his whole life leaving. It was as if the fairy dust that had been sprinkled over every aspect of his world was twinkling its way to its doom.

He saw a life of boiled potatoes on the table at the right time each night, clothes folded neatly in the drawer reeking of fabric conditioner and a TV guide with two or three choices circled in red pen tossed open on the coffee table.

"Diane! Wait…"

"Yes?" The answer was slow.

"Don't go."

"I have to; Harry's home."

"I mean, don't leave me… Can we meet again?"

"Oh, I don't know, David. Today has been probably the worst day of my life and all I want to think about at the moment is having a long bath, going to bed and staying there."

"Just to talk – to clear the air?" His energy was coming back to him as he felt the need to retain the sparkle in his life. "Friday night? At Louisa's place – she's out on some date or something. Please? Please, Diane?"

Diane stared at him and although it seemed against her better judgement, she said, "OK, I'll try. Friday. After work? I'll be there – if I can." Then the car door slammed and he watched as she walked brusquely up the drive, adjusting her skirt as she went and pulling her jacket together in an attempt to cover her indiscretion.

David felt himself smile and despite the depth of the shit he was in, he started humming to himself as he swung the car around in the hammerhead at the top of the estate and then headed for home.

CHAPTER 30

Tynnu nyth cacwn am fy mhen – to put a wasp's nest on my head (to do something that arouses anger)

Esther's day had been strange. The lack of hysteria that morning, particularly in comparison to earlier that week, had been noticeable and now she was sitting at a clear kitchen table sipping at a cup of tea and glancing at a magazine, and Louisa's car was only just pulling up out of the village. It was almost eerie – both sets of keys had been hanging on the hooks, packed lunches had been swept off the sides without complaint and the door had been shut *normally* – not slammed or banged nor left swinging, but just pulled to like in other houses the world round.

Louisa – well, she was obviously nervous about her date – she'd talked of nothing else since it had been arranged. Talked on her terms of course; Esther wasn't allowed to bring it up under threat of interfering. Part of her wished that she had the kind of relationship with her daughter which meant that they might discuss things like dates. Maybe they would develop one in the future, perhaps when Louisa had moved into her flat and her mother could call around for a chat (rather than have to try to maintain a warm relationship as she retrieved a pile of wet towels from the bathroom floor)? However, Louisa would actually have to move into her flat before she, Esther, would be able to pop round for a friendly coffee.

As for David, well, Esther still had *no* idea what was going on there. What could be the reason for a grown man suddenly putting his pyjamas on his pillow after years of kicking them under the edge of the bed? Why would he have polished his own shoes, rather than left them dirty side up, in the middle of the hall as a giant clue for her to find ten minutes before he desperately needed them? Why the difference between last week and today?

Esther was bored. There was no chaos to moan about, no clutter to pick up after. She vacuumed the clean carpets, she dusted the clean shelves. She even swept, then vacuumed the patio. She watched a little television, but her eyes kept being drawn over to her computer. She felt restless and knew that the devil was busy suggesting work for her idle hands...

Usually she spent her days being cross with David and Louisa. It was as if being a martyr to their thoughtlessness could occupy her mind better than anything else. She would pick up three shirts that had been tried on then slung onto a chair and roll her eyes. She would rinse a bit of David's beard off her toothbrush and think about how she might relate it to a friend with a resigned shake of her head. And she would probably peel potatoes knowing that they would be wrongly mashed, boiled or chipped.

Not having her mind filled with being cross with her nearest and dearest meant that she had time to be cross with other people. Like that Jan who ran the bakers in town. She'd queued for ages there yesterday, waiting patiently whilst Jan chatted with an old dear standing in front of her. It had given her plenty of time to look around and she had not liked what she had seen.

There had been dried-up cream on the inside of the glass counter above a load of cakes that didn't have cream on or in them. The floor needed a good sweep and then someone needed to get on their hands and knees and *scrub* it. She could see that the mop never made it into the corners and they were dark with grime and grease.

Esther had watched as Jan had patted her hair, hitched her bra strap up and then handled money before reaching for her, Esther's, provisions with the same hand. Then, blow me, if the bread wasn't rock hard and the pain au chocolat was surely a day old. The tin hat had been put on her visit with the sight of a few dead flies collected in the corner of the window display area, presumably just out of reach of the woman's cloth. Oh, she'd been cross...

Esther looked over again at the computer as the adverts flicked up on the TV screen. Perhaps if she just *wrote it down*, then she could put it to the back of her mind... She'd decided that the letters must stop, but it might be good to *clarify her thoughts*... She could practise her typing as she did it – that would be a good exercise: she didn't have to *turn it into a letter…didn't have to post it.*

She idly got to her feet and as she walked past, she just happened to turn the computer on. She went to the loo and walked back and jiggled the mouse. She popped into the kitchen and by the time she returned with a fresh brew, the computer was waiting for her.

The rest was automatic. Within ten minutes she'd drafted a full page of suggestions for Janet at the Crusty Bun. She read it back over: it was actually quite eloquent! But she wasn't going to print it out – it was only to allow her to practise her typing. She saved it under Typing Practice and wondered off to fetch her ironing board.

She re-read it a couple of times as she returned from taking clothes upstairs. The layout looked quite good. It would be interesting to see how it looked printed out – it was difficult to judge when it was just on the computer screen.

Eventually she pressed the button and a sheet spilled out of the printer. Yes, it was quite pleasing on the eye. She decided to stuff the ironing for the day and instead folded the letter into thirds and popped it into an envelope to keep it safe and went upstairs for a nap.

Her sleep was deep and her dreams were wild and very real. She was being shouted at by lots of different people – circus clowns, David, a zookeeper, Louisa and a group of children in school uniform. She was buttering a pile of bread as quickly as she could, but it wasn't good enough for them and as soon as she put down one newly buttered slice, it would be snapped up again and the plate was empty and the crowds were baying for more.

She dragged herself awake, half-sitting up in bed, the duvet pushed to the floor. She had to stop these daytime naps: they didn't leave her refreshed, just disorientated and sluggish. She opened the curtains and was disappointed to see sleet – damn, she hadn't been out of the house all day and she liked to get a little exercise – maybe she could just pop her coat on and go for a short walk. Maybe…maybe just to the post-box and back?

Twenty-to-five – damn, she didn't have long if she wanted to post a – that – letter. She struggled with her trousers and then went down into the lounge. She took her favourite fountain pen and with writing as unlike hers as possible, she inscribed the front of the envelope with

The Proprietor – it would be good for Jan to think that the writer didn't know her; Esther *knew* that Jan knew that she knew that Jan was called Jan and therefore she would never think that it was her…

As she pulled on her coat and hat and sat in the low chair by the front door to lace her shoes, the sleet buffeted against the pane of frosted glass. She was going to get frozen; but she did need to get her exercise, so she'd better just go.

She left the house at seven minutes to five and walked, her head down into the dusk. As she came out of her drive, a car purred down into Anweledig, its windscreen wipers on full pelt.

Esther saw an elegant gloved hand wave at her and she nodded in return. She struggled along, her stick slippery in her hand and was annoyed to see the lady in the car skip across to her, tied neatly into her polka dot mac.

"Hello!" the lady called through the weather, adjusting her red beret. "Horrible day isn't it? I wanted to introduce myself: I'm Katie and we've just moved in across the way. I've been meaning to come and say hello, but, well, it's been a bit chaotic!"

"Hello and welcome to Anweledig," smiled Esther, hunching her shoulders against the cold and wishing that they could do this another day. "I'm Esther – look, come over for a coffee when you have time – I must just take this to the postbox now; it goes at five, you see."

"Oh, let me," said Katie and she took Esther's letter from her and added it to a pile pulled out from her pocket, "I have to go too; I forgot on the way past."

"But…"

"It's no trouble, really! I'll see you soon for that coffee. Bye for now!" and Katie trotted lightly up the hill, her head down into the sleet and her heels defying the slippery road.

Esther watched Katie, her hand still out as if trying for a second chance to hold on tighter to the envelope, feeling a little out of control. What if Katie just got round the corner, then opened it and read it? What if she didn't ever post it, but instead took it home and kept it behind her mantelpiece clock for a year and then sent it? Damn her and her skipping heels…

Katie trotted up the hill, not noticing the exercise and glad to be able to do something to help her new neighbour. As she neared the postbox, she saw the post van screech to a halt beside it. A man in short trousers jumped out of the van and jogged to the box, his keys rattling in his hand.

"Coo-ee!" she called and waved her pile of letters in the air. She was out of breath now and walked the last twenty yards. "Thank you for waiting," she puffed, "I needed to get these in tonight. Oh, look – I've got them wet, and I've smudged the address on this one. Damn, and it's from my neighbour too! Can you still read it, do you think?"

"The – Crusty – Bun – yes, that's fine, I can read that – it'll be on my round anyway! Right, best get going: I'm bloody freezing in these shorts!"

"I'm not surprised!" said Katie, clearly bewildered at his attire. "Thanks then, and goodbye!" and she clattered off back down the hill, her curls now bedraggled and her shoes squelching a little.

Esther stood in darkness, watching from the window of her lounge. She had a feeling of impending doom. At last she recognised her letters for what they were – spiteful and cowardly and revenge taken on the wrong people. Jan Crusty Bun hadn't left ironed shirts in a pile on the chair, any more than she'd shaved her stubble off over Esther's toothbrush. She should have been shouting at Louisa and David, but instead she'd taken her frustrations out on innocent people who were just trying to earn an honest living.

Was it because she had secretly thought that *she* would be the one running a successful business in town and that in *her* establishment there would never have been dead flies left lying amongst the stock? Because *she* would have cleaned even the darkest of corners, is that why she felt it acceptable to criticise others who didn't?

She realised, sadly, that for twenty-odd years she had harboured a vision of a white shop housing a series of gleaming white display units with beautifully-made ceramic bowls or vases perched on top of them.

She would spend her days dressed in a painty kaftan and with a scarf wrapped around her hair – which highlighted the ageing of her dream – turning pots in the workshop in the back of the building and then firing them in her kiln. She would then sit in the shop window and paint delicate designs over her work and people would watch from the pavement in awe and then pop in, saying that they just *had* to buy one.

The trouble was that she had never made a pot... Never painted anything more elaborate other than a picture of a rainbow alongside the child Louisa. She had no money to buy a kiln and no idea of how they worked. She had never looked into premises, business rates, taxation or the position of ceramics on the shopping lists of the average Tan-y-Bryn citizen.

It was far easier to criticise everyone else's efforts, but these were the people who *had* tried to make their dreams come to fruition. They had taken gambles and opened cafés, hairdressing salons and grocery shops. They had done their market research and learnt their trade. Even if they hadn't got their table legs all the same length, at least they had table legs. She'd done nothing but legitimise her procrastinations: Louisa was too small. The dog needed walking around the block twice a day. The house needed a Hoover-through. She'd had a stroke.

The irony of the stroke was that of course, that *did* provide a legitimate excuse for not pursuing her plans. Even the most dedicated artist might find it difficult to make and decorate ceramic pots with her disabilities, but because she'd never tried it, she had never actually found out.

Even now, she'd put it off again in order to write some spiteful letters. If she'd spent her time phoning up about ceramics or fine art courses, rather than writing to people about their pinnies, she might by now be on her way to an evening course. Instead, she was more likely to be on her way to gaol...

Louisa slipped through the door of Chez Nous and started leafing through the sale rail. She slid hangers along the rail, noting, but not inspired by the clothing on it.

"Can I help?" asked the shop assistant who'd mocked elasticated waist-bands on Louisa's previous visit.

"Um, just looking thanks..."

"Well if you need anything..." she murmured as she glided back across the room to her other customer who was struggling in the changing room.

"Do you have the silver one in a size ten?" Louisa heard a voice call from behind the curtain and then she saw Rachel's face popping round the curtain, waving a black top at the assistant. "Oh, hi again, Lulu! Out shopping?"

"Yes, I've got a, er, date tomorrow night and I thought I might get a new pair of trousers – jeans, y'know."

"Wow, lucky you! A date, hey? Yeah, you've got to get a new *something* for a date; it helps you feel all special!"

The black top was swapped for a silver one and put on. Rachel came out and stood in front of Louisa and the assistant; she looked stunning. She looked at herself in the mirror, "Hmm, don't know. What d'ya think?"

"Perfect," purred the assistant automatically.

"You look fantastic," whispered Louisa, almost in awe of how the halter neck top looked on her new friend.

"Thanks! Well, in which case, I'll have it! We're all going out tomorrow and I wanted to wear something a bit more, y'know, special?" She quickly got changed again and then dumped the top on the counter and the assistant started to pack it. "So, Lulu, what are you looking at?"

"Oh, I've only just started looking," said Lulu, walking away from the sale rail.

"Jeans is it? What about these? They're nice," and Rachel pulled out a pair of ripped jeans with a low waist. Louisa knew that if she bought them, she would need to buy some new underwear as well as her pants would be visible for at least six inches above the waist. And also a flesh-coloured girdle.

"Umm…"

"Or these, these are a bit more – classy," and a pair of indigo jeans were pulled out. "They would look really good with those great boots you had on the other night – really funky."

Louisa walked over to them. "Yeah, actually they're really nice!" She desperately looked for a size label; she certainly wouldn't be shouting for a pair in size ten. To her relief, there was a row of the same jeans all in different sizes.

"Go on, try these on whilst I pay for that top! See what they look like!"

Louisa grabbed a pair of the size she thought she *might* in her wildest dreams be, a pair in the same size as her elasticated-waist jeans and then a more realistic *allowing her to eat a pudding* size, and nipped into the changing room.

She put the largest size on as quickly as possible, desperately hoping that Rachel wasn't the kind of shopping friend who was so confident with her own body that she would whip the curtain open, regardless of the occupant's state of dress. Luckily she wasn't and Louisa had a few moments on her own to get used to the idea of the jeans. They were – nice. They looked – OK.

She opened the curtain and stepped out. "What do you think?" she asked shyly. Rachel and the shop assistant stopped what they were doing and looked her up and down. "I know they won't look great with my work blouse," smiled Louisa.

"No, nothing would look good with that much nylon."

"Turn around," said Rachel. Louisa did what she was told, hoping that no one would mutter, "*Jee-sus*" when they saw the size of her arse. They didn't.

"They're really nice," said Rachel in a considered way. "And they *would* look good with those boots. What do you think?" she asked the shop assistant.

"Perfect…"

"What top will you be wearing?"

"Oh, I've got a top sorted. A red one. A low-necked red one."

"Atta girl! What about accessories?"

"Oh. Don't know."

Rachel picked a chunky string of indigo coloured beads from the rack. "What about something like this? It would link the top and the bottom together?" Rachel was the queen of accessories and it *was* a lovely piece.

"I really like that," said Louisa. "Right. I'll have the jeans and the necklace!"

"Good for you!" called Rachel as Louisa ducked back into the changing room and the shop assistant upped her tempo as five-thirty neared. "Anyway, who's the lucky guy?"

"Well, not met him yet" Louisa said from behind the curtain, "I, er, met him online!"

"Wow! You're brave! Sorry, Lulu, I've got to rush off again, but have a great time – and, look, a few of us are going to the Dog and Duck before we get picked up for a party at about eleven. There won't be room on the bus for the party, I'm afraid, but if the date is naff and finishes before then, call in for a drink! Let us know how it went!"

"Thanks! Thanks for the offer – I might do – if it is naff." She actually hoped that she would be walking hand in hand along a moonlit riverside path after the meal, but it was nice to have a backup plan.

She paid for her goods with a big smile on her face. "Have a good night," the assistant said in an unconvincing monotone as she prepared to lock the door and turn the sign the millisecond that Louisa was over the threshold.

Louisa nearly danced down the pavement to her car – new clothes, the possibility of looking funky, accessories, and a backup plan that involved going to a pub to meet some friends! Fantastic! Maybe, *finally,* she was actually sorting her self out – and her dad hadn't organised any of it!

CHAPTER 31

Chwain y gof - the blacksmith's fleas (the sparks from an anvil)

It was Friday morning and the Crusty Bun was having a mid-morning freshening up. A broom swept most of the crumbs and fluff off the floor and pushed the rest into the corners for the mythical pixie that would surely come and finish that bit properly later. The proprietress, Jan, wiped a cloth over most of the surfaces, swerving not so neatly around the tray of bagged doughnuts, five for a pound, on top of the counter.

Sally their delivery driver pulled up in her white van outside and Jan went to greet her. "OK? All done?"

"Yes, all fine," called Sally, opening the back doors and grabbing the massive bread trays.

"Stick them there," said Jan, pointing to the shop floor, "I'll just go and make room for them out the back."

Sally grabbed the trays two at a time and clattered them onto the tiles. Then she grabbed the broom and went to sweep out the back of the van.

A lady wearing a black shiny coat with brilliant white spots on it walked into the shop and pulled her belt tighter around her waist in the attempt to keep the warmth around her.

"I'll be there now!" called a voice from the back.

"No rush; I shall just enjoy browsing!" the smart lady called back. She stood by the trays on the floor, her black patent shoes on tip toes to allow her to peer over them into the counter.

There was a noise behind her and she turned to see a postman with purple-blue legs encased in thick woolly socks walking in. She smiled and turned back to observing the cakes, then turned back to him, having remembered who he was. "Hello again," she smiled and he nodded to her as he assessed the clutter on the floor.

Jan came back into the shop, wiping her hands on her pinny. "Sorry about that. Now: how can I help you? Oh, hi, Tommy, do you want to pass those over?"

"Here, let me," said Katie and she took the small pile of post from Tommy to pass over the trays to Jan. "Oh, look!" she exclaimed, looking at the top letter in the stack, "isn't that funny! Here is the one I gave to you last night – look, there's where I smudged the ink! How strange is that; I could have kept it, steamed the stamp off and brought it with me this morning!"

"Don't do that," Tommy said, "you'll have me out of a job!"

Sally came into the shop. "Sorry, folks, let me just move those from the floor, get them out of your way. Hi, Tommy, cup of hot chocolate for you? You must be bloody freezing!"

"I am, and yes please," he grinned, adding to Katie, "this is the real reason I wear shorts – people who own cafés take pity on me!"

"Ooh, hot chocolate; that sounds perfect," said Katie, "just what I need in this weather."

"Well, sit yourselves down and I'll get you both one if you like," Sally said and motioned them to the small tables in the corner.

"Wonderful," said Katie and sat down, removing her coat and revealing a black woollen dress.

The trays were moved away and two steaming mugs of hot chocolate were brought in, their sides sticky with overflowing milk. Sally stood chatting to Tommy whilst Jan had another whip around with a cloth and then started on her pile of post. She was clearly intrigued by the envelope with the ink stain on the front and so opened it first.

She read it with a growing frown on her face and her eyes jumped back to the beginning a couple of times. She considered it, re-read it, then tossed it to Sally. "Read that," she said, then watched Sally's face as she too read it with increasing incredulity.

"Bloody hell!" Sally exploded when she reached the end. "Someone was in a bad mood!" She tossed it onto the table, and then looked at the woman in the black dress. "Hang on, you said you posted this – *you* wrote this? And you sit there, drinking my hot chocolate after you wrote us *this*?" and she pushed the letter towards her.

"Oh no," Katie said, "it's not *from* me; I posted it for my neighbour…" but she picked up the letter all the same and read it:

Dear Proprietor,

I am writing this with the best intentions to tell you about your shop. Sometimes I believe that it is useful for a purveyor to know how their customers see it. I hope that you will find it constructive and helpful.

Your shop is filthy and the corners are full of flies. The bread is hard, the croissants are stale and the bread puddings are days old. Your pinnies are stained and your fingernails need trimming. You chatter away to people when you have customers patiently waiting and the handles on your carrier bags rip or cut into your customers' hands.

As I said previously, please be sure to take this in the constructive manner it was intended.

With very best wishes,
A loyal customer

By now, Jan had tears rolling down her face and Sally stood to give her a hug. "Take no notice," she said, "it's spiteful and cruel." She turned to Katie. "I think you'd better go now, please."

Katie looked horrified, "No, no, you don't understand. I said that this isn't from *me*; it's from my *neighbour*. It was sleeting and the post was due, so I took it from her and ran. You remember," she turned to Tommy, "I'd smudged the address with my thumb from the sleet and asked you if you could still read it."

"It's true," Tommy said, distracted as he too was now reading the letter. "Yeah, she did say she was posting it on behalf of a neighbour.

Bloody hell," he said as he passed it back to Jan, "she must have had a jam-less doughnut…"

"Or a Chelsea Bun with no currants in…" Sally said, beginning to smile.

"Yeah, or even a ham roll with no ham – or roll…" Jan said dryly.

"Seriously though," Tommy said, "I'd take that to the police. Ask this lady to write a statement; I will as well if it helps. Was it Esther Harrison?" he turned to Katie.

"I don't know her name – fifty-ish, with a stick?"

"Yeah, that'll be Esther. No one else really lives there in Anweledig anymore. Well, well, I didn't think she was the type. Got to report it though – been a few sent out and they're terribly upsetting for people. And gives us posties a bad name, you know, shooting the messenger and all that. Right," he said, reluctantly standing up and grabbing his keys, "thank you very much for that; let me know if you need anything, OK?"

Jan and Sally nodded and they all watched as he left the shop, the hairs standing straight out on his mottled legs. Katie finished her hot chocolate and stood up, reaching for her purse. "Do you want to go to the police?" she asked quietly, "my car's outside – I can take you now if you want?"

Jan looked at Sally. "Yeah, you go, my love," Sally said, "I can look after here. Shop the nasty old bitch. Dirty floors – bollocks! Mind, saying that, maybe that corner is a *tiny* bit grubby…"

The post dropped through Esther's door just as she was vacuuming the hall carpet for the fifth time that week. Sometimes she would relish having a few bits on the carpet – made it more rewarding to make it clean again; vacuuming was pointless when you couldn't see where you'd been.

She clocked the two-for-one offers from the supermarket and the double-glazing leaflets on the mat, cursing that she'd have to make the journey to the recycling bin in the back porch. She gathered together the rest of the letters scattered across the mat and set off towards the kitchen.

On the top of the pile was a strangely-shaped quality cream envelope with beautiful handwriting scribed across the front, addressed to Mr and Mrs Harrison. It was thick and had the look of a wedding invitation: they hadn't been to a wedding in years and it would be just what they needed.

Esther sank onto the stairs, she'd have a job getting up, but she was too intrigued to wait until she reached the kitchen table, and she carefully unglued the flap so as not to rip the envelope. She peered inside and pulled out a sheet of paper, folded into quarters. The handwriting was old-fashioned copperplate, but had a few giveaway mistakes that made her think that the scribe was trying to disguise their handwriting.

Dear Mr and Mrs Harrison,

I am writing to you about your daughter, Louisa, as I think it would be helpful for you to see her as everyone else sees her.

She is fat and lazy and needs to make her own way in the world. You keep her at home for your own ends and therefore you are selfish. She needs to move out and get a life.

This letter is for your own good and for that of your daughter.

Yours truly,
  A well wisher

Esther gave an involuntary cry and dropped the letter as if it were on fire. Then she picked it up and read it again. No, no this couldn't be real: it had to be a practical joke – a sick one, mind, but a joke all the same.

Fat and lazy? Needs to make her own way in the world? Her heartbeat was rising and she felt a little faint. It was if someone had thrust a knife into her, but she couldn't see them to allow her to fight back. Why would someone do this? OK, so maybe Louisa was some of those things – but only on the surface: she wasn't *really* lazy, just a little unmotivated at times. *She needs to move out and make her own way in life?* Well, actually, she had a flat now – had had for three weeks – just hadn't spent a night in it yet. But there were reasons for that weren't there? What reasons? She couldn't be arsed…? The sofa at home was warmer and comfier than her own one would be? Esther groaned again and covered her face with her hands. She felt violated. The fact that the letter was actually, well, spot on, meant that someone had been watching *very closely*.

Who could have done this? Who would be so mean, so spiteful and so intimate in their detail? She looked out of the window, as if there might be someone hiding behind a bush to make sure that she had both received and read the letter.

Perhaps two people had masterminded it, having spent weeks sitting on their sofa in the evenings, mocking her and her daughter? Had they laughed as they'd written it? Had they spent days agonising over whether it was the right thing to do or had they just pinged it off on a whim?

Esther read it again, her hands shaking, and then she started sobbing: great big tears rolling down her face, her mouth open wide and yowling. She felt angry, humiliated and – the worst bit – impotent. She couldn't argue her case, couldn't tell anyone to stuff off and mind their own business. And the worst thing of all was, of course, that it was her own fault! Not only had she not quietly pushed her maturing daughter into making her own way in the world, she had started all this letter writing. It had been her that had made it the thing to do, and now it was only right that she suffered from her own brand of rough justice and, boy, was it rough…

She put the rest of the pile of post down on the stairs, took a big gulp, wiped her eyes and crawled off to bed. Sod the ironing of shirts, sod bloody everything.

Esther's sleep was poor. She lay there in her big bed in the blandly immaculate bedroom and tried to get respite from her thoughts: but, no chance. She alternated between visions of Louisa sitting on the sofa, wrapped in her chenille blanket, asking for something that she could easily have fetched herself and a faceless couple, sitting on a sofa bitching night after night about *her* and Louisa until they thought the only decent thing to do was to write a letter.

Then the thought struck her that maybe, maybe it would have been better if they'd written it fifteen years ago? She remembered back to the times before her stroke when she heard David telling Louisa to sit on the sofa and put the television on, as it was too cold outside for little girls. She would feel like shouting, *it isn't if you put a coat on her!* But she knew that in two minutes she would be creeping out the door as inconspicuously as possible with a flask of soup and some fresh sliced bread for one of her ladies.

She had always known that Louisa's lifestyle wasn't quite as it should be and that she should do something about it, but her thoughts were always that the current situation was temporary. When Harold gets out of hospital, he can feed his own cat. When Blod gets back on her feet, she can see to her own tea and when Social Services process their form, Lily and Elwyn can have proper care. Therefore, there would be no point in putting her foot down about David's obsession with a thermometer to dictate what Louisa should / should not do that day – notwithstanding how close she was sitting to the fire when it was taken – as in a couple of weeks, Esther would be free of her obligations and could gently put a stop to it.

However, the obligations seemed to be on a rolling programme. Blod rarely got completely back on her feet and so Esther would be phoning around for help for her and when she *was* on her feet, she couldn't open tins. Lily and Elwyn might get their visit from Social Services, but a neighbour would fall in the meantime and the picnics in the park with her daughter would get put off for another season.

"It's not even that you get paid!" David would rant. "If you got something for it, it would be a start."

"I do sometimes…" Esther would mumble.

David guffawed with incredulous laughter. "What? Like that tube of Toffees you got last week? And what was it you got from that skinflint, bloody Harold? A pair of his dead wife's socks?"

"They were very nice socks; they'd never been worn."

"She's been dead ten years! They've sat in her chest of drawers for ten years and the miserly old sod opened the drawer rather than his wallet and gave them to you! What's that rate of pay? An inch of sock per hour of work?"

"I don't do it for the money."

"Yeah, but *I* have to work for five days a week for the money; we can't all be as altruistic as you, can we?"

And so it would go on.

238

Esther mentally enacted the inevitable scene where she had to tell David about the letter… "Well, you didn't think of *that* whilst you were ironing someone else's Y-fronts, did you? Are you seriously going to throw that in my face after all those years of doing my best? That it's all *my* fault for not letting Louisa out to play? Thanks a bunch. And why tell me tonight, for God's sake? Don't ruin Friday night for us as well, Esther, you *know* there's a Frost on…"

Every now and then a wicked thought came into her head – perhaps she should show *Louisa*: might make her get off her fat arse and take a bit of a gamble in life…

Eventually she decided to do nothing immediately, but to mull it over. Maybe she could unearth a few clues if she asked Louisa and David some pertinent questions about who might hold a grudge or who kept offering "advice" to them about Louisa's lifestyle choices or her default setting.

Eventually she dragged herself back out of her bed and made it for the second time that morning. She was due at the hairdressers at three-thirty and the taxi was coming in an hour. Time enough for a quick lunch and tidy round and to make herself look passable enough to bear sitting and staring at for an hour in front of a well-lit mirror.

At five to three, she was composed and sat on the bottom of the stairs waiting for her taxi. The letter had been hidden in her underwear drawer and no one ever went in there. She absentmindedly picked up the remaining pile of post and leafed through it, three for David, one for Louisa and two for her. She recognised her catalogue bill and left that for later. She opened the other one with one eye out of the window for her cab. The contents made her cry, "No! Not another one!"

This time she held a typed sheet of flimsy paper that had been popped into the style of envelope that one might pinch from work. Her breath was shallow as she read it:

Dear Mrs Harrison,

As a long-standing acquaintance of yours, I think it is important that you are told that your husband, David, is having an affair. It is with Diane Dawson from admin and they were caught in flagrante *in the store cupboard at work. I don't know where else they meet and do not know how long it has been going on, but suspect that it is for a number of weeks.*

I trust that you find the courage to sort things out.

Yours truly,
  A well wisher

A well wisher? Not another effin' well wisher! She could really do without being wished so well so often. Esther gasped and then groaned and then laid her head on the side of the banister and groaned again. Her life was falling apart. What on *earth* was going on? This morning she had been a somewhat disgruntled contented person who felt that life needed perhaps a little re-papering, but not wholesale redevelopment. Within a few hours the guts of her world had been ripped out, chewed around and spat out onto the pavement.

David? Her David? Having an affair with Diane Dawson? Surely not! David had been giving Diane Dawson a lift twice a week for eight years – had they been doing *in flagrante*s all that time? Oh good God, had she been ironing his shirts so he could look good for *her*, so that they could be ripped off again in a dusty store cupboard? Should she be screaming with rage? Sobbing with remorse? Maybe she should be hunting for a gun or a kitchen knife with a long sharp blade that she could go and charge on to the factory floor and stab him with, then walk into the office and stab Diane bloody Dawson before giving herself up to the police and accepting her life sentence with dignity and the conviction that she'd done the right thing and that justice had been achieved...

Parp parp! The sound jolted her from her spinning thoughts. Damn – the taxi. That meant it was time to go and have her hair styled, supposedly so that she could look nice sitting next to her loving husband at the golf dinner the following evening. Oh, God, how could she just go and sit draped in nylon – or cotton as it was now – and have someone ask her about her holidays after having had the kind of day she'd had?

She pulled herself to her feet and steadied herself on the banister. She'd have to, wouldn't she? She had to keep a pretence of normality until she had decided what to do – the decision to stab everyone or to remain dignified needed to be thought through. But how could one make a thought through decision when the bottom of their world had been spat onto the pavement and smeared in filth? *Parp parp!* In a daze, Esther pulled herself to her feet, collected her coat and handbag, threw her shoulders back and opened the door.

Esther always booked with the same taxi firm and more often than not, Shane was the driver. She would sit beside him and they would chatter away about the usual taxi things, ending the journey a little more right wing than when they'd started it.

This time, Esther crawled into the back seat and sat behind him, mumbling in response to his chirpy "How are you today?" that she was a little out of sorts.

They drove along in silence, Esther staring out of the window alternating between feeling sick, angry, confused and in despair. After a while she felt the car slow down and Shane cursed, "What a stupid bloody place to park. Look at that – right on the brow of the hill!" and he shook his head at two guys who were loading a sofa onto the back of a removal lorry. A couple were standing next to the open van, the man with his arms wrapped around the woman, as if he were trying to soothe her tears.

It was the house on the hill along her bus route. It was the house with the lack of blinds. Esther bit her lip. Perhaps they were moving out because they felt violated in their own home? Perhaps they felt that everyone was watching them or criticising their lives and that they could no longer live there?

Esther stared out the rear window until the lorry was just a dot on the horizon.

They arrived on the outskirts of Tan-y-Bryn, with Shane mumbling about plans for a new one-way system for part of the town; Esther was only half-listening.

"Yeah, and it'll start at the Market Road and come out at Friar Street, you know, by the Tasty Bite Café – well, the Tasty Bite Café that *was* anyway…"

"That was? Why, has it closed for refurbishment or something?" Esther was listening with full attention now.

241

"No, shut full stop. End of last week. Real shame – I used to have my lunch in there sometimes, really friendly place. Good food too."

"Oh. Why was that then? Are they – moving abroad, or opening a new…boutique or something?" Esther was hopeful.

"Nah, all closing and they're going on the sick. They'll live above the café. Nasty business really – they got one of them spiteful letters and, well, Pat Marshwood said that she's lost all her confidence."

"I read about it in the paper – but, I thought they *appreciated* the letter? Y'know, said it made them look at their business with fresh eyes?"

"Well, she said it did for a while, and then they just felt sick that they had been baking and cooking and serving someone as nasty as that and they hadn't realised. Made her think about who else had been sat there, thinking it was dirty or moaning about it to their friends. Couldn't face going in there in the end, made her feel tearful and sick apparently. Shame though. As I said, a nice couple; tried really hard…"

Esther leant back against the seat. She felt as if she might be sick. What had she been thinking? She had just ruined two people's livelihoods and made them ill and for what? A staleish cake and the failure to wipe the table with something more effective than a bottle of cheap cleaner and a used cloth.

"Here we are, my love," Shane said as they pulled up alongside the hairdresser's. "What is it today? Shaved head or just a bleach blonde?" It was his little joke and she usually replied, "No, just a Mohican" or "I thought I'd have a purple rinse…" Today, however, she mumbled about not being sure yet, and thrust a tenner at him and stumbled out of the car.

"Esther Harrison," she said to the new girl on reception, "I've an appointment with Mona?"

"OK, you'll be with me, then. Mona's off sick at the moment, so I'm doing her cuts. Would you like to come and take a seat?"

Esther tagged along behind her, feeling dizzy and slightly out of control. "What do you mean, off sick? Is she OK? Has she got flu – it's been doing the rounds, hasn't it?"

The girl fastened her into a gown and started brushing through Esther's hair. "No – she's not very good apparently. Had a bit of a breakdown – got obsessive compulsive disorder or something like that…"

"Obsessive compulsive disorder?" whispered Esther.

"That's right, obsessive compulsive disorder. She can't stop washing herself or something – sounds a bit odd, doesn't it? Came from nowhere apparently. She's trying to get treated, but there's quite a waiting list, so she might be off for some time – you can't have someone in here changing their clothes every half hour, can you? Gets nothing done! Now, what are we doing today?"

"Just a tidy up and set," Esther mumbled weakly. She could feel the sweat beading on her brow and her guts were churning. Obsessive compulsive disorder? A bit of a breakdown? It was all like a bad dream.

"Are you OK?" asked the girl, as she led her to the sink.

"Just had a bit of bad news today, it's shaken me up a bit," replied Esther, trying to pull herself together.

"Oh, that's tough. I had some bad news once..." and the girl was off. Esther knew that she could just sit and nod occasionally and she could get through this. Just don't be sick or faint, she told herself. Please:don't be sick or faint...

Esther was settled under the heat-lamps and had a pile of magazines thrust onto her lap. She leafed through the contents pages; because she'd never had a weight problem, so many of the articles were simply of no interest to her. *Improve your Zest for Life!* No, not at that point yet. *Coping with Loss* – nor that, but maybe she should rip out the article and take it home – could be useful for future reading.

Page 43 – What To Do If You Suspect He Is Cheating? Ah, now, this was more like it. Coming in for a haircut was obviously fate. Esther flicked to page 43 – quickly looking around her to check that no one was reading it over her shoulder.

Weight loss, increased care with appearance, unexplained outings or things taking longer than usual were listed as the signs. Right – now she was getting somewhere. Anger, rage, disgust, dismay, anxiety, incredulity and depression were the symptoms felt by the cheated partner – yes, she had run the gamut of those in the last hour and a half alone.

What to do: now, this was the useful bit. Unfortunately, it wasn't a simple checklist: shout, scream, cry, cut off his testicles, shred his suits, and get a good lawyer. She needed to consider it first – what did *she*

243

want from it by way of a result? *Separation, Reconciliation, Revenge, Release?* Esther gave up and put the magazine to the bottom of the pile. At the moment, she just needed a way through the rest of the day.

Right, she thought, think clearly. Her scalp was beginning to burn, and that meant that she was nearly done. Presumably the first thing was to clarify the truth. If it were just malicious rumour and plucked from the air then she was worrying about nothing. Having a romp in a works cupboard didn't sound like David's style, although when they were first courting, they'd done it in her parents' downstairs toilet – not very salubrious, but then they didn't seem to need salubrious in those days...and opportunities to be alone together were rare.

Perhaps she should meet him at work, wait for him in the car park. Catch him off guard and confront him. It could be sorted by the time they got home. *Hang on, wasn't he planning to pop to Louisa's flat after work tonight?* Why on a Friday night? Perhaps he's meeting *her* there?

Esther dived back to the pile of magazines and rummaged, pulling out the one she had read earlier. She flicked back the pages and checked the checklist: *unexplained outings or things taking longer than usual.* Right, David Harrison – show time!

She paid, tipped, said it looked lovely having barely having taken in what the girl had done to her, and then turned back to ask that she pass Esther's best wishes on to Mona. Louisa's flat on Market Street was only 200 yards from the hairdresser's and Esther reached it at 4.40p.m. She settled herself in a café window seat across the road and ordered a large mug of tea and a scone and prepared to wait.

The police car shot past the turning that led to Anweledig, then reversed back and dipped down into the hamlet. PC Janet Taylor checked her notebook and then stopped outside the Dingle. She strode up the drive, her radio bleeping and chatting to her as she went. She knocked smartly on the door. Then she rang the bell, then she knocked again, then she peeped through the lounge window.

Having ascertained that there was no one in, she returned to her car. Funny business this, she thought. Esther Harrison was that woman who used to be involved with the Guides several years ago. She remembered going to see them when she was a Community Officer to talk to the girls about self-defence and remembered Esther as being just like *her* old Guide leader twenty years before. She'd never have put her down as a malicious writer, but then, nothing would surprise her anymore.

Right, back to the station for an hour of paperwork before heading out to start the early Friday night drinkers' deterrent presence.

And so the only police car that had visited Anweledig in the last fifty-five years purred out of the hamlet and headed back to the badlands of Tan-y-Bryn.

Esther was on her second mug of tea and was dotting up the crumbs of her scone when she saw her husband's car pull up across the street. She felt the sweat break out on her forehead and she had to take a grip of herself to stop involuntary whimpering. She leant back into the shadows, although David was twenty yards away and not likely to see her. She watched as he checked his new *hairstyle* in the mirror and blew a breath into his cupped palm. He rummaged in something lying on the passenger seat and then she saw him squirting something on to his neck: aftershave! Since when did David Harrison use anything in addition to a squirt of Tesco's own in the morning?

Another check in the mirror and then he got out of the car. He suddenly seemed to be very tall and actually quite handsome as he brushed himself down and checked that his shirt was tucked in.

As she watched him, she felt a wave of sadness wash over her. Perhaps this was all her fault? Perhaps she'd become blind to him and his handsome looks, his sense of fun? She'd certainly not treasured him for at least a dozen years or so – mainly out of spite for him not treasuring her, but even so… Maybe she'd driven him into another woman's arms, a refuge of comfort where someone actually thought he was worth making an effort for? Could she be watching the final moments of life as she knew it?

Tears pricked to her eyes as she saw him look up and down the street and then open the door to the flat at the side of the pound shop. He did look furtive, no doubt about it; there was definitely *something* going on.

Esther was dabbing at her eyes with a rough corner of a serviette when she saw someone else who was distinctly furtive walking down the street in the January night. She looked like a high-class prostitute – a madam, maybe. A faux fur coat, done up top to bottom, red stiletto-heeled shoes and – surely not, not in Tan-y-Bryn – fishnet tights. The madam's head wasn't quite as fitting as the rest of her, being a little bit jowly and a little bit plain, even though it had a fair bit of make-up on.

Esther's curiosity turned to horror as she saw the madam stop outside number 40B. Oh God – surely not prostitutes? Not in their own daughter's flat? Not *fur coat, no knickers*, not for her husband? Esther half got to her feet and then slumped down again and groaned as the madam pushed the door open and slipped in, gently closing the door behind her.

Esther felt sick as she imagined the fur coat climbing the stairs, the heels sashaying slowly towards Louisa's flat. She imagined David hanging around the door, nervously checking his appearance again and again, cupping his breath and doubting the strength of his deodorant. She bet that he'd be a gentleman with madam, offering her a drink first before gratefully partaking of her wares.

Would David feel guilty? Probably, but he'd no doubt be able to justify it. Esther wasn't interested in him anymore and a man did have urges and far better to pay for it up front, an honest transaction, than to have an affair? But, there was still that letter burning away in her bag – the one that said he *was* having an affair – and with his regular lift.

Esther's stomach suddenly flipped – surely that woman wasn't Diane Dawson? Mumsy neat blouse and pencil skirt stuck round her fat arse Diane? Surely not? Could Diane Dawson have bought a prostitute's outfit and clacked down the road in it in her own town?

Esther fled her surveillance window and hobbled to the loo. She looked into the mirror and saw a grey sallow face with a bouffant blow-dry halo peering at her. Her round-neck white top was brilliant white, but depressingly sexless. Her grey cardigan was seriously warm, but would never light the loins of any man, especially one who was turned on by fur coat and no knickers.

So, now what…? Nothing else for it: she had to go and sort it out. She washed her hands, dried them, washed an imaginary spot off them again, and then admitted that she was playing for time. She took a deep breath, left the toilets, paid her bill and walked out into the cold night.

PC Janet Taylor was walking down the corridor of Tan-y-Bryn police station towards the entrance foyer.

"Taylor? Where you off to?"

"Just off out, Sarge. Gonna walk past the pound shop on Market Street and turn left into Morris Street. Thought I might leave now – you never know, I might just stop someone making the mistake of their life!"

"Not yet you won't. Can you just come here for ten minutes – I need to ask you something..."

The gas fire was blazing and the inhabitant of the fur coat was getting hot.

"David," she whispered, "don't say anything. Let's forget what happened the other day, yeah?"

"Yes," David whispered back. "All forgotten." He reached out to touch the woman, but she moved back from his hand and instead put a red-nailed finger over his mouth.

"Sh, all done. Now..." and she undid her top coat button and slipped the shoulder off to reveal naked flesh, " ...we both know that it all has to stop. I'm not going back to work, but I can't leave Harry, so this will be our last time together. OK, lover?" David groaned and nodded hungrily. "We'll just have this one last hour and then we'll go back to our normal lives and never mention it again, OK?"

"OK."

"But..."

"Yes?"

"We can think about it, OK, lover?"

"Oh, yes, we'll certainly be thinking about it..." And the fur coat fell to the floor. David leapt at the mass of bare flesh that it had covered. If it was their last time, then he needed to make sure it was memorable.

Louisa had left the bank at five p.m. spot on, with many giggles and good lucks. Doreen had clucked around her all day, teasing her excitedly about her special night ahead; it was the best thing that had happened to the employees in that bank for years. The moment the numbers flicked over to 17:00, the staff all piled out the door, Louisa being allowed to do her key first and then run as fast as she could along the pavement with lots of calls and whoops following behind her. By the Argos five doors down, she'd slowed to a fast walk.

She'd driven past Doreen, still waving in excitement for her usually miserable friend. All the way home, Louisa had felt special, turning on the radio to see if someone had asked for a request to help on her way to a great evening out. They hadn't.

She wasn't really sure which part of the evening she was most excited about: the date with this Iestyn bloke or having a drink with Rachel and Rosie and their friends if the date didn't work out. The party afterwards might be a step too far, but a drink with a few people in a pub – well, she was sure she could handle that. Half of her wanted to forget about Iestyn and just go for the drink. A blind date was so much more momentous than anything she had arranged for herself before and she thought that the only reason she'd entertained the idea of it was because it was so far-fetched so as to be impossible.

However, with her new found drive and determination to forge through into a new life, she was going to give it a chance at the very least. If he was naff – or perhaps more likely he thought her naff and ran off after the starter – then she could do both drink and date.

She pulled into Anweledig a good ten minutes before she normally did. Strange: no lights, no open gate and actually no banners or balloons either. Louisa felt miffed having to get out and open the gate; it was raining for God's sake and she *had* been working all day…

The house was in darkness too; what was going on? The only thing that she could think of was that her mum must have met her dad from work and they had popped to the shops to buy her a gift – something to make her evening extra special. Something new, something blue or whatever the saying was. Well, although it was very nice of them, it still meant that in the meantime she'd have to make her own cup of tea and probably a sandwich to keep her strength up – she didn't want to show herself up by being ravenous on a first date…

Esther pushed open the front door that was still on the latch and began the long climb up the green swirly-carpeted stairs. Perhaps Diane was a teacher in her spare time and was giving David French lessons before making her way to the Prostitutes' Club afterwards? Perhaps she was a chiropodist and under that coat was a white uniform – no, uniforms were still dodgy. Maybe she was also a plumber as well as an administrative assistant and had just popped by to fix the fire? The possibilities for a happy ending were infinite.

She needn't have tiptoed as the inhabitants of 40B were pretty absorbed in what they were doing. She was able to watch them for long enough to allow every detail of the scene to become ingrained in her mind's eye and hence to allow it, with all its rich sounds and scents, to be replayed in great detail at any future point in her life, day or night.

The sight of her husband giving it his best, and to a woman lying on a faux fur coat, her stockinged legs pointing straight up in the air and tipped with bouncing red patent shoes, could have been comical, had it not had such horrendous implications. Maybe it was feminine intuition, maybe it was boredom, but the woman – now very definitely Diane – stopped chewing David's ear and drawing blood from his back with her painted nails and looked around. "David," she hissed, trying to push him up from her.

"Call me Scamper," he urged.

"Scamper?"

"Yes?"

"It's Esther..."

"No, call yourself something different..."

"No, *it's* Esther, *she's here*." The buttocks stopped pumping and hovered mid-thrust.

"Too fucking right it's Esther," roared Esther from her position in the doorway. "Scamper...? Get up, you fucking idiot!"

"Esther?" David turned, more shocked by the transformation of his wife into a cursing fishwife, than he was by the sight of her there, staring at his duplicitous buttocks.

"What the bloody hell do you think you're doing?" raged his wife. "And you..." she spat at Diane who was now rolling herself back into her fur coat, at least lucky enough not to need to put her knickers back on this time. "What the hell are you doing screwing my husband?"

David was now spluttering like a naughty boy, clearly out of his depth in the face of the wrath of Esther. "Esther, love, it won't be happening again," he said, tucking his shirt into his trousers and squatting slightly to re-adjust himself.

"Well, David," she stormed, still holding the room in her command, "don't worry on my account, you can screw this harlot as much as you like – and Diane, I'm so ashamed of *you*. I thought you were a bloody *prostitute* when I saw you walking over here, got up like that. Anyway, David: you won't be coming home. Our marriage is over. You can just ask Louisa if you can sub-let your shag pad from her and then you can play 'Scamper and The Whore' to your heart's content. And, if you are wondering how I found out, take a good look at this…" She rummaged in her bag for the letter, tore it from its envelope and threw it at him. Despite her venom, it fluttered gently to the floor to rest by her feet and sat there gazed at by two pairs of confused eyes as they clocked its contents. She could tell that they were itching to grab it and analyse it, but instead had to make do with reading it from afar, both squinting and looking as if they wanted to fetch their glasses. "Shagging in a bloody store cupboard? At work? Yuck: look at the state of you both. I hope that whoever it was who discovered you was offered counselling… Goodnight!"

Esther picked up the letter again and stuffed it back in her pocket. "Just in case I ever feel a wave of kindness and feel like I might want to let you come back," she explained, and then she turned and felt for the door frame. She was unsteady on her legs and had to grope her way to the top of the stairs.

"Esther, are you all right, love?"

"Yes, I'll be OK, thanks. Just need to get a hand on the banister. There. OK, done now, thanks," even in Esther's mood, her habitual resilience remained.

She hobbled down the stairs feeling shaky and sick. She was not sure how that had gone – as expected, perhaps? Maybe not. But then, how could you ever predict how one might react in such a situation.

She reached the front door and clutched for the handle, pleased to feel the cold of the air as it hit her flushed face. She stepped out onto the pavement and stood for just a couple of seconds, trying to gather her thoughts about what had happened and what she was to do now.

"Hang on a minute – Esther Harrison? Is that you?" asked the voice of a woman who had just screeched to a standstill on the pavement next to her.

"Pardon? Er, yes, I am Est—"

"PC Janet Taylor. What a coincidence, I've just been thinking about you. Would you like to accompany me to the station? We need to have a chat..."

"No, not now actually. I'm a little tired and could do with—"

"*Now*, Mrs Harrison, if you don't mind... It's not far, just round this corner; here, see the sign? Good. Come along... "

In the dingy sitting room with the dusty green carpet, Diane and David gathered their composure, both bright red with humiliation and probably both wishing the other gone from the face of the earth, never mind number 40B Market Street, Tan-y-Bryn.

"Caught with my tits out twice in three days..." muttered Diane. "This has *got* to stop."

David didn't reply. He looked green. That letter – he wished he'd been able to read it properly, to study it, so that he could work out a defence. He didn't really want to discuss it with Diane, he wanted a clear head to think. "Did you manage to read that letter?" she said, "what did you think it said?"

"A bit."

"Well, what did you think it said?" asked Diane, now clearly irritated by him.

"Something about being *in flagrante* in a store cupboard and that it had been going on for weeks."

"*In flagrante*? Who the hell would have said *in flagrante*? I just saw my name and something about it being from a long-standing acquaintance."

"Well, what ever it bloody said, that's it, isn't it. All over. Finished." He walked to the window, yanked open the curtain and leant his forehead onto the cool glass. "Twenty-odd years of marriage, thirty years together – and all over. Just like that."

Diane was frowning at him, "Well, if it had been *that* good, you probably wouldn't have been here tonight with me."

"That was different. An – aside – perhaps."

251

"An aside? An *aside*? I thought you said it was the most wonderful thing you've ever experienced. *I've never felt so alive,*" she finished, in a mocking voice.

David shrugged. His head was in turmoil. What should he do now? Go home, stay here, shag Diane again, or get chips? In four short weeks his life had been turned upside down. He was a laughing stock at work and there was no way he was going to keep his job as team leader; it would be untenable with people smirking behind his back. Whenever he spoke to someone, someone else would reach round them from behind and fondle their chest, and then everyone would fall about laughing.

Louisa would hate him. Esther already hated him and everything he'd worked for over the years was fluttering away in a haze of dusty-carpeted lust.

Diane's phone rang from the depths of her handbag; they both froze.

"Who is it?" hissed David.

"How the hell do I know?" said Diane and she strode over to have a look.

"Shit, it's Harry."

"What does he want?"

"Well, how the hell should I know? I haven't answered the bloody thing, have I?" The phone stopped ringing and they looked at each other for fifteen seconds until it bleeped to signify that a message had been left.

"Shit," Diane said.

"You'd better listen to it; he might be – I don't know, coming round?"

"Don't be ridiculous. He doesn't know I'm here. As far as he knows, I'm out for a power walk."

"In nothing but heels and a fur coat?"

"I got changed, stupid..."

David mumbled something to himself and returned to the window. It seemed to take forever hearing Diane phone her answer machine and finally hear the message. He heard her swear and chuck the phone down.

"He said," she said with tears in her voice, "that he's had a letter and if I'm with you, then not to bother coming home. And he knows

I *am* with you, as why else would I have taken my make-up bag, a kit bag and a car out with me on a walk..." She turned to David with tears rolling down her face. "Oh God, it's such a mess. I thought he was in the bathroom when I left. Oh, poor Harry."

Poor Harry? thought David, what about poor David? Homeless, probably soon to be jobless and with a wife that hated him. If she were really that bothered about poor bloody Harry, *she* surely wouldn't have been here in the first place either...

Louisa stood in front of the full-length mirror on the inside of her wardrobe door and turned to the side. That red top – *why* had she said that she'd definitely wear it? If *only* she'd double-checked it first. When she'd last worn it, it had looked quite nice, floating comfortably over her stomach and hips. Now it clung a bit, settling around her rounded stomach and then sitting, as if resting on a ledge, on top of her hips. Bloody Mum; she must have put it on too hot a wash or something; she was sure that she hadn't gotten any plumper – not much, anyway.

Where the hell was Esther anyway? And her dad? She wouldn't have wanted them fawning around her, making a fuss about her date – it was only a date after all, but it would have been nice if they could have taken a *bit* of interest, reassured her that she looked OK and that she'd be fine.

She hung the top back on the hanger next to her new jeans and went for a shower. She still had two hours to go, but she didn't want to be in a rush.

Esther stood at the front desk of the draughty police station while the duty sergeant took all her details. Finally she was offered a seat where she sat and stared at the patchwork of posters that covered the wall, stating the obvious: don't drink and drive, say no to drugs, *don't be so bloody stupid as to write malicious letters...*

She was shivering from the cold, but also shaking from the various shocks of the day. She felt sick and didn't know what to do. She would normally phone David. Yet, how could she ask him to prise his penis out of Diane Dawson and come and rescue her from a cell for doing something so unpleasant. When he finds out, he'll probably be relieved to be able to correct people and say, "No, you mean my *estranged* wife: we're not together anymore. I'm now called Scamper and live in my daughter's flat with a whore."

She'd watched *The Bill* enough times; she should know by now what would be happening, but she felt like a small child sat outside the headmistress's office. She knew she was going to get told off, but had no idea as to how bad it would be. The clock on the wall ticked to 6.30, then 7 p.m.

"They won't be long now," the duty sergeant had called to her a couple of times but she knew it was a tactic to make her sweat, to wear her down – and it was working. The one consolation was that Louisa had her date tonight and wouldn't need anything to eat – otherwise, she'd probably have phoned the police by now out of sheer indignation at being left to her own devices. Esther had turned her phone off; she didn't feel like talking to anyone or answering any questions as to where she was and why.

She felt like she'd had enough of other people's input. She knew she shouldn't be here. She knew she shouldn't have done what she'd done. Thinking about it, she realised that she'd been feeling manipulated for nigh on the past twenty years and it had all finally boiled over into something stupid, nasty and vindictive.

She tried to think of the last time that she'd not felt like pulling her hair out. It was probably when Louisa was young, before she'd gotten swept up in her do-gooding, as David used to call it. Before that moment she'd felt like she had a good balance in her life. She enjoyed her job and working just three days a week allowed her plenty of time with Louisa, but still a little autonomy.

Then, just as she was thinking it was time to put her ceramics plans into action, her phone had begun to ring. Was there any chance she could just pop to number 23? Margaret had taken a fall and needed some shopping. Of course she could. Before long, it seemed that her phone number had been stuck on a card in a phone box, but instead of saying "Oral sex given, 24 hours", it said, "Domestic and emergency help given for free; no advance notice needed. Please feel free to take the piss."

She knew that she had been doing more than her fair share and that it had extended beyond neighbourly helpfulness, but it was very difficult to say no. However, the do-gooding had started to cause a rift in her marriage. David began with little mutterings and tuts, then moved on to remonstrations and finally to asking her what sort of mother she was if she preferred sorting out Mavis Stratton's fat-roll ulcers to supervising her own daughter's progress in her spelling test.

"Well, *you're* here; Louisa does have you…" she would mumble, "if I hadn't gone to Mavis tonight that dressing would be black by now and she'd be back in hospital…"

"Maybe then someone would be able to give her the attention she needs!" he would yell in frustration.

"But then I'd still have to look after her cat…" David would storm out and Esther would wash the dishes or get Louisa's clothes ready for the next day in silence.

As she sat on that hard chair in the police station, Esther tried to think about what benefits her charity had brought her. It was obvious really that David had as good as insisted that they move to Anweledig to call a halt to her constant running around. The irony was, of course, that her stroke would have stopped it anyway – and maybe she would have had a little of her investment in her neighbours paid back. It was as if the gods were about to take care of it, but David forgot to tell them he was making alternative plans and so she was given a stroke, but in a place where no one else lived, where she had no friends or support mechanisms and the bus only went past twice a day.

The stroke had been a bolt from the blue. She'd always tried to look after herself; she'd never smoked and rarely indulged in anything that might encourage such a condition. Unlike the old guys, the ones whose pissy bathroom floors she'd been cleaning, who smoked twenty rollies a day, had thick butter on their toast and went down the Legion six nights a week for a few nips. It all seemed so unfair.

The saving grace – if there could be such a thing – was that David was so good with Louisa. And what could she have said? She couldn't have offered to do more herself, so it would have been a pretty pointless conversation.

They'd never really spoken much about her stroke. Yes, they'd had conversations about the medical prognosis, the rehabilitation and the practicalities of general living, but they'd never really discussed how it made her *feel* or what he *thought* about it. It was as if they were living with a diseased dog – there was lots of debate about how to keep the sofa clean, but not a lot about having a dog in the house in the first place.

"They *really* won't be long now," said the duty sergeant as he walked past with a tray filled with steaming cups of tea and a plate of chocolate biscuits. Esther only just managed to stop herself bursting into tears and pleading for a cuppa herself…

Menna stood in the shower and let the water flow over her. Her face was turned to the showerhead as she rinsed the day's grime from her body. She had her hair slathered in deep conditioner, she had already shaved her legs and had removed all the old nail varnish from her toenails. Her bathroom was wonderfully warm and Marvin Gaye was being piped out from the speaker in the corner. It was as if all the pampering that she had given herself in this room over the months had been just a trial run: this time other people were going to see the outcome.

She was nervous about the night ahead. She was nervous about her new dress and she was nervous about how she was going to manage to walk in her new shoes. "Wear them about the house for a couple of weeks," Sima had suggested, "you'll soon get used to them!" But what if people laughed at her? What if her efforts made her look worse than usual? What if Iestyn preferred her dressed as a waiter?

Tonight felt as if it were the start of a new chapter in her life. She felt like a caterpillar that was starting to nibble through her chrysalis. Sima had said to just act as she normally did. Accept the compliments, as there were sure to be dozens, and take them all in her stride. "People will no doubt look at you, but if you act as if, *well of course I look beautiful tonight; it's a big party* then you won't feel uncomfortable. Make it *their* big deal, not yours. And just enjoy it; it's all going to be fine!"

At last she was free from soap suds and so she stepped from the shower, wrapping herself in a huge towel and then sitting on the chair. She had plenty of time and she wanted to get everything right. Make-up first, then hair, then finally dress. And what of Iestyn? Was he going to look all dashing and suave in his dad's funeral suit again, or would Joe have brought him something else to wear? Would he seek her out, or would he be too busy at the bar?

She felt that after the cringing lunch that he'd had at her parents' place and the fact that he was *so* embarrassed and desperate to explain about the rabbit ears night, that *surely* he must fancy her? She knew that he had in the past and – well, she'd blown him away for reasons that he would never know – so, maybe tonight, she might be able to take another step towards re-kindling something?

Softened by body lotion, she stepped into her bedroom and sat down at her dressing table.

In the Bevan household, things were a little more confused than usual. Joe and Sima had their party clothes all ready in a plastic travel sleeve, but Sima wouldn't let them be put on until the last minute. "They'll be filthy in no time," she'd glared at Joe as she sat with her face perfectly made up and her rollers still in, wearing a pair of jeans and a button-down-the-front blouse.

Tomos was still in the far barn and hadn't been seen for hours. Isla was running round in an ancient dressing gown muttering, "Where the hell is he? Why's he taking so long? Iestyn, love, go and find him. Tell him to get his skates on, we'll never get there at this rate – and he should really have a shower too before he goes…"

"Should?" laughed Joe. "Even Dad can't go to a dinner covered in cow shit and straw, surely! *I'll* go and find him; Iestyn's on a date, *he* can't risk being late and keeping a lady waiting."

Sima glowered at him, "Don't you *dare* get stuck into something. Promise me? *Promise!*"

"It's OK, I'll just wander over and drag him back by his wellies – although he did ask for a bit of help with that tractor gearbox… Only joking," he laughed, hands held up and he grabbed his coat and the torch and barged out of the door into the night.

"Oh, I don't know, Sima, love, what *is* it about men that they can't get themselves ready for a simple night out? Now," she said, before Sima could reply, "where on *earth* might my best shoes be? I was certain that I put them back in the box after last year's dance…" Sima rolled her eyes: she thought the Bevans were wonderful people, but my goodness they were useless at some things…

*

"Mrs Harrison?" PC Taylor put her head round a door. "Would you like to come in now? We're ready for you." Esther nodded and got to her feet. Her leg was aching from the strain of so much more walking than she usually did and also the effect of all the stresses on her soul that day. She was sat at a cold table next to a draughty window overlooking the car compound. She could see the backs of the properties that lined Market Street. Louisa would be making her way to the reataurant pretty soon. Esther was sure that the red glow from one of the windows would be the back rooms of the China Palace.

Sitting across the table from Esther was a smartly-dressed man in his fifties and also PC Jan Taylor. Esther was cold, she needed the toilet and she was desperate for a cup of tea, but she didn't feel that any of her requests would be looked on favourably.

PC Taylor turned the tape player on to *record* and stated the circumstances of the interview. The smart man turned out to be Detective Arnold. Esther was reminded that she wasn't arrested, but under caution. Her miserable nods were pounced on with a "Please speak up for the benefit of the tape."

"Right then, Mrs Harrison, what's been going on?"

"What do you mean?" *Letters? Affairs? Useless daughter?* "Mrs Harrison, we have twenty-seven malicious letters in our possession all posted from within Tan-y-Bryn to properties within the Tan-y-Bryn area..."

"Twenty-seven?" Esther was flabbergasted: she'd only written, what twelve, thirteen tops!

"Yes, although we don't believe that they are all from the same person, Tan-y-Bryn seems to have, I am afraid to say, a bedrock of spiteful people who, once the idea was put into their minds, found it the ideal outlet for their small-minded prejudices." PC Taylor shuffled a pile of bagged letters, all individually labelled. "And yours, Mrs Harrison, we believe started it all off." She found a plastic wallet with Esther's first letter to the Tasty Bite Café. Esther went pale.

"Envelope A11. One of yours?"

Esther nodded, tears now rolling down her face.

"For the tape, please, Mrs Harrison."

"Yes."

"And this one, A12?"

"Yes."

"And this, A13?"

"Yes."

"What about these two, A15 and A16?"

Esther didn't recognise the font or the pink paper. "No, those aren't mine."

"Didn't think so..."

The list continued and Esther winced her way through it, now aware of the human misery that she had caused; a café closed with a hardworking couple losing their livelihood, a family moving house, a hairdresser unable to work because of OCD.

When she could bear no more, Esther picked her bag from the back of her chair. "I received some too..." she whispered. The PC and the detective exchanged smirks and Esther wished she'd kept quiet.

"The other is at home..." she said.

"Mrs Harrison is handing over a letter," said PC Taylor for the tape, but Esther could see that she couldn't wait to read it. The WPC read it out for the tape, knowing that she was delighting the man at her side. Esther suspected that this could well be the lowest point in her whole life.

CHAPTER 32

Taflu'r llo a chadw'r brych – to throw the calf and keep the afterbirth

The Lamp had done itself as proud as it was ever likely to bother to do; the floor tiles were shining as throngs of people in out of date finery hurried into the hall. The air was filled with the sound of farming ladies used to wearing plenty of layers, now having to suffer with naught but a sequined shrug to protect themselves from the chill, and gents whose dress shoes wouldn't fit over their usual two pairs of woollen socks. Although the snow was thawing fast, there was still a biting wind to whip up under their net petticoats or through the cloth of their threadbare party and funeral trousers.

"Blo-ody hell, it's cold out there!"

"Evan! Language!"

"Well," now a whisper, "it bloody is…"

"Jee-sus, there'll be brass monkeys with no bollocks all over tonight!"

"Hywel! Please! You said you'd behave!"

"Sorry, love, but there will be."

"Fuck it's cold."

"Yeah, it fuckin' is."

Menna's parents, as usual, had been the first to arrive. When an invite said seven o'clock, they would be there at seven o'clock. It meant that they had plenty of time to look around, comment on *everything*, and to welcome every single person into the large hall.

"Evening, Alice, cold tonight!"

"Evening, Cled, cold enough for you?"

"Evening, Alun, cold, eh?" And so on.

To her mother's dismay, Menna hadn't wanted to travel with them. "But, Menna – it says seven o'clock, look!"

"Mam, that's just a guide. No-one'll be expecting you to be there at precisely that time."

"But, Menna, you don't want to be late…"

"Mam, m'n, I'll follow you down. Don't worry about it. It's not a big deal."

Menna had been getting more and more cagey about what she revealed to her mother recently. She'd shrugged when Jean had asked her what she was wearing. She hadn't let her iron it, whatever it was and she'd resisted her calls to "hang all our things up together", or "put them next to each other to make sure we won't clash."

"We won't, Mam, don't worry," Menna had grumbled.

She was up to something, Jean thought. She would never normally hide outfits or keep secrets.

"I'll follow you over in the truck," she'd said. *Follow them over!* What point was there in that? An extra ten miles in diesel – twenty if you included fetching the truck the next day if she decided to have a couple of drinks and get a lift back with them. *Madness!*

Jean loved the Annual Sheep Breeders' Dinner. It was her one glamorous occasion of the year and she wouldn't miss it for the world. It was a last fling before the onslaught of lambing, which kept people tied to their farms for a good six weeks. It was the chance to meet up with all her neighbours and have a good old chinwag and to catch up on the gossip of the last year. Jean was a sociable person, but she worked too hard to spend much time visiting people or going out for lunch with friends. Ladies that lunch? Not her: more like a lady that washes, irons, bakes, cleans, feeds, mucks out and makes sure that all around her have everything they need to go about their jobs on the farm.

The hall was filling up. Jean was getting a bit nervous; if Menna didn't arrive soon, she'd be *late* and there'd be nowhere for her to sit and she, Jean, couldn't hang on to an empty seat all night as they were trying to sit opposite the Burtons...

Iestyn stood in front of his mirror frowning. He was dressed in one of Joe's shirts with a pair of Joe's jeans on. He had Joe's silk socks on, last winter's good shoes and Sima had even thrown him a pair of Joe's Calvin Klein boxers "in case you get lucky!" She might have been joking, but he'd popped them on anyway and they were a hundred times more attractive than his old raggedy turquoise ones...

He'd had a haircut and Sima had slicked his hair into shape with some hair wax that gave results a million miles from those he used to get from the dusty can of mousse on the bathroom windowsill.

"You look gorgeous!" she'd said as she'd stood back to admire her work and he had to admit that he very nearly did. Somehow, the same barber that he'd been to since he was a lad had finally done something other than simply *cut it* and, under Sima's instructions, he actually had a style. He wasn't sure that he could recreate it on his own, but it was nice to know that he did brush up well with a little effort, even if that effort had to be made by someone else.

He should have been standing wondering what his date would be like, what they would talk about, whether they would get on, but he wasn't. He was thinking about Menna. He'd seen her in her truck in town and that had made him nervous. Then Sima had had to rush from the barbers and he was sure that he'd seen them walking up the street together, going God knew where.

It was a shame that Menna couldn't see him now, looking as good as he did. She normally saw him covered in mud/briars/axle grease or eating her father's lunch, and it would be nice to show her that he could look good when the occasion arose. He'd kicked himself when he'd realised that he'd arranged this date for the night of the Sheep Breeders'. Typical: *absolutely* nothing happens for months and then there's two things on the same night.

"Perhaps I could re-arrange Lulu?" he'd suggested to Johnny Brechdan.

"You're joking, aren't you? The first decent date you've had in years, with someone who wouldn't rather be out with me and you want to postpone it in favour of a night with your parents and a hundred other pissed farmers singing 'Hi Ho Silver Lining' and trying to remember how to rock and roll? Honestly, Iestyn, there'll always be next year and the year after that and they'll all be *exactly* the same!"

"S'pose so," he'd said, trying to ignore the recurring image of his mother trying to jitterbug.

So, he decided to go for it – the big date with Lulu. But Menna normally went to the Sheep Breeders'. Normally wore a pair of trousers and a shiny top, and chugged pints like a navvy, but it would be nice to see her. To try and sit near her. Make her laugh and try and catch the twinkle in her eye...

He heard a call from downstairs. "Iest – we're all ready! For God's sake come on before we lose Dad to the barn again; the bugger's been out chasing rats with a length of alcathene pipe all this time!"

"Aye, and I'd have had the big bastard if you'd given me another two minutes an' all."

Iestyn picked up his wallet and put it in his back pocket. He checked his hair once more and left the room. The others were waiting in the kitchen, Joe looking well-fed in an expensive suit, Sima looking devastatingly beautiful in a silver off-the-shoulder number with a black lacy shawl draped around her for warmth and Mother in the same dress that she'd worn every year for the past twenty years, but with brown lace-ups in place of the usual gold flatties. She spotted Iestyn's questioning gaze. "Oh, I couldn't find my dancing shoes, now, can we just *go*?"

Father stood at the door, washed and scrubbed in record time and looking dapper in the suit he'd got married in. "Come on, come on – your carriage awaits…" and he winked at his wife and took her by the arm.

262

They all climbed into Joe's Jeep and Iestyn hopped into the driving seat and quickly put the heaters on and soon they were all warm and snug and heading off down the track for their big night out. They stopped at the first gate. "Mother'll have to get out," sniggered Tomos. "She's got the right shoes on…"

"Oi, you," giggled Isla, but she jumped out into the slush and the darkness. Iestyn could feel Sima's glare at Joe.

"Well, I've got my suedes on," he claimed, a little wounded.

"Suedes?" laughed Tomos. "You'll be like Dancin' Dafydd!"

"Dancin' Dafydd?"

"No, it was Jiggling John; you remember – at the Lakeside."

"Jiggling John?"

"No, no, it wasn't the Lakeside, it was Beryl's uncle's place."

"Beryl's uncle's? No, she was the one with the hernia. You mean Phillip Evans. You know – Phillip and the cream cake…"

Sima looked out into the blackness: it could well be a long night.

Iestyn drove into the car park of the Lamp Hotel and pulled into a space. All around him there were 4 x 4's, some battered and ancient, others brand new and gleaming. Nearly all had had some kind of cleaning out for the occasion. Greying snow still lay on the ground and so most of the guests had reluctantly spurned their cars and opted to use their trucks instead despite the agricultural odours, which clashed nicely with the unaccustomed scent of Old Spice and Yardley's Lavender.

"Right," said Iestyn, "everyone out! Have a lovely evening and I'll call by on my way back and give you a lift home if you're still here. Text me, yeah, if anything changes," he added to Joe, "and thanks for the loan of the Jeep; it'll give me a bit of a head start and, by Christ, I need it!"

"Nonsense, you look fantastic!" Sima said. "Now, *enjoy* yourself, and don't worry about us. We'll just get a taxi home if need be."

"Taxi?" muttered Tomos. "You'll not find a rank at the end of this road, *bach*…"

Iestyn watched them go, two couples arm in arm. Joe supporting Sima and her unsuitable shoes across the snow and Mother supporting Father with her brown lace-ups and his worn-out soles. The last thing he heard was Father mumbling, "I hope they've got lots of spuds this year: I'm so hungry, I could eat a scabby horse raw…"

Iestyn checked his watch, still plenty of time to get to the restaurant to meet Lulu. He still wasn't sure how he'd find her. She'd said she'd wear a bright red blouse and that she had blonde hair. Sounded good to him and he assumed that the China Palace wouldn't have many women like that in it on a winter's night! He reached over and mucked about with Joe's stereo, pressing all the buttons and running through the CDs on his multi-changer. Joe's tastes had moved on a little further than his own had and he turned the volume up high, cocooned in his luxurious world, lit by a dashboard of blue lights and with climate control keeping him warm.

As he settled on CD number five, he noticed a lump on the seat next to him. Damn – Joe's wallet. He'd need that later, thought Iestyn; Sima had looked like she needed more than a little placating. He picked it up and jumped out of the Jeep, shocked by the difference in temperature as the chill wind hit him. He hurried across the car park, nodding to a few neighbours as they climbed out of their trucks, all exclaiming about the cold weather.

He felt a little self-conscious as he walked in, everyone else being in evening wear and wanting to stop and chat. He just wanted to poke his head in and go. The hall widened into a lobby – good, there was Sima just coming out of the Ladies, looking fantastic as usual and people all around were turning and staring.

"Sima!" he called. "Over here!" He walked over and gave her the wallet.

"Good," she smiled, "he'll – no, *I'll* be needing that later!" She thanked Iestyn and wished him a good night again, then mumbled about going in to face her doom and off she went, a picture of style and elegance amongst the smell of mothballs and past-its-expiry-date perfume.

Iestyn turned and headed back towards the door, just as it was pushed open and Menna Edwards walked in. Iestyn stopped in his tracks and stared: what on *earth* had been going on? In place of a woman in a pair of jeans and trainers, was a beauty in an orangey-red dress. She hadn't noticed him as she was busy untwining a lacy scarf from round her neck. The dress was a strapless thick brocade tube with ruches up the front and – oh my God – Menna Edwards had curves!

She had a gold necklace at her throat that complemented the dress and gave her a warm glow. Her hair was clipped up at the back, apart from a few wisps that fell around her beautiful, freckled face. She had make-up on, but only a little and she looked absolutely – stunning.

At last she looked up and Iestyn realised that he was standing, gasping, with his mouth open.

"Iestyn…"

"Hi, Menna – you look, well, fabulous!"

She smiled a coy smile, "Thanks! You, er, you do too!"

"Me? Oh, no, I'm not dressed for here – I've got to go somewhere else tonight, I'm afraid. Worse luck, eh?" He was aware that he was gabbling, "Yeah, I've got a date. Never mind, eh? It'll be the same stuff as last year and next year too I expect. 'Hi Ho Silver Lining' and all that, eh?" He thought he saw her face fall. He wasn't sure – but if it did, it had soon recovered.

"Well, I'd better, well, go on in – y' know, make sure I don't end up sat next to Bad Breath Ken again…"

"Sima's there – and Joe. Look, why don't I…I wish I was… Oh, I'd better go. Have a good evening…"

"Yes, and you. Enjoy your – date." And she flashed him a smile that made his heart jump and she walked past him, a little unsteadily due to a pair of orangey-red heels.

He turned and watched her go. He felt sick. Why hadn't he just followed his gut instinct and cancelled bloody Lulu? What was the point of seeing someone new when he *so* wanted to be with Menna? Why was he going to fart about with chopsticks when he could be dancing to *Shout!* and the Grease medley that DJ Dave finished every single one of his crappy discos with?

He watched as she sashayed up the corridor, looking so small and dainty now that she wasn't padded out with excess denim and a bulky rugby shirt.

Should he just stay? Brechdan would. He'd just text Lulu and say, "Sorry, can't make it," or maybe not even bother doing that. But then again, he didn't have a ticket for the dinner. Even if he did decide to blow Lulu out, he wouldn't be able to have a meal. He couldn't just perch on a chair at the side of a table in a pair of jeans, looking like he'd forgotten where he was supposed to be, just because Menna Edwards had a dress on.

Still he stood and watched, his neck craned round to see as Menna clicked open her little bag and fiddled with something in it. Then she threw her shoulders back and made to walk into the hall, first giving a tiny backward glance that shook Iestyn into action. He gave a half-wave and turned and strode back into the night.

Louisa looked at her mauve bedside clock: eight minutes past eight. Right. Time to go. Fifteen minutes' drive, five extra to accommodate the snow and then a bit more time to allow her to be a little late and oooh, so busy, I nearly didn't get round to coming. That was what they said, wasn't it? Not to be too keen? Well, she was keen. Very keen. But, this Iestyn bloke didn't have to know it.

She brushed her hair again, then changed her mind and ruffled it a bit – tousled hair, wasn't that the in thing at the moment? That's what Rachel had had the other day, anyway. She turned to the side again and looked at her new jeans. Rachel had been right, they did look good. She still wasn't so sure about the top: she sucked her stomach in and then the top fell nicely. Sod it: now she'd just have to suck it in until she sat down and then – look out! Maybe she shouldn't have a starter, or give pudding a miss? Or maybe have a starter as a main course? She picked up her handbag and clomped down the stairs. Actually, she was quite peckish: perhaps she should just have all three if her stomach was going to stick out whatever...

Louisa took one last look at herself in the hall mirror, adjusted her necklace and gave a dazzling smile. "Right," she said, "goodbye Louisa, hello – *Lulu!* Oh Iestyn, you are a lucky boy..." Mind you, it would have been nice if her parents could have been bothered to be at home to wish her luck...what a pair of charmers!

Iestyn drove along the lanes towards Tan-y-Bryn. The music was loud, but he wasn't really listening. She'd looked gorgeous tonight, and even he'd looked passable – what a waste! There was still time... He could text Lulu, tell her he'd had a puncture or something. Drive back to The Lamp. Walk into the hall, scoop Menna out of her chair and then carry her, laughing, out and never put her down. Ideally he'd be wearing a white officer's suit and she'd work in a factory, but wearing Joe's trousers and rescuing her from Bad Breath Ken would be plenty romantic enough.

Brechdan would do it. Brechdan would blow out Lulu and go back and claim his girl. But then Brechdan would shag his girl senseless for two weeks, get bored, give her the clap and then go and apologise to Lulu with a large bunch of flowers and so it would go on. Just wasn't Iestyn's style, so he put his indicator on and glided into a parking space outside the restaurant. Somehow he'd managed to make it to the China Palace without being aware of any of the journey. Oh well. He was here now and might as well get on with it. Menna probably didn't want to be carried out into the night by a bloke wearing his brother's clothes anyway, especially if she hadn't finished her pint. For all he knew, she might be seeing someone else; perhaps someone else had bought that fantastic dress so that she didn't have to wear that white shirt and black trousers combo again?

Iestyn stuffed his wallet into his back pocket and jumped out of the Jeep, his landing splashing slush up his trouser legs. Great. Now he looked as if he'd peed on himself. He set off into the restaurant feeling as if he were going to seal his romantic doom.

Esther was sitting at the interview room table, crying in the cold. She had an empty bladder, a blanket wrapped around her shoulders and a mug of tea at her side. PC Taylor was writing her statement down as she spoke, in between sobs. Even through her distress it sounded pathetic and small-minded.

"So, because your husband left his shoes lying around, you decided to send a letter to a hairdresser to tell her that she smelled and to, in effect, ruin her confidence?"

"Yes, that's right."

"Ri-ight."

"And, your daughter wouldn't make her own hot chocolate, so you sent a letter to the Tasty Bite and, in effect, closed *their* business?"

"Yes."

PC Taylor's disbelieving shake of her head ground the rest of the Esther's self-worth into the tatty lino floor.

Iestyn was sitting fiddling at a table in the corner. He hadn't ever been on a blind date before and he was feeling nervous as he was very definitely way out of his comfort zone. Sitting there faffing with his cuffs, he now realised that it had all happened very quickly. He'd written a few witty remarks and then asked a stranger for a date. She'd written a few witty remarks back and then agreed to go on a date: was that right? Was that how it should happen?

Surely people should get to know each other a *little* before they arranged to spend a whole evening together? He wasn't sure if he'd invited her for a meal because he liked the sound of her – or because he wanted to get Sima off his back?

And why had this Lulu agreed to a date so quickly? Had his half dozen comments made *such* a huge impression that she desperately needed to find out more about him? Or was she being hassled by someone from her end? Was she desperate to go out with *anyone*? Quite probably all of those: this evening could be a big disaster for both of them...

On top of all that what could he possibly talk to a stranger about for two hours? Or maybe an hour and a half if he ate quickly? Joe had said to talk about whatever he would talk to the bloke behind him in the queue in Powys Farmers'. Sima had said that he was to do nothing of the sort, but that if he got stuck for conversation to ask Lulu something about herself. Brechdan had said to talk about the curve of her breasts, or to ask how she liked her eggs in the morning...

The restaurant was beautiful. It had rich furnishings, drapes on the walls and Iestyn had got to his table by walking over a little footbridge that spanned a pond with fish gliding about amongst the weeds. The gentle music slowly improved his mood and the aromas that swept over him every time the waitress walked past carrying someone else's supper made him feel very hungry.

He'd not eaten anything since an afternoon tea of mother's scones and three mugs of tea at four o'clock, and although Joe had remarked that he, Iestyn, had eaten enough to floor a rhinoceros, he was now empty again. "It's because I'm not clogged up with bagels or whatever it is that you city folk eat," he had retorted.

Joe had dismissed him with a smirk to Sima. "This is the guy that, until last week, called them 'baggels' as in waggles. Take no notice!"

The waitress brought over a jug of water with ice and lemon in and poured him a glass and he smiled at her. She was beautiful with long black hair and brilliant white teeth. Actually, he thought as he tufted his hair around again, he was beginning to feel quite good! Perhaps it was time to break out of Bwlch y Garreg occasionally and start to spread his wings. Maybe outside of Bwlch y Garreg, people *did* casually arrange to go on dates. Perhaps it was only in Bwlch y Garreg that people waited for fourteen years to approach someone they fancied? The door opened and a woman with blonde hair and a red top peered round it. Ah, the mysterious Lulu, must be! Iestyn got to his feet and walked over to greet her.

She was pale and soft and her hair was shining under the restaurant spotlights. She wasn't quite the six-foot sultry fox in spike heels and a red crop top that Iestyn now realised that he had been expecting, but she looked, well, nice. Not as nice as Menna, mind, she'd looked gorgeous...

Sima was sitting at a large round table as Joe joked and laughed about skinning knuckles on farming implements with five other ruddy-faced men. "Don't you dare ignore me this evening," she'd warned Joe, "I'll be more than pissed off if you disappear with all your old cronies to talk about splash marks on toilet walls and leave me sitting on my own..."

"Sima!" he'd said, incredulously. "Come on! I'll only know a few people there and I'll introduce you to everyone I speak to; I'll be so proud to be there with you and, anyway, I am sure that you have a few tales about splash marks of your own to tell..." However, despite the good intentions, Sima was left alone. Finally, just as the compère called to everyone to take their seats for dinner, she saw Menna walk in. Sima stood up and to her relief, Menna spotted her wave and walked over, pretending to be unaware of all the looks and nudges that her changed appearance was getting.

"Hi, Menna," Sima said, grasping her arm affectionately, "am I glad to see you! You look *fantastic*! Did it all go OK?"

Menna nodded, "Yeah, not too bad, thanks. I've just been in the Ladies now for ten minutes trying to sort out my hair and I'd had a bit of trouble with the heels in the snow, so I just wore my wellies down and changed in the car park!"

Sima laughed and told her about the suede shoes and Isla's lace-ups and Menna giggled in return. "Isla's a star; she won't mind at all – probably be so good for dancing that she'll wear them next year too!"

"Oh, and Menna, I'm sorry but I'm afraid that Iestyn can't make it tonight. I had no idea; Joe only told me tonight that he had something else on."

Menna shrugged. "It's OK. No worries. I saw him earlier anyway; off on some date or something." Sima wasn't fooled by the light-hearted dismissal, but realised that Menna's pride didn't allow her to dwell on it.

A waiter came to the table and Joe was retrieved from his friends. "Ah, the soup, please," he told the waiter. "Hi, Menna, you OK? Hey, Sima, that bloke was John Davies, you know, the one I told you about? The one with the dog with the orange blob?"

"What on earth are you talking about?"

"You know, I said that he had a spare seat in his car? In the boot?"

"Joe – I don't know what you're on about…"

"No, it wasn't the spare *seat*," corrected Menna, "*that* was John Evans. John *Davies* had the funny trousers – you remember, at Jack Tarn's house?"

Sima declined a starter and instead laid her head on the tablecloth and groaned.

A loud cheer from around the room brought Sima back up to sitting position and everyone craned their necks to see what was going on. Johnny Brechdan walked into the room, his hair coiffed with gel and his handsome face beaming with pride. Clamped to the front of his stylish suit, by one enormous hand, was little Gwennie Shackles, oblivious to the looks that her "dad" was receiving: unbridled joy on the faces of the older ladies, hilarity on the faces of his male friends and complete despair and disbelief on the faces of some of the younger ladies in the room.

Tansy walked at his side, with a coy smile, and they sat on the spare chairs at Nain and Taid's table, with Nain taking Gwennie whilst Johnny got himself settled, and Taid taking Tansy's coat. A wave of people flocked over to them and Gwennie was cooed over and Tansy was introduced to a dozen people whose names she would never remember.

The air in the hall became thick with questions: "So, is that baby supposed to be one of his then, or what?" "That woman – is she supposed to be the one blackmailing him then?" and "Have you managed to shag him since the baby's come? No, me neither."

Menna popped another garlic mushroom into her mouth and took a sip of water. Bit of a pointless night now that Iestyn wasn't coming, aside from the hassle and expense of the new dress and haircut. She might as well not bother drinking and then she could just sneak off whenever she fancied. Otherwise she'd have to wait for her parents and they *always* stayed until the bitter end and she didn't feel like sitting in a puddle on the floor in her new dress, doing *Oops Upside Your Head* or whatever ridiculous thing Dave the DJ thought was bang on this year.

It was nice to be with Sima and Joe, though, and she had waved at Nain and Taid Brechdan and Johnny and Tansy on their table at the other side of the room. But, really, she wasn't in the mood for partying. Seeing Iestyn like that had been a bit of a shock. All that dress hunting, all that trying on of shoes, practising with curling tongs and trying to find out how to keep lipstick where it was supposed to be was, well, for his benefit really. To find out that he wasn't staying was such a disappointment and one that she hadn't actually considered. But, to find out that the reason he wasn't coming was because he had a blind date just twisted the knife. Sima had apologised, but it wasn't *her* fault.

She, Menna, had allowed herself to build up the night into one big romantic shebang and it was almost bound to go all curly: things tended to in her case. So instead of dancing slowly to 'Lady In Red', nuzzling her head into Iestyn's strong shoulder, she would instead be getting pestered by her mum to "Come on and dance! Don't be shy!" That'd be only slightly better than the year that Pissed Brian had put her over his shoulder and run around the room with her.

However, the night had a long time to run yet and she needed to put a brave face on it all. No point in sitting looking like a smacked arse all night; no, she needed to *try* and enjoy it – for Sima's sake as much as her own – Sima looked like she might appreciate a friend to talk to who didn't keep running off to talk to blokes about John Davies' funny trousers and the like.

She took a little sip of wine from the glass at her side, "So, Sima," she smiled, "tell me who else you've been sorting out recently?"

"Well," replied Sima, "my favourite at the moment is an older lady who… Hang on, who's this then? Grand entrance number two! Return of the prodigal son or what?"

There was another buzz developing in the room and Menna heard gasps and the scrapes of chairs as people stood to see what was happening.

"Well, *look* who it is now!"

"Well, bloody hell. Look who's here…"

"Well, welcome home, boy!"

"Fuck me – did *he* do that to her?"

She craned her neck to see what was going on and through the throngs of people now standing, she could just make out a couple at the door. She saw a man in a dark suit and a woman in a very clingy white dress – perhaps they were a local couple that'd just gotten married and had popped by on the way to their reception? She was just about to turn back to Sima when someone moved and the man at the door came into view: Paul Morgan. Paul the Neuadd. Five years older and more handsome and expensive-looking than ever and with a woman at his side. A beautiful woman. Younger than him, smiling up at him with a gaze that needed no words. One hand was adorned with a large ring that glistened in the soft lights and the other rubbed itself over a swollen, pregnant belly.

Menna gasped and dropped her fork. Paul the Neuadd? Paul the bloody Neuadd? Tonight of all nights? She hadn't clapped eyes on him or spoken to him or even received a note from him for years and now he turns up without warning, with a beautiful bride who looks as if she's ready to give birth right there on the carpet.

Menna could feel the good vibes in the room as her neighbours welcomed home one of their favourite sons. She'd heard through the grapevine that he rarely came home now and that he was a successful estate agent in Manchester, but she hadn't heard that he was married or that he had fathered another child.

She could also feel eyes from around the room turning her way to see how she was coping with the surprise arrival. They would all have known that she and Paul had once been an item, although no one knew why they had separated – but they would have made up their own theories.

She felt sick to her stomach, but knew that if she did as her gut instinct was telling her to do and bolted, they would all be watching that too. No, she thought, stay dignified, disinterested and show no emotion. If anyone was going to squirm, make him squirm. With an effort, she planted a smile on her face, turned back and said, "Sorry, Sima, you were saying about that older lady?"

Iestyn smiled again at Lulu and struggled with his chopsticks. They'd pretty much exhausted the "I'm just crap at chopsticks" gag as had they the "how's the IT course" and the "what do you normally do on a Friday night" conversations. Iestyn thought Lulu was nice enough. She was pleasant to look at in a soft dumpling kind of a way. She smelt nice. She smiled quite a bit, but she was a little, well, *passive*.

He wasn't brilliant at small talk, but surely there were a few things that she could ask back? There was the weather to talk about, he'd broken his arm three times and that was usually good for at least fifteen minutes, and he worked a bloody great farm with 350 sheep and each one had different things that happened to it but they were still waiting for the main course to arrive.

However, although he was not feeling Lulu's sexual vibes, the waiter obviously was; he'd been constantly looking over to their table and Iestyn had spotted at least three winks that had been given to a blushing Lulu as he'd walked past with a tray of dishes. Perhaps it was actually *his,* Iestyn's, problem. Maybe Lulu was a real catch, but it was *him* that was lacking. Was she sitting there thinking, "For God's sake, stop talking about your bloody sheep – you didn't *really* think I was interested? I was only pretending! Tell me about the time you skydived or rowed across the Atlantic, like every other bloke I've dated has. At least try and look at my breasts; everyone else thinks they're magnificent, but you've just looked at the lanterns on the wall."

Lulu sat and watched Iestyn. He was very handsome and she was a little tongue-tied. He had those smart clothes on and a very trendy haircut and she combed through her own hair with her fingers as she smiled at him again. He'd seemed quite chatty, quite interested in her and her job. She wished that she'd stuck a little more closely to what she'd talked about in her blog – or actually, maybe it would have been better if she'd actually *lived* what she'd written about in her blog. She should have dived at her flat with a paintbrush and a pair of denim dungarees and painted it herself. Iestyn was sitting there with knuckles chipped and grazed and a black thumbnail all because he'd got stuck into something. She didn't have a drop of gloss in her hair or even a chipped fingernail to show for her endeavours to "do up a flat". She felt a bit of a sap and she realised that she didn't have a great range of things to talk about.

"So," she managed, "do you have your own dog? Or do you all share the general ones – y'know?"

Iestyn squinted up at her as if he were struggling to comprehend whether she'd actually asked that or not. "We all, well, we all use them all really, although I have my own favourite."

"What's he – or she – called?"

"Nancy."

"Oh." Louisa put on her deliberating face as if she were weighing up what she thought about a dog called Nancy. Instead she was desperately trying to think of something witty or incredibly interesting to say. Come on, come on, what would Rachel say? As her untrained mind ran through its usual topics – her work, the weird woman at her work, mucking up the balance-up *again*, reasons why her diets didn't work, the new forensics series on BBC1, and her dad nearly reversing into the woman from across the yard's BMW, she realised that she simply wasn't ready for this.

She hadn't *really* wanted the flat or the new exciting leap from her cosy nest. She was actually quite content sat on the sofa each night, her dad making sure that she was snuggled up with a blanket and her mum ensuring that she was well fed and watered. What did she *really* want with a draughty first-floor flat, sitting there, night after night on her own? She was a sociable creature and sociable creatures wanted company, conversation and someone else to make the tea.

She popped the last of her rice into her mouth and muttered an "Excuse me," and popped off to the ladies for a break from the uncomfortable silence.

274

The roast lamb came and went and a big cheer went up as the waitress announced that it was from Phil Arnold, the Cwm, and Phil sat looking pleased as punch at the raised glasses (all the while hoping that they hadn't gotten that sinewy old mutton that he'd persuaded the new guy from the abattoir to put through with the younger ones).

Menna chose the chocolate gateau with cream for dessert and she sat feeling cold, awkward and very uncomfortable. She'd always known that there was unfinished business between her and Paul. In her more charitable moments, she thought that perhaps she'd missed the boat on her right to respond to his churlishness. She should really have insisted on sorting things out properly – the *two* of them, not just her having to do all the hard work. Maybe that would have allowed her to move on a little faster. It had taken her five years to put on a sexy dress and (sort of) make a play for another man – albeit another man that was completely unaware of her efforts and instead was having a great time on a date with another woman.

And there was the last man she'd gone out with, sitting – typically right in the middle of her field of vision – chatting, laughing, greeting old friends and introducing them all to his new wife who, incidentally, he was treating like cut glass.

She was obviously far more his equal than Menna had ever been. She was beautiful and confident and happy and the only time she took her hands off her flaming belly was when they were replaced by Paul's hand, caressing the bump with loving, fluid movements.

Menna knew that Paul had seen her – if only because he looked everywhere but in her direction. *Should I walk over and throw my drink into his face*, she mused. No, childish really and it would ruin everyone else's night. Should she try and speak to him? Maybe later if he was alone... But what would she say? "Hello, you shit, how's it all going?" Also, it wouldn't be fair on his wife; she probably had no idea about what had happened and it wouldn't be fair to drag her into something as unpleasant as this at such a late stage in her pregnancy.

"You OK?" Joe had reached across and prodded her arm as Sima had turned to talk to someone walking past behind her. Menna managed a watery smile and a nod and then demanded some more cream before he drank the lot straight out of the jug. "Sorry," he grinned, "I thought it was just for me!"

Yep, just stick it out until the tables were cleared and then she could slip away unnoticed, leaving with her head held high and her dignity intact: maybe she could just scrape his car with her keys on the way past? Or perhaps pop a little dog shit under his door handle as she left…

The ladies' washroom in the China Palace was not as palatial as the rest of the set-up; it had a little more of the British terraced house about it. Chipboard doors painted pillar-box red gave a headache-inducing glow and squeaked open onto tiny cubicles. Louisa chose the one nearest the window as it looked as if it might have a little more space. She didn't actually need the loo, but instead eased open the tiny Crittall window, glad for the rush of cold air that blasted the self-conscious flush from her face.

The window opened out onto the police yard and Louisa could see a line of police cars parked facing the gates. She could see shadowy figures in the windows of the rooms opposite, blurred by the steamed up windows and she allowed herself a bit of a diversion by guessing at what these people might be doing.

She imagined seasoned coppers striding around interview rooms, banging their open palms onto the tables, the accused cowering under the attack. Yep, she decided, some of those shadowy figures that she could see were on their way to the slammer. But, never mind, eh, she thought as she squeezed back though the red chipboard, serves 'em right! She washed her hands and shook them over a plastic plant rather than use the damp towel stuffed through a hoop.

As she wasted time faffing about with her hair in the mirror, her stomach churned at the thought of going back to the table. Surely dates were supposed to be easier than this, otherwise no one would ever, ever, go on them? Iestyn seemed like a nice chap and she was a nice girl and yet they were sitting there as if they had nothing in common and nothing to say to each other if it wasn't through a keyboard. She had to accept that although Iestyn was younger and more handsome than the person she'd thought he might have been, he was far less indulgent than she would have liked. Maybe he'd been expecting someone rather different too?

She knew that she was looking at least relatively attractive because the waiter kept winking at her and when he saw her struggling with her chopsticks, he'd rushed over with a knife and fork: shame really, as the chopsticks were pretty much providing the substance for their conversation and they hadn't really got back on track since.

She tripped over the vacuum cleaner that was squeezed into the corner and went out to join her "date". Only pudding to go; it surely had to get better over pudding?

Maybe by the time they went for a moonlit walk, hand in hand along the riverside path, everything would have moved onto a more playful plane? She hoped that chocolate gateau was on the menu if they were going to go for a walk in this weather – she'd need something substantial to keep her strength up…

Menna made it through her dessert. Good, she needed the toilet; that would kill another five minutes. She might take her chances and see if she could sneak out just after the speeches – or maybe during them if Chairman Jon Jones was going to bang on about statistics like he did last year.

She excused herself from the table and, remembering her bag with its facial repair kit, wove between the diners to get to the lobby, greeting people here and there and receiving lots of compliments. By the time she'd reached the lobby, she'd actually cheered up; perhaps it was good to be out, to be amongst friends – to lance the boil on her arse that was Paul the Neuadd.

She caught a glimpse of herself in the huge, gilt-framed mirror in the hall and was pleased with what she saw. Usually by this time in the proceedings, she'd have necked so much lager that her face would be blotchy and her pores *enormous*. Instead now, she was sashaying slowly along, enjoying her new ability to walk in high heels. She heard footsteps behind her…

"Menna – Menna, stop a minute. Can I talk to you, please?"

Menna stopped dead. Then she carried on walking and just turned her head. Her brain was spinning at a hundred times faster than her feet, so by the time she'd said, "Oh, hi," she'd already decided to play it cool. Play it calm and dignified. "How's things?"

"Menna, Menna, hi, yes, I'm good thanks. How are you? Well, you look great – fantastic actually. You look fantastic. What's new? What you up to?"

It was, of course, Paul. He had almost jogged up to her. A good suit; nice cut and a good fit. Unlike the ones that he used to wear, shiny, off the peg, chosen by his mother.

"Nothing much. You know, the usual." Menna was cool and still very much on the way to the toilet, but just gave him enough time for a chat. "Nice to be back?"

"Yes, well, OK I s'pose. Don't come back too often. Busy – you know? Up in Manchester?"

"Yes."

"Well…"

"Right, if you'll excuse me…"

"Menna…" Suddenly he had a purpose. "I've written you a note. I hoped I'd see you here. Maybe. Well…I…you know… Sheep Breeders' and all that? Menna – I've written you a note." He fumbled in his pocket, looking over his shoulder back to the party as he did so, as if wanting to be sure that no one else saw him. One more check and he pulled out an envelope. "Look, it explains everything. Everything. I'm so sorry, Menna, I'm really *so* sorry…"

He thrust it into her hand and clutched it for a moment. For a while, Menna just stared into eyes that drilled into her soul, deep with meaning – one she couldn't comprehend. He held the envelope in both her hands, his eyes imploring that she got it this time - was it pain? Remorse? Guilt? Or convenience? She simply didn't know.

He looked over his shoulder again, then once more. Then he grabbed her shoulders and kissed her full on the lips. Then he pulled away, another of those fathomless looks in his eyes. He shook his head, "I have to go. I'm sorry, Menna, but I have to go." Menna watched him walk away, then looked at the envelope in her hands. It had obviously started off as big and expensive, but was now crumpled and greasy from uneasy fingers. She held her dignity until she saw him halted by another crony and then she dived into the Ladies. As she sought the doorknob, she realised that her hand was shaking.

She sat on the loo for support as her legs felt like they might give way. She took a few deep breaths and turned the envelope back and

278

fore. It was quite bulky, so obviously it wasn't just a short note inside. It felt like a lengthy and, having seen his face, perhaps tortuous ramble. There was no name on the front, presumably so that if his wife had seen it, it wouldn't require an explanation – not good to be writing notes to an ex-girlfriend when you're about to have a baby with your wife, especially if it were a tortuous ramble. Why had he waited until now, she thought as she picked tentatively at the sealed flap. Why, if he wasn't going to talk her through it, hadn't he just posted it? Mind, knowing Paul, it could still yet be a newspaper cutting about a nutritional supplement for a bull or a way of reducing foot rot in hill sheep…

Menna listened as a crowd of women crashed laughing into the toilets. Stuff them, she thought, there are two more cubicles, they'll just have to wait: this is important.

She could feel her heart thumping hard; she wished she were at home now, in the privacy of her own lounge, not sitting on a loo listening to women talking about how Johnny Brechdan was still lush, even though he had a girlfriend with a baby. Maybe she should go to her truck and read it? But what if he were lurking outside, waiting for her reaction? Well, it was a little late to be worrying about her feelings…

On the Thursday night after the fateful altercation in the Neuadd's cowshed and in accordance with her usual habit, Menna had skipped dinner with her parents in readiness for her curry with Paul. That night, however, she had been more than glad to; lamb chops…even the smell of them cooking made her stomach churn.

She'd sat on her bed and prepared to pull off her work trousers – shapeless jeans with a saggy arse and a low crotch. She felt exhausted and even the thought of taking off her trainers was tiring. She'd never felt fatigue like it and it was all consuming. The pains in her stomach were getting worse and she really hoped that it wasn't going to be like this for the next six and a half months. She'd read that it was an uncomfortable time, but she could really do with someone to talk to, someone who could explain it all to her – someone who didn't want to be an estate agent…

She felt her insides gurgle and she was relieved to undo the button of her jeans. The pains must be being heightened by the unforgiving denim. She'd dragged her jeans down and then cursed as she realised that she still had her trainers on. She'd tried to tug the trouser legs over the top of the shoes, but they got stuck. She'd wrenched at them, getting hotter and more frustrated. Trying to stand, she'd tripped and then slid to the floor, landing awkwardly on her ankle. Pain had washed over her and she'd burst into tears, tears of frustration, anger and hormones.

She'd slumped against her bed, sitting on a rag rug that she'd made for her mother's Christmas present fifteen years before, but which had somehow found its way back into her bedroom.

As the tears flowed and her mind had darted from one futile scenario to another, her body seemed to make up its own mind and with one huge cramping pain, it expelled the tiny form from her body, wrapped in a cushion of blood.

And so the little life that had begun on a careless night, oiled by a little too much Tiger beer, had ended in a puddle on a badly-made rag rug. Paul never arrived that night and nor did he come again for Sunday lunch. He'd never come back for his post-thumper, either, nor did he bring back the newly-greased crankshaft.

Menna hadn't spent the evening watching at the window for her beau, instead she'd spent it sat in a state of shock on her rag rug, watching as the blood seeped from her.

She'd waited until her parents had gone to bed, exhausted with debate about what could possibly have happened to Paul the Neuadd. She'd ignored their calls from the bottom of the stairs and mumbled about being tired in reply to her dad's knock on her door. She'd drunk the cup of tea that was left outside her door, but not until it was lukewarm. She had then replaced the cup outside the door, as empty as she felt.

When all the lights had been switched off and her father had done a last check of the stock, Menna had crept out in a pair of navy tracksuit bottoms and her boots, clutching a bloody hanky rolled into a towel.

She'd taken the torch and tip-toed out of the back door, whispering loudly to the dogs, so as to stop them barking. She'd walked across two fields and climbed over the fence into the woods and then tripped and stumbled down through the trees until she'd reached her favourite childhood spot.

Menna had found a stick and foraged about amongst the tree roots until she found a small gap. Sobbing, she'd dropped to her knees in the mud, unrolled the towel and pushed the damp parcel into the hole and then back-filled it with moss and leaves. As she'd stood up, she'd nudged the torch with the back of her foot and it had rolled off down the hill. She'd left it shining a beam into space and then stumbled back up the hill in darkness, tears dripping from her face. They weren't tears from broken dreams of romantic happiness, but the tears of empty plans and the realisation of how much she'd come to love something so small in just a matter of weeks.

Somehow, Jean had managed not to berate Menna as it became apparent that Paul was going to eat his Sunday lunch on his own from then on. She'd obviously seen how upset Menna was by the split and therefore she hadn't had the heart to express her annoyance about her daughter blowing a fantastic opportunity both for herself as an individual and for the family in terms of the future success of their farm and their standing in the community. Unfortunately, she hadn't had the soul to comfort her daughter either, or make sure that she was all right.

As time had worn on, Menna had slowly recovered: physically quicker than mentally, but she had been left with a hollow spot… A sense of unfairness and an emptiness in her soul, and she couldn't really work out why.

She'd desperately wanted to see Paul, to tell him what had happened, to scream at him that he was a wanker, to sob on his shoulder, to tell him coldly that he need not worry about her or the baby. However, she'd felt washed out, exhausted and tearful: when she confronted him, she wanted to be in control and on fighting form. She hadn't wanted to be sobbing about the loss of something that he'd never wanted; she needed to be calm inside, even if on the outside she was a screaming banshee. But the time had never felt right. She'd *never* felt calm and strong enough for such an altercation. It was hard to plan how you could make someone else feel worse than you did by giving them the information that you knew they craved.

A week had passed, then two. His silence strengthened Menna – at least he would be worrying about what was happening. Her only power had been in knowing the truth: he must have been terrified that the next time he saw her, she would be sitting at his kitchen table chatting to his mother and rubbing her hands over a large bump. *Let him think the worst is yet to come,* she'd decided. *Don't let him off the hook that easily...*

As the years had rolled by, Menna had come to know herself better and she'd concluded that her emptiness was more to do with the weight of the responsibility that she and Paul had taken so lightly, than the sadness at the loss of a child. It seemed wrong that an extra bottle of Tiger had resulted in a fumbling with a condom and that had resulted in a life. A life that, had it not failed, would now be a little child asking non-stop questions around its mother's knees. It may have grown up to find the cure for cancer, or discovered a new breed of fish, but one little blip in the building blocks and – phut – nothing. It seemed to Menna that she should be ashamed of her lack of responsibility, her previous sense of fun and light-heartedness should be gone forever.

Menna had buckled down to work, as much to avoid her mother's disappointed glances as to embrace an honest toil. She checked the animals, she scraped up shite, she mended fences and pleached hedges. She got cold, wet, sunburnt and sunstroke. She trimmed feet, removed bollocks, lanced boils and wanked off a bull. She got tired, exhausted, strained and kicked. She started to spurn the fripperies and fancies that she'd enjoyed as a teenager, thinking them wasteful and unnecessary. Instead, she became well known in her community as a hard worker and a great stockwoman.

She'd started entering her stock into competitions and she'd begun to win. Paul may have been a git, but she had picked up many tips from him and they'd started to pay dividends. Her father struggled with his health and had been happy to relinquish more and more responsibility to Menna and instead toiled on the more predictable elements of the farm – the buildings and the land.

As Menna's reputation and autonomy had grown, she'd begun to enjoy her work again, but this time with a pride and a determination to succeed. Glascwm had grown more successful financially and through competitions, and it began to be the place that neighbours would drop in for a bit of advice or to borrow a more modern bit of machinery.

Menna had heard that Paul had gone away to university early and that it had devastated his parents. They had apparently been getting ready to hand over the reins and had been shocked to the core by his revelation. He'd rarely come home, apparently throwing his energies into his studies, but Menna had known that it was also due to guilt. Not just for the way he treated her, but also for his parents who had been relying on him. It wasn't his fault that they had always assumed that he wanted to take over the farm without actually asking him, but it might have been fairer if he'd not waited until his bags were packed to give them the first clue...

Back in the toilets in the Lamp, she turned the envelope over and over in her hands. Half of her was desperate to see what he had to say, the other half felt like flushing the whole thing down the toilet and pretending that whatever Paul had to say didn't matter one jot, so there was no point in reading it.

Eventually, the desperate half won. She tore the envelope open and peered inside. There was money, lots of money. She took the wad out and fanned the fifty-pound notes in her hand. They were clean and new with successive serial numbers – had he really stopped at the cash point on the way here, with the wife in the car thinking he was going to get enough for a few drinks and a loaf of bread in the morning? There must be a couple of thousand pounds in her hand!

Menna stuffed the money back into the envelope and pulled out the letter and unfolded it. She remembered Paul's writing well and the familiarity struck her as odd after all this time. Although he'd never been one for letters or poems or indeed *anything* sentimental, she remembered how he used to write – spidery writing creeping slowly across the page. He must have copied it from a draft, as there were no mistakes or crossings outs. His handwriting had always been slow and painful to watch; this must have taken him hours!

The door of the Ladies squeaked open and then was slammed shut to the sound of, "and if that bitch whispers at me to fuck off because Brechdan's taken again, I'll cut her tits off..." and the girls' chatter subsided to a distant shrieking. At last Menna had the peace to read what Paul the Neuadd had to say to her.

Dear Menna,

I trust his letter finds you well? I've always felt that we separated after difficult times and perhaps we have a little unfinished business to attend to?

Menna blew out a breath of amazement at the understatement.

I've wanted to contact you for all this time, but haven't had the chance and now it's more difficult, what with being married and expecting our first baby.

I felt that, when you got yourself pregnant, we were very young and probably didn't handle it very well, which sort of shows how we would have been as parents?

I admit I was relieved when I found out that you must have had yourself a termination and I have always wanted to thank you for making that decision and going through with it. You could have told me at the time and I would have stood by you and helped out.

I've always wanted to put things right by you and I hope that we can let the past be the past and all of us concentrate on our futures. I have since looked into it and I hadn't realised how expensive such treatments are, so I would like to start by making amends in a financial way – therefore I have enclosed £3,000 for your costs.

I hope that there are no hard feelings between us and I wish you well. I heard that you'd got Best in Breed for your bull at the show last year, so well done.

Yours sincerely,
Paul

Menna sat back, stunned. She shook her head in confusion and then read it again. It was like a cross between a standard business letter and one from a fourteen-year-old boy. *Yours sincerely? I would have stood by you? Got yourself pregnant?*

Menna felt the rage well up inside her. Rage that should probably have exploded five years ago, but had not had the chance. How *dare* he? *Termination? Helped out?* Was he mad? He'd walked away from the girlfriend that he'd impregnated – and you couldn't get much more shitty than that – but then to have his conscience pricked into paying for it five years later, via a *note*, when his own bride was sitting twenty yards away swollen with child? Could he get anymore insulting?

She got to her feet and slammed open the bolt on the door, catching her knuckle in the lock. She saw her reflection in the mirror opposite and she barely recognised herself, her eyes were dark with rage and her cheeks white, aside from her new blusher, and her orangey-red lips were pursed near to extinction.

She tucked an escaped curl behind her ear and swung out of the Ladies' and back into the corridor.

As she stalked the fifteen yards down the corridor, she had no idea what she was going to do. She could hear her heels clattering on the tiles, but she didn't associate the noise with herself. All she was aware of was the rage and anger within her, knowing that it was about to blow and hang the bloody consequences...

Sima was listening to the speeches with glazed eyes and a fixed smile on her face. Funny how so many women were wearing black and gold blouses, she mused, it would have been nice to have a little more of a splash of colour around.

The speaker was a dull old fart. He had already apologised twice for not being able to read his own handwriting and here he was fumbling again with his glasses, trying to remind himself what twaddle he was supposed to say next; Sima wished that she'd had an hour with him beforehand and pushed him through her intensive Public Speaking With Confidence course.

The audience waited with baited breath. The only sound was that of high heels approaching down the corridor. Sima turned – oh, good, it was Menna on her way back. Someone to giggle with through the rest of this guy's tedious announcements would be good.

Strange, Menna had stopped half way back, she was standing over a man perched on a chair. It was that Paul bloke, the one with the very-pregnant wife. Joe had been starting to tell her something about him, but had been distracted by one of his old fishing buddies. Hang on, Menna looked absolutely fuming…what was that about?

The crowd was beginning to turn away from the mutterings on the top table and look towards Menna and the visitor, nudging each other and raising their eyebrows, as if they had been waiting for something to happen.

Eventually the man must have sensed that something was up and he turned from whispering to the guy next to him to face the thunderous eyes behind him.

"You *bastard!*" Menna shouted as soon as she had his attention. "You BASTARD!" Her voice was high and full of emotion and Sima could see that she was shaking. "Firstly, *you* got *me* pregnant – I did *not* get *myself* pregnant. *We* did it. Between us. *Then* you wouldn't let me see anyone, not even a bloody midwife. *Then—*"

People were beginning to stand so that they could get a better view. The guy on the top table put down his notes, aware that he had lost his flock to more interesting pastures.

"you *dump* me. Without even telling me. Then…*nothing* for five years and then *this?*" Menna shook an envelope around Paul's face and he squinted away from it as if it were tainted. "Money for an *abortion?* Was that supposed to make up for dumping me?"

Even under the dim lighting, Sima could see that Paul had gone white. His mouth dropped open as he gazed up at Menna as if trying to comprehend what she was saying and whether she was *really* saying it to him, or whether it was a bad dream. Menna's hands were balled at her side, one with her bag and the crumpled envelope in it and the other a balled fist ready for action. Her face looked as if it were about to explode with rage. She seemed absolutely unaware of her surroundings, of the people who were now craning to hear, people who weren't daring to breathe in case they missed something important.

"Well, Paul, just to let you know, I *didn't* have an abortion…" Paul's face fell into an *oh my God I'm a dad already* look of horror. "I lost the baby, that night actually. So you can keep your three grand as I didn't need to spend it." And Menna took the wad out of the envelope and threw it in the air and it floated around Paul like confetti.

Sima looked at Joe; he was also getting to his feet. *Damn that bloke behind them who'd pushed his chair back so that he could see better and had blocked them in.* Sima could see Jean scrambling from her seat in the opposite corner and hear her calling, "Menna, Menna!" with a look of horror on her face. Menna's father, Bill, was sitting with his mouth open.

Paul looked as if he'd been slapped, but he hadn't: shamed, embarrassed, destroyed maybe, but not slapped – yet. *Crack!* Now he had been... Right across the cheek and finally some colour was brought back to his face.

Menna started to turn on her heel, then stopped and turned back, now with a sneer on her face. "And, yours *sincerely?*" she spat in disgust. "You cock." And she turned once more and walked smartly away.

The room echoed in the silence, apart from the whimpering of Paul's wife who was being comforted by her neighbour. Paul looked like a beaten man. He sat, stunned, with a handprint on his face and a fifty-pound note sitting on his shoulder, staring into space. His helpful companions quietly picked up the rest of the money and thrust it into his hands.

Finally he looked over to his wife, obviously desperately hoping that she hadn't seen any of that. But, of course, she had. She jumped to her feet, her whimpering being replaced by rage. She pushed her chair back and there was a crash as it landed on the floor. She grabbed her purse and her shawl and struggled through the tables towards the doors at the opposite end of the hall. Just as she reached them she turned, the whole room watching her with baited breath: this was just getting better and better! "Well," she shouted at him, her hands planted on her hips and her face screwed up with anger, "now's probably a good time as any to tell you! *This,*" and she pointed to her belly, "is *not* yours." She crashed open the bar on the fire exit and stormed out into the night.

Paul finally seemed to gather his wits and jumped up, "Hazel!" he called to the banging door. "Wait! I can explain..." He ran round the outside of the room and people sucked their stomachs in and leant forward to give him room. He followed his wife through the door with another bang and the last that people heard from him was his breaking voice calling, "Hazel! Hazel, come back!"

Iestyn drove along the lanes in silence. He couldn't handle any music; he needed to get his thoughts sorted. The lanes were empty save for his massive truck and he drove slowly, out of choice as much as for the road conditions, which were not good.

He bit his bottom lip. He'd made a right mess of that, hadn't he? He'd only left ten minutes ago and he could hardly remember what Lulu looked like or anything she'd said. She'd just become a doughy ball in his mind, a smiling ball of dough with blonde hair, yet he knew that there was probably more to her than that.

Poor Lulu, he hadn't really been concentrating all night. His mind had been elsewhere – mainly at the Lamp, in a chair next to Menna Edwards. He'd been wondering since the meal began whether he could skip the main course – but of course he couldn't – then he thought perhaps the pud. But Lulu had been talking about chocolate pudding since she'd sat down. He'd managed to decline the option of coffee and luckily Lulu had too and he'd asked for the bill instead.

He thought that she might have muttered something about going on for a drink afterwards, but he was glad of a ready-made excuse about having to get back. "I'm afraid I'm giving a lift to my parents and my dad doesn't like being out too late." Lulu had nodded, understandingly – she'd gone on about her parents enough for him to feel that he could drop them into the equation without being ridiculed. However, he knew full well that his father would be busy doing a cross between a moonwalk and the mashed potato as he spoke and by no means ready for his bed.

Iestyn had insisted on paying; it was the least he could do seeing as he'd enticed her out on such a miserable night and under such false pretences. He noticed that Lulu didn't argue, instead just mumbled that she'd provide the tip. He'd had a discreet peep as she plonked some money behind a chocolatey bowl and had seen a measly two-pound coin. Two quid tip for a fifty-pound meal? Christ, if they stayed together he'd be like his dad in thirty years time, joking that "Mother" kept a coin on a piece of string for just such occasions…

There'd been an awkward moment as they'd hovered by the coat stand, her carefully doing up every button and him now itching to be off. He knew that he should really be asking whether she'd like to meet him again sometime, if she wasn't too busy, maybe next Thursday? However, he was too intent on returning to the Lamp to sort his life out to be bothered about even keeping his options open. Brechdan would keep a toe in the door (or some other available orifice) for a possible future dalliance. Iestyn's only urge was to bolt any door other than Menna's well and truly shut.

"Right," he'd said as she wound her scarf slowly around her neck. "Thanks for a great night; I'll see you again, no doubt. Good luck with the course and all that…"

"Yeah," she'd replied, looking a bit desperate. "Good luck with your – your farm."

"Thanks. OK, bye." He'd held the door open for her and waved her out into the slush.

Good luck with my farm? Good God, does she not read the Farmers Weekly*?* Iestyn walked Lulu to her car, but then she'd changed her mind and said that, actually, she might go and join a few mates in the Dog and Duck across the road. "Oh," he'd said and walked her there instead and she'd clutched his arm to stop herself slipping and been more animated in that two-minute walk than she had been for the whole evening.

"Bye!" she'd waved as she skipped in through the door. It would seem she'd spent the evening wishing she was somewhere else as well, which was a relief.

As he walked back towards Joe's truck, Iestyn looked through the window of the pub and saw Lulu squeeze into a seat alongside a dozen or so people sat around a table. Actually, that did look like as if it might be more fun than sitting with a bloke talking about how he broke his arm in two places and the personalities of his sheep. He imagined the hilarity that would break out when she told them all about the date and that she'd never spent such a boring night with such a boring bloke. "Iestyn Bevan?" someone would say. "Yeah, he *is* a right boring bastard. Can only talk about sheep or show you his blackthorn splinters – God, Lulu, how *did* you put up with an evening of that?"

Oh well, perhaps in the future he should write-off doing things that other people suggested. Especially if fools like the New Improved Coupled Up Brechdan thought it a lovely idea. One down, one to go, he thought as he took the road towards the Lamp. Let's just hope that the rest of the night was a little more successful.

Suddenly headlights flashed, full beam, into his eyes and he realised that he was heading straight for the front of a large truck. He wrenched the wheel of the Jeep into the verge and he bounced over the grass and missed the other vehicle by inches. A horn blasted at him as a dark shadow hurtled by.

Bloody hell that was close! He looked in his rear-view mirror and saw the tail lights of the truck at a tilted angle – obviously up on another verge twenty yards down the road. Christ, perhaps it hadn't been his fault after all – or, not completely anyway? Maybe it'd just come from the Sheep Breeders' dinner after having had a few too many? Better be careful, he thought, quite possibly there'd be a few more of those around tonight.

After driving a little more sensibly around another corner, he saw the lights of the Lamp and he pulled into the car park. Right, take a few breaths, compose himself and – hang on, wasn't that Sima? Out in her little dress, splashing about in the slush? And now Joe – were they looking for something? Iestyn pulled up next to them and fiddled about with the controls, opening the sunroof and changing the colour of the interior lighting before finally lowering the window.

"What's up?"

"Have you seen Menna?" asked Sima, her voice shaky and higher pitched than usual.

"Just got here…"

"Hang on," called Joe, "her truck's gone. She said she'd nearly reversed into a tree on coming in and here, there's a space by this tree. It would be bound to have been filled otherwise – ages ago. She must have gone."

"Actually," Iestyn said, trying to picture the vehicle that had nearly run him off the road, "I think she might have just passed me. Why? What's up?"

Joe quickly explained as Sima stood shivering and close to tears. "And then, she just left," he said. "It's carnage in there now; God only knows where Paul and Heather—"

"Hazel."

"Hazel – whatever – have gone. Jean's crying. Bill's striding around like a mad man threatening to kill Paul or kill the bloke who'd sat next to him or the waiter who took his plate away – anyone really."

"But where's Menna gone?" blurted Sima. "We have to find her. She'll be in a right old state…"

"I'll go," Iestyn said. "That OK with you?"

"Yeah, just go. We'll sort something out for a lift home. Brechdan's here, so he can take us."

Iestyn opened the sunroof, ground the gears, turned the lights off and then found reverse. "Sorry!" he grinned. "See you later!" and there was a splatter of slush onto Joe's trousers as the Jeep hurtled backwards and then bounced off across the car park.

"F'fuck's sake: careful!" groaned Joe, looking down. "Great. Now I'll be walking back past the Gents looking as if I've pissed myself."

"Don't worry," said Sima, taking his arm, "you won't be the first one tonight…" They walked back into the turmoil that was the Annual Sheep Breeders' Ball and it flittered through both their minds that perhaps that would be it for the speeches tonight; maybe every cloud did have a silver lining after all?

Iestyn sped down the lane heading back in the direction that he'd come only minutes before. He soon passed the bit of road, with gouge marks on the verges on both sides, where they'd nearly crunched into each other. He drove as fast as he could, now, fully concentrating on the road in front of him. Part of him wanted to stop and find some good loud music to fit the atmosphere – something like the opening track to *Trainspotting* perhaps – but he knew he hadn't got time to waste.

After four or five miles, he reached the open hill, bumping over the cattle grid. Right: better slow down here, it wouldn't help Menna if he shot off the side of the unfenced road and the Jeep didn't have the tyres for such conditions, even if it looked as if it should have. As he reached the top of a slope, he looked down the dark valley in front of him and saw a couple of stationary red lights about half a mile in front of him. Good – they looked big enough to belong to a truck rather than a car. Perhaps she'd stopped at the side of the road to give herself time to calm down.

Poor Menna, he thought from what Joe had said, it sounded as if she'd had a really rough time. That Paul the bloody Neuadd, well, what a tosser – and to Menna as well; didn't he know when he had it good?

Actually, thought Iestyn, what Joe had just told him finally made sense. God, no wonder she had blown him away that time...

Iestyn had been racing the old quad bike a little faster than Tomos would have liked and therefore he was doing it on the other side of the open hill. He'd gone up to check the sheep and had been carried away by the simple physical pleasure of flying along with the wind in his hair and the sun warming his face.

Iestyn's days rarely allowed time for mucking about; there were always dozens of things that he would be better employed doing. However, although this was certainly the case now, he was still young and energised enough to think *sod it* occasionally. In his mind he was thinking he could justify it by saying he was looking for the ewe with the mark on her face and the gash on her leg. He'd not yet spotted her and he wanted to be sure that her wound wasn't becoming infected. It was excuse enough to scatter hill ponies on a beautiful May day!

As he sped along the ancient tracks that had carried his ancestors on ponies or by foot for centuries, he went over a particularly large bump and the resulting jolt caused the petrol gauge to crash to zero. He saw it out of the corner of his eye and cursed – it had gotten stuck a couple of times recently, once causing his mother to have to walk a couple of miles home in her wellies and two bobble hats, which hadn't gone down at all well.

Iestyn groaned. He was miles from home; why had he let himself stray so far for the sake of a pathetic speed buzz? If it conked out now, he'd be a couple of hours walking back and then he'd have to confess to Tomos that he'd gone much further than he needed and therefore wasn't back where he should have been: at the farm scraping chicken shit off a rutted concrete floor.

He scanned the horizon for other vehicles – most farmers usually kept a spare can of petrol in their trucks in case of emergencies. Nothing. Then he drove over the brow of the hill and looked down into the valley – great, Menna's truck was parked up by some woods.

Perhaps she was doing some fencing – probably where they used to climb over as kids, until her dad got fed up with them stretching his wire and put a little stile in.

Iestyn's good humour had returned at the thought of getting away with it *and* seeing Menna to boot, and he set off to the gate leading from the open hill down onto Menna's family farm. Halfway down the track towards the woods, the quad bike sputtered, stalled and ground to a halt. Bollocks, thought Iestyn. He freewheeled a little way, but eventually he gave up and jumped off; it was no distance really as the crow flew.

Once on foot, he decided against following the track with its giant zig-zags taking out the worst of the steepness. Instead, he dived into the chest-high bracken sending a few hiding sheep scattering. As he gambolled down like a carefree child, going just a little bit faster than he had control over, he'd felt like whooping with joy! The fronds of the bracken, which his grandmother had said could kill a man if enough were ingested in a tea, slapped against him and their leaves stuck to him.

He vaulted the fence into the wood and carried on through the trees, expecting to jump the stream and then come upon Menna working on the fence on the far side of the woods.

He hadn't been in this wood for years; he and Menna used to spend hours in it, trying to find ways of crossing the little stream (that he now hopped across with no effort at all). They'd had tyres hanging from trees, death slides, camps and seats. Their favourite tree was a stumpy old oak, full of places where two little children could find a comfy seat.

In fact, thought Iestyn as he started to puff, now climbing the steep slope up from the stream, *there* was their oak – about a third of the size that he remembered it, mind, but the shape was unmistakable; the dip in that one branch which had been his favourite place to sit and whittle out knots, with a penknife that would have had him arrested had he carried it anywhere else but Mid Wales. And there was the other place where Menna used to lie back and pretend to be really comfortable.

But, hang on, there was someone there now, sat at the bottom of it – surely, surely that was *Menna,* sat with her head resting on her knees, her long hair loose for a change and flopped over her arms as they cradled round her knees.

Iestyn had stopped: was she OK? It looked like a private moment, but she was by *their tree!* Perhaps she did feel the same as him? Perhaps she would come over here to sit and remember happy times and think about what might be if only she could dump that arse from the Neuadd!

Iestyn took a deep breath and scrambled up the rest of the slope towards her. "Menna?" he called, not wanting to startle her. But he had and her face jerked up from her knees. She saw him and then looked away.

"Menna," he puffed, arriving beside her hot and breathless from the exertion but also the excitement. "You OK? What are you doing here?"

She looked up again and stared at him. Her beautiful pale blue eyes were red ringed and swollen from crying. "What's the matter?" he whispered, dropping down beside her. "Menna – what's wrong? The family? Are they OK? Has something happened to…Paul?"

Menna scoffed and turned her face away again. "What are you doing here?" she sniffed, trying to wipe her eyes without him seeing.

"I ran out of petrol…saw your truck. Look, can I help? Do you want me to fetch someone? Ring your mum or someone else? Paul?"

"Paul?" she sneered. "You're bloody joking aren't you?"

Iestyn remembered how his heart had leapt at this comment. "Why?" He had to ask. "Are you not – well – together anymore?"

"He's a fuckin' idiot," she snarled and then buried her head once more.

At last, Iestyn had thought, at last! She's dumped him and has come to sit by our old tree! It was him, Iestyn, that she was in love with after all! *Now* was his chance; it was now or never. Fate had brought him here on this beautiful day, had made him run out of fuel and then had made him find her here, waiting for him.

He'd missed his chance, that time in the beer tent. An hour and two pints had meant that someone else had stepped in and – bam – three years wasted. It may not be the ideal timing, the first flush of just dumping someone – or even worse, having just been dumped – but, he'd have to take the risk. What if she popped into the shop on her way home and met Brechdan? Bam – another, well, another fortnight wasted, plus the eight months for the STD quarantine to pass. No, he needed to grasp his opportunity and jump in.

He had taken a deep breath and gone for it.

"Oh, Menna, Menna," he'd said, grasping one of her hands with both of his. Her head snapped up in surprise.

"Iestyn? What are you *doing*?"

But it was too late now for him to reconsider; this had been on the tip of his tongue for years.

"Oh, Menna, I'm here now; we can be together at last! I'm so glad that you feel the same as I do!" He kissed her hand as the only thing even remotely available to him and the smile of fresh love burst from his face.

"Iestyn!" Her voice was confused, horrified even. "What the hell are you doing?" She had pulled her hand away and jumped to her feet.

Iestyn remembered looking up at her, expecting to see love shine from her to him. Instead, it was a snarl that signified anger and maybe even distaste.

He was shaken by it, jumped to his feet and stepped backwards so as to lessen its intensity as it ground into his heart. "But...Menna...I thought – our tree?" As he said it, his puzzlement sounded pitiful.

She laughed. A cruel, harsh laugh. "*Our* tree? You're joking aren't you? You thought that I...? God, you men just haven't got a bloody clue have you, not a *bloody* clue." She made to walk off but turned back for one last twist of the knife. "Why on *earth* do you think that I'd be interested in you *at a time like this?* For fuck's sake, Iestyn..." Then over her shoulder she called, "Fuel's in the truck; help yourself." Her dismissive tone told him that she was so completely unimpressed by his declaration of love that it was forgotten and she walked off into the woods, swinging her jumper over her shoulder, apparently enjoying the birdsong coming from the trees.

Iestyn watched her go, walking sure-footedly over fallen branches, not even noticing the cluster of nettles that wrapped themselves around her bare legs.

His face was burning so hot that he reached his hand up to feel it. What had happened then? What *had* he been thinking? Iestyn ripped off his jumper, the heat from his exertion coupled with his embarrassment becoming suddenly unbearable.

295

He rubbed his hands through his hair and set off up the hill thankfully in a different direction from Menna. His hands and legs were shaking but he strode off as fast as he could, stumbling over a tree root as he went, another kick of disloyalty from *their* tree.

He found the fuel in the back of Menna's truck and pulled it out. He decided against short-cutting back through the woods in case he bumped into her again and instead he walked along the track, his boots now rubbing his feet, chafed from the earlier gambolling down the steep bank. Despite that, all he could think about was Menna looking at him with as much distaste as a woman could muster. *Why on earth do you think I'd be interested in you?* As he finally made it to his quad bike, filled the tank and headed for home, he had taken a hard look at himself and what he represented. Stubbly faced, probably extreme body odour (given the gambolling), knackered quad bike, holey wellies, scraggy sheep...

Yeah. Why on earth would anyone?

Iestyn drove slowly as he contemplated the past in the present's new context. Suddenly it all made sense; his timing on that occasion couldn't have been any worse! No wonder Menna had retreated into the world of all work and no play. She'd been shafted good and proper and lost a baby in the process – and then he, Iestyn, had piled in asking if they could live happily ever after, and just made it worse.

So, how would she be feeling now he wondered? Would she be elated by her performance? Cleansed and ready for a bit of impromptu canoodling, or would she be sitting, sobbing, over the wheel of her truck?

And what should *he* do? Iestyn drove even slower as he pondered his actions. Probably best just to be a friend. Check she was OK, get her home, change into his white officer's suit and— No. Take her home, make her a cup of tea, listen if she wanted him to and then go and collect the family and write off the whole night as a bad job, maybe moving to start a new life in Australia in the morning.

Hang on – Iestyn squinted. It seemed as if the tail lights in front of him were moving again. Shit – he should have driven faster. They jumped back onto the road and then seemed to veer off left again and he could see the lights bouncing up and down as the vehicle went over rough ground.

That wasn't the way to Menna's farm. Perhaps it wasn't her after all? Perhaps she'd gone into town and was sitting having a giggle and a Martini with Lulu in a bar as a guy played *I got the Iestyn Bevan Blues* in the corner?

Unless – surely that wasn't the back lane to Menna's farm? There was an unsurfaced green lane that had served the farm and which forded the river. Menna's grandfather had been one of the first people in the area to get a car and, not wanting to risk driving it through a ford, he had cut a new track to join the council road and make use of their bridge. The family still used the lane sometimes, but only with a four-wheel drive and in summer. He and Menna had driven her dad's Land Rover along it, practising driving, as kids. Bill had rollocked them for "cutting the surface to buggery". But Iestyn also remembered later overhearing Bill telling Tomos, with pride in his voice, that he was amazed that the two twelve-year-olds could cross a ford in such a clapped out old vehicle!

It was technically a short cut, but only if the ground were dry and the river was low. But, early February? Ground dry and river low? Tonight? No chance. He'd better get moving...

Esther put on her coat and stood outside to wait for the taxi; she couldn't bear to be inside the police station for another moment. She stood as far back into the shadows as she could, as much for her own privacy as for sheltering from the bitter wind. Convenient as it might be, it would never do to hitch a lift home with a passing Louisa, eyes full of sparkle from her evening with a new beau.

She felt as if she'd been in a washing machine, battered, spun, disorientated and emerged a wrung-out rag. What should she do now? Did she tell people what had happened, what she had done? Get her version out before it appeared in the papers? Mind, her version would not be any less seedy than a write-up in the local rag – how could one turn a wad of spiteful letters into something less despicable than what it actually was?

A taxi pulled up and she walked towards it, feeling as if her legs might not make the five yards. A familiar head opened the door to her.

"Mrs Harrison? You all right? I wasn't expecting to pick *you* up again today – and especially not from a police station!"

"Oh, hello, Shane. No, it's not been a usual day today for me. Can you just take me home, please?"

"Course, love. What's been going on then? Been fighting? Grand theft auto? Or just a bit of GBH? Heh, heh."

Esther climbed into the back seat and rested her head on the window and tried to ignore Shane's delight in his repertoire of jokes about criminals and policemen and their truncheons.

They drove along the street, the slush skitting out from under the car. Esther looked out the window as they passed 40B Market Street. There was a light shining through the green curtains. It all looked very cosy in there considering it was such a foul night. She imagined David – sorry, Scamper – cuddled up with the Whore on the sofa. Diane would be wrapped around Scamper and they wouldn't really be watching what was on the television – they'd probably only have it on to drown out the noise of their antics for the sake of the occupants of other flats in the block.

Would they be laughing at her? Probably. She could imagine Diane saying, "Did you see her face? Oh, priceless! Oh well, at least she knows about *us* now. It was getting too difficult to hide the way we felt for each other." David probably wouldn't speak; he would just hide his face in Diane's warm folds and be happy that he had someone soft and jolly and in love with him to cuddle, instead of someone like Esther, who was tolerant of him in a cold, bony and irritated manner.

Tears slid from Esther's eyes as she stared back at the window and they continued to fall until she was dropped off, in silence, in Anweledig.

The Jeep's enormous headlights managed to pick out the lane easily and Menna's tracks were visible through the few remaining stubborn drifts of snow, now grey with age.

Luckily the grass soon turned to a stony track and Iestyn's truck managed to grind along it without his city tyres sinking into the mud. The route was filled with great lumps of stone and he winced as the chassis grated and clunked. Every now and then he would hit a muddy patch and slide into a hedge, or spin dangerously near a ditch.

Twice he ground to a standstill, his wheels spinning in the sludge and he had to climb out and throw a few rocks under the tyres, wading though the brown water that ran down the ruts, soaking his shoes and muddying his trouser legs.

Joe's truck was soon filthy and he hoped that he hadn't dented it where it had slid into a branch sticking out of the hedge. In addition, every time Iestyn got back into the seat, he brought a slurry of red-brown mud with him and he knew that he had covered the mats and the seat in sludge.

Sleet started falling and Iestyn fumbled for the windscreen wiper, finding the stereo volume stem first and making himself jump out of his skin. The track rounded a bend and then started heading steeply down hill. Shingle had been laid on the slope to make it easier to traverse and the truck slipped and slid down it. Where the hell was Menna, he thought as he put the diff-lock in. He was hoping that he would have caught her up by now, but that was unlikely really considering her head start and her not being worried about driving her brother's forty-grand Cherokee. Eventually the slope was too much for the Jeep and Iestyn slid the remaining ten yards to the river – sideways – with his heart in his mouth.

He glided to a halt parallel to the river which was just yards from him. *Thank fuck for that,* he breathed. Any faster and he'd be heading off down the river in it by now! He sat waiting for his heartbeat to slow down and wondering what on earth he should do next.

He put the windscreen wipers on high speed and strained to see out of the side window to gauge the state of the river. To his dismay it was a raging torrent of blackness. How was he ever going to get through that? The shallow ford he remembered as a kid had been engulfed by a deluge of melted snow that had picked up mud and stones as it went.

How stupid he had been – he should have guessed that the river would be in spate. At this rate, Menna would be home, in bed drinking cocoa and he'd have to ring her and ask her to come and pull him out!

He looked back up the track at the shingle slope. Although that too was enveloped by blackness, he knew that he would never get back up it in the Cherokee without off-road tyres. It was either through the ford *within* the vehicle, or through the ford *without* – or walk back up the lane, right round by road and then back down the proper farm track – probably about three and a half miles. No, he really didn't fancy that either, especially in this stupid bloody get up; he'd be hypothermic by the time he got anywhere with any heating. He could sleep in the truck, and though, knowing Joe's penchant for extras, there would probably be a mini bar and a plasma television screen in the back it would still be a grim night – especially for a six-foot-two-inch bloke in a bad, and worsening, mood.

He checked his phone – no, of course not, no reception. Bollocks: stuffed. Well and truly stuffed. He decided that it wasn't going to get any easier and so he made the decision to get out and quickly check the river – then he could either cross it, or dismiss that option and bed down for the night in the truck. He took a deep breath, turned his coat collar up and plunged out into the night.

The cold bit through his clothes and his feet, which were already chilled from their earlier soaking, had a new trickle of water run across them to replace that he had valiantly warmed up a few degrees. The sleet slashed against his face and he hunched himself over as he walked down the rest of the slope to the river. He stood and watched it, his eyes adjusting to the darkness as he saw sticks and fertiliser bags that had been dislodged from the river banks by the increased flow, floating by.

He looked upstream, knowing that it narrowed and therefore would be a deeper channel. Downstream, well, that might be possible? Then his eyes spotted something – surely a light? Was it Menna's bungalow? Her truck might be stopped by a gate? No, surely not; it looked different to that. More like – *shit!* – more like the interior light of a vehicle.

Without hesitating, he ran towards it, glad of Joe's truck's headlights as he slipped and tripped along the river bank.

"Menna?" he shouted, knowing that he was competing with the sound of the river. "Menna!" He tripped over a rock jutting out of the grass and he fell headlong, sprawling into the sodden mud that had been churned up nicely by sharp hooves as cattle had stood and drank from the river. He scrambled to his feet, mud sticking to his shoes and doubling their size and making moving difficult.

300

He could see the light plainly now – good God, it *was* an interior light, he could see the outline of her truck now, *and it was in the river!*

His eyes had acclimatised a bit and he could see the vehicle's silhouette at a tilt and the water raging and foaming around it. Shit, what on *earth* had happened? He fell again, this time knee deep in slurry and one shoe and then the other was sucked off. He could either waste time delving up to his shoulder in the mud or just go on without them: he went on without them, knowing that Joe would think it no loss.

Finally he got to the truck and stopped dead as he surveyed the scene: a tree had fallen across the river and the truck was wedged within the branches. The river was raging halfway up its doors and the back was lifting up and down as if just another few inches of torrent would tip it up onto its nose.

"Menna!" he screamed again, "Menna!"

Through the noise of the water he heard a scream in return, a terrified, hysterical cry that made his blood run cold. He saw fingers clawing out of the sunroof that was about two inches open and was prevented from opening any further by a chunky catch.

He shouted to her again and quickly assessed the situation. If he scrambled along the fallen tree, he could climb up onto the bonnet and then wrench that roof open. It didn't look easy, but it was his only chance – and hers by the look of it.

He leapt up the root ball of the tree – that was the easy bit. Then he edged his way along the lower trunk, cursing the lack of grip from his socks. Then he started going out over the water and he could feel himself getting more and more tense and therefore less and less agile. *Don't look down, don't look down,* he told himself as he looked down into the spinning, foaming torrent.

He was thankful to reach a few jutting out branches and used them as handholds, as his feet, with sodden socks hanging off the ends, slid about on the ivy. Eventually he was above the truck and could see one of Menna's hands pressed white against the inside of the windscreen. He kept shouting to her, telling her that he was on his way and that she'd be fine, but he had no idea whether she could hear him or even knew that he was there.

What had happened? Was she OK? What if she was trapped within the actual truck? It was too much to contemplate.

Finally he sat on the tree and inched a foot down onto the bonnet. He tested it for stability and it seemed stuck fast within the branches. The nose must be wedged, being pushed under the tree by the weight of the water coming along behind it.

He could hear Menna screaming again as he carefully put his full weight onto the bonnet, having tossed his flapping socks away into the water. Crouching low, he crawled up the bonnet and made a dive for the windscreen, hanging onto the wipers as he caught his breath, his heart beating wildly within his chest.

Iestyn pulled himself up to the roof and shouted through the sunroof, "Menna! Are you OK? I'm here now; I'm going to get you out, OK?"

He could hear her crying inside, sobbing and then a shout, "Iestyn? I'm OK, but just get me out!" It rose to hysteria as he grabbed at the sunroof. Damn – it was stuck fast and was too tight to the vehicle to get any purchase on it to lever it away.

Menna started banging the underside and he yanked the top, but the mechanism was strong and it wasn't budging. Iestyn felt desperate. He could feel the truck moving about a bit as he struggled with the catch – perhaps it wasn't wedged as tightly as he had first suspected.

"Find something! Something heavy – I need to lever this off or break it." Ages seemed to pass and he shivered as he spread his weight across the bonnet, after feeling the vehicle shift when she moved around inside. Eventually a shoe poked through the gap.

"No!" he shouted, "something bigger, heavier!" He heard her screaming something at him, but he couldn't make out the words. He tried to lever the top off with the shoe, but the heel cracked off. He tried to knock the mechanism sideways, but it was no good. He was getting cold and tired from hanging on and the rain had run all the gel from his hair into his eyes and was making them sting.

"Fuck it!" he shouted, rubbing his eyes and rattling at the sunroof. Then a slim stainless steel Thermos flask was pushed through.

"Fantastic!" he shouted and on the third crash, was able to knock the catch sideways and prise the flap upwards. By the time he'd righted his balance, Menna's arms were out of the gap and her head and shoulders quickly followed.

Had he not known who she was, he would have struggled to recognise her. The moon had peered around a sleet cloud and he could see that her face was swollen and distorted with terror. "Just get me out of here!" she screamed. "Get me out!" The truck shifted its position and Iestyn knew that they had to be careful.

"Menna," he shouted, holding her shoulders as she struggled to wriggle out through the roof, "wait, *listen*, we need to be *careful*, OK? Don't bounce, don't jump or we'll be tipped up, OK?" He gripped her tightly to make sure that she listened.

She stopped wriggling for a couple of seconds and her eyes looked at him, great big dark hollows peering out from a white face with teeth that chattered so hard that he was sure that they just *had* to fall out.

Right, he thought, take control. Be quick, but not slapdash. Firm, but not rough. Menna looked so traumatised that he felt that she would disintegrate into hysteria at any moment and that would be no good to anyone.

"OK, push yourself up as far as you can and then I'll grab around your waist and lever you out, understood?" Menna nodded and Iestyn could see from the concentration on her face that she was searching for a foothold. "Try the steering wheel, or the gear stick?"

She obviously found something and pushed herself upwards, and Iestyn rejoiced for her slightness as her chest, now enclosed in a filthy, saturated red and orange dress, wriggled free.

"Lean over my shoulder," he ordered and he grabbed around her waist and desperately tried to drag her up through the roof. He could feel her efforts as she wriggled this way and that, desperate to get her hips through the gap. Eventually they did and she popped out like a cork from a bottle and Iestyn fell backwards onto the bonnet, pulling Menna back on top of him. They slid down the bonnet with screams and cries of fright. Miraculously, they ended up in a pile at the bottom, still on the bonnet, just, but entangled in branches and ropes of ivy.

"Now, get on that tree trunk. Ready? Go!" Iestyn grabbed around Menna's thighs and bumped her up onto the tree, pushing her backside until she was safe. He could feel the truck was moving more

303

now, as if it were being lifted by the weight of the water and he knew that they didn't have much time.

"Go!" he shouted, "that way," and he pointed her to the opposite bank from where his truck was, no point in going back to that; her bungalow was only a few hundred yards away now.

He watched as Menna started to crawl along, hanging onto branches and clawing at the ivy, whimpering as she went. "Keep going!" he shouted, knowing that if she stopped, they would be done for; the tree just wasn't wide enough for him to help her along it.

As soon as she had gone far enough to give him room, he clambered up behind her, his final bounce from the bonnet being enough to dislodge it from its position and the back swirled round, crashing into the tree. Menna screamed again as it rocked the tree and Iestyn could see the water damming up behind the truck, which was now wedged sideways against the branches. "Quick! Quick!" he yelled, glad that Menna was as strong as she was and he scrambled along behind her, both of them crawling, grabbing for branches, slipping and sliding on the ivy and praying that it was strong enough to withstand their tugging.

Finally they reached the point whereby the tree was over land and Menna ground to a halt. Iestyn was able to climb around her and jump to the ground. He put his hands out to her and, like a child, she half-rolled into his arms and he lowered her to the ground, an exhausted wet pile in the soggy grass.

"Come on, Menna," he shouted, "we *have* to keep going. Now. Come on!" Menna was sitting on the ground, her teeth chattering, her whole body shivering uncontrollably. He knew that she would be in shock as well as freezing from the water in the truck; she must have been waist-deep in it for a good ten minutes.

"Come on, take that off – off, *now*," he cried, and fumbled for the zip on her dress. She wearily submitted and his freezing fingers struggled until it was down. He pulled her to her feet and holding her under the arms with one hand, pulled and tugged and yanked the dress off with the other – not greatly unlike he had done to Judy outside the Young Farmers' dance that night long ago. The thick brocade material was sodden and she'd be frozen by the time he got her home. Trying not to notice that she was now sat in a puddle of mud on a freezing February night in only a pair of knickers, he ripped off his own clothes. He quickly put his T-shirt on her and then fumbled with his rucked up shirt, which was incredibly difficult given his freezing fingers. He gave up on the buttons and just wrapped the ends further round her. His bloody nonsense fashion jacket was slung over the top and stuffed under her arms to stop the ends from flapping.

Menna managed to smile and mutter a *thank you*. Although the clothes were caked in mud, they were dry – well, dryish, anyway – and the residual warmth from his body had to be better for her than a sodden, strapless dress.

"Right," he said, the wind now biting into his naked torso, "come on, we're off," and he manhandled her to a half-standing position and then humped her into his arms. Iestyn fought his way out of the rest of the tree branches, getting poked and prodded as he slid around in the mud and he half-carried, half-dragged Menna up the slope.

His relief when he reached the old shingle track was immense and he felt like weeping as he carried his love, her arms wrapped around his neck and her face nestled into his naked shoulder, over the stones.

"Iestyn," she whispered, "you came for me!"

"Of course I did; I love you," he mumbled, and he felt her squeeze him tighter around the neck, "and anyway, it's what I do: I trim hooves, I look after sheep and I rescue maidens…"

As he stumbled off into the darkness, his bare feet were knocked and stubbed by the builder's rubble that had been dumped on the track over the years where it had become too muddy, but he was oblivious to the pain, partly because of the cold making his feet numb and partly because of the elation he felt at the crescendo of his adventures. He wasn't quite dressed in a white officer's suit, but he had done something far better than rescue his lady love from life on the production line.

He saw the roof of her bungalow silhouetted against the moon in the distance. They'd nearly made it! They were going to make it! After all those years of thinking about this point (albeit in a *slightly* different context) all that trauma and freezing cold water, it was going to be OK! As he bent his head and shed a few tears into Menna's sodden hair, she clutched her shivering arms around him just a little bit tighter…

Iestyn had been confident that the bungalow would be unlocked, and it was. The only problem now, he thought, would be that, knowing Menna, the fire would be out, there'd be no milk in the fridge and he'd have to wrap her in an itchy old blanket that she'd nailed up across the window to keep the draughts out. Perhaps they'd be better to go on the extra half mile to the farmhouse where at least there'd be some creature comforts?

As he stood in the porch and deliberated, Menna twisted in his arms and found the light switch. Iestyn gasped as the hallway was lit up: surely they were in the wrong house? He shut the door behind them to keep the wonderful warmth in. The deep red rug felt beautifully soft beneath his battered and frozen feet.

Three hours later, Iestyn finally felt that he could risk some sleep. He was the most comfortable he'd ever been in his life and he felt as if he'd really earned some shut-eye. The fire in Menna's lounge was pumping out heat as he'd stacked it full of logs and opened the vents until it had roared. He'd plonked Menna onto the sofa and then dragged it over closer to the fire. He'd wrapped her in the fur throw and fetched her duvet and quilt from her bedroom and any other blankets he could find, but she was still shivering in a way that shook her whole body.

"Menna, I need to get those things off you and get you warm, OK? Are you happy for me to do that?" She nodded and mumbled that she needed a shower to get warm. He ran off and stopped only for a second with an open mouth to stare at the exotic opulence of her bathroom. He put the shower on to run warm and noted the wonderfully soft towels to wrap her in afterwards. He helped her to her feet and they walked, her leaning against him, into the bathroom.

They stood and looked at the shower. "I'll leave you to it then," he said.

"OK," she replied, trying to hold onto the towel rail. Her legs, bleeding from the crawl across the tree trunk, buckled and he just managed to catch her before she hit the deck. Menna managed a giggle. "Just help me in. I don't mind you being here – after what you've done, I think I can trust you!"

Iestyn smiled and suddenly felt awkward – *OK, but he wouldn't look...* "Right, arms up!" and she obliged and he lifted the clothes up over her head. He helped her into the shower and she leant against the wall and let the warm water run over her.

She put an arm up to wipe the water from her face, but slipped and landed painfully on the floor. Oh God, thought Iestyn, she's never going to manage on her own. He looked around as if hoping to see a lady from a Moroccan hammam standing in the corner ready to step in, but there was no one but him.

Menna tried to stand up, but slipped again, this time bringing all the bottles of shower gel and shampoo clattering down around her.

Iestyn took a deep breath, "Menna, I'll come in too, OK?"

"OK," she said feebly as she struggled to pull herself up. He really wasn't sure about this, but quickly undid the jeans that were now cold and stiff from the mud and pulled them over his feet. Suddenly his feet hurt. He hadn't realised, but there was blood on the wet floor trickling from the cuts on his feet that had been made as he walked back carrying Menna.

He opened the door of the cubicle, feeling more than a little uncomfortable in just his boxers (although he had time to quickly thank Sima in his mind for slinging them at him earlier that evening, as otherwise, he'd be standing there with a pair of washed out turquoise Y-fronts hanging halfway down his backside through lack of elastane) and he helped Menna to her feet.

Eventually he'd stood in the corner and she leaned back against him, finally relaxing as the warm water poured over them both. He helped her wash her hair with a beautiful citrus shampoo and groaned inwardly as he saw the suds run down over her freckly shoulders.

After far too short a time, he helped her out, quickly removed her panties and wrapped her in three towels and sat her in the chair in the corner of the bathroom. He jumped back into the shower and saw to his feet, soaping the grit and the gravel out of the cuts as gently as he could, then gave himself a quick once-over with the shampoo. He wrapped a towel quickly around his waist, turned the water off and then turned his attention back to Menna.

He helped her back to the sofa, spread her duvet out over the seat and the back and snuggled her into it. He fetched another duvet and wrapped it over her and made sure she was completely covered from head to toe. He made two cups of tea each for them and loaded hers with sugar, ignoring her protests that she didn't like sugar in her drinks. Then he phoned both Joe's mobile and his parents' house and left messages to let them know that everything was all right and that he'd tell them about the Jeep tomorrow. After getting Menna's agreement, he also left a message at her parents' farmhouse.

Then he came and perched on the end of the sofa, still wrapped in his own towel. He felt drained, emotionally and physically, and his feet were hurting. The soles felt as if someone had rubbed a cheese-grater over them and he was sure that he'd broken at least one of his toes.

He looked over at Menna, wrapped like a caterpillar in her down-filled chrysalis. "How you feeling?" he asked softly. "Warm yet?"

"Nearly," she smiled.

"Actually, you've still got your towel round you; it'll be wet. Go on, take it off, I'll go and get you some pyjamas or something."

"Iestyn…"

"Yes?"

"Come here. Come and sit behind me. Sit in the corner by here, yeah?"

"Well…OK." He wasn't quite sure what she meant and thought it might be perhaps too soon to shout *Yippee!* toss his towel in the air and pounce on her. Instead, he shuffled into the corner where she patted the sofa and leaned into the duvet. It felt slightly damp, but still warm and scented with the wonderful fragrance of that shampoo that he'd rubbed so happily into her hair.

"Now, put your feet up, twizzle around a bit. Come on, Iestyn!" He did what he was bidden. When he was settled to her liking, she picked up the second duvet again, dropped her towels to the floor and nestled onto his lap, so that she was leaning sideways against him, but still could see his face.

Iestyn's eyebrows shot up high as the duvet was draped across them both. "Come on," she said, tugging at his towel, "play the game!" He gulped, then squirmed until his towel was also free and tossed down the back of the sofa.

He pulled her close to him and kissed the top of her hair. Everything was wonderful. He didn't feel sexual – he was too physically and emotionally exhausted for that – he just felt soft, warm, knackered, in pain, but simply completely overwhelmed with the feelings of love for the woman who was snuggled into his nakedness.

"How did you know to come after me?" she whispered.

"I heard what had happened – and you nearly ran me off the road and I wanted to get your insurance details in case I'd scuffed Joe's mudguards – no, I wanted…I just wanted to check that you were all right."

"Am now. Oh, but it was hideous. Actually, the whole night was bloody hideous! Paul, the money, your date – all of it!"

"My date *was* pretty hideous, to be honest," he grinned. Menna wriggled around a bit and found one of his hands and she held it in both of hers, working her way around it, stroking his rough patches, the nail he'd crushed on the tow hitch and a tiny soft area on the knuckle of his little finger.

"I sat for ages by the river, debating whether to try and cross it or not," Menna said, "I knew that it would be deep, but eventually I thought *sod it* and gave it a go!"

"Why didn't you use the road bridge?"

"Dunno. Adventure I s'pose. It'd been such a shit night, to crawl home and just go to bed would have been the ultimate in crap endings. I felt like I needed a little something to take my mind off it all being so shit!"

"What, like floating down a river in a four-by-four?"

"Don't joke; it was horrible. There was a big rock in the middle of the ford that I couldn't get over – must have been washed down with the flood – so I went round it, but I must have gone too far round as suddenly I was moving and there was absolutely *nothing* I could do! The whole truck just bobbed away down the stream as if it were a can of pop. I thought it would roll, but it swung round then crunched into that tree."

Iestyn could feel her beginning to shake and her voice trembled into tears, "And then, and then it started to fill up and I couldn't open the doors, nor the window and that bloody sunroof, well, well I couldn't open that either…" Iestyn pulled her tighter to him and cradled her still-damp hair. "…and just when I thought I was going to die in there – you turned up!" She smiled a watery smile at him and planted a kiss on his cheek. "Thank you!"

"You're welcome, and, as I said, it's what I do!" Iestyn looked at the clock. Two-thirty a.m. "Come on," he said, "go to sleep now, tell me about it again in the morning. Are you warm enough?" Menna nodded. "Comfortable enough?" She snuggled down and put her head on his shoulder and nodded again. "Good."

He wrapped his arms around her and pulled her tight to his chest, so enjoying the touch of her warm skin against his own. He felt her fall asleep almost immediately and he just lay there, listening to her breathing, stroking her hair, occasionally brushing his lips back and fore across the top of her head and just inhaling the whole idea of lying, naked, on a sofa in front of the fire with his love in his arms. Finally, the happiest man in Wales fell fast asleep.

CHAPTER 33

Naw chwyth cath – the nine breaths of a cat

It was a big crowd that stood at the riverside and surveyed the scene the next morning.

"Fuckin' hell."

"Jee-sus."

"Oh my goodness."

"*Dieu, dieu*, Menna *bach, dieu, dieu.*"

It was drizzling lightly as they stood in a huddle, sinking slowly into the mud. Iestyn was dressed rather absurdly in one of Menna's pairs of tracksuit bottoms, baggy and long on her, but like a pair of ballet tights on him. He had a tight red rugby shirt that *just about* reached the top of his ballet tights and a pair of her dad's split wellingtons that she'd found in the bottom of a cardboard box filled with spiders in the garage. However, he stood surveying the scene very seriously with his arm tightly around Menna's shoulders.

Sima and Joe had opted for designer countryside and Isla wore what she always wore, but with an extra hat on. Tansy was sitting perched on a rock on top of Johnny's coat feeding Gwennie who was wrapped in so many blankets that she looked like a bundle, rather than a baby. Johnny sat next to her, occasionally pulling the blankets back to make sure that Gwennie could breath.

"Bloody hell, Menna," said Joe quietly, holding on tightly to Sima's hand, "how on earth did you manage to get out of that?"

They were all staring at the tree, still lodged in the same place it had been the night before, but now it had something wedged upstream of it that made the water swirl in an unusual way. All that was visible of the truck was one of the back corners, with about eight inches of rear bumper poking out of the muddy water.

Sima exclaimed and then ran to pick up what remained of Menna's dress, now a filthy piece of material trampled into the mud. "Oh, Menna, you poor thing! You are just *so* brave – both of you, *so* brave." She had tears running down her cheeks as she stood on the other side of Menna and gave her a hug. "Tell me again…"

Menna pointed again to the ford that was now completely unrecognisable, as the track either side just ran into a torrent. She explained quite simply what had happened, making it all seem rather matter-of-fact. Iestyn then filled in his part of the tale. The two sets of parents stood and listened, nodding or whistling whilst Sima provided the dramatics (which was good, as someone should have): groaning and clutching or uttering *oh my God* every now and then.

"Look!" she cried, as Iestyn got to the bit about how he ran along the bank and fell in the mud. "There's one of your shoes!" and she pointed to the opposite side of the bank.

"Oh, yeah!" he grinned, "I'll go and get it, see if I can find the other one!" He made to go back to cross by the tree, but Menna grabbed him.

"No! Don't," she said, "you can't." The look of terror came back to her face and he walked straight back to her and resumed his position at her side.

"Sorry – of course I won't," he said quietly to her. Menna had started trembling again, tears welling into her eyes and rolling down her cheeks. Everyone could see how upset she was and called a halt to the event. "Come on," said Jean, "everyone fancy a cup of something hot and a piece of cake at the farm?" Apart from Johnny and Tansy who said they'd join them after Gwennie had finished, the others all mumbled *too right* and shuffled off towards the big house.

"Joe – your truck…" started Iestyn as they drew parallel to it.

"Don't worry about it, mate," said Joe immediately, "whatever has been damaged can be repaired. We'll pull it back up the track later. Don't even think about it; the important thing is that Menna – and you – are safe."

"Thanks," mumbled Iestyn and Menna in unison. Everyone knew that Joe loved his truck, but to see him barely look sideways at it as they walked away, parked on the opposite side of the river, splattered in mud with its flickering headlights sucking the last of the power from the battery, was quite an acknowledgement of the risks they'd taken.

"Well, it's only a vehicle after all, isn't it…" started Sima.

"Oi, easy now," growled Joe, "there's no need to get carried away…"

Menna cried off the tea and cakes invite and Iestyn said he'd accompany her back to her bungalow. They waved goodbye to the others and set off slowly to Menna's home, Iestyn hobbling on his battered feet and Menna slow and subdued. The tea and cakes fraternity watched them going, all trying to hide their desperate interest as to what was *really* going on with those two, but knowing that things were too traumatic to enquire or joke about, even in a light-hearted way. Sima looked as if she was about to explode and Jean was biting her lip and looking very uncomfortable.

Eventually, Jean broke away from the crowd, tapping her husband's arm and muttering, "Bill, I'll catch you up," as she went, trotting along with her collar turned up and her hands dug deeply into her pockets. "Menna! Menna, love, wait please…" and she scooted around to the front of Iestyn and Menna who had been walking back in silence.

"Menna …" she said, trying to get her breath back, as much for her nerves as from trotting fifty yards. "Menna, love …" She looked at Iestyn with a little embarrassment.

"Do you want me to go on?" he asked. "So that you can, er, have a word?"

312

"No, it's fine," said Menna, looking directly at her mother.

Jean looked uncomfortable, but desperate to speak, "Menna, love – all those things you said last night – to Paul – were they, were they *true*?"

"Of course."

"I didn't know."

"No. You didn't ask."

"Menna …"

"Mum, you were so disappointed that I wasn't going to be part of the Neuadd that you didn't stop to think whether there might be a good reason for it."

"I know, Menna, love, I know and I'm so—"

"You gave *me* a hard time when I'd been dumped, pregnant, because *you* wanted me to live at a bigger farm. How do you think that made me feel?"

"Oh, Menna, I'm sorry, *so* sorry, *cariad*…" Jean looked close to tears and it was the first time that Iestyn had seen her anything other than strong and in control.

"But, actually," Menna shrugged, "it's OK now. I think I got a little of my own back last night – I didn't mean for anyone else to hear, mind, but, well, these things usually happen for a reason, eh?" Then Menna seemed to have a change of heart and patted her mother's arm. "Anyway, Mum, you weren't to know, were you? After all, I didn't tell you, so how could you have guessed?"

"A mother should know, Menna, a mother should know. Your Dad and I, well, you should have been able to tell us. Next time, you tell us OK? Promise?"

"Hopefully there won't be a next time, but yes, OK, Mum!"

Jean managed a hint of a smile and made to go. Then she turned back and gave Menna a desperate hug. "Oh, *cariad*, seeing that truck, oh…you're so important to us, we do love you so much, so *so* much…" Somehow Iestyn got sucked into the embrace, "and you, Iestyn, you saved her life, I don't doubt that. Thank you, thank you…" She planted an out-of-practice kiss on each of their cheeks and then gave a nervous shrug and scuttled off. "We'll see you later, OK?" she called over her shoulder and headed off after the others.

"Bloody hell! I'll have to have a near-death experience more often!" Menna said, obviously pleased by her mother's unexpected outburst. "I don't think she's said anything more personal to me than *take your shoes off* in years!"

Tansy and Johnny sat on their rock in silence, save for the noise of the water swirling around the truck and Gwennie's occasional snuffles. "You warm enough?" asked Johnny.

"Yes, thank you," smiled Tansy, "I don't think anyone could feel cold when they have as many coats on as you made me wear!"

"Just to make sure – you can always take one off…"

"I bet Nain used to say that to you?"

Johnny smiled sheepishly. "Funny isn't it, how the things that you let wash over you for years and years suddenly become relevant. I'll be saying that *a hat keeps in 70 per cent of your body heat* next, or *get your feet warm and the rest will follow*…Hear that, Gwennie? Keep your feet warm and the rest will follow! And when you're five, I'll be saying, *Listen to your teacher*… and then when you're sixteen, I'll be saying, *You can always phone me and I will pick you up wherever you are*…"

Tansy leant back into him and smiled as his arms wrapped around her and little Gwen. "And I'll be saying, *Hey, listen to your father…don't take that tone of voice with me,* and *You are* not *going out in that,* if anything my parents said to me still stands!"

"Nah, we'll be great parents, won't we? I'll show Gwennie how to race quad bikes and you can tell her, I don't know, about fish or hamsters or something!"

"Johnny, my love, I think you still have a few things to find out about me if you think I am going to spend my time teaching our daughter about hamsters… Come on, she's finished now. Can you pull me up and let's go and get a piece of that cake Jean was on about: I'm starving!"

After tea and cakes had turned into a hearty lunch, Joe, Sima and Bill took the tractor and tow rope out and headed for the truck. Bill drove the tractor and Joe and Sima sat either side of him, leaning against the doors. Joe was amazed that Sima had wanted to come, but she had been quite stirred by what had happened the night before. "Menna is just so strong," she'd said, "I don't know what I'd have done in the same situation."

"Probably talked the truck into reversing back up the river and onto dry land…"

"Don't be silly, Joe. It just makes me think – Menna's got a *real* life up here. Mine is all smoke and mirrors really. Getting paid an awful lot of money to just spout nonsense to people…"

"Sounds bloody marvellous to me," grunted Bill. "Joe, get out and open the gate will you, please?"

Just as Joe was about to climb down, Sima called, "I'll do it!" and started fiddling with the door, then took an age to scramble down from the tractor. She slipped and slid over the muddy bits in her flowery wellies, rather than sticking to the stones, fiddled with the gate catch and then made a huge show about lugging the gate round as it had dropped on its hinges.

"F'Christ's sake, Joe, you do the next one, will you?" Bill mumbled, and he waved kindly to Sima as he bumped the tractor through the gateway and then watched in disbelief as the process was reversed and Sima closed the gate, then hauled herself and her white mac with black stitching and a couple of mud splashes back into the cab.

"Quite hard work all those gates, aren't they?" she gushed, rubbing a mark on her hand.

"S'pose so," he said, "especially when you add them to three hundred sheep, a hundred and fifty cows, hens, ducks and the Ministry…"

They spent the rest of the afternoon hitching up the rope onto Joe's Jeep and dragging it back up the track, manoeuvring it round and then towing it back along to the road, slipping and sliding through the mud, its wheels thick with clay. Sima insisted on driving it and seemed to be quite enjoying herself as it occasionally bounced off a hedge or clonked over a rock.

The truck left muddy tyre tracks the length of the tarmacadamed road with clods of earth being flung off it as it went. It then got dragged back along the proper farm track, with the tractor picking up speed and Sima concentrating hard as she tried to avoid the drops into potholes and the worst of the ruts.

"I think we'll leave Menna's truck for the time being," Bill said, looking done in by the events of the night. "It'll be knackered anyway, so there'll be nothing to be gained from struggling with it now."

Joe nodded and thanked Bill as he put the battery on charge. "We'd better go and see if Iestyn wants to come home."

"Yes, definitely!" Sima said, setting off across the yard, desperate to know what was going on in the little bungalow.

What *was* going on in the little bungalow was that Iestyn and Menna were pretty much in the same position that they had been the night before. The sofa was still in front of the fire and the fire was stoked up high. There were a few cups and a plate of half-eaten sandwiches lying on the floor beside the sofa, but basically there were two people entwined and chatting quietly.

"Who was Lulu? Well, Lulu was someone I suppose I met over the Internet!"

"Over the Internet!" laughed Menna, stroking one of the sore and swollen feet draped over her lap.

"Well, I don't know why I arranged it, really. I wasn't really wanting to, you know, meet someone else – I suppose it was after something that Sima said."

"Sima?"

"Yes, she was always on about me and the lack of women around me, and she suggested that I look under my nose a bit more – so I typed Tan-y-Bryn into the internet and that's how it started!"

Menna laughed, "I've got a feeling that I know what she *really* meant! But, why weren't you – er – 'wanting to meet someone else'?"

"Because of you, silly!"

"Why did you go through with it then? Why not just ask me?"

"Because you didn't seem interested."

"But I was…"

"But *I* didn't know that, did I…"

It was the kind of conversations that lovers have when they have first let their guard down and are desperate to know how much the

316

other one is in love with them and to know that they always have been, preferably to the exclusion of all others.

Iestyn had another pair of ballet tights on; this time some of Menna's white pyjama bottoms with red checks on. They were stretched across him and were the reason that Menna kept dissolving into giggles. Menna had a stretchy vest and a pair of contrasting red pyjama bottoms with white checks on that fitted her much better – and very nicely too, in Iestyn's eyes.

"And I cannot believe this place," said Iestyn, looking around.

"Do you like it?" Menna asked nervously.

"I love it! It's so, well, it's so *you*, when I think about it."

"Really?"

"Yeah –I *knew* that you wouldn't be rugby shirts and wellies *all* the time – you always smelt so wonderful you see!" Menna smiled, very glad that he hadn't teased her or made a big thing out of her domesticity.

Sima and Joe arrived, made them more tea, fed them with Jean's cake and then left them in peace. Sima had *loved* the bungalow, with Roberta Flack playing throughout and the warm glow of the furnishings. "Just the thing to be wrapped in on a cold winter's day," she'd enthused. "Come on, Joe, let's book into a hotel for the afternoon…"

After Joe and Sima had left, Joe promising to bring new clothes later that evening, Iestyn and Menna sat on the sofa for the remainder of the afternoon. They'd snuggled, dozed, whispered nonsense and drunk tea. Menna was emotional and occasionally she would shed a few tears as she thought about the rescue or the event in the Lamp and Iestyn would relish the act of pulling her back deep into his lap and wrapping her in a bear hug that would always be there for her.

Epilogue

Nefi blw! Navy blue! (goodness gracious!)

Eighteen months later...

It was a beautiful June day and the sun baked down on the gathering as they lounged on a couple of blankets under an old lime tree.

"It's hard to imagine how this tree got to be blown into this shape when the day is as still as today, isn't it?" said Tansy as she scooped together a pile of little stones and watched as Gwennie painstakingly put them into her bucket, then toddled over and emptied them into the brook nearby.

"Gwennie, you'll divert the course of the river if you carry on," yawned Iestyn as he stretched back and closed his eyes.

"You used to do that," smiled Isla as she passed around the glasses of squash – a nice clear tall glass for Sima first, then in worsening degrees until eventually Iestyn was thrust a faded blue beaker with the remains of a Bambi sticker on the side. "I'll just go and get yours, Menna, love, the kettle was only now coming to the boil."

"I'll do it," said Iestyn, getting up. "You sit here, Mam, and try and get a suntan on the gap between your skirt and your wellies... What'll it be this time, Menna? Broccoli and banana tea? Grapefruit and sausage?"

"Eugh, don't," groaned Menna, rubbing her swelling belly. "No, I'll have elderflower and lemon. No, lemon and ginger."

"Not camomile anymore?" asked Sima. "It's good for settling the stomach."

"No, I must have overdosed on the stuff; now it just makes me feel worse."

"When I was pregnant, all I wanted was crisps and lemonade!" said Tansy.

"Mother just craved scones," smiled Joe.

"Oh, and Iestyn, now I think of it, there's a plate of them on the side; bring them out too, will you?"

"Just make sure you don't give them to the workmen, won't you," said Sima, "it's hard enough getting them to do anything anyway,

318

without them – er – sitting down to enjoy them too!" she added diplomatically.

The others laughed, "OK, lemon and ginger tea and the scones it is, then," said Iestyn as he walked away from the group and headed back towards the kitchen.

The lace on his boot came undone and he dropped down to tie it up. Then with the sun shining down on his neck, he had one of those rare moments where one takes a few seconds to consider things.

Ahead of him, the old barn was shrouded in scaffolding and several workmen, their backs the colour of hazelnuts, worked in the sun as the radio blasted around them. The re-pointing of the stone on the north wall was nearly complete and the first of the windows was being fitted. The whole project was a credit to Sima's organisational skills as she walked around the site with a clipboard, immaculately presented and the only one wearing a hard hat.

It wouldn't be long before her studio was finished. She and Joe had already moved into their barn conversion half a mile up the lane and it was a shrine to careful interior design: sensitive to the vernacular yet complemented by the most modern of fittings.

Once the studio was finished, work would begin on the old farmhouse, the clutter of rooms on the top floor being converted into four en-suite bedrooms, perfect for a small group of clients to come on her courses and stay in a traditional working farmhouse. Sima wasn't entirely convinced that Isla would cope with the portion sizes required by genteel ladies but, as Joe kept reassuring her, they could always leave some…

Joe had loved being back on the farm and, under the guidance of Tomos and Iestyn, he'd dived into the work, relishing the hard slog and bringing new ideas and practices to a slightly stale business. Mind, he hadn't been there for a winter yet, but he had a few more months before the real weather struck and the last of his sushi lifestyle was whipped away by a cow skidding on his foot in a minus-twenty wind chill.

It was all change on the Brechdan farm too. Nain and Taid had finally been persuaded to retire, although they both came to the farm every day and put in a full day's graft. In the evening, however, they returned to Tansy's old house in Cefn Mawr where they were lodging whilst their new bungalow was being built at the end of the Cwmtwrch track. Tansy had, with Nain and Taid's financial help, bought Greg out of the house and this had allowed Nain and Taid to move out of the farm and for Johnny and Tansy to – notionally, anyway – take over the reins.

Nain loved being in a more modern house, being near her sister and within walking distance of a couple of shops. "Mind, not that I'm ever there during shop hours, but it is nice to think that I could walk to them if I wanted to," she would say. Taid enjoyed his power shower at the end of each day and apparently sat down with his pre-bed cocoa like a fledgling, his face bright red, with his dressing gown on and his grey hair all fluffed out at the sides.

Iestyn knew, however, that they were looking forward to being back on the farm and that Johnny and Tansy would feel better then, too – Nain and Taid would probably have a more restful time being on the doorstep where they could pop in and out, rather than feeling that they had to finish all the jobs they wanted to do before they made a move to go home. The bungalow was almost finished with its two large bedrooms – one for Nain and Taid and one for Gwennie and the rest of the future great-grandchildren when they come to stay!

Johnny and Taid had sneaked over to Cefn Mawr one afternoon and tackled the garage. They had giggled as they ripped labels of the walls, pulled nails and hooks out and then whitewashed the plywood. When Tansy had found out, she had been so touched that she'd given Taid such an enormous bear hug that she picked him off the floor, tears in her eyes. "Christ, m'n, you'll break my spine!" he'd said, but Iestyn could see that he was moved; he'd developed a real bond with Tansy, a quiet enjoyment of the woman who had made his grandson so happy.

As for himself, Iestyn couldn't be happier. He turned to look back down the slope and saw his wonderful family and friends sitting together, chatting and laughing under the full branches of the lime. His beautiful Menna was sitting stroking the belly that cocooned their baby. She was stunning, dressed in a golden-coloured sundress – chosen by Sima of course, but worn with rigger boots as she insisted on helping out.

"It's good for her," Isla had said, "let her carry on as long as she feels comfortable. I was splitting logs the day that you were born."

"Too right," Tomos had muttered, "wasn't up for doing the bloody ditching though…"

He and Menna lived in Menna's bungalow, and he revelled daily in the luxury of Menna's fixtures and fittings. Together they had added a few things, but Iestyn had said he so loved what Menna had already done that he didn't want it any different. Together they were learning how to cook and they ate their supper to the sounds of soul music. Iestyn had never really had a taste in anything, so he happily latched onto what Menna liked, simply enjoying the fact that it was already there for him and that it was warm and it worked.

He would sing as he showered after work each night, indulging himself in strawberry soaps or oatmeal scrubs – still such a happy contrast to showering with Tomos' wellies, and cleaning himself with a squirt of Isla's washing-up liquid. Afterwards, he would wrap himself in a luxurious towel and then sit chatting to Menna as she chopped carrots or scrubbed potatoes.

Menna's pregnancy was the icing on the cake. They had had a conversation establishing that they both wanted children about a week before Menna realised that she was two weeks late. Iestyn would bring toast and a cup of tea in to Menna each morning as that would keep the sickness at bay and then he would keep out of the way in the afternoon in case she needed to sleep off some of the desperate tiredness. They had already painted the spare room and Tomos was stripping the lead paint off the ancient cot that had been dug out of the old barn. "Bit of lead never stopped ours growing," he'd grumbled as Isla had sent him back out to make sure *all* the paint was gone. "Looking at them, the lead probably made them grow more…"

Everyone said that Menna had also blossomed since the night of the Sheep Breeders' and Iestyn was pleased that he might have had something to do with it – although he had loved her as she'd always been and wouldn't have worried if she'd worn tracksuit bottoms every day for the rest of her life. Saying that, however, he did love her new fitted tops and her floaty skirts, and he loved the fact that her feet had freckles on because they'd finally been touched by the sun…

The plan was that Iestyn would carry on working at Pencwmhir, showing Joe the ropes and then start doing a day or two a week at Menna's farm, slowly moving over to work it with her in order to be full time there when the baby was born. Menna's father, Bill, was glad of the extra help and it meant that between him, Bill and Menna they could get the place working like clockwork.

Menna's mother, Jean, had been softened by the whole ordeal of the night at the Lamp, the revelation about what had really happened between Menna and Paul the Neuadd and that terrible incident in the river. She would be forever grateful to Iestyn and had found a growing gentleness and indulgence towards her daughter and, as if making up for her years of cool and rather controlling parenting, the occasional bunch of flowers would be dropped off at their kitchen or a little pack of toiletries left on the doorstep.

Menna had embraced this new maternal relationship, especially with the baby due, as she felt she finally had so much more in common with her mother. For some reason, Menna had said that she never wanted to have Sunday lunches at the farmhouse, but that was fine with Iestyn; he was quite happy practicing his own roast chickens with scones, jam and cream for dessert…

Iestyn was jolted back to the here and now as the group of men on the scaffold burst into song, accompanying the radio blaring out "Bohemian Rhapsody": it was bloody awful. He carried on up the slope and shut the kitchen door behind him.

Esther was sitting at a table full of women drinking afternoon tea and playing cards when a tall woman with cropped black hair came into the room carrying a cake with a candle on the top.

"Ladies, ladies, could I have your attention please?" The chatter stopped and the women looked up to Lucinda and then across to Esther, all with smiles beaming across their faces.

"Now," continued Lucinda, "we all know that this is Esther's last day today and we're all very grateful for everything that she has done, aren't we?"

"Yes, yes," they all mumbled, nodding their heads and looking back and fore between Esther and the cake.

"Now, we all know that people do community service for having committed a crime and that crime isn't good." Everyone nodded and Esther looked down, her face red with humiliation. "However, I think we also all know that there are usually reasons why people do those things and Esther isn't an exception to that rule, isn't that right, Esther?" Esther shrugged, then thought a little and nodded.

"Exception, no, no you're right there, no exception," mumbled the other women.

"But the good news is that Esther has more than repaid her debt to society and I think you'll all agree that she has been brilliant here, helping us and probably learning a few things herself – am I right, Esther?" Esther nodded gratefully at Lucinda. "The other good news is that we won't be saying goodbye to her as she has agreed to carry on working here, two days a week, in place of Jen who is leaving next Friday. Isn't that wonderful?"

The women nodded, beamed and clapped and Esther blushed again, this time out of joy.

The thought of being assigned the day centre as her community service hadn't pleased Esther, but the whole experience of the court case and the resulting publicity about her letter writing had been so hideous that she didn't really care; she just wanted it all over. Her plan had been to keep her head down, do what was required and then move on – move somewhere and start again in a place where she wasn't known as the Tan-y-Bryn Spiteful Letter Writer.

Yet, as her old friends had shunned her, not understanding how she could have done something quite so offensive (despite having agreed with the sentiment of the letters' contents wholeheartedly), the women at the day centre had become her friends and they didn't seem to judge her. Jules had done time for persistent shoplifting and had lost her kids. Bethan, who had had a breakdown after her husband had left and now couldn't cope very well with life, knew exactly why people did things that weren't rational: she had smashed up the wrong car after seeking revenge on her ex-husband's mistress – collateral damage perhaps, but not *really* her fault. So who were they to judge anyone else's mistakes?

Therefore she'd spent three afternoons a week for the past year organising activities that were intended to help move the women forward in their own lives. She showed them how to cook and to budget and helped them fill in forms. It had become the focus of her week and she regularly arrived early and left later than her hours stipulated.

In the long term, it had been great for her relationship with Louisa, which had become very cool after the letter writing saga and the revelation of David's affair – which was somehow also Esther's fault. At last, Esther wasn't hanging around, waiting for Louisa to come home every evening. Instead, even when she wasn't at the day centre, she was planning activities, researching games that had a lesson or two in them. It seemed as if in Louisa's eyes she'd became a human being in her own right overnight, albeit one that had done something that wasn't very nice. She'd changed from being someone whose sole purpose in life was to make her daughter's day function a little easier to being someone who quite obviously had a mind of her own and better things to do.

She'd also done some community service of her own volition. She'd gone to the Tasty Bite and humbly apologised. She'd been received suspiciously at first, but then with appreciation. She was glad to hear that the couple were to go and start a fresh life in Spain.

Her reception at the Crusty Bun had also been received cynically and she had nearly crumbled under the derisive stares of Janet and Sally. However, they had accepted her offer of coming in once a week to help and with a slight sneer, Janet had suggested that perhaps she'd like to clean the place if she thought that she could do a better job.

Esther had accepted the challenge and early each Tuesday, she would scrub and scrape and polish whilst Janet and Sally cooked in the back kitchen before the shop opened. At first they were cool towards her, but after seeing that she was working very hard – and effectively – they started to mellow, inviting her to join them when they stopped for coffee, then giving her a loaf and a couple of cakes for tea, and finally paying her taxi there and back.

For the last three months she had been officially part of the team. Sally would collect her on her way to work and she was paid for her hours. Although the work was hard and unglamorous, Esther would bask in any comments that were passed on from customers about the place looking fresher.

Esther's divorce from David had made the front page of the local gazette: *Affair husband divorced from Tan-y-Bryn's most spiteful woman* the headlines had said and it sent a barb through her whenever she passed an A-board outside a newsagent or saw the papers fluttering on a wire rack outside a shop. She didn't read the papers anymore; they made her feel sick.

Their relationship had disintegrated almost immediately, as all she could see when she thought of him were his bouncing buttocks and Diane's red shoes bobbing in the air. However, as their life together was slowly untangled by the divorce courts, they had managed to get some of their old friendship back. He would come over to collect some things and they would share a pot of tea together and chat about what they had been up to. Sometimes he would ask if he could disappear into the new conservatory for an hour with a paper, "just for a bit of peace" and she would happily let him, sometimes bringing him a glass of elderflower cordial and a piece of shortbread, possibly with slightly disingenuous motives – more to make him enjoy it in a "how stupid was I to throw this away?" way, rather than an "ooh, this is nice" one.

She never asked about Diane, but would drink in his occasional comments about her not doing anything around the flat or how she just watched daytime television all day. Or how he'd driven her to the beach hoping that they could walk through the waves but instead, they'd sat in the car and drunk a Thermos of tea between them, then driven straight home again.

In a rather sad, reflective moment, he'd referred to the happenings of the last year or two as a huge mistake and apologised to Esther for taking her for granted for so long. Esther had graciously accepted the apology and said that, well, she'd probably taken him for granted too.

He hadn't asked whether he could come back and she was not sure if she would want him to. She felt as if for the first time in many years she was enjoying *her* life and doing what *she* wanted and feeling really valued and useful; she wasn't sure if she wanted to go back to making packed lunches with the wrong sandwiches or being grunted at for not guessing that someone fancied mashed rather than boiled potatoes tonight.

She had done an evening course in art and another in pottery, but had found that not only did she not really have much natural flair, it also was too long-winded for her. Part of the excitement of the course was discovering things about herself. She realised that she liked immediate achievements; perhaps that was why she was so good at housework and had been so effective at her do-gooding all those years ago. Harold needed a cat fed? Harold got his cat fed – tick.

Waiting for a layer of paint to dry on a pot before being able to paint the next part was not for her – she couldn't clear everything up and put it all away if a pot had to stand and be left in peace until it had dried. It hadn't taken much market research to work out that not many people in Tan-y-Bryn would want a plain blue or a plain red pot, even if they wanted a pot at all.

She was, however, even more pleased to discover a few things out about Diane too. Mainly that Diane wasn't as exciting as the fur coat and no knickers had first suggested: David had asked if he could pop some of their washing in the tumble drier whilst he cut her hedges, rather than spending the afternoon sitting in the launderette and she'd been happy to see that Diane's knickers were as high waisted and comfortable as her own…

Louisa was lying on a lounger in the warm Anweledig sun. She had a plate of sandwiches on one side of her and a can of Diet Coke on the other; it was lovely to have a day off now and then just to enjoy the weather and recharge her batteries a little.

Her plan had been to go with the conservation volunteers and clear that overgrown bridleway, but she'd woken up late and missed the minibus. She could have driven after them in her car, as the site was only five miles away, but she had recorded something on Sky Plus and now that she was going out a bit more, her television schedule was tighter and it made it difficult to catch up on things she'd missed.

Perhaps she should have made the effort after all: that Daniel chap in the conservation group seemed quite nice and Carrie and Sarah would probably have managed to make it. So far she'd managed to go to three planning meetings in the evenings, but had not made any of the practical days. She'd sat next to Daniel at the last one and he'd laughed at her when she'd apologised for not making the ditch-digging day as something had come up.

326

"Yeah, a duvet," he'd laughed, but it had not been unkindly and although her blushes had probably shown it was true, she'd managed a giggle in return.

She still saw Rachel and Rosie occasionally and they always stopped for a chat if they passed in town. They'd turned out to be perhaps a little too wild for her, but through them she'd met Carrie and Sarah and they were a little more her type. They would meet for lunch each week and Louisa would babysit for Carrie's baby occasionally to allow her to go out with her husband.

It was the same with the flat. Despite the divorce being such a period of turmoil, it had been a bit of a relief when her father had sheepishly asked if he and Diane might stay there for a few months until they had sorted themselves out. She'd agreed with as much false magnanimity as she could muster, whilst feeling her spirits rise at the thought of not having to bother living there herself. She'd done enough: getting the flat and overseeing its decoration had been a satisfying adventure for her and now that she knew she could do it any time she pleased, the urge to prove anything to herself or others had evaporated.

She and Diane had not managed to make it to being friends yet, much to the sadness of her father. Louisa had shunned Diane's first attempt at civility and had then been surprised to find that Diane had not bothered again. It was very trying to maintain the moral high ground when the cuckoo that had ousted her own mother from her nest didn't seem to give a monkey's.

As Louisa took a bite from her sandwich, she frowned at its dryness. Esther always said that a sandwich should have three fillings in it, but she, Louisa, had only put cheese in hers that day. Louisa thought back to the days when her mother would have made her a packed lunch for such a day, plus there would have been a few extra things under cling film for snacks. However, the difference was that now Louisa knew the score – if you want a nice sandwich, *make* a nice sandwich. If you can't be bothered, don't – but don't moan about it or wish it better. Either get up and go back to the kitchen and chop up a tomato, or just eat it and take a swig of your drink to wash it down. She deliberated about it, then ate it and then took a swig of her drink to wash it down...

Iestyn walked back across the yard with a tray laden with scones and Menna's lemon and ginger tea. 'Bohemian Rhapsody' was reaching a crescendo and the builders had started an octave too high and were beginning to struggle.

Joe and Johnny Brechdan were walking across the yard, heading back to the barn after their break. "Oh, gis one of those scones," said Johnny as he grabbed one from Iestyn's plate, "Pencwmhir wouldn't be right without having my stomach lining stuck together with one of these."

"Yeah and me," said Joe, trying to find the biggest one, "Sima's not looking, *and* she made me drink oat grass or something again for breakfast."

"I think that was meant for the cows," said Iestyn. "I'll be with you in a moment; I'll just give Menna her drink."

The others grunted at him and went back to the barn to carry on their task of chipping out the old crumbling mortar from between the stones on the far side of the barn, ready for it to be re-pointed by the professionals.

Iestyn sat down by Menna, passed her her tea and took a swig out of his Bambi cup.

"Thank God Joe's gone back to work," said Sima, politely passing on the plate of scones, "he'd be after the biggest one with the most butter on if he were still here!" Iestyn kept quiet.

"Actually, while I remember," said Isla, picking a couple of currants out of hers, "anyone up for going to Cefn Mawr show this weekend?" Menna and Iestyn exchanged glances and sneaked a look at Tansy to see if there was a reaction; there was nothing.

"Yes, I think it's on a Saturday this year," continued Isla. "You ever been, Tansy, when you lived in Cefn Mawr? Little Gwennie would love it!"

Iestyn and Menna cringed in unison. "How's the re-pointing going?" said Iestyn to Sima, trying hard to change the subject.

"On schedule," she replied. "Sorry, Tansy, did you say you'd been before?"

Tansy shrugged and Iestyn was glad that Johnny was out of earshot.

"Actually, no, I haven't been to *Cefn Mawr* show…" Iestyn and

Menna swapped confused glances, then looked back to Tansy, trying not to look too interested. "…although I did go to *Pwll Du* show once, but to be honest I'd rather not think about what happened there – put me off shows for life…"

"Had a dodgy burger or something, did you?" said Isla, concerned. "Tomos did once there, wrote him off for days."

"Something like that," mumbled Tansy, and she pulled Gwennie towards her. "Come on, Gwennie, shall we go for a little walk? Take all these plates back in?"

She stood up and walked away with a tray in one hand laden with cups and dishes and leant over to hold Gwennie's little hand with her other.

Iestyn looked over at Menna, her mouth open wide in disbelief. Something came over him and he started to giggle. He thought back to the night of the Cefn Mawr show and imagined the Viking with Johnny: perhaps in hindsight she *hadn't* been as tall as Tansy. Maybe her cheeks had been a little *ruddier and her eyes less startlingly blue*? He looked up at Johnny on the scaffold, a hammer and chisel in his hands, bandana on his head, tanned and fit in the sunshine and singing along to whatever shite was on the radio at that moment. He couldn't tell him – ever. Brechdan loved *his* daughter, he loved his new fiance. He was a changed man, relishing family life.

Iestyn looked over at Menna and put a finger gently to his lips and gave a slight shake to his head. Menna nodded back and winked at him, his giggles now infectious. "Right," he said, "pass us one of those scones and then we'd best get back to work…"

THE END!

ABOUT HONNO

Honno Welsh Women's Press was set up in 1986 by a group of women who felt strongly that women in Wales needed wider opportunities to see their writing in print and to become involved in the publishing process. Our aim is to develop the writing talents of women in Wales, give them new and exciting opportunities to see their work published and often to give them their first 'break' as a writer.

Honno is registered as a community co-operative. Any profit that Honno makes is invested in the publishing programme. Women from Wales and around the world have expressed their support for Honno by buying shares. Supporters liability is limited to the amount invested and each supporter has a vote at the Annual General Meeting.

To buy shares or to receive further information about forthcoming publications, please write to Honno at the address below, or visit our website: www.honno.co.uk.

Honno
Unit 14, Creative Units
Aberystwyth Arts Centre
Penglais Campus
Aberystwyth
Ceredigion
SY23 3GL

All Honno titles can be ordered online at
www.honno.co.uk
or by sending a cheque to Honno.
Free p&p to all UK addresses